A Recipe For Murder

By

C T Mitchell

A Collection of Short Cozy Mystery Reads featuring:

Lady Margaret Turnbull
Kate Mackenzie and
Selena Sharma

A 13 'Bakers Dozen' Culinary Cozy Mystery Box Set

Copyright

Table Of Contents

Lady Margaret Turnbull Cozy Mysteries

Murder at the Fete

Chapter 1

Unlike the name implies, Bangalow, New South Wales is probably one of the most serene communities in the county. The name actually appeared to have come from an Aboriginal word meaning "a low hill" or "a kind of palm tree", and what better to be named after than a palm tree?

The small town is a beautiful destination for day-trippers who want a gorgeous small town to visit; it had the most darling village streets filled with shops and boutiques, and cafes bragging about their locally grown organic produce.

Like most of the little villages in Australia, it boasts a hotel and pub, a church, a police station run by Constable Greenaway, its own mayor's office, and a small dance hall adjacent to the primary school. The town is set up so that the people who live there don't have to travel far to do the things they need to do. It's one of Australia's smartest and quaintest regional centers, and Maggie Turnbull loves it.

She and her husband had visited friends in Bangalow two decades ago on the way back from a business trip, and she'd always wanted to come back and settle down. When her husband passed away, that's just what she did. Admittedly, she still stood out a little with her thick British accent, and occasionally people would be brave enough to tell her that her voice and the way she carried herself made her seem a little pretentious. But those who know her realize nothing could be further from the truth.

Eventually, though, she didn't let it bother her. Maggie, or Lady Margaret Turnbull as she was properly called, could have moved anywhere in the world when her husband passed of a heart attack, but she settled in New South Wales for the latter part of her life. The late Mr. Turnbull, a dot com millionaire, sold his sold email service to British Telecom for 157m pound, leaving Maggie to do as she pleased.

As she pleased, it turns out, was a newfound passion for cooking and eating healthy foods as a way to stave off poor health for herself. She loved it so much that she was eventually inspired to teach others, as well. She purchased Lawler's Loft, an architecturally designed hilltop acreage home with old world charm and commanding views across the valley to the mountains in the west and Pacific Ocean to the east. Shortly after making her purchase she decided to teach others to live a healthy lifestyle, and the town's bed and breakfast, became synonymous with the beloved busybody, Maggie Turnbull. Busybody in a kind way. Maggie was not your stereotyped, doddering fool type. Quite the opposite in fact.

Running the bed and breakfast, teaching her patrons to cook wholesome food for their own wellbeing and igniting a passion for food in others provided most of her satisfaction in life, but everyone needs an extra hobby; at least in the mind of a busy Maggie Turnbull.

In her spare time, her favorite thing to do was to irritate Detective Inspector Tom Sullivan; albeit not intentionally. It wasn't her fault she had such a knack for knowing other people's business before he did...maybe it was just woman's intuition? Although the high academic marks she'd received all her life would suggest her brain was simply superior to his, which always made her grin.

As much as he tried to like her, it really did bother him to constantly be chasing her hunches. No matter how much Tom tried to do things by the book, he couldn't ever figure out a way to beat Maggie to solving the crime. Tom's uncomfortableness was evident particularly around Maggie, often getting a twitch in his eye. And that could be seen by all and sundry, something the locals would pick up on.

And she was the only person who drove him batty, even though he was thought highly of all over Bangalow. He did his job exceptionally well, which Maggie actually respected. The man had a real passion for justice after witnessing a hit and run when he was in high school. Tom's best friend was killed, and it triggered something in him that took precedence over what he thought would be a future as a fisherman like his father. As it turned out, fishing was how he spent his downtime. He had the uncanny knack to balance work and family life, which so many people lack, and was well known in town for being a great family man. He spent almost as much time with his family as he did in his work, and in his moments alone, took to the outdoors for solace. Maggie always imagined he spent his off days fishing and contemplating revenge for her spoiling his arrests.

Once, when he was certain he'd caught the killer of Julie Duncan, a primary school aged girl, it was Maggie's eye for detail that nailed what seemed like a random passer-by as her killer. Tom never would have even suspected; in spite of his thorough yet traditional investigation. Once again Tom's inner anxiety was heightened; at least this time he could hide it from prying eyes.

"Morning!" Melissa Shepherd, the baker's daughter sang as she waltzed through the doors of the bed and breakfast. She was here to do two things: break Maggie's train of thought and deliver the morning's pastries. Guests at Lawler's Loft looked forwarded to their early morning croissants and Danish pastries; something the guesthouse had become known for with travelers who were food connoisseurs.

Maggie smiled and threw her arms around her, as she did everyone who walked through the doors. Maggie maybe a Lady in title but she was no stuffy aristocrat, rather a warm and endearing person that people naturally gravitated to. "Morning, dear! You know where they go." She pointed toward the kitchen and followed Melissa through the foyer. "How's Constable Greenaway?"

Everyone knew Daniel Greenaway, the town constable, was in love with Melissa. And why shouldn't he be? She was as sweet as they came, very pretty in a plain sort of way, and as quiet as a mouse. Perhaps self-imposed as Melissa, born and bred in the district, had never ventured far from its borders and was not aware of worldly delights that lay beyond. It embarrassed Melissa when Maggie mentioned his name. The poor girl was smitten with the constable, but was too naïve to really think he fancied her back, and Maggie teased her endlessly about it.

"I'm sure he's fine," she answered, her cheeks reddening as she hurried to the kitchen. "He came by the bakery this morning and looked well enough."

"I'm sure he did, dear." Maggie pulled the dish towel from her shoulder and popped Melissa with it. As a woman who had her fair share of male suitors of the years, Maggie knew that Constable Greenaway had more than strawberry tarts on his mind whenever he visited the bakery.

If she was any good at setting people up, she would make it her hobby to get them together. They'd be perfect for each other, as the constable was also a quiet sort of fellow. He didn't speak unless he was spoken too, and was generally revered as a vanilla kind of gentleman. He wasn't much to look at, Maggie thought, but when he was around Melissa his eyes lit up like a schoolboy in a candy shop and it was adorable.

~

"Are you going to the charity fete?" Melissa asked, changing the subject.

"Well what else will there be to do in this town next Saturday, dear? Of course I'm going. I'll bet the constable will be there, too," she teased.

"Alright alright! That's enough out of you. What are you, my grandmother?"

"Is your father ready to become mildly rich with that prize money?" Maggie knew when to change the subject, and it made her giddy thinking that old man Shepherd would finally be acknowledged for his wares. The man knew his way around the kitchen better than any female Maggie had ever met, and she'd been all over the world. No one, however, held a candle to Jack Shepherd's scones and tarts, and he made one hell of a flat white sponge as well. Maggie could spend all day, every day in his bakery if she were of the mind to gain an extra few pounds a week. But being in her early fifties, Maggie knew that putting on those pounds was far easier than taking them off. She cut a trim, toned figure for a woman of her vintage; not unnoticed by quite a few of the town's male folk; single or married.

Melissa laughed and nodded her head. For a shy girl, she knew her father had more talent than most and was fairly confident he'd win every category. There was to be a purse of five hundred dollars for the best strawberry sponge cake, two hundred dollars for the best English scones, and one hundred dollars for the best fruit tart.

"Who's the weird old fella that's putting it on, again? I can never remember his name," Melissa asked.

"Mr. Stewart, that handsome old Scottish coot with all the money." He obviously appealed to Maggie's eye; albeit he was probably thirty years her senior.

"How'd he get so much money, anyway, Mrs. Turnbull? I don't remember ever having a benefit before he showed up and it's like he can just afford to do….anything."

"No one knows, dear. But he doesn't seem terribly strange in a bad way, so no one really cares!" Maggie laughed and imagined Mr. Stewart probably made money as a voice-over actor in secret, what with his thick Scottish accent. It drove the ladies mad and he found great joy in really working it when he was in front of a microphone. Maggie suspected that was why he did things like throw galas and benefit picnics, to fight the boredom of being incredibly wealthy and give the ladies something to fuss over. He probably considered himself to be a bit of a Sean Connery, although Maggie could never see His Majesty's service employing him. Mr. Stewart was not the most athletic man she had ever laid eyes on. She couldn't quite be sure he cared terribly about the Bangalow Boarding School receiving all the benefit money either…the man had never even stepped foot in the town's home for disadvantaged and delinquent children.

~

For the last four years, the fete has been renowned for its good food, fun rides, and fantastic baking prizes. Everyone in the town loved going, as it gave them something to look forward to every year. All the proceeds from rides and games went to whatever charity or organization Mr. Stewart chose, and the soirée even attracted people from many neighboring villages of Byron Bay, Clunes and Lismore.

Even though Maggie was not a baker, herself, every year she was a guest judge of the baking contest. And every year, she vowed to learn how to bake properly, though her apple pies and the occasional lemon meringue were the extent of her efforts in that regard. Her big dream was to have a famous guest chef run a cooking school at her Lawler's Loft bed and breakfast. Jamie Oliver was her ultimate wish, but she'd settle for some local Australian talent to mesmerize her guests with their culinary skills.

Her nephew, Simon, would be driving into town for the festivities and to spend some time with her. Maggie loved her nephew, he was a fine young man, but she wished he would get his act together quickly and settle down with a nice girl so she could have a little one to bounce on her knee.

That was the only thing she lacked in life, family with little ones running around. She loved when people brought their young children to the bed and breakfast, though it was mostly older couples or couples on vacation without their kids that came to stay. Occasionally, though, there would be five or six little ones running through the halls and racing up the stairs, and Maggie loved it. Simon was her best chance at having young ones around to spoil, and she couldn't quite convince him to settle down.

~

When Saturday finally arrived, Maggie helped Melissa unload the truck with her father's contest entries. They were there early enough that it was very quiet, though everything was already set up and ready for enjoying.

The children's rides were set up overnight, the caterers had already set up the restaurant tent and snack bar, and the local carpenter, along with the assistance of several farmers, had set up the stage and judges table inside the large food tent. Maggie followed Melissa carefully toward the table along the far side of the tent that was labeled Baking Contest Entries, and a young boy held the rope aside for them to pass by without dropping their pies and tarts.

~

Maggie is quite impressed with the range of pastries and delicacies offered at this particular fete. It seems that the village ladies have outdone themselves this year. Once the judges will have awarded the prizes, she has already put her name down to purchase six of Mrs. Grant's scones. "Her scones are the best in the county," she tells her nephew, keeping her voice low so as not offend old man Shepherd who considers himself this year's champion scone maker. Simon, whose favorite meal is a hamburger and fries, shrugs but smiles at his aunt's delighted face.

"Thank you, dear," Maggie crooned without looking at the young man.

"You're welcome, Auntie."

Maggie spun carefully to see Simon, who had arrived early to spend time with her before the festivities got started.

"You little! Come here and give me a kiss." He leaned toward her, careful not to knock the pie from her hands, and kissed her on the cheek. Maggie walked past him and set the pie on the table, eyeing the other entries. "Wow, they've really outdone themselves, this year. Mrs. Grant's scones are the best in the county... will you put me down for six of them, sweetie? I'm going to ask Melissa what else she needs."

Chapter 2

It was nearly lunchtime when the winner of the sponge cake was declared, and it was well-deserved. Mrs. Davies would take home first prize and the five hundred dollars and, much to the dismay of Mrs. Grant and Maggie, Mrs. Neddles took the honor of best scones. Apparently they were "smoother to the palate" than Mrs. Grant's, which Maggie highly disagreed with.

As for the fruit tarts, Melissa Shepherd had actually entered and won in that category. The look on Constable Greenaway's face when she was announced the winner was the only consolation Maggie had after Mrs. Grant scones were snubbed. The boy looked positively in love.

As he had taken to doing every year, Simon walked Maggie to the restaurant tent to have lunch with her. It was Maggie's favorite part of the day, because she could catch up on the gossip from Simon's small town, which wasn't too far away. She filed this information away systematically, to be retrieved later if needed.

Usually, the two of them would have hamburgers and chips, but today Maggie caught her nephew drooling over the Bangalow pork belly with plum sauce, so she suggested they each get a plate of that instead. Between that, the roasted potatoes, steamed broccoli and tea, the two of them were perched happily under the tent for the better part of an hour. For dessert, they each had a slice of fruit tart from Melissa's award winning tray. Maggie knew she would have to do a few extra laps of her ten acre property tomorrow to wear off the extra calories she devoured today.

As Maggie was scooping the sauce from her last bite of pie, there was a commotion near the back of the tent. Someone was choking, and apparently no one knew what to do anything besides sit and stare. That is, until Mrs. Davies stood up and knocked her chair over, causing Jane Neddles to scream at the sight of her friend writhing on the ground for breath. At that point, people started clamoring around her, unsure what to do.

"Someone find Detective Sullivan!! Or a doctor!" Jane screamed, trying to pry Mrs. Davies hands from her face so she could help. Soon, though, the woman stopped thrashing, and relaxed her hands, then relaxed her whole body into Jane's arms.

"Oh my God!" Jane cradled her friend, pushing the hair back on the top of her head as if she were petting a cat. "No no no....."

"How can that be?" Mrs. Grant whispered as Maggie trotted up behind the crowd.

~

Tom Sullivan rushed through the front of the tent. He'd been visiting the fete with his family, just like everyone else, but was happy to help. Frantically, he searched for the choking victim. All he'd been told was to get to the food tent immediately because someone was choking. Pushing through the crowd, he knelt down next to Jane and lovingly helped her stand up and passed her off to a nearby onlooker.

"You there!" He pointed to an older woman who looked as though she could speak well enough. "Which table was she at?"

The old woman pointed to her right with a shaky hand.

Tom spoke loud enough for the entire tent to hear. "No one touches that table, you understand? Don't even pick up your purse. Leave it there; I don't care if it's inconvenient. Don't touch it." There were a few grumbles, but everyone stayed away from it.

Constable Greenaway trotted into the tent, and Tom gave him some sort of signal to manage the crowd, which he did.

"Excuse me, ladies and gentlemen," he said only loud enough to be heard. "You heard the man. Stay back."

Tom opened his mobile phone and dialed the only funeral parlor driver in town. Carmichael's Funerals had been a part of Bangalow since 1949, a family run business now in its third generation. Since the town was small, it didn't have its own autopsy facility or morgue, so Mrs. Davies would have to be transported to Lismore, some thirty kilometers away, for evaluation. Tom was pretty certain he was dealing with an elderly woman that had choked on her food but needed to be sure.

It was very sad, but hardly the reason to make people wait any longer than they had to. He would take some snapshots and get a few statements and let everyone get back to the event if that's what they wanted. The crowd was already growing restless.

It wasn't twenty seconds before Tom's eye was twitching. The body had only been gone a few minutes, and already he saw Maggie set into motion. The woman was a dear soul, but nothing irked him more than having her know things first. Tom didn't want to be shown up again by Lady Margaret Turnbull, Bangalow's would be amateur sleuth, over a highly trained, academy graduated detective.

"Stay here if you want, dear. I'm going to talk to Mrs. Grant. That woman's up to something." Maggie patted her nephew on the shoulder and rushed away, but not before the Detective Inspector grabbed her gently by the forearm.

"Leave it alone, Maggie. It's nothing."

"It's Lady Margaret Turnbull to you, Detective. And I'm just going to talk to someone. It's nothing." She winked at him and hurried away. Detective Sullivan sighed in frustration knowing that anything involving Lady Maggie wasn't just about nothing. She was acting on one of her hunches again and they are usually right, much to the displeasure of the Detective.

"Aunt Maggie!" It was Simon, trotting toward her, looking as though he was saddling up to say something brave. "Don't go," he suggested, taking her by the hand. "I know you like to help the police, but can't you just sit this one out?" Simon knew his aunt had a reputation for getting caught up in police matters, and it didn't matter if she figured things out first or not, she was still a bit of a nuisance to the police force.

Maggie kissed him on the nose and walked briskly to the other side of the food tent, sliding in and out of mini crowds that had formed and making her way through them easily. She was in pretty good shape for being in her fifties; he had to hand it to her. Simon watched her briskly stride out from under the tent; she really was cut out for her favorite hobby.

Mrs. Grant was startled when Maggie sat forcefully into the chair next to her. "Hey there!" Maggie said loudly, patting the woman on the leg. I heard what you said back there, why was that? What made you say "This can't be?"

The color drained from Mrs. Grant's round face. "I have no idea...did I say that? Probably something I mumbled from shock."

Maggie didn't buy it. There was still plenty of time left in the day to have a cup of tea with the woman and sort things out, so she suggested just that, recommend-ing a little trip home to Mrs. Grant's house to help her deal with her shock. Surprisingly, Mrs. Grant agreed, and the two women walked arm in arm right past Tom Sullivan on their way to the parking lot.

He stood up and looked at them, eyeing his nemesis as though it would change the fact that she was taking a witness home with her. If he tried to stop her, she would only cause enough of a fuss to delay his entire day, so he let her go and returned to questioning witnesses at the table closest to the crime scene. It didn't seem to be going well; all the people at the table could say was how shocked they were that anyone would want to kill Mrs. Davies.

Chapter 3

The Detective Inspector wouldn't be going home tonight. Everyone else would probably stay at the fete in order to shell out their money to happily give funds to the children's shelter. Tom, however, tossed the keys to his wife and rented a hotel room at the Bangalow Gardens Motel, on the edge of town. Thankfully they had a room for him.

"I find it strange," Maggie said on the phone with Tom once he'd reached his room for the evening, "that Mrs. Davies was poisoned in the food tent."

Tom sighed; he was going to have to hear her out, one way or another. And after all, she had helped him on quite a few cases, so the woman at least deserved a hearing. "Why is that, Mrs. Turnbull? A food tent seems like a perfectly normal place to poison someone to me." He pressed his eyebrows together with his forefinger and thumb and sat down in the desk chair in the motel room. It felt like it was going to be a long night.

"Poisoning someone is a private affair, Detective," she said plainly. "One never randomly poisons somebody. It's usually targeted and personal."

Tom waited for a minute, processing his response. He didn't want to blow her off or seem ungrateful for her assistance but once again she was meddling in police business. And he didn't want to make it seem like this was news to him, but he had to admit, she had a good point. She went on to talk some sort of nonsense about Mrs. Grant mumbling a phrase under her breath at the crime scene. Maggie seemed to think that Mrs. Grant assumed she, herself, would be the victim. The idea struck Tom as the most ludicrous thing he'd ever heard, but he nicely mentioned that it was "far-fetched" at best and promised to appease her and keep her posted.

"No need, dear. I'll figure it out." And she hung up. Tom sat back in his chair, shoulders slumped thinking to himself, 'here we go again.' He looked to the ceiling of his room, sipped his tea and grimaced at the thought of Lady Margaret not only being involved but right.

The next day, Tom decided to investigate Maggie's hunch and take a trip to Mrs. Davies' cottage. Yet, before he had the chance, the forensic science team from Lismore called him stating that they'd found a threatening letter in her study desk. He wondered if Mrs. Grant had received a similar sort of letter, and told them to wait for him at the cottage.

Chapter 4

Maggie called the Inspector from her house at eight o'clock that following morning, having already put several more hours in on the case, and she felt more energized than she had in months. Maggie was an early riser most mornings preparing breakfast for her guests, taking delivery of Melissa's pastries and pottering around re-arranging the fresh flowers that adorned the lounge and hallways in the house. But sinking her teeth into a case, invited or not, gave her an extra spring in her step.

"You see, Detective, I went straight to Mrs. Grant's house yesterday after the festival. I knew you'd trust me with her, and you were right to do so." She loved rubbing it in the Detective's face that he pretty much let her have her way with things, and she waited for him to respond to her jab.

"And?" he asked impatiently, letting out another sigh; something he would do often around Lady Margaret. It sounded like he was traveling somewhere, and she didn't want to actually waste the man's time, so she hurried through the account of the previous night.

"When we got there...I told her I just wanted to have tea with her and would buy some of her delectable scones, hoping the idiocy of the timing would catch her off guard. It worked, of course, and she let me in. We weren't five minutes into the tea and pastries before she started to shake. I really am good, eh?"

"Oh yes, the best Lady Turnbull. Can you tell me why she was shaking or are you just going to leave the story at 'I made an old woman shake'?"

"Now listen here you little smarty, she isn't much older than me, so watch your tone. And of course there's more. She fetched an odd letter from a stack of papers in her kitchen and let me read it. It just said 'Lying is a mortal sin.' What do you make of that, Detective Sullivan?"

"I've no idea." She could hear him put his rackety car in park and shut the door, and was sure he'd hang up soon, so she blurted out the rest.

"The only other thing she asked me was what kind of poison was used to kill Mrs. Davies. Since I'm not privy to autopsy reports…yet…I told her I thought it was probably arsenic. A few drops in her tea would have sufficed, don't you think? Anyway, before I left, Tom…she said something strange."

She just said "There were three of us… Mrs. Grant immediately looked as though she'd regretted saying anything at all, but when I turned around to ask her what she meant, she merely crumbled into my arms in a sobbing heap. I couldn't really make out much more of what she said."

Tom was quiet for a moment.

"You might want to get it from her before she destroys it. She's a bit off her rocker at the moment. And you may want to visit Mrs. Carrington, as well. She's a cantankerous old bat who probably won't let you in the door, of course, so I would be more than happy to accompany you if you like?"

"Mrs. Carrington?" he asked, sounding out of breath.

There was a knock on Maggie's door, so she switched the mobile phone to her other ear and straightened her blouse. It felt good to be this active in the morning. She opened the door just as Tom was flipping his mobile phone closed. He slipped it into his pocket and gestured toward the inside of the house, asking to come inside.

"Well I never! Come in, Detective. Anyhow, Mrs. Grant and Mrs. Carrington testified to a crime some years ago; carrying the conversation on now face to face. Before you and I were ever in this area. Whatever the old case was, the suspect that was accused didn't commit the crime. Mrs. Grant refreshed my memory, but that's really all she'd tell me."

"Isn't she an invalid or something? My wife visits her for church, I think." He followed Maggie through the foyer of the bed and breakfast and she poured him some tea. They adjourned to the verandah and took in the view of the grassy valley to the distant mountains, where they discussed their next move; Lady Margaret now firmly entrenched in the case regrettably accepted by Detective Sullivan.

"We need to get over to Mrs. Carrington's place" Tom exclaimed finishing his tea and retracting his attention from the engulfing view and re-focusing back on the job at hand. "Let's see if she has received a letter also?"

Chapter 5

After ringing the doorbell at Mrs. Carrington's house for the third time, the Detective shot Maggie a knowing look and walked quickly toward the back of the house to check the other door. "Wait here," he instructed. And, as she sometimes did, she did as she was told. Before long he opened the front door and informed her that Mrs. Carrington had, indeed, met her Maker. Maggie was aghast.

"Was it poison?!" She yelled, pushing past him and searching for the kitchen.

"No, no," he replied.

"Are you sure? How can you be certain?"

"I know for a fact it wasn't poison because she was stabbed with a letter opener."

Maggie pulled to a stop before entering the kitchen. She didn't need to see that to be helpful to the police force, so she turned to Tom.

"Detective," she said, adjusting her slacks. "Was it her letter or someone else's? And did you find a strange letter, as well?"

"I didn't see one, no. I came to let you in. But I'd be willing to wager that we will. And as to whether it was her letter opener, well hopefully there are some fingerprints on it we can lift."

~

Tom Sullivan dropped Maggie off at her home, and she immediately phoned her friend at the Lismore's Northern Star newspaper office. She was trying to obtain a copy of the article about the trial Mrs. Grant was speaking of. And even though she had little hope of the gentleman finding it anytime in the next few hours since it happened nearly thirty years ago, he mentioned that he knew the case quite well.

It was apparently one of his first journalistic feats, and he even attended the trial, which he remembered clearly. On a year or two into his sentence, the person who was found guilty committed suicide, yet the story didn't end there. A full twenty years later, the witness of the crime came forward and said that they hadn't seen the criminal's vehicle properly. The women— Mrs. Davies, Mrs. Carrington, and Mrs. Grant— were even charged with perjury.

"Of course, they never went to jail," her friend said. "But I'm pretty sure suffering their own conscience was punishment enough! That poor man that hung himself, it's so tragic."

Maggie thanked her friend and hung up, walking to the window to think clearly. The day was clear, hardly a cloud in the sky. Momentarily Maggie's mind drifted back to her days in the UK; dark, dreary, cold wet days and thanked her lucky stars she had made the decision to move to Australia where the sun and clear blue skies were in abundance. But back to the case in hand.

Someone is making those women pay for wrongly accusing an innocent man, she thought. But who would do such a thing?

She put her teacup and saucer in the sink and decided to go for a walk to clear her head. And a call to Detective Sullivan to update him was in order, as well. He took notes on everything she said, and meekly thanked her for her contribution. The two of them agreed that Mrs. Grant was next on the list, if they were worth their weight as detectives, at least one was officially, that she needed to be protected. He arranged for Constable Greenaway to stay with her until they could sort things out.

"We'll wait for the forensic report on the letter opener and go and catch our killer," Tom said.

"Awwww, Detective. You said we. I'm flattered."

"Alright, now. Don't go getting a big head, Lady Maggie." Tom mentally cursed to himself to be more careful when freely talking about the case using the collective 'we' in the conversation. But at the same time he did have to give Maggie her dues; once again.

On the way home, she would pass the cemetery and decided to take a look at the headstones of the victims from thirty years ago. Maybe she could find some inspiration or direction there. It was all she could think to do while they waited for the report. Surely, something would come to her, it always did.

As she walked past the graves, she poured over the names carefully, trying to remember details from stories she'd heard over the years about the case. Leaning against a tree, she took in the whole place for a moment. The cemetery had a commanding position in the town with many old tombstones of the districts early settlers and pioneers. That's when she saw the fresh flowers. On one of the headstones, a bouquet of fresh flowers was arranged neatly on top of the stone. It caught her eye because she'd seen an identical bouquet of flowers at the fete the day before, though she couldn't remember whose they were.

Chapter 6

"**M**elissa Shepherd!!" Maggie shouted into the air. Melissa Shepherd had received a bunch of flowers identical to this one! Daniel Greenaway had given them to her for winning the baking prize at the fete!

When she approached the headstone that the bouquet was laying on, she exhaled sharply. The script was as plain as day.

"Lying is a mortal sin and you never did, Sam Connors. May you rest in peace."

"Oh bless you, Simon, for this wretched mobile phone. I've used it more today than I ever thought I would!" She kissed her mobile phone held in her shaking hands and dialed Detective Sullivan's number.

"You can't be serious, Mags—I'm sorry—Lady Maggie…I mean Lady Margaret. You can't be serious."

Yes Maggie insisted that he get Constable Greenaway out of Mrs. Grant's home immediately. He could tell from her breath that she was running somewhere and she seemed quite worked up about the Constable, so he decided to humor her. She hadn't been wrong yet, though he couldn't quite understand how the quiet Daniel Greenaway could manage to kill as housefly, much less an entire human. Two humans, no less!"

"Oh thank God!" Maggie leaned on the fencepost of Mrs. Grant's house to catch her breath, more than relieved to see that Mrs. Grant was standing on the front porch with Detective Sullivan. "Where's the Constable?" she demands immediately.

"Oh he's gone to get some milk at the store, dear. He's such a sweetheart," Mrs. Grant is as clueless as ever, yet here she was, standing there bragging about the kindness of a man who was going to kill her.

She looked to Tom. "If he thinks he's been found out, he'll run."

"I still don't underst...." as Tom was cut off by Maggie.

"He's our murderer, Detective. Mrs. Grant would have clearly been his third victim."

Mrs. Grant put her hand to her mouth to cover a gasp, though the news did not come as a complete shock to her. Seeing the look on Tom's face, Maggie offered her explanation.

"Mrs. Davies, Mrs. Carrington, and Mrs. Grant committed perjury during Sam Connor's trial thirty years ago. Their statements sent Sam to prison for life, where, as I told you before, he committed suicide. Ten years ago, the three of them admitted to their perjury about the suspect's vehicle and Sam obtained a pardon posthumously.

"However," she held up her index finger in the air. This was her favorite part. "The ladies' admission of guilt came too late as far as his son was concerned.

Daniel wanted them to pay for what they'd done to his…. father. Yes…father!"

"His mother, you see, suffered the wrath of the town gossips for years until she eventually reverted to her maiden name—Greenaway. She and her son moved away, embarrassed and ashamed, but Daniel wanted retribution for the loss of his father. He's been planning this for a very long time Detective. Remember what I said earlier – poisoning is not random. It's a private affair and in Daniel's case it's very, very personal."

Within moments, Tom had called in an arrest of Daniel Greenaway at the local convenient store, where he was reported to have been picking up gasoline and matches. Later on while going through his wallet, a worn, crumpled portrait photo of Sam Connor would be found; the father he had lost because of the actions of Mrs. Davies, Grant and Carrington. Now he would pay for their injustice.

News spread fast in the small township of Bangalow; shocked at the arrest of their local police constable. But life must go on. Melissa still managed to show up on Monday morning with the delivery of baked goods from her father. Never once had she considered, she told Lady Maggie, that Daniel's interest in the older women of the town was anything but harmless. Murder never is though.

Murder in the Village

Chapter 1

Lady Margaret's birthday was coming up, and it wasn't something she was too keen on thinking too hard about. There wasn't anything wrong with birthdays, really, she just didn't feel as old as her birthday cards told her she was, so she was disinclined to open them. She'd have the cake, but the reminder of getting older? Not so much.

She was drinking her first cup of tea of the day, standing in the large kitchen of her bed and breakfast property, Lawlers Loft, she ran on the outskirts of town, reading the paper. There wasn't really anything noteworthy happening in the small town of Bangalow, New South Wales. One of the quieter cities in Australia, it was an old favorite of Maggie's and her late husband's during their many travels over the years from the UK. For some reason it struck her as the perfect amount of quaint and city life, kind of a cozy village and it suited her perfectly since she decided to move here after her husband passed away.

She bought the bed and breakfast on Lawler's Lane, and was the strange mother-figure of the small town. Everyone loved her, even though she was a bit forthright. Her posh British accent, not to mention her knighthood, was much the talk of the district and it certainly helped in getting onboard with the local community councils; great venues for Maggie to listen in on the town's gossip.

Disappointed in the lack of enthusiastic news reporting for the week ahead, Maggie refreshed her tea and strolled over to the little picture window over the sink. Clad only in her bathrobe, she was caught off guard by the knock at the door.

"Who on Earth would be ringing me at this hour?" She wasn't expecting any deliveries for the inn, and the mailman would never ring her so early for fear of catching her in her bathrobe. And Lord knows that even though she was in decent shape for her age, she was pretty sure no one wanted to see that. After all, it wasn't proper.

Nevertheless, whoever was at the door was knocking so adamantly that they couldn't be kept waiting. She hurried to the front door, careful to look quickly through the foyer to make sure no guests would see her in her robe, and shuffled to the door. When she opened it, she gasped a little, greeted by the flushed cheeks of Inspector Tom Sullivan of the local police force.

"What's the matter, Tom?" she asked, making sure the robe was closed all the way and pointing to his reddened cheeks with her free hand. "Cat got your tongue? Or has it just been a while since you've seen someone other than your wife in a bathrobe? Don't flatter yourself, dear. I'm not interested."

Inspector Tom cleared his throat mid-laugh and

asked to be let in. He didn't look, Maggie thought, like he was really in the mood for joking. Though she was glad she got that one in, because seeing his cheeks flus was worth all the flack she would catch for it later. She waved her arm out in front of her and gestured for him to go into the kitchen quickly.

He did as he was told and shuffled in with a medium sized box under his arm.

"Tom, you're soaked, hun. Do you want some dry clothes? I'm sure I can find you something around here?"

"Aaah, no thanks, Maggie." The thought was going through Detective Sullivan's mind as to how Lady Margaret would have some men's clothing in her possession considering her husband had passed over ten years ago. Anyway he thought better of it to ask.

"I hate when you call me that. So what do you need? Anything at all, you know that, Detective. Let me take your coat."

Tom let her remove his coat, and she draped it over the back of one of her kitchen chairs. Eventually, when she saw that he wasn't going to stop pacing her kitchen floor, dripping wet, without saying anything, she made him a cup of tea. Maggie tapped him on the shoulder, breaking his train of thought. Tom grumbled a bit and nodded his thanks to her, taking the saucer from the older woman's hands.

"Thanks, it's been raining all night, and I just never dried out. I appreciate the warm tea, Lady Turnbull."

He made a fake salute to her with his small tea cup and hoped she would appreciate him using her proper name.

"Well, hopefully you don't catch pneumonia and die an old fart. You really should take better care of yourself. Now what brings you here? Do I need to call the Mrs. and let her know where you're at."

"No thanks, mam. I appreciate the sentiment. But I'm not really speaking to anyone at the moment."

Maggie's eyes perked up and one eyebrow danced across her forehead. "Oh really?"

"Yes, really. Don't go getting all excited about it, it's nothing like that."

Maggie grinned widely at her friend. "Oh I think it's exactly like that, Tom! You know me, and it's nearing my birthday, even! This must be your gift to me, a juicy secret case to be solved on the quiet. That's very kind of you." She dipped her head to him and he half-chuckled, "Now what have you got for me, here?"

"My socks are soaked through, Lady Margaret. I'm freezing and I don't want to be here all day, I'm knackered. I came to you because I don't want to be airing out my dirty laundry all over town. I'd much rather come to you, since you have a way with these sorts of cases, than to have it broadcast all over town. It's from my Aunt in Byron Bay, she sent it in the post and I wanted you to have a look at it before I took it to the Station."

"Alright alright, cool your horses. Settle your spirit, love. You look shaken, what's going on? Why do you want me to look at it first?" Maggie asked.

Tom handed her the box, and Maggie eyed him carefully. Whatever was in the box has him pretty worked up. "It's probably a book of some sort, I'd imagine."

She pried the lid off with one hand, and half expected there to be an old sandwich or something inside of it. When the lid finally came loose, Maggie swallowed hard. Nestled into a crimson-colored piece of fabric was a jar. The jar was cloudy inside, and had a liquid in it, held securely by a firm piece of cork. Inside the bottle, which Tom looked away from as soon as she opened it, was a slender finger. It was floating in some sort of liquid, and upon a quick smell of the bottle, Lady Margaret assured him that it was formaldehyde. She could see the color in the Detective Inspector's face grow lighter, and he looked as if his stomach was a little queasy.

Lady Margaret regained her composure quickly and squared her shoulders at the kitchen table. "This is not what you were expecting, I take it?"

The Detective shook his head and brought a fist to his mouth, looking as though he were about to be sick. "No!" He shouted, suddenly upset. "I thought it was an old book or something that she'd gotten you for your birthday!"

Only a few moments later, Maggie was showing him to the front door. Detective Tom apologized profusely for the interruption and confusion, and excused himself to the police station at Lismore to try and figure out what the package was all about.

Maggie watched as he went back to his car, not quite fully dried out yet, still holding the plastic bag under his arm. He had barely wanted to wait for her to wrap it up, but she'd insisted, so that he could maintain privacy. Those goons at the police department had no business asking questions about a beat up old shoe box; just yet anyway.

Chapter 2

Lady Margaret Turnbull, beloved bed and breakfast owner and part time sleuth of Bangalow, New
South Wales, freshened her tea and returned to her
kitchen table. No sooner had she grabbed her pad of
scratch paper and begun to doodle on it, her mind raced
with all the things she'd taken in.

She wasn't given much time before the Detective
had replaced the lid on the box, but in that short time,
she'd gathered that it was a young woman's finger. It
was a ring finger, probably belonging to a woman in
her twenties. Tom was no spring chicken, and his aunt
must surely be in her sixties, so she imagined that it
belonged to a young engaged woman, since the finger
was still adorned with an engagement ring.

Getting dressed quickly in something she could be
seen around town in and be proud, Maggie hopped into
her car. The darling car, a 1968 Mercedes 450 SLC,
red with white leather, perfectly engulfed everything
that was Lady Margaret Turnbull in a nutshell. It was
classy, fun, sporty, and full of life at any age. And it
turned heads, which she loved.

She climbed into it and checked her hair in the rear
view mirror. She couldn't get the "ring finger in the
box" out of her head, and she wanted answers. Those

answers sure wouldn't be coming from Detective Sullivan, as soon as she'd opened the box, the man had clammed up like a school boy on his first date. This left the ring, itself, as being the only other lead in the case.

She'd seen many rings like this one advertised on television; it was no ordinary engagement ring. An expensive jeweler in Lismore had been advertising rings exactly like these for months. They were very unique, and Maggie admitted to herself that she'd envied them on more than one occasion.

With wedding season approaching, the jeweler had been offering the rings at a reduced price. Nearing the shopping center where Lismore Family Jewels was located, Maggie pulled into the car park located underground. She usually hated driving around in town, mostly because people were in general impatient arses, but this morning the drive had not been so bad.

Trotting up to the entrance of the shopping center, Lady Margaret was pleased to see that the early morning crowd was much thinner than normal today. The shops were opening one by one, and she took a seat on a bench outside the jewelry shop. It was one of the last ones to open, which Maggie took note of. She was careful not to look as though she was staring, and she carefully eyed the man inside the shop who was directing the other sales clerks to their stations. It was time to have a chat with the man.

Meanwhile, as Lady Maggie rose to confront the jewelry store owner, Inspector Tom Sullivan was leaned over his desk at the police station with his head cradled in his hand.

"Auntie, auntie….listen…" he said quietly.

"No, you listen, dear. I sent you no such package. I'm certainly not dead, and I have all of my fingers! So whatever you found in a jar inside a box has nothing to do with me. And quite frankly, you're making me nervous. You sound quite shaken up. You should get some sleep…or make a cup of tea."

As he was trying to hang up the phone, the Detective Inspector's Sergeant bursts through the door and tries to interrupt his conversation. The young officer had no tact when it came to when and where he was invited to speak, and was always in a hurry. Tom liked the guy, but Sergeant Daniels always seemed to be running late, and everyone else's time suffered for it. He hung up quickly and turned to Sergeant Gerard Daniels with a sigh.

"Sir," the young man was breathing heavily, as though he'd jogged down the hall….and everywhere else he'd been that morning.

"Sir, I've only found three women reported missing in the last few weeks. These are the only three that fit the description from the forensics lab." Gerard handed him three pieces of paper fresh off the printer. The finger apparently belonged to a Caucasian woman in her early twenties.

"She's had a manicure pretty recently," Tom said aloud. "Now we just need a body to go with this finger."

Chapter 3

Back at the shopping center, the little bell on the door dinged as Maggie walked in. The man she assumed was the manager looked surprised to see her for some reason, and checked his watch absentmindedly.

"Are you open?" she asked.

"Yes, yes ma'am," he replied. "We'll be here until six."

"Ah very good! I'm in a bit of a hurry and was wondering if you could be a darling and show me one of those rings you advertise on television."

The man eyed her curiously, wondering if this woman in her mid-fifties was about to be proposed to.

"Oh no, no dear. It's not for me! I just wanted to ask you a few questions about them. They're so pretty." Maggie watched as he decided whether or not to humor her, and when he returned with a tray of rings similar to the one in the jar, her face lit up. "Oh, they're beautiful!"

The man went through the usual list of reasons to buy such beautiful and unique rings, but Maggie stopped him mid-sentence.

"Do you remember, perhaps, selling one of these to a woman sometime in the last month or so?"

Taken aback, the manager took two actual steps back. "Why on earth would you want to know something like that. Have we met before?"

"No of course not, I just…one of my friends had one just like this and I was wondering if you were the one that sold it to her." After another half hour of clever fibbing, Lady Margaret left the jewelry store with three names and addresses of men who had purchased a ring from the tray in the last three months.

One of the names, Maggie noticed, was for a young man who lived on the same street at the Detective's aunt in Byron Bay. It might be a coincidence, but Maggie doubted it. These things were seldom coincidences; they were generally revered as juicy, wonderful details that led her to solving a crime that the police department couldn't handle.

Returning to her car, she threw down the top and pulled out of the park way, headed for the police station. When Detective Tom Sullivan saw her breeze through the station doors, a picture of class, his skin crawled a bit. He knew he shouldn't have involved her in this, though knowing her she already had the perpetrator tied up in the trunk of her car begging to be fingerprinted. He hated when she came to the station, why didn't she just phone him with her hunches as she usually did? No time for personal insecurities, Tom needed to talk with Lady Margaret.

Chapter 4

Just as Tom was approaching Maggie, Sgt. Gerard Daniels rocketed out of an office door.

"Sir! A woman in her twenties was just pulled out of the river…she's missing her ring finger."

Tom nodded to his sergeant and kept walking toward Maggie. As much as he hated involving Lady Margaret on cases directly, he had to admit she'd been an incredible amount of help on many occasions. He'd be a fool not to ask her.

"Well," he said when he reached her. She jumped a bit when he came up from the side, and it made him happy to have startled her. The Detective imagined that it probably didn't happen very often. "Let's go."

"What's that, officer? Are you taking me in?" A sly smile wandered across her face and she put her hand to her chest dramatically. "I'm sure I didn't do anything…"

"Alright, alright." Tom grinned and laced his hand through the crook of her arm. "Come with me. Something's just come up…literally." Maggie's eyebrows danced across her face and Tom shot her a grin. "In the river."

He knew she loved this part, where things were just starting to get interesting for the normal police force was the part where Lady Margaret Turnbull started working her magic. As much as Tom hated to admit it, the little boy in him loved watching her brain work.

"Happy to go along, Detective! But I'll take my own car if you don't mind." Maggie turned her nose a bit in false protest. "It's much more stylish than a police panda car."

"That may be perfectly true, Lady Margaret. But I won't be able to debrief you if we're in two separate vehicles." Maggie looked disappointed, but ultimately caved pretty quickly. "It'll be fine, your car will be fine here, and we'll come back and pick her up later. The boys will make sure she gets lunch." Tom winked at her.

As soon as they pulled out into traffic, Lady Margaret pulled three sheets of paper from her purse and waved them at Tom while he was driving. "Let me debrief you, first. These three gents all bought rings like the one we discovered. And one of them lives very near your Aunt. What do you make of that?"

Unexpectedly, Tom grabbed the papers from her and pulled out the one that lived near his hand, he folded it up and slid it into his jacket pocket while steering with one hand.

"No offense, Lady Margaret, but I really don't want you getting involved in the case in this way. This perpetrator seems to be especially vicious, and I don't need to lose you due to your lack of police training. It was dangerous going and getting these." He looked at her, and rolled his eyes at the grimace she was sending across the cabin of the police car. "What?! It was dangerous. How did you even get anyone to—you know what. Never mind. I don't want to know."

Before long they pulled up to the pier on the banks of the Condamine River where the body had been discovered. There were a handful of officers walking around and some police tape being strewn about in places that didn't make any sense to Maggie. She loved the excitement of the scene and started to get out of the car.

"Huh uh. You stay here." Tom pointed his finger to the seat like he was instructing a toddler. "I'll come get you when I need you. It's dangerous down there and you're in proper shoes. No sense in dirtying them up if you don't have to."

Reluctantly, Maggie agreed, but not without a significant amount of scoffing. Five minutes later, though, as Tom was getting his bearings on the scene, he saw Maggie traipsing down the embankment toward where he was standing. There really was no telling that woman what to do. He should have diverted her by saying she had to come down. Then she would have stayed put.

"Lady Margaret, seriously! You're going to break your ankle! Didn't I tell you to stay in the car?" He trotted out from under the pier and up to give her a hand. She accepted, as any lady would do, and didn't say a word until they were settled underneath the pier again.

She motioned for Tom to get back to whatever conversation he'd been having, and after rolling his eyes a few more times, he did just that. She undoubtedly just didn't want to miss any details, and Tom couldn't fault her for that.

When he was done talking, Maggie turned to him.

"I noticed something in the mud up there on the hill." She pointed to where she had walked from. "I didn't want to disturb it because I knew the forensics team would want to get a picture of it in situ, but it's worth looking at." Tom was always impressed when she used proper police terms, but he always immediately pictured her reading Nancy Drew novels late at night.

"Show me," he said.

The two of them climbed back up the hill some ways and Maggie pointed to the ground. "I believe that's a ring box, Detective Sullivan."

"Stay right here." He started back down the hill and stopped mid-stride, turning back to her and reaching his hand out in kindness. "Please."

Moments later, he came back with a forensics photographer, and when they gotten what they needed, he slipped on a latex glove and pulled the box from the mud. Turning it a few times in his hands, he didn't say a word, and then dropped it into a clean evidence bag. On the outside of the box was the name Lismore Family Jewels.

Chapter 5

The Detective and his team confirmed that Pete Evans, one of the names on the slip of paper that Maggie managed to rustle up, had purchased the ring on the severed finger. Once they reached his house, Evans told Tom that he purchased the ring at the jewelry store in town.

Apparently, and Tom wasn't even the slightest bit convinced of his story due to the trademark shift eyes of the person telling it, he'd asked Alison Clay to marry him on the river bank where they had found the box. The two of them walked back to the restaurant on the promenade where they then had a lovely dinner to celebrate their new engagement.

They drove home separately, and since it was a week day on the evening he proposed, Pete assumed Alison had driven back to her parent's house. That was, as he claimed, the last time he saw her. The next day, Alison's mother listed her as a missing person.

In Tom's mind, there were too many unanswered questions in the case. Maggie wondered why sending the package to the Detective personally was something the perpetrator chose to do, it seemed a bit bold. And why did the attacker use his aunt's address? Maggie suggested to Tom that it could have been done on accident, or possibly to derail the investigation. It was, she thought, a strange thing to do for a serial killer, though.

The following day, Tom phoned Lady Margaret to inform her that there was a second body with the same description.

"Have you received a shoe box for this one, too?" Maggie asked.

"No, I sure haven't. Not that I've seen, anyway. Maybe it was a fluke?"

"I doubt it. Strange things are rarely a fluke. Hold on a moment, please." Maggie walked to the door where the postman had just come in. She'd seen him there, in the foyer of her bed and breakfast, a thousand times.

Today, though, the sight of him stopped her in her tracks. He was holding a shoebox and the clipboard he normally carried when she was required to sign things. The only person that had her address that would have anything to do with the case, other than the Detective himself, was the owner of the Lismore Family Jewelry Store. "Send a car to Lawlers Loft. Immediately. I'll call you back."

She knew that within ten minutes there would be a car at her door, so she sat tight with the box and readied herself for whatever was to happen next. A fresh coat of lipstick and a pair of earrings later and she opened the door for the officer. The young man, whose name Maggie could never remember because he was a very forgettable face, sat quietly with her and sipped his tea like a timid gentleman in training until Detective Sullivan arrived.

"Okay, Lady Margaret. A lot has happened in the time since you had me send the car. Branson, you're excused. Thanks so much."

The young man thanked Maggie for the tea and set his cup and saucer in the sink before leaving as quietly as he'd come in.

"This guy is killing these girls because he was refused; at least that's my theory. His own proposal to his girlfriend was refused, and the profiler and I truly believe he's acting out on other people because of it. It's pretty basic, but you get the drift.

Anyhow, he bought the three rings at the jewelry store in the mall, and when I swung by to question the manager you spoke to, he wasn't around. The other workers mentioned that he'd gone on an unscheduled vacation."

"Mmmm…do go on."

"Yeah, my thoughts, exactly. Should've called in sick, because you can't get much more suspicious than that! I've got his name and address. Want to ride along?"

Maggie nearly jumped from her seat. "Do I!"

At the apartment complex, the landlord informed the two of them that Mr. Bruce Diamond had not gone on vacation as far as he could make out…he'd left altogether. Mr. Diamond had moved out three days ago.

"He was never a problem," the landlord said. "He even paid the last month's rent. He mentioned that his girlfriend had taken a job out of town and he wanted to follow her. Seemed a good enough excuse as any, I'd say?"

"No way is she moving for a job. That woman's been abducted," Maggie whispered to Tom as they walked down the hall. "I'd wager these three killings are a warning to her that she'd best accept his proposal...or else! He's probably obsessed with her and can't stand to see any other woman with a similar ring on their finger."

Tom scoffed. "That seems a bit far-fetched even for you, Lady Margaret."

Maggie raised an eyebrow as they walked. "Does it?? Then give me another explanation that better describes a crazy person."

"Nah....you're probably right as usual. It'll be faster if I just admit that out loud. If you're right—"

"Don't tease me, Detective. You know I'm right."

"—then he won't stop until he's killed his girlfriend. We've got to find her before that happens."

Chapter 6

"Perfect! You did perfectly, thank you so much." Tom slammed the phone down and jumped from his chair, slinging his jacket over his shoulder. He quickly dialed Maggie's number with his free hand.

"Lady Margaret! The clerk at the Byron Bay Jewelry Store just phoned to say that Mr. Diamond ordered a ring. He told him yesterday to come back today to pick it up. And he's phoned us this morning. Sergeant Daniels and I are on the way to apprehend him. Daniels is going to pose as a clerk and I'll be waiting outside when he shows up."

"His girlfriend is probably being held somewhere in town, Detective. Did you ever get any information on her?"

"I sure didn't, but I'm hopeful we'll get it out of him. That's why Daniel's is posing as the clerk, he'll try to get her name and address before we grab him. He's wearing a wire so I can hear the address when he does, I'll send a team out immediately after."

An hour later, Daniels is in place, and Diamond walks into the shop. The other clerks were on lunch, and Diamond strolled right up to the counter, where the Sergeant did his job exactly as he was trained. He asked for the name and address of the girlfriend for insurance purposes, which is something that Bruce Diamond knew to expect as common practice. In this case, however, Diamond actually refused to give the information.

"I'm the one buying the ring and I'll use my information for it. I value our privacy." Diamond told him. "If she refuses the ring, it will still be paid for, and I'll keep it as a keepsake."

Daniels did not argue, as he knew that would only raise Diamond's suspicion. Detective Sullivan, however, heard the whole conversation in his earpiece and simply waited for Diamond to come out. When he left, Tom would simply follow him, convinced he'd lead him to the girl.

While he was waiting, however, he received a call from the Lismore Police Station. The desk sergeant reported a woman had called in a reported that her daughter didn't come home last night. She was worried, and the daughter's name was Libby Carter. Her boyfriend's name was Bruce Diamond. The hairs on the back of Tom's neck stood up, he thanked the sergeant and gripped the steering wheel.

As soon as Bruce exited the store and pulled into traffic, Tom followed him at a safe distance. They were headed to the downtown area as best as he could tell. Something about the direction they were headed didn't feel right, and sent goose bumps down his arms. The central business district was busy, even for a popular seaside tourist town and he didn't want to lose the guy in traffic. He called in to have a few unmarked cars dispatched to assist in an eventual chase, just in case.

A full half hour later, Diamond dropped down into a car park below the popular Byron Bay Hotel in the Byron Bay CBD. Tom followed and watched him exit the vehicle, and he received word that a Byron Bay police constable was on site near the car park elevator. Carefully, the officer followed Bruce Diamond to his room and radioed Tom the location: Room 651 on the sixth floor.

A few minutes later, Tom and the Hotel security officer met the constable outside the room. He listened for any noise, and when he heard a faint string of muffled sounds followed by a very audible scream, he used the security officer's master key to open the door.

As the three men burst in, they saw the young woman being held over the balcony railing by Bruce, who was holding her left ring finger in front of her face. Libby Carter fainted just as Tom reached her, luckily he grabbed her arm firmly enough that he could swing her back toward him and she collapsed into his chest. The Byron Bay police constable slammed handcuffs onto Diamond and forced him to the ground.

Since her finger was severed shortly before she was rushed to the hospital, Libby's finger was able to be reattached.

That evening, after a long day of filling out paperwork and then filling Maggie in on the details, Detective Sullivan left to stay the night at his Aunt's house in Byron Bay.

In the morning, they would go shopping together for a special book for Lady Margaret's birthday. It would be a tall order, Tom thought, because it would have to top the early birthday gift of her being able to help on another case. And he knew it would be hard to top that.

Murder in the Cemetery

Chapter 1

A muffled scream was all the emanated from Valerie's beautiful mouth as the knife pierced her
heart. Here, nestled in the heart of the last resting place
of so many, Valerie was finally given what she deserved.

A few rats scattered about in the corners, hopefully
not to be seen, and the whole place smelled of mold.
The air was still, but cool, and felt good on his arms as
he moved her around.

Valerie's dress, purchased not long ago for fear she
ever wear the same thing twice, was immaculate as it
should be, except for the large stain down the front. She
looked like a doll, like a museum doll in a pleasant little
house of horrors, and he was happy to have helped her
meet her end on a day when she was wearing green.
It made the whole scene more exciting, somehow, not
that anyone else would ever see it.

His tormentor for as long as he'd had memories,
Valerie would torment no longer and her assailant
breathed a sigh of relief as he adjusted her body to its
last resting position. On the outside, she looked better
than him in every way, but it wasn't for lack of trying
on his part. His miserable existence was because of her,
with her out of the scene, perhaps now he could find a
new way in life.

Her hand fell when he placed it across her lap, so he laced her fingers together and she looked as though she were thinking about something. By the time he was finished with her hands, and had adjusted the last bit of her skirt, her face had fallen a bit. She no longer looked frightened or surprised.

Dear Lord, why was she surprised? She had to have known this day was coming. It should have happened ages ago, but he was suppressing his will to see it through. Still, she shouldn't have been surprised. Now, though, her face looked calm. It looked pleasant, even. And he reached up and pressed on her cheeks with his fingers until there was a slight smile on her beautiful face.

Never again would she hear someone tell her how beautiful she was. And she was, to be sure, with porcelain skin and silky hair, but the inside didn't match the hypocrisy of it all drove him up the wall.

No one else seemed to be able to see how cruel she could be. It made him relatively sad that the truth of her character would never see the light of day, but it didn't matter. Down here in the cool, damp dwelling place of busy rats and those who'd had their chance at living, at least she couldn't hurt him anymore.

The man stood, wiping the sweat from his thick forehead, and trudged up the stairs into the light. The smell of the crypt soon left his nostrils, and he strolled through the cemetery, blood still dripping from the knife he held loosely at his side.

Chapter 2

Bangalow, New South Wales, Australia is probably one of the most serene communities in the county – having nothing to do with its name. A village like many others throughout Australia, is boasted a hotel and pub, a church, a small dance hall adjacent to the elementary school, and a small, well-appointed cemetery.

Lady Margaret Turnbull, one of the most popular town citizens, was the owner of the bed and breakfast in town called Lawler's Loft. Lady Turnbull moved to Banaglow after the passing of her husband, an internet millionaire, and has lived there for the last ten years.

When her husband passed in the UK, Lady Margaret turned her talent to cooking classes and running the bed and breakfast because it gave her the freedom to do what she loved, and also the freedom to be an amateur sleuth; something else this busy body loved to indulge in.

The latter was very much to the dismay of Inspector Tom Sullivan of the Lismore Police Department. Lady Maggie always loved a good mystery, and unfortunately for the entire police department's detective team, she was very good at solving them.

Maggie had decided to go for a walk that morning since there were more people than normal bustling around in the gathering rooms of her guesthouse. Someone's family reunion was in town, and the lot of them were not Maggie's type of crowd.

A nice, leisurely stroll through the neighborhood, though, provided all the entertainment anyone ever needed. With only twenty minutes of walking, one could get to just about anywhere in town they needed to go. Maggie especially loved this about Australia, that each section of the cities were divided up into miniature towns that held everything a full sized town would have.

You didn't even need a car here; you could really just walk everywhere. It was wonderful, and Maggie enjoyed it immensely. The warmth of the autumn sun on her back reminded her of vacations with her husband, and something tugged at the back of her throat. She was nearing the town's cemetery, and could see someone standing just inside the far gate near a tree. The breeze from the ocean teased the last leaves on the tree.

When Maggie neared the entrance of the little cemetery, she noticed that her dear friend Jennifer Langley was visiting a gravesite. It was probably her late husband's site, he had died two years ago from a heart attack and it left her shaken.

They had lived very long, happy lives together, but Jennifer still had a lot of life in her. She had finally gotten her visits down to once a week or so, and talked about the visits often in the quilting club that met at

Lawlers Loft on Monday mornings.

Maggie often overheard, and took part in, these conversations. It was like talking to someone with a newborn child. Only another parent can really understand what they're going through. Maggie would go to her friend and stand with her as she talked with her husband, it was the least she could do and was something she'd expect of anyone else.

Making her way through the little gate, Lady Turnbull noticed that the door to one of the mausoleums was ajar. It was open enough to get her attention, and she decided to take a look into it when she was finished. After all, that family reunion certainly didn't need her presence, and she was in no hurry to return.

Jennifer was especially cheerful this morning, and spent about half an hour recounting several good times she'd had with her husband to Maggie. Maggie listened intently, and hugged her friend as she was leaving, although she had been secretly eager to get over to the open mausoleum the whole time.

When she came up to it, finally, she pushed it forward and it creaked under her palm just like an old movie. Maggie felt like a grown-up Nancy Drew, and she grinned a bit as she propped the door open enough to light the first few steps. After that, she used her mobile phone to light the way.

It was cold and dark in the crypt, but nothing out of the ordinary for Lady Margaret, as she lived for this sort of mystery. Something about the way the hairs on her arm stood up a bit told her that she would find something unpleasant down in the bottom of the tomb. Unless someone was servicing it, there was really no good reason for it to be open.

Down the steps, just at the end where two large tombs of what Maggie assumed to be a husband and wife buried next to each other, was the body of a beautiful woman in a lovely green dress. Well, lovely, except for the giant red stain down the center. The woman's face was left untouched, and her mouth was turned up in a gentle, yet awkwardly out of place smile. Except for having obviously been stabbed in the heart somewhat recently, she looked as though she might have been pleasantly sleeping.

Maggie walked quickly over to her and ran her fingers through an outside portion of the blood on the woman's gorgeous dress. It was still very wet. Maggie knew that Detective Sullivan would be displeased that she'd touched the body, but she always played by the rules. Just this once, she wanted to bend the rules a bit and gather more information before hand. She'd risk the lecture just this once.

Not normally one to be shaken by such a sight, for some reason the death of this particular girl struck Maggie as a very sad thing. Her insides were beginning to knot up, so she stood for a moment at the young woman's feet. She took a few steps back and tried to take in more of the scene.

The young woman's Italian-made shoes, which

Lady Margaret recognized in an instant as being delightfully overpriced and a status symbol for many of the upper-class women, were caked in mud. Though her face was beautiful, and Maggie hadn't noticed it at first glance, her make up did appear to be smudged from tears.

And her lips, bright red with lipstick, were actually bleeding. The woman had bitten her lower lip. Maggie called the Lismore Police Station. Constable Donaldson answered on the first ring, and listened to Maggie's discovery. Her instructions, as always, were to wait at the scene and touch nothing until a police officer or two could get there.

Twenty minutes later, she had given her official statement to Constable Donaldson and another officer of the law and was free to go home. Maggie walked home unnaturally slow, wishing she had something stronger than sherry waiting on her in the cabinet at home. A shot of whiskey to ease her shaky nerves wouldn't be out of the question, today. She couldn't quite figure out why the image of the young woman had upset her so, but she didn't care for it.

Chapter 3

Maggie poured some cooking sherry into a tea class and sipped it as she strolled through the kitchen of her sprawling colonial home. She could still hear the sounds of the large family reunion out on the verandah and she shook her head a few times to clear the noise from it.

"Why was the woman smiling? Why did she look like she was having a good time?" Maggie asked herself. There was no way in hell that girl was having a good time being stabbed in the heart. Something was amiss.

By the fourth time the image of the girl's laughing face haunted Maggie's mind, she heard someone knock at her door. It was Detective Tom Sullivan, the man who was always reluctant to admit what a huge help she was in solving cases, but always seemed to keep coming back for more.

This time, though, Maggie secretly wished he would ask her to stay out of it. This time, she would listen. Tom took his usual cup of tea when she offered it to him, and he made a mental note of the way her hands shook when she handed it to him.

"You okay, Lady Margaret?" He asked, taking a sip. She nodded but said nothing. "Okay then," he said hesitantly. "Well, we've found out that your victim is named Valerie Chambers. Ready for the run down?"

Chills ran down Maggie's spine, but she nodded because she knew that's what she normally would have done. At the moment, she was acting on instinct, and her instinct told her that she should be interested...so she faked it.

Tom opened his small notebook with a flick of his wrist and began reading. "Thirty eight years old at the time of her death. Single. Lived in Clunes, New South Wales. Owned and managed a spa and beauty parlor for the past ten years.

This, however, is exactly where her story stops, if you'll believe it. No one at the Station has been able to find a trace of her existence before she moved to Clunes....which I find very strange."

Maggie nodded. "Strange, indeed." Her silence afterward told Tom to continue. When he started to, she raised up her finger to stop him. "No wait...why would a beautiful, well dressed woman wander into the Bangalow cemetery in the middle of the night?

"Perhaps she came with whoever killed her to look at a tomb? To look at the tomb she was found in, maybe? Maybe she was forced into it. Who knows?" Tom shrugged when Maggie didn't say anything else, and then continued on with more theories. "Maybe she came to Bangalow to re-kindle an old friendship, and then things took a turn for the worse?"

"—wait right there, Tom." Tom grinned. He loved when Maggie interrupted him with her theories, though he would never admit it to her. "You may be right on any of those accounts, but she wouldn't have done any of those things in the middle of the night. That's not something a lady would do."

"Clunes is only 15 kilometers from Bangalow. Do you think she may have a special male friend here? A love interest, perhaps" Maggie enquired.

Chapter 4

Tom didn't know, but no one seemed to have any information on her, or anyone fitting her description who had relocated in the last ten years.

"Well I've definitely never seen her face before. And she has such a striking one—or she did—that I would have remembered it, I think."

"Didn't you say you knew the Pemberthy's?" Tom asked. Maggie had mentioned during her statement that the tomb the woman was found in belonged to the Permberthy's, who had been semi-frequent guests of her cooking classes at the bed and breakfast.

"Yes, I did. And I know what you're thinking. They had a boy and a girl, but they both drowned in a boating accident years ago. They were twins, and their bodies were never found. That was my first thought, as well."

"Well, I had one of my detectives look into the matter, because quite frankly, the manner of death for the parents was some cause for concern."

"Follow me," Lady Margaret said. "And keep talking, I'm listening. I'm just going to grab something." As Maggie tried to picture what the Pemberthy's children would look like, an image of Valerie Chamber's face Kept popping into her head, interfering with all other thoughts. Frustrated, she marched up to the little attic of the bed and breakfast, Detective Sullivan trailing behind her.

"So anyway, Jane and Charles Pemberthy, as you probably know, because they were in your cooking classes, died relatively closely to each other, time frame wise. Within a year or so of each other, they each had a stroke. I remember it striking me as odd, kind of like Johnny Cash and June Carter. It's sweet, but it doesn't happen all the time. What are you looking for up there?" Tom steadied the attic ladder Maggie had pulled down, when she didn't answer him, he just kept talking.

"Valerie's face is really haunting me, Tom. I can't remember exactly what Mrs. Pemberthy looks like…" She backed down the ladder and tore out a paper from an old cooking school yearbook. "Can you do me a favor and run this through some fancy science machine and let me know if this looks anything like what Carol looked like."

"Carol, their daughter, yes?"

"Yes. I'm sure you have something that can do that, don't you?"

"I can do you one better, I'll run the pictures through the aging program and let you know what the Pemberthy's daughter would have looked like, had she grown up. I'd imagine we'll at least get close that way."

After Tom left, Maggie decided to take a walk around her property. Stretching her legs and a bit of country fresh air would do her good; and her mind wonders. The reunion had quieted down and had given her time to think. Unfortunately, all she could think about what Valerie's face. It was so haunting how she'd been smiling.

The next day, Tom let Maggie know that her hunch was correct, as usual. For some reason, though, Maggie didn't delight in it as she usually did. Valerie was, indeed, Carol Pemberthy, all grown up.

The medical examiner also confirmed that the young lady had had some facial reconstruction surgery, though Maggie couldn't for the life of her figure out why. The woman had good genes; she would have been gorgeous either way.

It was certainly a twist in the case. As far as Maggie could tell, all they would have to do would be to retrace her steps from the day she supposedly drowned in the river. Her body was said to have been washed down stream, which was verified by someone on the scene. What happened after that was the big mystery.

"What about her brother?" Maggie asked as Tom picked her up to take her to the police station that morning. She'd insisted on driving and he reminded her that it would be very hard to catch her up on things while they were in two separate cars. Detective Sullivan had mastered the fine art of talking hands free on the mobile phone while driving, but Maggie still insisted that it was very dangerous.

"Do you think he survived?"

He did, but he doesn't use the name Pemberthy. He goes by Thomas Kilkane these days. The Lismore Police Department is looking for him right this moment. From what I can tell, though, he doesn't really fit the profile of a killer.

Most of what he has going against him are minor robberies and such. And even those are just from being poor and down in life. Not something we'd really classify as dangerous. One of the times he was picked up, he was asked if he was a drug addict. He joked that it was a luxury he couldn't afford! I thought that was a pretty clever way of saying no."

"Did any of his crimes occur in Clunes? That would be a good enough reason to link the two of them together."

"No, no. I don't think either of them knew the other one was alive. Again, I could be wrong, and I'm sure you'll tell me if I am…but as far as I can tell, no. And all of his crimes were in the Lismore area, none of them were in the countryside or even anywhere near Clunes. Next question."

"Perhaps, from his experience with his parents, he was afraid to venture too far away from where he was used to. Why, do you think, did neither of the children contact their parents when they were taken to safety? Why would you not do that? Were there any reports of child abuse in the home? I mean, I can't really imagine Jane or Charles doing anything like that…they seemed like the nicest people. But as you know, Detective, it's usually the people who seem the nicest that do the strangest and most terrible things."

"I'll look into it."

Chapter 5

Later that afternoon, when the police finally get ahold of Thomas Kilkane, he was completely stunned to learn about the death of a sister they said he had. As far as he knew, he'd never even had a sister. He claimed he'd never heard of a Valeria Charmers, had never been to Clunes, and was certainly never anywhere near the Bangalow cemetery.

All of this seemed fine enough, but when Lady Margaret arrived to the police station and asked to go into the interrogation room, the young man immediately changed his stance. He sulked in his chair, and cowered away from her as she entered the room. Under his breath he started a string of panicked mumblings that seemed to be directed at Maggie. Something along the lines of I'll never be late to cooking class again, I promise! He looked positively scared, and like he was about to be punished.

Maggie was very confused, and was eventually asked to leave the room by the psychologist on the case, who was finding it more and more difficult to get the man to answer questions while she was in the room. Once the meeting with him was over, the psychologist closed the door behind her and stepped over towards Detective Sullivan and Maggie in the hallway.

"Well he has certainly had some sort of childhood trauma, folks. But he isn't insane, and he's not belligerent. I also really don't think he is capable of murder. He's got a pretty sweet spirit, I think he's just been broken by life and been dealt a really unfortunate hand. That's certainly heartbreaking, but doesn't make him a murderer. The only things to be dug into are the fact that he can't recall having a sister at all, and can't remember where he's last seen Lady Turnbull. I'll send over my final report by morning, but until then, that's my off-the-books answer for you. Have good day." And with that, she was gone, her heels clacking on the cold tile of the police station floor.

"Well it seems we are at an impasse, Lady Margaret. If he can't even remember having a sister, or he's blocked all memory of her from some sort of childhood trauma, then I don't really think he could hold a grudge against her long enough to kill her. Any other ideas floating around up there in that inquisitive mind of yours?"

"I'm really more concerned with the parent's obvious disregard for their children's lives, here. Aren't you, Tom? I mean...who could just assume that their children drown, and then carry on with everyday life?"

"They basically just told everyone, that their children were dead and then retreated back into their cocoon. Seems odd, don't you think? They must have abused them in some way, I'm sure of it. There had to be something like that going on for Carol and James... or Valerie and Thomas, as it were...to never have contacted them after having survived the boating accident. There simply has to be an astounding reason for that." Lady Margaret stated.

"You know, I've been thinking back to when the two were in my class when they were younger. I recall them being a very timid, couple of people—very reserved. I also remembered earlier today, in the interrogation room, that Carol was always trying to better her brother in some way. Maybe she continued that on right into adulthood?"

"Yeah you may be right, there, Lady Margaret. You usually are. But why would she completely refuse to acknowledge him after all that time. Do you think she even remembered that she had a brother? It certainly looked like she was okay in the head enough to do well for herself in life. I mean, that was a pretty fancy dress as far as I could tell…and everything we found on her from the last ten years or so suggested that she did pretty well for herself. Why would she leave her brother to live in abject poverty while she so obviously lived the high life? That hardly seems fair, maybe she was abusive after all?"

Just then, Detective Alfred Logan walked in with a few files in his hands. "Excuse me, Detective, do you have a minute? There's a break in the case."

"Sure thing, I always have a minute for that; what have you got?" Tom took the papers he was being handed and listened intently.

"Well it seems that Charles Pemberthy has a sister, and she lives here in Lismore. Her name is Helen. I thought you might want to pay her a visit. These days, sir, she's known as Alice Kilkane.

When they arrived at Alice's house about an hour later, the questioning went relatively quickly. She let them know that she did, in fact, see Thomas after his disappearance. A few days after he had supposedly died in the boating accident, he showed up on her doorstep. She was in complete shock, and when she offered to take him home to his parent's, he would have nothing to do with the idea.

Soon after that, Helen moved to Lismore and settled down, changing her name to Kilkane and raising Thomas as best as she could. The boy had gone to school and done fairly well, but suffered nightmares. He told his aunt how much his sister made him suffer, and Helen recounted stories of what a vicious child Carol was.

"Under a mask of cleverness and gentleness, she was evil, Detective. When he showed me his scars, that sealed the deal for me. That's why I took him away and raised him on my own. No one should have to live through that, it's inhuman."

A few hours later, back at the police station, the other detectives managed to track down the foster parents that took in Valerie after the incident. They'd found her wandering the streets of Lismore eating discarded food and trying not to be noticed.

Under the watchful care of adoptive parents, she eventually went to beauty school and did quite well there. The foster parents explained that they had no idea about her antecedents and could shed no light on why she might have been murdered and stored in her parents' crypt.

Chapter 6

On the way back to the station with Lady Maggie, Tom phoned the former Helen Pemberthy to ask her if she thought Thomas could ever act upon his nightmares. Apparently they were often about harming his sister, and Helen couldn't be sure. She hadn't ever seen any signs of acting out on them, but she wouldn't consider it impossible.

Detective Sullivan concluded to Maggie that this behavior probably contributed to his homelessness. The psychologist also called and let the two of them know that Thomas did have a deep-seated childhood trauma, along with some schizophrenia.

"You know," Maggie said as they drove. "Maybe they found each other by accident? Twins can find each other while being blindfolded, you know."

"I think you're right, Maggie. I think that Thomas Kilkane killed his sister, and has no recollection of it due to the schizophrenia. His alter ego just doesn't acknowledge that it happened, because to him…it didn't. The poor guy, can you imagine not remembering doing anything, much less murdering your sister?!"

"So how do you think it happened, Detective?" Maggie tried to keep the conversation light because normally she enjoyed this part. The look on that girl's face, though, still haunted her.

"I hope we get to know, Lady Margaret. It could be months before he assumes his other personality. That's the only real way to get any information out of him."

Several months later, Inspector Sullivan was interrupted during his morning coffee at the police station. Detective Hodges walked up to his desk and handed him a statement. It was from Thomas's alter ego, and he had given his testimony of what had happened that night in the crypt.

Apparently, as the statement read, Thomas was begging on the street for alms when his sister walked by and dropped some coins into his bucket. He didn't recognize her face at all, and the detectives concluded that Valerie suffered from the same schizophrenia that Thomas did because she didn't appear to have recognized him either.

The two of them would have passed in silence, as two ships not even acknowledging each other's presence, were it not for a small spark. Though Thomas didn't recognize her face, since she'd had facial reconstruction surgery, he did recognize her hand. Something about the way her hand twisted and let her wrist be exposed, he remembered it from the years of being tormented by her as a child, and something inside of him snapped.

Under the pretext of forgiving his sister and forgetting the past, he took her to their parents' crypt. She went willingly, and Thomas believed that was because she wanted to return to the abusive sister he always knew her to be.

She was stuck in a semi-healthy cycle where she could at least hold down a steady relationship and get through life. When she saw Thomas, though, and saw that familiar vulnerable look in his eye, she snapped back to being her sinister self.

Thomas believed that she would attack him again, and when they neared their parents' tomb, he took her inside and killed her before she got the chance to harm him.

Maggie, as Tom was retelling the story, imagined that's where the look of satisfaction had come from. In her mind, she was planning on returning to the evil version of herself the whole walk down to the crypt. It was only because Thomas acted faster that she was killed. Had he not acted quickly, she likely would have done the same.

When the story was finished, and Detective Tom Sullivan had given Maggie the very last detail, she was happy to have the case out of her system. Never again did she want to think of those two children as something other than the slightly timid people from her cooking class.

Now back home, she took the class yearbook up into the attic. She tried her best to let herself know she didn't do anything wrong. Everything in her told her she should have done something for those two kids. That she should somehow have been able to spare them their pain, and she couldn't.

Getting this emotionally involved in a case wasn't something Maggie had ever let herself do before, but this time it felt personal. It felt sadder. And Maggie was ready to be on to the next case, which would hopefully be a murder case that was a bit more upbeat. Even that is a little sad.

Murder in the Valley

Chapter 1

Maggie Turnbull stood on her sun-drenched veran-dah. In one hand she held a mug of coffee, with the other she shielded her eyes from the sun's glare. She enjoyed the moment to look out from her hilltop home that was known as Lawler's Loft. It was a beautiful area that always had fresh air and warm sunlight to provide for her and any guests that she entertained.

Privately, Maggie felt blessed to have found such a good guest house in Lawler's Loft. In the beginning, the house was in sore need of a protector who would give it new life. There were some hopeful buyers who avoided or even rejected it for the shape it was in but not Maggie. She refurbished and turned it into a bed and breakfast. Business was slow at first but soon began to pick up as news and word of Maggie's hospitality spread.

Lawler's Loft always had sun and warmth in great abundance. Maggie never suspected Australia would be so warm and enjoyable compared to the cold and bleak days of her time living in the United Kingdom. If she had known Australia was so inviting, she would have moved here twenty years ago instead of ten. What Maggie did miss – or who rather – was her late husband Malcolm, a dot com millionaire, who passed away from a heart attack far too early in life. She was grateful for his financial prowess and ideas that enabled her to live on her own even without him.

Maggie looked up when her thoughts of Malcolm's memory were interrupted by a loud knock on the door. Maggie walked through the plush, comfortable rooms of Lawler's Loft's main floor as the pounding on the door became more frantic.

"Coming, coming!" Maggie called. "Don't knock my door in. I'm coming." Maggie opened the door to reveal the hunched form of one of the locals – Lucy Broad. She gasped. "Lucy! Goodness, whatever is the matter?"

Lucy's shoulders shuddered as she struggled to take in a deep breath. She lifted up her face to reveal a wet, puffy, red face. Her eyes were practically swollen shut from all the crying. Her hair was a disheveled mess and her clothes were wrinkled.

"Did someone try to attack you?" Maggie asked when Lucy just stood shaking on her doorstep instead of telling her what was the matter. "Please, Lucy, you know you can tell me."

Lucy took several deep, gulping breathes before saying: "I—I almost got into an accident while coming to Bangalow! I didn't know where else to go but I need to talk to someone! It's so strange! It's too strange!"

"What's too strange? What happened?"

"The police in Lismore are absolutely useless! Useless! They couldn't find a window in a room even with a map!"

Maggie guided Lucy into the house, through the main hall, to the sitting room. "Please, take a seat," she said. "I'll pour you a cup of tea."

"Thank you," Lucy whispered as Maggie deposited a box of tissues in her still trembling hand. "I knew I could count on you to not judge and just be supportive. You're a true gem, Maggie."

"Every person is worth our time and understanding," Maggie said before disappearing to the kitchen to pour the tea. Under different circumstances, she would have gotten a tray to carry the tea cups and saucers out on but these times did not allow themselves for formalities. Instead, she carried one cup and saucer in each hand as she returned to the living room.

"I brought you your tea," Maggie said kindly.

"Thank you." Lucy reached out for the cup to take a sip. "I suppose you're wondering why I turned up on your doorstep like this."

"I am," Maggie admitted as she sat down across from Lucy.

Looking up again, Lucy gave Maggie a small smile. "You don't know me that well, Lady Margaret, so I feel there are some things I should explain to you. Just so you understand everything, that's all."

Maggie nodded. "Go on."

"My husband Winston and I live north of Bangalow in Federal, New South Wales. We live on an acreage estate that's Winston's property. We inherited it from Winston's grandfather. It's a lovely place but, like any old estate, was falling apart. Winston used to be a stock broker for Barclays UK. He ran the local branch office here and that's how we were able to renovate our house last year."

Maggie normally was quite good at learning the latest gossip around town but Winston not working at Lismore anymore was new information for her. "Used to be?" Maggie asked.

"Winston resigned from the firm in Lismore?"

"Yes, three months ago." Lucy's hands tightened around the tea cup to the point her knuckles almost turned white. "I didn't know that he had quit until I phoned Barclays UK in Lismore and found out that he left! He never told me or even dropped any hints!"

As if sensing what Maggie was about to ask Lucy continued as she gripped the cup in a death grip. "I don't know where, if anywhere, Winston is working now. He goes to work somewhere as usual every morning and comes back at night. That is except for last night when he didn't come home."

Maggie knew a little about Winston Broad from her usual sources of gossip in town. He was hand-some, well liked (or lusted after) by the ladies and could convince anyone of anything. She wouldn't be the least bit surprised if he went into town every morning to hide some ongoing affair and came home to his wife at night. Winston definitely came across as the type of bloke that wanted to have his cake and eat it too.

"Do you think Winston could have been seeing someone else?" Maggie asked as tactfully as possible. Now that she had Lucy calmed down, she didn't need to send her into a fresh torrent of tears.

Lucy shook her head. "No, Winston would never have an affair. It's not in his nature at all. We were planning our five year anniversary last weekend. He wouldn't do that to me. He just wouldn't."

Lucy's pink cheeks turned a deeper pink as she realized how forceful and in denial that must sound. "I'm sorry, forgive me. I just get so frustrated as those are the same questions that Detective Tom Sullivan asked me when I went to see him this morning. No one wants to believe me when I say Winston wouldn't have an affair. It's the likely conclusion so of course everyone jumps to it."

"Why did you come to see me about it?" Maggie asked.

Lucy looked up and blinked her red, tear bright eyes. "Because you need to help me prove it."

Chapter 2

"Help you?" Maggie blinked wide eyes at Lucy. "I. . .I don't make it a habit to play detective."

"But you have before, so why not again?" Lucy set her cup of tea down. "You don't have to tell me one way or the other now, but just promise to think it over. Please?"

"With any luck, there will be nothing to investigate." Maggie patted Lucy's hand in a motherly gesture that usually got the locals to spill all juicy details they knew about town happenings. She didn't mean to know and see all, it was just part of being known as a good hostess and even better listener. "I'll bet dollars to donuts that Winston is just being forgetful and will come home."

Lucy frowned. "I have my doubts that he will return but never mind that. A lot can happen in twelve hours. That's when the Lismore Police will let me file an official missing person report."

She sighed. "Twelve hours. I don't know if I can wait that long. Not knowing where he is or if he's safe or not is driving me mad."

"The police have procedures for a reason." Maggie picked up the empty tea things in one hand and gestured for Lucy to follow her. She deposited the cups and saucers in the kitchen before leading the way to the front door. "I'll think about what you're...requesting...but only after these next twelve hours pass with no word from Winston. Do we have a deal?"

The offer of help – even the delayed offer of help – seemed to calm Lucy. Her whole body relaxed as she stepped through the door onto the front porch. "Thank you, Lady Margaret. Thank you."

"Don't thank me just yet." Maggie leaned against the door frame. "There's no case yet."

"Oh, there will be." Lucy tried to straighten up her disheveled hair and clothes. "There will be."

Once Lucy was gone, Maggie shut the door. Something about Lucy's story and her behavior seemed, well, off to Maggie. She kept an eye on the drive way and once Lucy had driven away she left the room to go to her computer. There was bound to be information about Barclays UK stock online. Maggie knew if she could find out what the connection was she was certain she could tell Lucy and put this horrible question behind them.

She was a natural sleuth and wasn't about to let the question of what happened to Winston just fade into the background. Not when his life could be at stake. As she stated before, a lot could happen in the matter of twelve hours. Maggie wasn't willing to find out what exactly 'a lot' translated in Winston's case.

"And more Lucy was beside herself with worry," Maggie muttered to herself as she started sleuthing online. You could find just about anything online as long as you knew where to look. Maggie started out by looking for information on Winston's stock. Barclays UK was a rather large organization, and in some regions, branches went out into debt collection. If someone owed a large amount of money and saw Winston as their enemy, that would be an excellent motivator to cause him harm.

Maggie's excitement at finding a possible motive evaporated the longer she searched online. As much as she dug and searched into that side of the business, she kept hitting brick walls. Barclays protected their inside information tighter than Fort Knox. Frustrated, she got up and paced around her office. Why was there little to nothing to be found? Was everything locked up in restricted files? Fat chance of getting clearance to that unless she made nice with an employee.

"Now there's a thought," she said out loud.

Who could she find that worked in that department of the firm. Whoever was working in that part of the business would want to keep a low profile as debt collectors were often frowned upon as much as tow-truck or repossession companies. She couldn't think of anyone who liked to advertise their efforts or their success in that regards. It would be easy for some disgruntled person to try to cause them harm.

Despite the bad guy persona, repossession and debt collecting was a lucrative enterprise that existed since before the Roman Empire and would continue to exist long after they were all gone. Is that what happened to Lucy's husband?

Could Winston be involved in debt collection and a disgruntled person harmed him?

Chapter 3

Lucy Broad sighed as she returned to her home in Federal. She really didn't want to go home after Winston had gone missing. She didn't want to deal with the stares and whispers she knew would follow. The stares and comments would include pity, disgust, wonderment, and comments about her marriage to Winston.

It made her sick just thinking about it. Was it so hard for everyone in town to accept that Winston chose her? Sure, he could have had his pick of women – he probably still could – but he chose her. Lucy knew how lucky she was. She didn't need everyone reminding her that they thought Winston was just bidding his time until something or someone better came along. Lucy let her shoulders slouch as she pulled into her drive way. At least Maggie was kind to her. It seemed like no one else was willing to extend her that same courtesy during this trying time.

Climbing out of her car, Lucy headed towards the door but, before she could reach it, she caught sight of something that hadn't been there before. For one horrifying moment, she thought her door was covered in blood. Closer inspection revealed that it was red paint. Red paint that someone used to send her a message –

"You move or else!"

Lucy gasped. She couldn't stop herself from reading the terrible words over and over again as if they would somehow change the more she looked at them. Who would be so cruel? Who would write such a thing at a time like this? Her husband was missing. She didn't need to worry about vandalism and threats on top of it all.

For a moment, Lucy debated calling the police or venturing inside her house to see if they vandalized more than just the door. Would the police be of any help at all since they were no help at all when she tried to report Winston's disappearance? Why would they be any help now? Would they accuse her of writing the words herself for attention or sympathy?

Lucy struggled to build up her courage before she cautiously ventured inside her house. She couldn't hear any signs of life or anyone around. She hoped that meant the vandals had long since left. She took a deep breath to calm her nerves before pushing the door open. What she saw made her gasp more than seeing the words scrawled on her front door did.

The house was destroyed! It was an absolute mess. There were large red paint splashes over every piece of furniture in the living room and kitchen. It looked as if someone set a red paint bomb off in her room!

Tears stung Lucy's eyes as she teetered between despair and fear. Who would do such a thing? What had she ever done to anyone in town besides try to live her life as quietly as possible? She didn't like drama – Winston was the flashy one in the relationship – but it seemed like, no matter what, drama followed her.

Lucy fled the house and ran to her car. She sat in the driver's seat, hands gripping the steering wheel and took deep, gulping breathes to calm herself. Once her hands stopped shaking, instead of driving off to report the crime, she fumbled for her phone and dialed the first number that came to mind – Maggie Turnbull's.

"Maggie, it's Lucy. I'm sorry to call you like this but I'm in trouble," Lucy said after Maggie picked up. "Someone broke into my house and wrote 'move now or else' on my door and all my windows. They threw red paint over everything. My furniture, countertops, walls...It's horrible. It's just horrible. At first...At first, I thought it was blood." Lucy broke down in tears. "Who would do something like this? I don't understand."

"I can think of a few whose and what fors but I'll save that for when you're here instead of there" Maggie said. "Come to my place and stay here for a while, Lucy, or at least until this affair is sorted out."

"Are you sure?" Lucy asked. "I wouldn't want to put you in any danger."

"You should be safe here. I have plenty of room at Lawler's Loft and it's quiet at the moment. I only have one guest so that will leave lots of room for you."

Lucy didn't take long to think things over. She didn't want to be alone right now. Maggie offered her a cozy place to stay and company. How could she say no? "Alright. I'll be there shortly."

"I'll put some tea on for you."

Chapter 4

After Maggie hung up with Lucy, she immediately dialed Detective Tom Sullivan. "This is Sullivan," a man's voice said.

"Detective Sullivan, Maggie Turnbull here," she said. "Do you have a few minutes?"

"Yes, of course! Is something going on? To be honest I'm surprised to hear from you," Sullivan said. "Are you alright?"

"Yes, it's not about me. It's about Lucy Broad. She said she's told you about her missing husband but you wouldn't file and missing person's report. She was most upset about it."

"I'm sorry to hear it, but I don't make the rules," Sullivan said. "Protocol says that we still have to wait a few hours before filing a missing person report."

"The thing is, Detective, it's not just a missing person's case anymore. Lucy's house was vandalized this morning while she was away. She's scared out of her wits, poor thing."

"I'll send a forensic team to see if they can lift any prints from inside her home," Sullivan promised. "Maybe it will lead us to wherever Winston has gone."

"I hope so," Maggie said. "I dearly hope so."

Not long after Lucy was settled into one of the guest rooms at Lawler's Loft, Maggie went to answer a knock on the door. It was Detective Sullivan along with a colleague named Detective Jim Patterson. Detective Patterson was a member of the Lismore Police Department, and fortunately for Detective Sullivan, Detective Patterson was very familiar with the people of Federal and the rural areas surrounding Federal.

They had questioned everyone in and around Federal to get more information about Winston and Lucy Broad. They found out that Winston was a quiet and responsible man. He was popular with the ladies, but that didn't mean he did anything with the opportunities. He loved golf and often played at Ocean Shores Golf Club.

During the summer, the Broads would invite a few friends over and enjoy a backyard barbeque. There was nothing out of the ordinary which made it even more difficult to figure out what happened to Winston. It was time to interview Lucy.

"Detectives, please, have a seat, Lucy will be right in." Maggie motioned at the plush couch.

"Can I offer you any refreshments?"

"We won't be staying long, Lady Margaret," Sullivan said. "We just need to talk to Mrs. Broad."

Lucy entered the room and sat down next to Maggie in the couch facing the detectives. "Have you found out anything about Winston?"

"That's what we wanted to talk to you about, Mrs. Broad." Sullivan flipped open a small note pad and readied his pencil to take down her answers. "Mrs. Broad, have you heard of a scheme that has been going around recently?"

That was not what she was expecting. "What scheme?"

"There is a scheme where a person pretends to be interested in buying multiple properties over a large area of the valley. Have you heard about it?"

"There were rumors going around about some property developer examining all these properties for a resort going up in the valley but that's it," Lucy said. "If you hadn't have mentioned it, I wouldn't think it would have any connection to Winston's disappearance or someone vandalizing our home."

"Do you remember the name of this alleged property developer?"

Lucy shook her head. "I don't. It was only a rumor. No one really talked about it much and then it sort of faded away. Or at least I think I faded away." She shook her head again. "I never heard of it at any rate beyond the initial buzz."

Detective Sullivan raised an eyebrow but said nothing. It was rather strange that this rumor seemed to be so strong but no one spoke of it.

"Do you know of anyone who has moved away from the neighborhood recently?" Maggie asked.

Lucy shook her head. "I haven't heard about anyone moving. I have heard of a couple of foreclosures and even one lady was going to file for bankruptcy shortly."

Detective Sullivan jotted down some notes and asked Lucy a few more questions about Winston's habits. It was more of asking about Winston's schedule and where he may go from time to time. Was he always punctual about showing up at certain times or did he sometimes attend other places after work?

Lucy answered as best she could. As far as she knew, he left for work in the morning, stayed there all day, and came home the same time every night. He saved the week ends for golf and getting together with friends.

"Thank you for your time, Mrs. Broad. We understand it is a difficult time for you." Detective Sullivan closed his notebook and looked over at Patterson. "We should be off. A detective's work is never done. Even in a quiet town like this."

The detectives and Maggie rose from their couches. "I'll show you the door," Maggie offered.

"This way, please, gentlemen." She motioned for them to follow her. Instead of going straight to the front door, though, she stopped just out of Lucy's hearing. "I discovered some information on Winston," she confessed.

Detective Sullivan's notebook was out again in a flash. "We're listening. Lady Margaret is our resident sleuth," he explained to Patterson. "We've formed a partnership of sorts. It's easier to work together on a case than apart."

"I went online and looked up the company that he worked for," Maggie began. "I saw Winston might have received a debt collection package. He might have felt the need to work freelance on collecting debts and, or maybe even, executing foreclosures on behalf of the local banks. If he was, he could have been clearing an area of interest for that developer."

"Mr. Broad's firm and the developer would be able to force the residents to sell their property or run the risk of going bankrupt, Patterson added as the idea caught on. "That would allow them to pick up all that acreage for a very cheap price."

"It makes you wonder who this alleged developer is," Sullivan said. "For something that big, it's very strange that no one is talking about it out in the open. We should pay a visit to the banks. Maybe they'd know something since they're the ones that ultimately control the money."

Maggie nodded agreement.

"I hope following the trail to Barclays UK breaks the case wide open. Shall you talk to them or shall I?"

Chapter 5

"We'll work the Barclays angle," Sullivan promised. "You just figure out if Lucy is hiding anything."

"It's a pleasure doing business with you, gentlemen," Maggie teased in a sing song as she led the way to the front door. "Three heads are better than one, don't you think?"

"We'll find out soon enough." Patterson tipped an imaginary hat Maggie's direction. "Till we meet again, Lady Turnbull." Maggie smiled. "Likewise, Detective Patterson." She closed the door behind them.

Once back in the car, the detectives reviewed what they knew of the case. "What do you mean that it's strange that the bank would entrust Winston with foreclosures?" Sullivan asked.

"It's odd that a reputable stock broker or bank would entrust collection or foreclosure duties to someone as experienced in that department as Winston Broad." Patterson tapped the dashboard with one finger in time to the music playing on the radio. "His experience isn't in collections and he hasn't been in the bank for that long. Why give him that sort of responsibility? It's a thankless job even if you are making money hand over fist for the bank. Collections always gets some person seeking retribution."

Detective Sullivan nodded. "Do you think Winston Broad have access to account holders personal information? He had to know something for someone to want to foreclose on him."

"If he had clearance from the bank, he'd have access to personal information. Now the question is what did he do with it once he got his hands on the debt collection package. He might have begun to play some rather profitable game rather than play by the rules."

"If he had, it would be very dangerous for him," Detective Sullivan said. "I'm going to call the brokerage firm when we reach the station. Their manager should be able to tell us what happened to Winston at the bank. If he was stealing, then that would be an excellent motivation to disappear so suddenly. Being missing is better than being in prison."

~

Once back at the station Detective Sullivan found a quiet corner to call the stock brokerage firm. He expected to meet some resistance with the higher ups once he identified himself and told them why he was calling but, to his surprise, the company was more than happy to talk about what happened. The person doing the talking identified herself as Sybil.

Sullivan didn't know if he lucked out and encountered someone new to the company who was spilling secrets or if the higher up decided to make an example out of Winston Broad. Either way, he wouldn't complain. Cooperation was hard to come by in his line of work.

"Well, it all started when he stole something from the firm," Sybil said matter-of-factly.

"And what was that?" Detective Sullivan asked.

"A package." Sullivan heard rustling around as if Sybil was searching for something. "That's all I can really say, though. First the package gets stolen and then Winston goes missing. It's a little too convenient, don't you think, Detective?"

"You tell me."

"Well, we thought so, so we sent someone to...investigate if you will. We thought if we roughed up his house a bit we'd find something or he'd come out of hiding. Either or. We weren't going to be picky which."

"The company hired someone to vandalize Winston Broad's house?" Sullivan blinked, shocked. That was not what he was expecting to hear. A firm with a hired tough? And in a place like this? What are the odds?"

"We only wanted to scare him into handing over what the stock brokerage needed," Sybil insisted. "I admit, it's not my favorite way of dealing with a situation, but it is an effective way."

"Yet Mr. Broad and the package are still missing."

"Yes, there is that," Sybil said. "I didn't say it was a foolproof way, just normally an effective way."

"If you think of anything else that is important to the case, give me a ring, Sybil."

"Of course, Detective."

After hanging up the phone, Sullivan gave a heavy sigh. Patterson looked over from his desk.

"Bad news?"

"No, politics." Sullivan sighed again. "Remind me never to get involved in stock brokerage."

Chapter 6

Quietly, Maggie was suspicious of Lucy's story but dared not to voice her opinion just yet. She worried that if she did, Lucy would clam up and not say anything to anybody. Maggie suspected Lucy did know something more than she claimed about Winston's disappearance, but was hiding it for reasons not yet known to them.

"Lucy, I have an idea," Maggie said cheerfully after finding Lucy reading quietly in the sitting room. "Why don't we go to the shire's urban development and planning office today? I know that doesn't sound like the most exciting outing, but it will get you out of the house and away from this terrible situation for a while. It may help distract you from thinking of Winston's disappearance or the vandalism."

Lucy struggled. "I suppose anything is worth trying once."

As they drove, Maggie made small talk but didn't let on to her suspicions about Lucy or North Federal Resort Development Company. She'd bet dollars to donuts that they had their fingers in this pie. Maggie suspected they applied for construction permits to build a resort and townhouses on the plot of land in the rumors circulating around town. It just might be the string they needed to tie the company to Winston's collections scheme.

Maggie knew she needed to play her cards right if she was going to gleam any information from the development company. She wasn't the police so she couldn't just barge in with a warrant and extract information that way. Still, she was well known and trusted in the community so someone in the company may be willing to let secrets slip that way.

After parking the car, Maggie turned to Lucy. "Just follow my lead in here, alright? If my hunch is right, the North Federal Resort Development Company is tied to Winston's disappearance."

Lucy sucked in her breath. "Do you really think so?"

Maggie winked. "We're about to find out."

"Good morning, we have some questions about your latest development project." Maggie smiled as bright and charming as possible when they stopped in front of the reception desk. The receptionist's name plate read 'Susan Chase.' "Can you give us a hint about this land?"

"It's going to be developed," Susan said. "North Federal Resort Development Company applied for multiple development permits in and around the rural areas near Federal. "

"Is that so?" Maggie made a point to sound interested. Showing any bit of interest in someone's job usually got them talking more. "Why are they trying to buy up the rural areas?"

"No one would miss that little plot of land and the benefits to the company are huge. Once we finish up buying all the pieces of property, construction will begin."

"I don't suppose we could take a peek at what the company has in mind, could we?" Maggie asked.

"I'm afraid not, but I don't think the company will be upset if I tell you there's a plan to build a great resort on it," Susan said. "It'll be huge. All we'll have to do is sit back and watch the money roll in. It will be a boon for the area too," she added as if she realized that all this talk of money, money, money for the company wouldn't sit well with a couple of locals.

"Well, we can't wait to see what all the excitement is about." Maggie plastered a big, insincere smile on her face before backing out of the office with Lucy close behind her. They certainly seem eager to get started," Maggie said once they were out of hearing.

"With the money they're set to make on the deal, I can see why," Lucy said. "I think just about anyone would be tempted in that situation."

"Just about," Maggie agreed. Was Winston tempted? Is the land development project the reason he disappeared without a trace? "Let's touch base with Detective Sullivan. Maybe we both can fill in some gaps for each other."

Lucy frowned. "But they're the police. What if they already know about the development plans? We'll be wasting time we could be spending looking for Winston."

"We're all working as a team, Lucy. The sooner we make sure everyone is on the same page, the sooner we find Winston."

~

"Hello, Detective Sullivan!" Maggie waved as they entered the police station. "Any new information to share?"

Sullivan looked up from a stack of papers he was pouring over. "The stock brokerage firm was surprisingly forthcoming with information. It seems Mr. Broad was in possession of a large debt collection package when he was last seen at the company. Did you know anything of his moonlighting with collections, Mrs. Broad?"

Lucy shook her head. "I had no clue! Winston wasn't acting suspiciously or anything when I last saw him. I certainly never saw him come home with any sort of package. Could the people who broke into our home have been looking for that?"

"It is the most possible scenario," Sullivan said. "We still don't know where or from whom Mr. Broad got the package." He motioned at his stocks of paperwork. "Patterson and I are trying to figure that out now."

"Perhaps that land developer gave the package to Winston," Maggie said. "If this package is worth that much money, he could've been lured into some kind of lucrative scheme. The property owners who still needed to leave their land would be forced to do so if they couldn't repay their bank mortgages or credit card debts."

Lucy's already pale face drained of all remaining color. "I can't get over the idea that someone would go to such lengths to buy someone's property, let alone vandalism."

Detective Sullivan's eyes softened in sympathy. "I'm sure this is just an extreme case, Mrs. Broad. We'll find who did it and that should lead us to your husband."

Maggie, however, was not surprised at what the land developer would do to collect up valuable properties. Similar things were taking place in other parts of Australia. It may be a long shot, but it was possible that all the cases were linked together.

"I can't believe my husband would be willing to participate in such an awful and underhanded scheme," Lucy said. "Someone must be threatening him or-or using his good name. I won't believe it. I just won't."

"I don't mean to be difficult but do you know how lucrative and tempting debt collection can be?" Detective Sullivan asked. "When a credit card company is unable to get payments from their clients they often sell the debt to a collector for rather cheap. If the debt is $5,000 the debt collector says he will buy it for say $1,000. He then approaches the credit card owner and offers him to wipe the debt clean for say $2,500. If the person chooses to pay the collector the quoted amount the collector has made the amount and an additional $1,500."

Lucy still stoutly supported her husband's innocence in the scheme. "It's not in Winston's nature to do such a thing...no matter how much money was in it for him or anyone else."

"Do you have another theory?" Detective Sullivan humored her."

Lucy bit her bottom lip. "I....It could be a way to get many of the struggling land owners or even hobby farmers who own their properties in the area to sell their land. But I don't understand why Winston would just up and disappear? Is he hiding somewhere to do the job?"

"I'm sure Winston has disappeared of his own accord; otherwise your house would not have been vandalized," Maggie told her.

"Why are we talking land deals and collections when Winston is still missing?" Lucy asked. "That should be your focus – nothing else."

Detective Patterson appeared. At first he looked surprised to see Maggie and Lucy standing next to Sullivan's desk but soon got over the shock because of the weight of the news he carried.

"Forensics found some prints in the Broad house and a receipt for $500,000 from Winston's brokerage firm. He purchased the debt collection package from his firm for $500,000."

"But where would he get that sort of money to buy anything?" Lucy asked. "We don't have that lying around. If we did, we wouldn't be buying debt collection packages, that's for sure."

"You don't have that sort of money laying around, my dear, but the land developers do," Maggie said.

"We already have a team on it following the paper trail," Patterson said. "The better question is where is Winston? Did he run away with the package and plan to go over the developers' heads and contact the debtors on his own?"

"It is a strong possibility," Maggie agreed. "But why would he get mixed up in such a scheme? By all accounts he made a good wage and owned a house and property."

"We didn't want for nothing," Lucy said. "Winston saw to that."

Maggie started to pace Sullivan's small office. What were they missing? What could be the motive? You don't just run off with a $500,000 debt collection package for no good reason. There had be to be something more in it for Winston, not to mention the land development company. Maggie stopped pacing suddenly and looked over at the detectives. "I think I got it. Can you bring me a map?"

Patterson left and soon returned with a map. He unrolled it onto the desk and drew a pencil circle around the development area. "This is the area the company wants to buy up for the resort."

"Just as I thought." Maggie pointed at a spot in the middle of the map. "Lucy, your house is smack in the middle of the proposed resort development. If you can't buy them out, scare them out."

Chapter 7

Lucy sat down heavily in the nearest chair. "Do you think...do you think they did anything to Winston?"

"It's possible." Detective Sullivan didn't bother to sugar coat the news. "At the same time, it's possible he's hiding out in one of the empty houses in the valley." He pointed out several possibilities on the map. "It's a long shot, but they should be searched. Once Winston decided to freelance with the debt collection package, he put himself and everyone around him in danger."

"Which means, you ladies need to return to Bangalow and wait for word from us," Patterson said.

Maggie set her lips into a firm, determined line. "We're in this together, remember, Detective?"

"We can't have either of you put in more danger than you already are," Sullivan said. "None of us know for sure where Winston is or what he'd do if he's found. The land developer also seems like a vicious type who will stop at almost nothing to get what he wants. If he wants Winston's property that badly then it's the lynchpin of the project, he'll stop at nothing."

Sullivan led Maggie and Lucy back through the station to the lobby. "I'm sorry, but you'll have to trust us, ladies. We'll let you know as soon as we have anything solid to tell."

~

At Patterson's prodding, the detectives ate lunch at the golf course country club. They weren't in it so much for the food, but for the gossip. Some guests were more than happy to talk about assorted details of the land development scheme but learning about Winston's recent activities took a little prying.

Once one person started talking, it was like a dominos effect where others also began to spill their secrets. The kicker was one patron's insistence that Winston had been in hiding for three months. How could that be when Lucy claimed he came home every night? The detectives thanked the guest and climbed into Patterson's four wheel drive truck to explore the abandoned houses in the valley. Was Winston hiding in one of them? They were about to find out.

The first house they came to was an eyesore. Everything was boarded up tight. A notice stuck on the window said it was set for demolition next week.

"There's no way anyone could live in there," Detective Patterson said. "The doors and windows are boarded up tight. If Winston managed to get in, let alone stay, I'd be very impressed."

"Let's mark it off and move on to the next one," Sullivan said.

The second house on the list was in a similar state

of disrepair with boarded up windows and doors and a demolition notice in the window.

"Next," Patterson sighed. "With our luck, there won't be any sign of life until the very last abandoned house in the Valley."

Fortunately, they didn't have to wait that long. The third house wasn't boarded up and showed some signs of life. The detectives exchanged glances. Could this be the big break they were after?

"Let's check the back," Sullivan said.

The detectives creeped around to the back of the house. To their surprise, and good luck, the door was unlocked. Both drew their guns and pushed the door open to enter the house.

Sullivan instantly covered his nose when a wave of hot, putrid scented air hit his face like a fan circulating stale air. Patterson held his sleeve to his nose as they explored the rag tag living room and kitchen. That's when they saw it or, more appropriately, him.

Winston Broad laid dead on the floor, half in the walk in pantry and half on the kitchen floor.

Chapter 8

"Yes, thank you, Detective, I understand." Maggie hung up the phone.

Lucy fidgeted on the couch beside her. Everything about her was a ball of nervous energy. "They've found him, haven't they?" she asked quietly. "He's not hiding out, but dead." Lucy blinked back tears. "Don't soften the blow for me, Maggie. Just tell me out right – like tearing a band aid from a wound."

"The detectives believe Winston was in the way of that developer so he had to die." Maggie sat down beside Lucy. "It would be the only way for the developer to get the house. That debt package was simply a way to lure him into working for the developer. If Winston had seen the benefits he would get from the debt collection and working with such a powerful ally, I imagine he would let go of his home and land. What the developer didn't expect was Winston was honest and compassionate. He must have been preparing to forgive the debts instead of demanding payments."

"The developers never approached us," Lucy said. "If they had, we may have sold."

"That $500,000 must be a drop in the bucket to them. They clearly wanted the property. You said he owned it out right – that it had been in his family for generations. The only way to get it was to kill him."

"The developer can't get his hand on the land by killing Winston," Lucy blurted out. "It's been mine from the beginning. I asked Winston's put it in my name as soon as he acquired it outright. It was a way to...safeguard...the property and not tie it directly to him. Now I can do whatever I want with it."

"That was certainly a convenient break." Maggie bit her lip and tried not to let any suspicions shine through. She always had her doubts about Lucy but now this complete lack of compassion after finding out about her husband's death, increased these doubts tenfold. She could cry at the drop of a hat for any other thing about the case but not shed one tear for Winston's death?

Something was going on.

Lucy smiled, though it was far from a warm gesture. The best word Maggie could use to describe Lucy's smile was calculated. "Isn't it though? Now I can sell property to the developer, move out of this horrible village, and retire to the Cayman Islands. "

"So soon?"

"Why not?" Lucy suddenly became defensive. "Wouldn't you want to leave an unpleasant chapter of your life behind you? You moved here from England, now I'm going to move far, far away too."

"Are you sure you've been telling us the whole story, Lucy?"

Her nervous fidgeting returned in force. "I don't know what you're talking about."

"I think you haven't been telling us the whole story," Maggie said. "I think you lured your husband into the scheme yourself and might have even killed him during one of the latest visits at the abandoned house.

You knew where he was all along, didn't you, Lucy? It was all part of the plan. Except Winston got cold feet. You couldn't have that. Not with all your dreams of getting away from the village hanging in the balance."

Lucy opened her mouth to deny it, but the words wouldn't come out. She opened and closed her mouth like a fish gasping for air before finally spitting out: "What do you think you know?"

"Plenty."

Maggie felt in her pocket to make sure her cell phone was handy. If Lucy was a killer, she didn't need to be the latest victim. "You're not as good as covering your tracks as you think you are. I knew you already owned the house instead of Winston. All that took was some public records searching. On top of that, your reaction to hearing news of Winston's death was not one of grief. You knew. You knew before any of us did." Maggie stood and moved across the room.

Even with one hand on her cell phone, putting more distance between her and Lucy wouldn't hurt any. She hit the re-dial button while keeping the phone hidden. The last person she called was Detective Sullivan. He picked up on the second ring. Maggie made sure to speak loud and distinct so Sullivan could hear. She needed witnesses or it would just be her word against Lucy's.

"I admit, you had even me fooled early on, Lucy. You were quite good with the waterworks," Maggie said. "But the waterworks can't hide the truth. Winston wasn't your first husband, was he?"

Lucy denied it, though denial was getting her nowhere fast – and it certainly wasn't throwing suspicion off of her. "I don't know what you're talking about. I loved Winston."

"But not as much as you loved Quentin."

Lucy's face drained of all color. "How did you... How did you find out about Quentin?"

"You mean your first husband?" Maggie knew she had Lucy on the run now. Just a few more well placed reveals and they'd have the case solved.

"You'd be surprised at how much information you can gather from talking to the right people. Quinton worked with Winston at Barclays UK. He even went so far as to introduce you to Winston. He even came up with the plan to divorce him in favor of marrying Winston, didn't he?"

"But the land was worth so much money," Lucy finally confessed. "Quintin and I struggled. I know a lot of people struggle, but Winston – or more like his land – was our ticket out of struggles. Winston would have done anything for me. He proved it when he signed over the property to me. Once it was mine, Quintin put the bug in the land developer's ear that now was the time to build. In order for me to have full control over the profit of the sale of the land, Winston had to die."

"And you were just the one to do it, weren't you?" Maggie asked. "He trusted you and you led him to disaster."

"I didn't do it." Lucy shook her head emphatically. "It was Quintin. I got cold feet. I wanted the money, but I wanted it on my terms. I've spent my whole life beholden to a husband and hoping he can provide for me. Not anymore. I wanted to make my own decisions and control my own money. Quintin couldn't accept this. He --"

"He vandalized your house in the hopes you'd come running scared back to him."

Detectives Sullivan stood in the living room doorway with Patterson directly behind him. "He underestimated your determination, though, Mrs. Broad. You weren't going to share the money from the sale of the house any more than Quintin was going to share you with Winston. But you see, Quintin has the last laugh after all."

"What do you mean?" Lucy's hands trembled.

"When Quintin realized you were going to cut him out of the scheme, he came down to the police station and wrote out a confession. He signed it in front of witnesses."

"What does that have to do with me?" Lucy was still grasping at straws to stop her boat from sinking.

"He named names, Lucy," Patterson said. "You're at the top of the list. Lucy Broad, you are under arrest for conspiracy to murder Winston Broad...."

Murder at the Manor

Chapter 1

Major Roberts held his breath as best as he could, but ignoring her was difficult. Her dark, slanted eyes, her skin as silken as an ocean pearl, her black hair and gorgeous lips were almost too much for him to handle. She enticed him more than any other woman he'd ever met, and he wouldn't be satisfied until she was his in all the ways he imagined. Natasha watched him as he fidgeted in his leather chair in front of the inactive fireplace. He always grew restless this time of night, and she would be wise to make haste with her chores and go to bed. Major Roberts really was kind to have let her live with him all these years, but his increasing efforts to flirt with her were becoming alarming. There was no denying the attraction, but if she were being honest with herself, lots of men were attracted to her. None of them, however, made her feel as uncomfortable or scared as Major Roberts did.

Natasha tucked her hair behind her ears and continued dusting the grand piano on the far side of the living room, under the watchful eye of her adopted father. If anything should happen, Adrian would be only in the next room or so.

All I need do is scream, she told herself.

Soon enough, she was lost in her thoughts. Lady

Turnbull had her weekly cooking class that focused solely on traditional English breakfasts coming up the next morning, and she would want to be ready for it. Natasha loved Lady Maggie so much, and always considered her the adopted mother she would have chosen for herself. During her stay in New South Wales, Australia, Lady Maggie was the only person to seek her out every week and try to make sure she felt like she fit in. Of course, with the famous Lady Maggie as your friend, one couldn't help but fit in.

Wondering what the menu would be for the next morning, Natasha busied her mind with thoughts of cinnamon and eggs and butter... three of Lady Turnbull's favorite ingredients. "You can make anything with these lovelies, anything at all" she would say every week. "The world, and every man with a stomach, is putty in your hands if you know how to use them properly!"

The sound of footsteps crossing the room didn't register to her until the grasp of a strong hand was wrapped around her tiny bicep. Major Roberts spun her around and put his face in hers.

"That's it, temptress! I'll have what I'm owed, now."

Not understanding, Natasha's eyes darted back and forth between his, and she noticed how wild his pupils looked. The man appeared to have suddenly gone positively crazy, and she needed to figure out why. Had she done something wrong? He was always quite cross when she did something wrong.

"I know you can't be so naïve as to think I brought you all the way back from Vietnam all those years ago just for the hell of it, eh? Or out of the kindness of my heart?"

Unsure of what to say, she remained silent and waited for him to get to the point, though her shoulders began to tremble.

"What's wrong, love? Are you afraid of me?" he spit in her face through gnashed teeth. Natasha didn't dare move. Maybe if he spoke loudly enough, his wife would hear. Or possibly Adrian. Where was he, anyway?

Major Roberts noticed her eyes darting and lowered his voice. "You think I'm stupid, aye? Well think again." He lowered his voice again to almost a whisper and his warm, foul breath washed over her face as he spoke. "I know you're smart, Natasha. I know you've come to realize over the past few years that I didn't take you out of Vietnam because I was a friend to your mother. Or because I'm an overly nice guy. I wanted you for my own…and I certainly didn't bring you to Australia to live with me so you could marry that good-for-nothing nephew of mine!" He spat on his own carpet as if to prove how disgusted he was. She only found it disgusting because she knew she'd be the one who had to clean it up later.

Major Roberts moved his hand up to her throat and put his left hand on her waist, moving it ever so slowly toward her back. Her small waist fit in his hand like a tiny, breakable ornament. His large palms, warped and mangled from a difficult but prosperous life, could crush her in only a moment. Yet if she held still long enough, surely he would calm down.

Major Roberts stepped closer to her, pinning her small frame against the bookshelf and slid his hand from the front of her throat around to the back of her neck. He forced her head backward and pressed his lips to her neck. Natasha couldn't help but let out a yelp, which was a terrible idea as it caused him to return his hand to her throat.

"DON'T make a peep. I deserve to collect on my good deed, and you'll behave properly." His yellowed teeth were barely visible under his large mustache as he leaned in closer and pressed his lips to hers. It was so forced and so hard-pressed against her mouth that those awful teeth of his cut into her lip. She didn't dare scream, she rather valued the use of everything attached to her waist, where his grip was continually tightening. Just as he pulled back and she was about to chance screaming just once, his nephew, Adrian Delahunty burst through the double swinging doors that led from the dining room.

"Get off her!" It didn't take four steps with Adrian's long legs to put him directly in front of Major Roberts, and only one arm's length to knock him to the floor. The man got up, regaining his footing quickly, and rushed his young nephew. The two men grappled in the living room, knocking over the two end tables on either side of the sofa and one recently-filled vase on the coffee table. They made quite a ruckus, and before too long, Lady Maggie herself came barging in through the same swinging double doors.

"What on earth is going on in here, gentlemen?!" she demanded. "You stop that right now!"

Adrian turned toward Lady Margaret in a sign of respect, and Major Roberts took that as a sign to land a cheap shot across his right cheekbone. When Adrian stood up to return the blow with a young, feisty version of his own, Lady Maggie stepped in between them like a professional referee.

"I said, that'll be enough of that, Digby Roberts."

Chapter 2

Natasha was due to be in Lady Margaret's kitchen for school any minute. Maggie put the finishing touches on the set up for the day and waved to her when she finally entered. Natasha always loved to arrive early to help her set up, and make sure everything was neat and tidy before the students arrived.

Bangalow, New South Wales is the lovely town that Major Digby Roberts and his wife, Elizabeth, decided to retire some years back with their adopted daughter Natasha. Robert's nephew, Adrian Delahunty, came to live with them shortly after because Adrian's parents had been killed in an unfortunate road accident. Natasha was first raised in a Catholic convent in Hanoi, and grew to be a devout Christian woman. The sleepy village of Bangalow, also home to the locally infamous Lady Margaret Turnbull, was a perfect place for well-to-do people to retire and spend their time. Ten years a dot com millionaire's widow, Lady Turnbull took young Natasha under her wing at Lawler's Loft bed and breakfast and cooking school.

Lady Margaret had taken to her right away because she was so polite, a character trait that Lady Maggie appreciates quite a bit. She thought that you could be as terrible a person as they come, but you could at least be polite. And Natasha was that, in spades. She won over everyone she met, both with her good mannerisms and genuine kindness, but also with her physical beauty. The girl was so strikingly beautiful that she held most people's attention without saying a word.

When Adrian returned home from serving in the war in Iraq, he was happy to have a place to stay with his uncle and aunt, but once he met Natasha, his feelings toward his uncle changed quite a bit. The man was positively harsh toward most people, which was reason enough not to like the man, but his actions toward Natasha bordered on unacceptable most of the time and made Adrian uncomfortable. And not just because he had designs on Natasha, himself!

Lady Margaret, herself, was no blind woman. She knew that Adrian had feelings for Natasha, and encouraged him as often as she could to pursue her. The two were quiet, exceedingly kind, and loved by everyone that truly knew them. In other words, encouraging them to pursue their affections for one another didn't exactly make Maggie a professional matchmaker; it tickled her just the same to see them together. As Natasha twirled around the kitchen, whistling while she laid out spoons and flattened the aprons on the table tops, Lady Margaret couldn't help but smile. There was to be a surprise party for Natasha tonight to celebrate her twentieth birthday. Maggie had been invited by the Roberts themselves, and would be going with her dear friend, Mrs. Cartwright.

The house was the biggest one on the block, Major Roberts made sure of that. When they had moved to

Bangalow, he commissioned a mansion much like the one he'd had in Hanoi so the family would feel right at home. Even driving by it, one would feel the lap of luxury literally lapping over into the street. The place was downright ridiculous, though it did remind Lady Maggie of some of her friend's homes overseas. She was no stranger to mansions, and had even owned a few in her lifetime, but this house took the cake every time she saw it. There were at least fifty steps leading up to the front entryway, though no one ever used that entrance. All guests had to use the side entrance, which was only about twenty feet away. The silliness of the extra entrance for guests always made Maggie laugh, but she used it just the same. Whatever made the Roberts family feel important, she was happy to oblige for Natasha's sake.

Inside the entrance, after their coats were taken and they'd had a chance to remove their shoes, Lady Margaret passed the giant stuffed tiger on her way to the living room. There, in the main foyer, was an actual tiger, mounted and looking like it was ready to pounce on everyone that came by. It was one of Major Digby Roberts' prized possessions, and always a conversation piece during dinners. Lady Margaret gave the animal a quick pat as she always did, and made her way to the sitting room.

Dinner consisted of cream of mushroom soup, roast lamb with spring potatoes and snow peas, and birthday cake for dessert. Afterward, everyone retired to different areas of the mansion. The gentlemen went to the study and the ladies to the library. Before long, the doorbell rang. Elizabeth Robert's brother, Alan Montgomery, strolled through the front door unapologetically, handing his coat to the butler without making eye contact. Alan apologized for being late, as he was apparently supposed to have arrived earlier that afternoon.

"Stop at the bar on the way here, did we, Alan?" Major Roberts strolled through the foyer just in time to administer an insult before casually placing his pipe in this mouth and wandering back toward the study. Alan huffed and adjusted his jacket before turning his attention to the ladies.

"Good evening, everyone. I see I've missed dinner, but it's no matter, I'm not that hungry anyway. Where's the birthday girl? I have her pressies." He held out three large bags and Lady Margaret walked forward to take them, noticing the twinge of alcohol on his breath. It wasn't her place to judge, and at least he wasn't showing up to a five-year-old's birthday party smelling of booze.

A few hours later, after everyone except Lady Maggie had gone home for the evening, the fight between Adrian and Major Roberts took place. Lady Margaret, after having walked in on them and separated the two men, didn't feel it was safe for her to go home. Luckily, neither did Mrs. Roberts. Elizabeth Roberts asked Lady Maggie to stay with them overnight, partly so they would feel a bit safer with Australia's favorite super sleuth in their home, and partly so she could have some adult lady company. It was no secret that the Major had feelings for Natasha, and Lady Margaret gathered that this is what the fight had been about. Elizabeth probably wanted to gab about it a bit, and that was just fine with her.

"What worries me most," Margaret told Elizabeth over tea in the kitchen while the boys cooled down, "is why Natasha went to her room before the cake was even served. Wasn't she excited about it? I mean, we baked it especially for her from the design she picked out in the catalogue."

"I don't know, Lady Turnbull. Maybe she didn't feel well. You know how she gets around my husband." Mrs. Roberts rolled her eyes. "You know how everyone gets around my husband, he's not exactly dipped in sugar."

"Yes, well it was certainly nice of Adrian to apologize for his behavior, wouldn't you say? Not every day you meet a young man upstanding enough to apologize for hitting an old prat in the head." Lady Maggie held up her glass to toast her friend and they touched them together before finishing the last of the wine.

Chapter 3

"I'll set up the guest room for you, my dear," Elizabeth says as she gets up from the kitchen bar. "It'll only take us a minute to—"

"Nonsense, I'll sleep on the couch in the library if it's alright with you. I rather like it in there. Nice and quiet." Without waiting for an answer, Maggie hugged her friend and grabbed an afghan from the sofa in the living room before heading to the library to retire for the night. Once settled in, Maggie patrolled the shelves for something to read before nodding off. The evening had left her too knackered to care much for starting a long story, so she chose a book on taxidermy from the shelf nearest the desk and thumbed through its pages. The stuffed tiger in the foyer had always been of particular interest to her, in that it was the only stuffed animal she was ever around these days. Something about him reminded her of her travels to Asia, which if she weren't mistaken, is where Mr. Roberts had killed the animal.

Fifty pages into the book, there was a picture of an identical tiger. The animal was marvelous, and was arranged just as the one in the foyer was…ready to pounce. Maggie shook her head, sad that such a magnificent animal would never again be able to pounce in real life, and shut the book before closing her eyes.

The next morning, Lady Margaret awoke to the sound of someone screaming. She lept from under the covers and slid her shoes on before trotting up the stairs. It wasn't the scream of desperation; it was the scream of a deed that had already been done, so there was no use running around without her shoes on. No doubt she would be on her way to Lismore within the hour and she didn't want to have to take any more time than absolutely necessary. A quit trot up the stairs and Maggie turned toward the master bedroom. Elizabeth had her hand over her mouth, staring at her husband's body, which lay lifeless on his bed.

"I came to check on him and he…he—"Her hands trembled as she tried to find the words.

"It's okay, dear. It's okay." Lady Maggie rushed over to the Major's side and checked for a pulse, as she'd seen Inspector Tom Sullivan do a thousand times. He was, indeed, dead. Maggie stood and looked around the room. "Where's Natasha."

Soon, Lady Margaret had everyone in the house gathered in the living area and had made all the appropriate calls to get the dinner guests back to the house. She made a fresh pot of tea while they waited for everyone to arrive. One last phone call to Inspector Sullivan and everything could be sorted out. Lady Margaret let Elizabeth make that phone call since it was her husband. No more than half an hour later, and everyone was on the scene. The forensics team was busy upstairs, taking fingerprints and doing their job quietly, and the officers would be on site soon. When Tom

Sullivan walked through the door of the front room, his notepad and pencil in hand, he noticed Lady Margaret sitting on the sofa near the corner of the room.

"How did I know you'd be here?! Shouldn't you be readying yourself for cooking class this morning?" He shouted, surprised to see his best citizen Detective at the scene already.

Cool as a cucumber, Lady Margaret answered without emotion. "My star pupil is in charge for the day. Lucy Jones, she'll be fine on her own for the morning.

"Right, right," Tom said, quickly regaining his composure and clearing his throat. "I mean, I'm so sorry for your loss, Mrs. Roberts. How can I help, this is everyone who was present last night, aye?" The detective eyed Maggie as he crossed the room to lean on the fireplace. He reached down and patted Elizabeth's hand before getting straight to work.

When no one answered him, he turned to Lady Turnbull. "Well I guess you'll be the most help, as per the norm? Is this everyone?" Lady Maggie nodded her head but said nothing else. Mrs. Roberts rocked herself slowly in the rocking chair near the unlit fireplace, and Lady Maggie would occasionally reach over from the sofa to pat her arm and let her know everything would be okay. Adrian and Natasha were perched on the sectional adjacent from them, and Mrs. Cartwright stood in the doorway, stroking her cup of tea nervously.

"Okay, let's start with you, Maggie. Did you have anything to do with this? Or can you tell me about it, please?" There was teasing in his voice, as he knew Maggie wouldn't hurt a hair on anyone's head, though she could certainly get herself into a fair bit of trouble. Detective Sullivan winked at her, encouraging her to let the comment slide just this once. Which she did.

"Well, Detective," she said matter-of-factly. "We were all over for dinner last night, Natasha here had a birthday you see—"

"Happy birthday, dear," Tom interrupted.

"Yes, not very happy as a matter of fact. Anyhow, she went to bed early, and then the rest of us went to bed. I woke up to screaming this morning, and that's what I know of the situation."

"Okay…..I've seen the body, and it looks like Major Roberts, God rest him, suffered quite a bit before his passing. And my chief forensics scientist tells me he's been poisoned by something. So my job here is to figure out if any of you have anything against this man. Consider this your first line of questioning in what could be a very, very long day if you don't help me out." Tom gestured toward everyone in the room with the back of his pencil before crossing his arms over his chest. "We'll start with you, Maggie. Since I know you're not afraid to speak. Did you have anything against Major Roberts?"

"Well," Lady Turnbull stated, looking at her friend who had just been widowed. Elizabeth nodded in understanding. "He was an arse."

Chapter 4

Tom stifled a chuckle and instead wrote something in his notebook. "Noted," he said. "Anything else to declare?"

"No, that's all," Maggie stated flatly.

"How about you, Alan? What were you up to last night? Did you hit the pub at all?"

Alan Montgomery, still hung-over from clearing out the mini bar at whatever hotel he'd stayed in overnight, leaned against the other side of the door frame leading to the front of the house. "I don't see what difference that makes, but yes. I was. Doesn't make me a killer, even if he DID never lend me a dime when I was trying to start my businesses."

"Now now, don't go getting all defensive, Alan. I'm just asking routine questions." Alan tucked in his shirt so as to appear more presentable and Tom moved on around the room. "Natasha, Adrian? What about you?"

"Now Detective, if you don't mind, they're pretty shaken up. If it's all the same to you, I can give you an overview?" Tom nodded at Lady Margaret and her request, readying his pencil. "Adrian, here, got into an altercation last night with Major Roberts."

Adrian's head jerked up at the mention of his name

and the possible implication that he had something to do with the murder.

"Calm down, son. I'm not saying you did anything. But these things need to be talked about sooner rather than later, or it'll look like you were hiding something. Now, as I was saying, they got into an argument yesterday over Natasha. Or rather, what Major Roberts was trying to force Natasha to do."

Tom looked at his friend, and Maggie nodded her head once to let him know whatever he was thinking was probably spot on. Tom cleared his throat and wrote furiously.

"Adrian, naturally, stepped in to help in whatever way he could. Turns out the old man took a bit of a beating, but I would venture a guess that it was merited. The boy has designs on her, for certain, but any one of us would have stopped him if we were there."

A tear rolled down Natasha's cheek, and Lady Margaret felt bad for her. No one should have to know anything of the evil of the world, especially not at such a young age. The girl had so much life left to live, and if she could spend the rest of it being loved by Adrian and not under the control of Mr. Roberts, then Maggie thought everyone should be so lucky. Adrian rubbed her back and held her hand in his lap. When she would cry a bit, she would hand her a handkerchief.

"Okay," Detective Sullivan said. "What about you, Mrs. Roberts? Did you have any reason to see that your husband met his end?"

Elizabeth choked up at the words and couldn't speak.

"If I may, Tom"

"Sure, Lady Margaret. Fire away."

"Elizabeth has recently discovered, she was telling me last night over tea, that Digby changed his will. It can pretty much be summed up in that he is leaving everything to Natasha. He didn't plan on making sure Elizabeth had anything upon his death. My guess would be, and this is only my guess, so you can put that pencil down right now, thank you very much. My guess is that he planned on leaving Elizabeth to try and make some sort of life with Natasha. Somehow trying to get away from life and his responsibilities, here. And also away from Adrian, who he knows would protect her to the ends of the earth. "

"So what you're telling me," Tom said. "Is that pretty much everyone here had a reason to want this man dead."

"Basically," she answered. "Now that you've got your notes, would you mind taking a short recess with me, Detective?"

Tom followed her to the library, where she picked up the blanket she used the night before and handed him the book she was reading. Maggie folded the blanket while he read the page she'd opened it to.

"Do you think this was the poison they used??" Tom asked.

"I think it very well could have been. It's pretty fast-acting, it sounds like. And isn't something everyone would think to look for. What do you think?"

"I think you're probably going to rub this hunch in my face when it turns out to be correct. Do you have a plan?"

"Sure do, I think you should go ahead and make an arrest. Make it be whoever you like, and I'll contact you tonight."

Chapter 5

Tom opened his mouth to speak but the look on Maggie's face told him he wasn't going to get anything further out of her. So he turned on his heel and went to the living room. Leaning over to whisper something in Adrian's ear, he tucked his notepad into his trousers and pulled out his handcuffs. Adrian flinched when the metal was secured around his wrists. Without flair, Tom read him his rights as they walked out the front door. Natasha was more than a little upset, and was nearly working herself into a vomiting fit when the front door closed behind them.

Later that evening, since Detective Sullivan said everyone was on house arrest until further notice, they had the butler prepare dinner as usual and they all sat down to eat. When it was time to say grace, Maggie dipped her head but did not close her eyes. As the prayer was being said, she noticed small white flakes being sprinkled into her soup. Without saying a word, once the prayer was over, she requested a new bowl of soup and went all the way through dinner as if nothing had happened. Excusing herself to the kitchen, she put a lid on the soup and stored it where she could give it to the detective later.

After dinner, Lady Margaret retired to the library early, but requested to speak to Natasha before going to sleep. Once Natasha had finished with her chores, she appeared in the doorway of the library.

"So…you know?" Natasha asked.

"Yes, dear. But my question is this: Were you trying to actually poison me? Or were you just getting my attention?"

"I wasn't trying to actually poison you, Lady Turnbull! I would never. You've been so kind to me. I wanted you to secretly know that it was me so you could help me figure out what to do. Adrian shouldn't be sitting in jail if I'm the one that poisoned Major Roberts. And I didn't know what else to do."

"Well tell me, dear," Lady Maggie said, patting the sofa cushion next to her. Natasha sat and rested her head in her hands. "Why did you do it?"

"He's just awful!" Natasha sobbed. "He's so mean, and he was always forcing himself on me. I can't even count the number of times he's kissed me, though I always fight it. I was so sure this time he was going to force more, and I just couldn't stomach it. I mean…
.I've never even…"

"Shhhh. It's okay." Maggie put her arm around the child, upset that she was in the pickle she was in. "I'll take care of it." She pulled the girl closer and let her cry it out on her shoulder. When she had finally calmed down a bit, Lady Margaret pulled out her cell phone. "Detective? I've found your murderer." Natasha jumped in her lap but Maggie soothed her by stroking her hair. "They poisoned my soup at dinner tonight, but

I was on to them. I've lured them to Lawler's Loft, and locked them in the basement. Please have them picked up as soon as you can, it's not good for business for me to have a murderer locked in the basement of my bed and breakfast. And send Adrian to me, as well, I'm sure he'll want a decent breakfast after that slop you served him in prison. Thank you." She clicked the phone shut and stood up, embracing Natasha one last time.

Once Adrian arrived at the bed and breakfast with Lady Margaret and Natasha, the two young ones held each other tightly, thankful that neither of them were in jail for the moment. Lady Maggie left for a moment to give them their privacy, and returned with something concealed in her hand. She reached out and took Adrian's hand, placing in it two sets of car keys.

"These are the keys to my car; I won't report it stolen or missing. Go and live life. Drive to the airport, by the time you get there, I will have arranged for your immediate flight to Sydney, and from there, you'll go straight to Cambodia."

"Cambodia" Adrian let out.

"No extradition treaty with Australia, dear , or perhaps you'd prefer to stay here and wait for Detective Sullivan" Maggie quickly reconfirmed to him; looking over her spectacles in a motherly like fashion.

The two children hugged Maggie tighter than she could remember ever having been hugged, and left for the airport. Moments later, Detective Sullivan arrived to collect his murderer.

Chapter 6

"I'm sure he was in here, somewhere," Maggie pondered, her finger to her mouth in false amazement. Tom's eyes widened in disbelief.

"Lady Turnbull, what have you done?" He walked over to the kitchen and leaned over the counter far enough that it brought his feet off the floor. "Lady Margaret, where's your Mercedes?" His tone was serious, but Maggie was steadfast. She said nothing, and merely looked at him with a straight face while he put all the pieces together.

"Lady Margaret Turnbull," the detective said slowly through gritted teeth. "You love that car. Where is it? Did someone.....steal it?"

"No. They sure didn't, Detective. Do you have any other questions or can I get you some tea? We've all had a long day."

Tom put his fingers to the bridge of his nose, unsure of what kind of paperwork he'd have to do over this case.

"They're on their way to Cambodia, if that's what you're worried about, Tom. If you'll just greatly delay any paperwork you've got rattling around up there in that head of yours, they'll be out of your reach anyway."

"Okay. I'm....I'm not gonna argue with you too much on this one because…" He fought for a minute as to whether or not it was right to say it out loud. He stuck his forefinger out and pointed at Maggie, speaking forcefully as if they were his own children. "Because I DON'T want to see that girl go to jail."

Maggie said nothing, but fetched them each a glass of tea and a buttered scone that Lucy Jones had prepared that morning. "You know, you're not half so hard as you think you are, Inspector. You've got a heart in there made of gold." She tapped his chest for good measure.

"So it was the powder for tiger's coat?" Tom asked. "She what, just scraped it off and put it in his meal? That stuff will do the trick, alright. I finished reading that section in the taxidermy book you handed me."

Maggie nodded once.

"That poor man, what a way to go." Tom shook his head. He then raised his tea cup to Lady Margaret. "Good thing you didn't eat your soup, I'd hate to lose my best detective."

Murder in the Frame

Chapter 1

Lady Margaret lives an active life. She is retired, but unable to just sit at home and wither away, she still loves to work and stay busy. With a very successful little cooking school on the outskirts of Bangalow, New South Wales, she was really enjoying this golden stage of her life.

Most of her life was spent residing in the United Kingdom, but when her self-made millionaire dotcom husband died, she decided to make the move to Australia. Margaret's husband had traveled with her all over the world, but New South Wales had always been that special someplace that held her heart.

While her husband preferred the business of city life, and the beauty of high rise buildings, Lady Margaret had always secretly loved the quiet pace of the smaller Australia towns. She just loved how they were all set up so that you could walk everywhere you needed to. In the big cities like London, you practically needed a vehicle to get anywhere. Every time she needed to go the doctor, she'd have to call for a cab or have a driver take her somewhere. While she did have a car that she loved, she also loved to walk to the shops whenever she could. And the people in the town were just superb. It felt like enough of a small town to be able to say hello to her neighbour, but not small enough that everyone was in each other's business all the time.

Nestled in New South Wales, Bangalow is bordered by Lismore to the west and Ballina on the coast. The country houses were perched on the rolling hills. All of the beauty was just what her soul needed, and she was looking forward to making new friends.

Now that Lady Margaret was living in a sweet country guesthouse, Lawlors Loft with her cooking school attached, she was always conscious of the safety and security issues of living on her own. It wasn't that she was scared, so much...it was more that she took pride in taking care of her own safety. She was quite capable of taking care of herself, and delighted in double-checking locks, giving the place a look-around before she shut the place up for the evening or when she went away. It was very liberating, and she was happy to do it. It would take a while to fully get used to living on her own, but she was on her way to being as comfortable as she ever was. Plus, she was too in love with the place to ever live anywhere else. Her guesthouse had a large living room, gleaming hard wood floors, a state of the art kitchen including an Arger oven, and the bay windows in her bedroom and living room were something that every girl dreams about nestling into with a cup of tea and a good book.

Her neighbours were interesting, but not too interesting, which is just as she preferred it. There was a dashing man in his fifties nearby with outlandish visions, every time she saw him, he would spout detailed dreams about the future of Bangalow and you couldn't shut him up about it until he was finished. She had only been here a week and he had already organized a party in her welcome. He was quite taken with her class and charm, it seemed, and so he should be, she thought. She had a lot to offer this town, and she loved that she already felt so at home.

It was a medium sized party, but with every attention paid to detail. It was in the little town square, and it really held its own as a party. Lady Maggie had been to plenty of high class parties, and this one was like a smaller version of that. There were a couple of tents, the nice ones that were sturdy and clean, and the poles were all wrapped in lights. The tables were covered in white linen, and the catering was by the region's finest, the Sugar N Spice Catering Company. She was sure they had thought of everything. There was even a picture of her late husband at the head table, and a place card at an empty seat next to hers. A little card between their seats said something sweet about their "new adventure". It was a beautiful gesture. Lady Margaret couldn't wait to have some fun here!

Lots of new faces made their way to her table, and she recognized lots of friendly faces that she knew from past visits to the area as well. After only a week, and with the help of some good food and drink, it already felt like home. Once the party was finished, Lady Maggie walked home satisfied, her tummy slightly bulging and a pleasant smile on her face. It was lovely that she could walk alone here, safely. That's one of the main reasons she chose this place to settle in. It was harder to walk in a place like London, for example. There were lots of people there, and she didn't feel unsafe, but it was so busy that it was hard to enjoy the journey. Here, though, it was just breathtaking. Everywhere she went, she could walk at a nice pace and take in the rolling hills and the lazy waters and friendly faces. There was no reason to hurry, and why should she? She had all the time in the world.

Once she made it around the side of her house, Maggie noticed the window open in the front. Her feet froze for a moment, she never left windows open when she went somewhere. Never. Being the curious type, she wandered right through the hedges and checked to see if anything looked suspicious. When she didn't notice anything out of the ordinary, she wandered inside. The front door was locked....and again, nothing looked out of place. Her bag was hung on the hook next to the doorframe and she sauntered over to lean over the back of the couch.

Hmmm, she thought. *It doesn't look like it's been tampered with. Perhaps I did just left it unlocked?* Not likely, but…

While she certainly didn't like even the idea of her privacy being invaded, she passed it off as something she must have overlooked, though she certainly didn't sleep well that night.

The next morning, Maggie set off on a long walk. Somewhere farther away from the village, perhaps, would give her mind some room to breathe. She loved a good mystery, and this was certainly a mystery. A long stroll across some adjoining grassy fields, she reached a hilltop that overlooked a little gathering area. There was a sun umbrella rolling across the grass, and sweeping away down the hill in the wind. Naturally, Maggie ran to catch it. Once she had grabbed it, she brought it back to where she'd seen it blow away from, closed it tightly, and leaned it against a tree. Hopping back up to the footpath she'd been walking along, she stopped short when she heard someone shouting at her. When she turned around, Maggie saw a young girl trotting up behind her, out of breath.

"Excuse me, lady?!" the young woman exclaimed. "Why would you do that?!"

Stunned, Margaret's mouth fell open, silently. The girl's wide eyes were impatient for an answer, so Margaret shook her head. "I...I was just trying to help. I thought the umbrella might be damaged." She pointed down the hill a bit, "There was no telling where it would end up, I just thought I'd set it back over there before it blew halfway to Lismore.

"Never mind where it was blowing," the girl barked. "Next time, mind your own business!" She turned on her heels and trotted back to the field.

Chapter 2

Later that evening, once Margaret had shuffled home, she quickly put her shoes away and went to make some tea. It was so rude of the woman to be upset with her for trying to help, why in the world would a person be upset over something like that? Of course Margaret wasn't afraid of a little confrontation now and again, but over something so silly? That wasn't acceptable at all, and it rather hurt her feelings on what was to have been such a relaxing walk.

Her tea came to a simmer on the stove and she went to prepare it, clicking on her television and computer so she could sit and check her emails for a while. With the small television on in the background for noise, Margaret soon sat down at her little desk and opened her browser window. On the first page that came up, which she had set to a local news website from her favourite station in Bangalow, there was a breaking news story that could not be ignored. A young girl had been killed...her heart pierced with the tip of an umbrella!

Lady Margaret couldn't believe what she was reading. The news page hadn't released any photos of the crime scene, but she knew it had to be the same one. The same girl. The same umbrella. There didn't seem to be anything of significance in the umbrella itself, as far as Lady Maggie could tell when she'd moved it. But she really wanted to find out why it was so important to the young girl. Maybe she could help...

Gathering her house keys and mobile phone, Lady Margaret made her way back to the hilltop where she'd seen the grumpy girl. Perhaps getting another look at the scene would lend some inspiration. When she arrived, the perimeter was cordoned off, and a white tent stood in the place where she had planted the umbrella against the tree. From where she could see, there wasn't a thing on the ground except a tartan travelling rug, stretched on the grass. No umbrella, anywhere. The wind couldn't possibly have blown it away, the trees were still now, and Maggie's wind chimes hadn't been singing since she'd arrived home. Disgruntled at her lack of finding anything noteworthy, Maggie decided to return home and make sense of things tomorrow, because something didn't seem quite right.

Just as she spun to head back to her house, Lady Margaret spotted a couple of people walking toward her. Not normally one to be nervous, Maggie did actually pick up her step because it was so late. No one else was around, and standing near a recently cordoned off police crime scene probably wasn't the wisest place to be so soon after a horrific crime. There was no telling what these people wanted, or even if they were the ones who had killed the girl. Maggie pulled her shirt up around her neck and bustled toward home. As the couple grew near, she veered to the right so they could pass, but they didn't. Instead, they cleared their throats and held up their hands to stop her, showing her a pair of badges as a good enough reason to do so.

"What are you doing here so late, ma'am." They said. It was more of a statement than a question, and Lady Margaret certainly didn't appreciate that. It made her hesitant to answer.

"This morning--" she began, slowly spelling out what had happened earlier that day. Surely that would be explanation enough for them, she thought. But she was wrong. As she spoke, the male officer simply stared at her blankly. The female officer looked more like she cared what Maggie was saying, but only barely. Neither one of them really seemed to believe her. But why? This was nothing more than a case of being in a strange spot at a very strange time. Yet they didn't seem impressed with her vivid description of the victim, and her knowledge of the umbrella. She possibly should have left that part out.

"Lillian Kennedy," the lady officer said pointedly, jutting out her hand for Maggie to take it. "This is my partner, Adam Williams. I'm sorry but we're going to have to bring you into the station and ask you a few more questions, formally."

Shocked, Lady Margaret just stared at her, not even glancing at Detective Williams.

"Miss," he finally said. "We don't have any other people wandering around here this evening, and you've just given us quite a load of information about someone you say you have never even met. Now I'm not saying that sounds suspicious, because I don't want to insult you. But it's....not nothing. So please, would you mind coming with us?"

Lady Margaret felt trapped, if there was no one else around, and they took her fingerprints which just happened to be the only set on the umbrella, then what? It would be completely logical for the officers to say that she would then jump to the top of the list of suspects. Margaret turned to follow them. It might be fun to ride in the back of a police car, she thought. I can check that off my list of fun things to do...and that'll give me plenty of time during a nice quiet ride to figure out what the heck is going on.

What of motive, though? It would be a stretch, in her opinion, for someone to paint her as an old bitty, with a bee in her bonnet, who just had to kill a sweet girl for no reason. Though would it be a stretch, really? She was new in town, so to speak, and she supposed anyone could be crazy. It would definitely take some doing to get to the bottom of all of this, but Margaret did love a challenge, especially a good mystery!

Once in the interview room down at the station, she took her mobile phone out of her bag so she could ring her neighbour, Andrew Hansen. After a few minutes of trying to convince him that she was not, in fact, telling him a story, he finally started to listen.

"There's just no way, Lady Maggie. No way. I don't personally believe you could hurt a fly, but who knows. You know, I did suspect you were a saucy one when you arrived, and now embroiled in a homicide investigation not two weeks into your new home!" He laughed over the phone. "And calling your new neighbour at ten o'clock in the evening from jail!" He laughed again, a big belly laugh. He was having a bit too much fun with her predicament, she thought, and simply waited for him to finish being silly.

"Don't worry, Lady Maggie," he added once he had finishing chortling to himself. "I'll get you out of trouble, if trouble there is! I'll see you shortly, dear."

Barely fifteen minute went by and Andrew came strolling into the station. "Welcome to Bangalow!" he shouted as he leaned on the door frame. A tall blonde woman wrapped her fingers around the edge of the door and whispered something in his ear. "OH. Well, apparently you're being held overnight, possibly for more questioning. Good grief, Lady Margaret, what did you do?!" And then he was gone. In the hallway, Andrew reached into his pocket and produced a mobile phone. Margaret couldn't hear who he was talking to, but she could see him through the window looking a bit too serious.

Chapter 3

"Well, Ms. Turnbull," Detective Williams sang as he tossed a pile of papers down on the table. "It seems that your fingerprints WERE the only ones found on the umbrella we've got." He raised one eyebrow, as if this statement were supposed to produce some spewing of guilt from her lips. She just stared back at him flatly. There was no sense in humoring him, it was very late and she would normally be turning in just about now. "Fine by me, then. You can have your lawyer present before you say anything."

"I don't ha--"

"That's fine," he holds up his hand to stop her. "We can certainly get one."

"THAT won't be necessary," chimed a large, bald man from the doorway. He wrapped his fingers twice on the frame and let himself into the interview room as if he'd been there a thousand times before. "Mr. Wallace, pleased to meet you. I'm Lady Margaret's lawyer. Detectives?" Mr. Wallace glanced at each one of them as if they were in his way. Surprised, they stepped idly aside and he took their place at the table across from Lady Margaret. Waving his first two fingers toward the door, he dismissed them, and they obeyed.

"Okay then," he mused, reaching his large hand across the metal table. "I'm Mr. Hansen's legal advisor. That's some neighbor you've got there, looking out for you so late in the evening." Maggie nodded and he kept talking, not missing a beat. "Anyway, depending on what you tell me, if I can't help you then I'll certainly refer you to the services of a criminal lawyer." He waved his hand flippantly in front of them when she gasped. "I'm sure it won't come to all that." Mr. Wallace glanced toward the window, where the two officers were standing in the hallway talking to each other. "They're just following protocol. I mean, who else was out there? No one. They were probably just bored and didn't have any other leads. Heck, I just met you and I'm fairly certain you didn't do anything wrong except walk by at the wrong time. So let's have it...what's your story?"

"This is really all going a bit too fast for me," admitted Lady Margaret. "I mean, honestly, I was JUST taking a walk. Then I was just picking up an umbrella that was flying away. Then I was just getting yelled at by some girl. That's really the whole story, I promise. This is all quite a lot to take in, especially at bed time." She sat back in her chair, hoping that Mr. Wallace would not recommend the services of another legal professional. That really would be the last straw. And what of sleep? How was she supposed to get any sleep if she had to stay in this crazy place? I mean, there were people walking around drinking coffee at eleven at night. It was all so exhausting, so Maggie laid her head down on the table, convinced that she couldn't possible tell her story again for the day.

"I honestly don't know," she mumbled into her arms that were folded in front of her. It came out so muffled that Mr. Wallace had to lean down and ask her to repeat it. "I just don't know why she was so upset with me...over a silly little umbrella." She shook her head in her arms, making her look a little like a school girl at a classroom desk. "There was no reason that I could tell that she'd be upset with me for checking on her umbrella for her, and taking care of it. I was just trying to be nice, and now she's dead and I'm stuck here at the police station lying on a metal table."

Mr. Wallace listened quietly, content to let her take her time. It was his experience that these things couldn't be rushed because people remember more details when they feel more relaxed. After he placed a fresh cup of ice water in front of his tired new friend, he went out to the waiting room in search of Constable Williams.

"There's really no way, as far as I can see, that Lady Margaret could have killed Lucy Davidson. I overheard you talking to your partner there about the autopsy report...." he gestured toward the doorway where they'd been standing when he walked up.

Williams cleared his throat twice in quick succession. "That's really none of your business, but yes. Since you already seem to know, it appears it would have taken quite a lot of force to kill Ms. Davidson. And I agree with you that she probably didn't have enough gumption or brute strength to do it."

Mr. Wallace slapped him on the back once, "Well then! Glad to hear it. So the part I didn't hear was just how MUCH force it would have taken to run a girl through with an umbrella hard enough to pierce her sternum. I mean, what are you looking for, here? A lumberjack?! Lucy appeared to be a pretty athletic girl, from the things I dug up on the internet on the way over here. She jogged regularly, that much was clear from a quick Facebook profile search."

Williams shook his head. "I'm not sure, really. Probably a full-grown man, for sure. It's anybody's guess for now."

"Well, good luck to you. Let me know if you need anything from me, personally." Mr. Wallace handed him a business card and turned to walk away, stopping mid-step. "Are you planning on keeping my client overnight?"

"No, I don't see why we should. She should stay nearby, though. Tell her not to go leaving the town or anything like that, in case we should need to question her again."

Mr. Wallace gave the officer a quick salute and disappeared out the front door of the station.

Hansen, her neighbour, offered to take Maggie home, since she had ridden to the station in the back of a police car. No doubt he would be holding that one over her head for quite some time, she thought. Not a fortnight into a new town and she already had a jail story. Honestly, it would probably make her laugh one day. Lady Margaret did love a good adventure. For tonight, though, it wasn't all that funny.

"I certainly don't mind being questioned during an investigation," Maggie told Hansen when they were almost to her house. "I do, however, mind being accused of a crime I couldn't possibly have committed. I mean really, couldn't we blame the older lady for some petty theft or masterminding a jewelry heist or something?" Hansen chuckled and lit a cigarette.

"Those'll kill you, dear." Maggie kept her eyes forward and scolded almost without thinking.

"Yes, ma'am," he answered. "Now Lady Turnbull, I'm certain this is just a case of you being in the wrong place at the wrong time. And I know that you're not entirely happy about it, and I do feel bad that you've been put out this evening." He pulled the car to a stop in front of her walkway. "How about you get some sleep and maybe they'll have found something by the morning. We can chat about it over tea?"

Lady Margaret looked toward her house and fiddled with her keys for a moment. "I did forget to mention to them about my window," she said as if she were merely talking to herself.

"Excuse me?"

"My window. It was open...I wonder if that had anything to do with the murder."

"I, uh-- I'm not sure why it would? Don't you leave your window open sometimes? Like when it's unseasonably warm or cool?"

Lady Margaret shook her head. "Never."

They sat in silence for a few moments, and she gathered her things and went inside. Scared or not, she was going to sleep well tonight due to sheer exhaustion. About five minutes after laying down on the couch, Maggie's eyes grew heavy. She looked around her new home, fighting sleep. She was certain someone had been through the place, but she couldn't prove it to anyone. Her eyelids drooped again.

That was a problem for tomorrow. For now, sleep.

Chapter 4

It was a long night. Maggie tossed and turned, and ultimately decided to get up around nine, which was about two hours later than she was used to getting up. It felt like half the day had been wasted already. No matter, there was a lot to do, always, and she decided to start her day with some shopping. The village center was just around a kilometer away. It would surely take her mind off of what had happened the previous day. The officers had instructed her not to travel far, and walking to the shops would probably not cause any harm. When she was about to enter the grocery store from its laneway entrance, she stopped dead in her tracks. Right there in the electronics shop window, there was a photograph of Lucy Davidson. There was a caption below the picture, stating that Lucy was a photographer of some note. Apparently, she was set to display some of her work at the Bangalow neighborhood gallery in about three weeks from now.

When she returned home, her head full of possibilities and running every situation in great detail while unloading her groceries, a woman approached her. The lady offered to help Lady Margaret carry her groceries inside, and then almost immediately asked if Maggie had happened to see Lucy Davidson's camera on the hilltop the previous day when she had "played" with the girl's umbrella.

"Excuse me?! Just who are you supposed to be, anyhow? First of all, how do you know where I live, and second, how do you know that I was even at any hilltop yesterday evening?" Margaret demanded.

"I--I'm sorry, mmm…iss. I'm Lucy's friend, Melissa. I just wanted to get the SIM card from her camera if you had happened to stumble across it." The woman fidgeted where she stood, tucking a stray hair behind her ear. "Lucy had, uh….taken some compromising photos. And I'd like to delete them before anyone sees them."

Margaret was surprised, to say the least. "Well, I certainly didn't see any camera. And even if I did, I would have turned it straight over to the police without even thinking twice about it." The woman looked disgusted.

"Well, I--"

"Now, listen. I am truly sorry that you have had some photos taken of you that you aren't proud of. Honestly, these days, that's all too common if you ask me." Lady Maggie straightened her collar. "But you DIDN'T ask me, so I will just say that if you do come across this camera, and you decide to delete some photos from it that were taken the night of the murder, then I do believe you'll find yourself in a fair bit of trouble. I'd think twice about that, if I were you. Being embarrassed is one thing, having someone accuse you of something you didn't do, such as deleting evidence or the like, is far worse. Trust me, I know."

"Well that's my business. I do appreciate your advice though, I guess." The woman backed away slowly, still obviously worried about whatever was on that camera.

"I did only meet your friend by accident," Lady Turnbull offered as the woman retreated to wherever she had walked up from. "I had no idea that she was even a photographer until I saw her picture in the electronics shop window just an hour ago. I have no idea where her camera might be, I'm sorry."

"Well, I'll give you my number, and if you think of anything or run across anything, would you mind giving me a call?"

"Sure thing, honey." Lady Turnbull waited patiently while she scratched her name and number onto a piece of paper from her small purse and bid her farewell, promising to keep in touch.

That evening, after many long hours spent working in the kitchen experimenting with some new recipes, Lady Margaret was ready to call it a day. She was about to open the oven to cook her steak and kidney pie when her doorbell rang. Exasperated at how much company she was having all of a sudden, her shoulders slumped and she made her way to the front door. I really do wish people would start keeping business hours, she thought to herself as she turned the handle. When she opened the door, she was quite surprised to see two detectives standing on her front steps. She welcomed them in, and offered them each a cup of tea...which they each politely refused. The very moment they sat down at her small kitchen table, they started in with questions.

"Did you know that Lucy Davidson was a photographer, Lady Turnbull? Were you aware of that before this moment?"

"Well, I'll tell you the same thing I told that woman that came by earlier. I went to the grocery store earlier this morning, and saw a picture of Miss Davidson in the window of the electronics shop. It was only then that I realized what her profession, or her hobby, was. Why do you ask??"

"Do you mind if we take a look around your place, Lady Margaret?" one of them asked.

"Is that actually a question, or more letting me know what you're fixing to do, type of thing?" she asked sarcastically. They didn't really answer her, and instead simply stood up and began walking through each room. There wasn't any good reason for her to stop them, since she didn't have anything to hide, so she tapped her foot and waited on them to finish. When they took a bit longer than she expected, she decided to go ahead and throw the pie into the oven, lest she be eating dinner at eleven o'clock again.

"What are you looking for, if I may ask..." she said, closing the oven door.

"We need to find Lucy's camera, or at the very least, the SIM card that was in it. We think some pictures on there might be of some help." Both detectives had on their white gloves, she noticed, and were carefully moving papers around so as not to disturb them too much. Each time they opened a drawer, they would stand back from it a little, scoot the contents around, and then close it and move on. Each book was removed from the bookshelves, and given a gentle shake to see if anything would fall out. It wasn't so much what they were doing that bothered Maggie, because they were being quite gentle about it. It was that they thought she had what they were looking for in the first pace that bothered her. She was literally just a passerby, and there was no reason for her to stash anything of consequence. Maggie wished that she had some sort of help for them, because she would much rather be assisting the police than being questioned and searched by them.

"Why don't you ask her friend?" she asked.

"What friend is that…" they both asked, spinning about to face her.

"The one I mentioned earlier. Oh, I'm sorry, were you not listening? Did you just assume that it was here and didn't really pay attention to anything else?" She rummaged around on the countertop for the young woman's name and number. When she found it, she marched it over and placed it into the gloved hand of the taller officer, the one who was looking smugger than his friend, and closed his fingers around it.

"Melissa," he read. "And who did you say this was?"

"Beats me, some woman who showed up here earlier asking if I knew where Lucy's camera was. I told her I had no idea, of course. But that I'd let her know if it turned up. She seemed quite shaken up about the fact that it was missing…" Lady Margaret thought it best to omit the part about the compromising pictures of Melissa, just in case it didn't matter. She wasn't one to go stirring up trouble where there didn't need to be any. "I tell you what, you come back tomorrow with a warrant in hand, and you can search every nook and cranny at your leisure. I'll even feed you while you work. But I do want a proper warrant, because I know for a fact that someone has been through my place recently. And I want everything documented properly, if you don't mind." The two detectives agreed, and left Margaret to eat her dinner in peace. Finally.

Chapter 5

The same two detectives returned the next day, late morning, with a proper warrant to search Maggie's place. Mr. Wallace was standing by to watch his new client's belongings being rummaged through, because he didn't want the detectives to assume the worst in the case that they DID find the SIM card in her house. Lady Margaret watched the whole search from the chair in her living room, and when they moved to the bedroom and den, she waited patiently. While she couldn't see everything from the living room, she could hear everything from there. She passed her hand between the armrest and cushion of her chair while she waited, just as absentmindedly as if she were thumbing through a magazine in a doctor's office. When she did, her fingers came in contact with something small and firm. She didn't want to pull it from where it was resting, she knew better than to say anything, so she closed her hand around it and stood up. The female officer that was in the room nearest her looked her way, but didn't follow her. Once she was safely inside the restroom with the latch locked, she placed the SIM card in her bra, flushed the toilet, wet her hands in the sink, dried them, and returned to the living room chair.

An hour later, satisfied that neither the card or camera was there in the home, the officers all left. Just before they drove away, one of the officers rolled down his window and shouted to Margaret that the forensics team might be by later to examine the window, if that was okay by her. She knew that it didn't matter if it was okay by her, that they would be by either way. She simply waved her hand toward them and they drove off. The last person she had to get rid of for the afternoon would be Mr. Wallace. He would no doubt want to go over everything again, and she really didn't have the mental energy for that. Though it probably didn't matter. To her surprise, he looked tired as well, and excused himself without having his tea refreshed. With a warm smile, he promised to be at the other end of a phone call should she need it, at any time.

Since the police hadn't confiscated her computer, tablet, or cell phone yet, she couldn't wait to see what was on the SIM card. As expected, once she pulled everything up, there were certainly quite a few sexual pictures of Melissa and Lucy, but they were very natural, loving poses in black and white. They weren't anything that could be considered offensive, or pornographic. The second set of photos, however, were much more intriguing. There was an entire collection of photos would certainly be of interest to the police, and not in Maggie's favor. They were all snapshots of the umbrella rolling down the beach, then a section of pictures in which Lady Margaret was grabbing it at that last moment before the wind gust would have lifted it and carried it down the hill.

Lady Margaret's mouth fell open. She certainly didn't expect to see herself in any of the pictures! Although the reason for Lucy being so upset with her did seem a bit more understandable now. If she was trying to get a photo of the umbrella rolling gracefully down the hill, then Lady Maggie certainly interrupted that. She thought for a moment about what that set of pictures would have looked like, were it to be displayed at the coming gallery. It would really be a nice set of pictures, she thought. Catching the umbrella's "take off" and "roll" patterns would have been quite lovely, if not a little boring and cliche. But who was she to judge someone else's artistic eye? Following the shots of the umbrella, there were several taken of the sky, then of the grass on the hill, one of someone's leg, and then nothing.

That was the killer...Margaret concluded. Since there was nothing else on the card she took it out of the slot on the computer and sat back in her chair. The obvious course of action would be to hand this over to the police, but they hadn't proved entirely helpful, as of yet, so she'd probably best think on it herself for a while. Slipping the card back into her bra, Margaret tried to think of who in the world would break into her house and hide a SIM card in her living room? That takes a LOT of thought, and a lot of planning, especially to have done it so seamlessly in the house of a woman who never left her windows open.

In a sense, Lady Margaret would have like the detectives to have found the camera card themselves, because it clearly showed that she didn't attack Lucy on the hill, and it did show what her intentions were with the umbrella. It was clear in the pictures that she was racing to catch it before it blew away. But now that she's seen all of this evidence, was there a way to get it to the police safely without them being suspicious of her? They did search the entire house that very day, and if she came up with it all of a sudden, that might not look so good for her. She pulled her cell phone from her pocket and quickly dialed Mr. Wallace's number. He would likely have just made it home, wherever home was for him, and she hated to disturb him.

"I promise, Mr. Wallace, I found it after the police left. Only just a few moments ago when I went to the restroom. As she was speaking on the phone, she had gotten another flash drive out of her drawer that she knew had some vacant room on it. She downloaded the pictures from the found card onto it, and deleted all the photos from Lucy's card.

"I'll turn around, I've only just pulled into the drive, and it won't be any trouble. Just put it in a baggie for me and I'll take it down to the police station so you don't have to get out and about again."

She didn't like that idea at all, and told him so. "I'll take it to the police myself, actually, I'm just getting in the car down to drive it down there," she lied. "I only wanted to let you know what I was doing with it, in case you needed that information. It's nearly lunchtime, now, anyway. Go on inside and make yourself something to eat. You can always meet me later somewhere when we all find out what's on this card."

It was nearly lunchtime, and Margaret's stomach was starting to let her know about it, so she decided to make a quick sandwich before heading to the police station with the empty card. When she got into the car ten minutes later, and began backing out of her drive, a car pulled to a screeching stop behind her, forcing her to slam on the brakes. Mr. Wallace jumped out of his car and walked in long strides around the front of Maggie's, holding a gun in front of him. Lady Margaret always hated this sort of grandstanding action, it always ended badly for someone and you could never tell who until it was too late. Although she was scared stiff, she knew that if she exited her car, Wallace wouldn't hesitate to grab her purse and snatch the SIM card out of it. As he stepped closer to her car, he repeated his demand for her to get out of her vehicle. He said it quite loudly this time and it gave Lady Margaret's heart a bit of a start. Instead of doing as he instructed, she bent forward slightly and placed the SIM card back in her bra, and remained down until she felt like he was only a few inches from her open car window.

Just as she heard him grab at the door handle to swing it open, Margaret sat up and sprayed him in the face with hairspray. Mr. Wallace staggered backward and fired a shot in the air. Only moments passed before there were sirens blaring in the background. A sigh of relief passed through her lips, and through Mr. Wallace's lips passed a whimper. He was now slumped over on her front lawn, weeping and holding his eyes.

She didn't blame him, honestly. Any woman who has accidentally sprayed hair spray into her eye knows that it doesn't feel nice, and Lady Margaret had really not been shy about how much she sprayed right in that man's face. Detective Kennedy was the first to arrive, and jumped out of her patrol car almost the instant it was in park, leaving her door wide open. Pointing her gun toward Lady Margaret, she demanded the woman put her hands behind her head. Lady Maggie did as she was told this time, letting the detective know that what she really wanted could be found in her bra. Detective Kennedy smiled and asked Margaret to lower her arms.

Chapter 6

An hour later, Margaret found herself in the police station...again. This time, Andrew Hansen was with her, both sitting across from the sergeant's desk. Sergeant Ashworth wanted Margaret to repeat everything she had said in her last interview, naturally. But this time, Lady Margaret did so gladly. She went through everything from the first time she realized someone had been in her home, through her window somehow, to the walk she had taken at the wrong time, to the person she had tried to help that didn't want any help, to being held at gunpoint. Twice. Sergeant Ashworth didn't look up even one time as she spoke, he only took notes enough to fill both sides of a report sheet and nodded his head once in a while. Once she was finished, Sergeant Ashworth asked her if she and her neighbour would like a cup of coffee, and then without waiting for an answer, motioned for two cups to be brought to his desk. Then he went straight into an explanation that Lady Margaret had been waiting for. Some more insight into the situation that had taken over her life for the past week.

"Lucy Davidson," he began, "was quite a famous young lady. Her photographic work, though not my taste, is quite popular around here, and even further inland she's got quite a following. She was very often attracted to the same sex when she worked, particularly the curves of women's bodies. That was kind of her "thing"." The sergeant made air quotes as if he didn't really care about any of this, but was just trying to explain it anyway. "She displayed several photos of nude ladies at the gallery in town from time to time, and these pictures sold very well. So well, in fact, that they gallery owner encouraged her to shoot some more life poses. Things that looked more natural. Apparently that's just what she did...with Melissa. Except--"

"She fell in love..." Lady Margaret interrupted, and the Sergeant nodded. "It happens to the best of us," she shrugged. "Continue."

"You see, the object of her affections was Melissa Wallace, the daughter of a highly respected lawyer in Bangalow."

Margaret and Andrew's eyes widened and they turned to each other. Margaret was both surprised, and irritated that her new neighbor had inadvertently gotten her even more mixed up in a bad situation than she already was, but she appreciated that he had tried to help her.

"Once Mr. Wallace found out about his daughter's love affair with Lucy, he was very upset. He is obviously very old-fashioned and wanted his daughter to break it off with her. His daughter ignored her, of course, they always do...and she continued dating Lucy Davidson."

"Mr. Wallace doesn't really strike me as the most sensible man, though," Maggie interrupted. "I don't imagine he would just let something like that go, whether he should or not."

"No Lady Margaret," he chuckled. "He's apparently a very stubborn man, I've had to deal with him a few times before, actually, in the court room. He's not my favourite guy."

"So when Lucy saw me on the hill, she must have thought her dad had hired me to sabotage her work? That would have given her the gumption to confront me. She didn't really look like the type who had a lot of experience with confrontation."

"Precisely, I'm sure it was something like that. There was a lot of drama going on there, there's no telling what sent her over the edge enough to come at you like that, I'm afraid."

"Why then," she asked, "would the killer come back to my house and plant the SIM card there? I mean, that's the only part of this equation that doesn't really make any sense to me?"

"Maybe they just wanted to tie you to the case somehow. Incriminate you."

Lady Margaret shook her head. "I'm not so sure about that. They could have picked anyone if that was the case, someone whose house was a little easier to break into." Maybe they left it as a cry for help, like how criminals sometimes want to be caught because they feel guilty? She thought. Or the pressure was too much? She didn't know how criminal minds worked, exactly, only that they did ridiculous things sometimes.

Either way, she was no psychologist, so she didn't share those thoughts with the Sergeant. "Who do you believe actually killed Lucy, Sergeant?"

"I'll reserve my answer until I have all the reports in, if you don't mind. I never like to speculate." Margaret certainly had her suspicions, but she didn't want to say anything until she heard more from the Sergeant.

The next day, Lady Margaret read on the front page of the paper in the convenience shop: MELISSA WALLACE ARRESTED FOR THE MURDER OF LUCY DAVIDSON.

That's nice and tidy, Margaret thought. And just as I thought. Apparently, Margaret read, when Melissa learned that it was Lucy's intention to sell the photographs that she'd taken of the two of them, she felt betrayed. Lady Maggie could certainly understand that, she would feel the same way. She must have just told Melissa about her intentions for selling them just as Lady Margaret was arriving on the scene. And right after she'd left, the young woman rushed to the umbrella, grabbed it, and planted it right into Lucy's chest. Promptly wiping her prints from it. While Margaret was out, Melissa had climbed through her window and planted the SIM card in the living room chair, assuming the police would find it and Margaret would be accused of the crime. Little did she know, she picked the wrong woman to tamper with. Lady Margaret was much too clever for schoolgirl crush shenanigans.

Margaret made a quick phone call upon reading

the story. Her only question for Sergeant Ashworth was finding out who had easy access to her place. He informed her that Wallace had a duplicate key made when he signed the sale documents on her home before she moved from England. While Margaret was at her welcoming party, he simply let himself in and went through her belongings. It really hurt Margaret's feelings that someone who didn't even know her would try to plant something on her. But in all actuality, it could have happened anywhere at all, and it didn't deter her in the least from her new hometown. On her way back to her house that day, she laughed at how much of an adventure she'd already had, and she was just getting started!

Kate Mackenzie
Cozy Mysteries

Deadly Vows

Chapter 1

K ate MacKenzie put the final cupcake on top of the tower and stood back to admire her handiwork. A crystal cake stand held layers of decorated cupcakes in tiers, hand decorated with cream lace icing and exquisite coloured flower petals glistening with tiny pearls. The display was pride of place at the Granger wedding reception being held in the swanky Byron Manor hotel.

The cupcake tower dominated the center of the function room, at the back of which the floor to ceiling glass doors led onto a cobbled yard and manicured gardens. A stunning view of Byron Bay lay beyond, the sea a sparkling blue on this sunny spring day.

Byron Manor was the most luxe wedding venue in Ewingsdale, and it was Kate's first wedding event there since her mother had passed away just weeks before. She pushed the thought of her mother out of her mind. The pain was still so raw, it hurt her chest just thinking about it.

As if reading her mind, a voice came from behind her. "They look amazing, Kate. Mum would be so proud."

Kate turned to see her younger sister Lucie smiling, her eyes were shining although they glistened with tears.

"Do you think so?" whispered Kate. "I hope so, but… "

"They're fantastic, Kate. Of course I do. Mum taught you so well. You're so good at this even if you don't realize it."

"Hmmph," snorted Kate. She wasn't great at taking compliments. Still, they didn't look too bad if she said so herself.

Cupcake catering wasn't what she'd envisaged as her career when she had left Ewingsdale years before, but when does anyone's life ever go according to plan? Her mother's illness had been the reason she had moved back to the local area two years ago, her lust for travel forgotten while she cared for her mother through her illness. She and Lucie had known their mum wasn't going to recover, but it still had been a shock when she finally passed.

Kate had fallen back in to the easy way of living in the town where she had grown up. A place where everyone knew everyone else and there wasn't much that got past the local grapevine. She had learned by now who to plant the seeds of a rumour with or who to avoid with confidences.

"Thanks for helping me today, Lucie." Kate smiled at her sister. In terms of temperament, Lucie was everything Kate was not. Lucie had inherited their mother's cool, calm demeanor, while much to her own annoyance; Kate shared her father's red hair and the hot headedness that went with it. She would have preferred to forget her errant father and the way he had let them all down over the years, rather than be reminded of him every time she looked in the mirror.

A noise from behind them snapped Kate out of her spell of contemplation and she turned around to see what was going on.

The sound of a spoon clinking a glass shrilled through the air.

"Ladies and gentleman," beamed the newly married Freddie Granger to the guests. He raised a hand to silence the crowd, and gazed down at his blushing bride, Moira, who sat by his side. "I would like to propose a toast. To my lovely wife, Mrs. Granger." Freddie raised his glass while the guests stood and followed suit. "Mrs. Granger!" they cheered in unison.

His wife looked a little awkward, Kate thought. Instead of appearing like she was going to burst with happiness, she seemed more embarrassed than anything else. She looked away while Freddie took a slug of champagne, sipping her own drink while the music started up. Freddie was quite the character and he was making his way across the room with one of the bridesmaids rather than stay with his bride. Kate raised an eyebrow and turned back to her cupcakes. She had been surprised that Freddie Granger was settling down, but rumour had it that Moira had a bun in the oven. That wasn't a reason to get married in Kate's opinion, but if it was true she would understand. Some families in the area were still quite traditional. Kate couldn't ever imagine herself getting married, pregnant or not. Not after seeing what her mother had gone through with her father. She would rather avoid that sort of toxic relationship at all costs.

"Now, now," muttered Lucie, catching Kate rolling her eyes at Freddie's antics. "Try and enjoy the wedding sis, even though I know you hate them."

"Well I'm not having much luck, am I," retorted Kate with a rueful smile. Sugar N' Spice, the cupcake company she had taken over from their mother, was booked out with weddings for the next three months. It was only because she had promised her mother that she wouldn't let any of the clients down that she was continuing the business at all. In Kate's book, honour was everything, and it was her mother's dying wish that Sugar N' Spice continue. There was no way Kate would let her down.

And even though Kate's creative talent leaned more towards self-taught digital art and design, she did find cupcake decorating mesmerising. If cupcakes were art then Kate's were Van Goghs. Renoirs. She could even throw in a Matisse for good measure.

"Hey, Sugar," said a smooth, sexy voice behind her, that made her knees tremble ever so slightly and her stomach lurch. In a good way. She didn't need to turn around to see who it was, but she did anyway, her face flushed.

And there he was. Lachlan Fitzgerald. Tall. Tanned. His eyes were sparkling blue pools that she could drown in. Even when he was all dressed up like to-day, his sandy blonde hair still looked messy and wind-swept. It must be a carry back from his surfer days, Kate thought to herself. She tried to keep a straight face as she scolded him.

"Don't call me Sugar!" she warned Lachlan in a low voice. "I'm your business partner, not your Sugar, okay?"

"Ooh, I love it when you get angry," laughed Lachlan, winding her up even more. Kate could feel the heat on her face and wished her colouring didn't make it so obvious when she was flustered. "Mm, now I know who put the spice in Sugar N' Spice," he smirked.

There was no winning with this guy. Just as Kate was about to think of a smart retort, another commotion ensued from across the room. A small crowd had gathered around the spot where Freddie the groom was lying on the floor. Fallen down drunk, suspected Kate. A murmur rippled through the crowd until someone screamed. A loud thump on the floor signaled that Moira the bride had fainted and fallen off her chair. She was a big girl.

"Call an ambulance," someone shrieked. "For Moira?" Kate didn't think that would be necessary. She rushed toward the top table to try and help Moira up.

"Come on Lachlan, you might need to help lift her," Kate said grimly, grabbing his hand and pulling him across the room. The warmth of his skin on hers sent a tingle through her arm and she liked the firm way he gripped her hand in his.

It was only when they got to the bodies that Kate realised the situation was far worse than she had thought.

Chapter 2

The NSW Ambulance service didn't take long to get there, even though the winding road to the Manor wasn't made for fast driving.

"Move out of the way, please," the paramedics ordered the guests, who cleared a path for the two medical attendants carrying a stretcher over to Freddie. The wail of a woman crying permeated the air and there was a general hubbub of people talking and whispering in hushed tones. While two men dealt with Freddie, a third went to see how Moira was coping. Sitting on the floor, she had come round and was in quite a state with tendrils from her up-do now poking out in all directions, and panda eyes from her tears. She was trying to crawl across the floor to Freddie, but had to be restrained by several guests holding her large frame back.

Kate watched in horror at the scene unfolding in front of her.

"Oh my God," she muttered to Lucie at her side. "This has got to be a bad dream. What the hell happened anyway, does anyone know?"

"I'm sure everything will be fine," said Lucie, putting her arm around her sister's waist and giving her a comforting squeeze. "He probably just fell over drunk.

Good old Freddie, we know he loves a drink. He'll be dining out on this one for years to come."

"I don't think so," Kate replied, as Lachlan stalked toward them, his face set in stone. Judging by the look on his face, it wasn't good news.

"Is he…?" she whispered as Lachlan stepped beside them.

Lachlan nodded, his lips pursed. "I'm afraid so," Lachlan replied with a sigh. "Freddie's dead as a dodo."

Before Kate could reply, they were joined by another female who had been standing observing the conversation. Selena Fox, Kate's assistant, was quite the fox herself, and she sidled over to Lachlan.s side.

"Oh, Lachlan," she purred. "You poor thing. Are you okay? Here let me get you a cold drink. I expect seeing a corpse has you all shaken up."

Lachlan turned and looked at Selena in surprise, and Kate had to contain a smile. Despite the gravity of the situation, the look on Lachlan's face was priceless. Lachlan Fitzgerald, ex World Surfing Champion and retired due to a shark injury, shaken by a corpse? Somehow Kate didn't think so. But good for Selena, she never missed a trick.

Kate's eyes narrowed as she watched Selena flutter her thick lashes at Lachlan as she leaned closer to him and laid a hand on his shoulder. Selena pouted as she shook her head from side to side, mock scolding him.

"Now, Lachlan, I really think you should sit down. Come with me." Before Lachlan could even reply,

Selena was dragging him over to the corner where she fussed and fawned over him. Lachlan caught Kate's eye as she watched them, and shrugged with a grin. Turning back to Selena, he almost seemed to be enjoying the attention.

"Put the green-eyed monster away, sis," Lucie laughed. "He's only winding you up. And it's working, right?"

"I don't know what you're talking about," huffed Kate. "As if I care who Lachlan talks to, you must be joking."

Lucie raised an eyebrow at her older sister.

"Playing hard to get is one thing Kate. But Lachlan's not going to chase after you forever. Not if someone else gets him first."

And with that, Lucie walked off to where Uncle Wallace was frantically waving to them from the doorway. This was a disaster for everyone, but especially for Uncle Wallace who had just launched his wedding business at the Manor recently.

"Oh my," said Uncle Wallace, wiping a clean white cloth handkerchief over his glistening brow. "This is a disaster. If word gets out that people are dying at Byron Manor, it would be the kiss of wedding venue death. No-one will want to have their wedding reception here again. Someone tell me this is not happening, please?"

"Don't be silly, Uncle Wallace," Lucie said kindly. "It's not your fault. These things happen. No-one can say it has anything to do with you or this lovely venue."

Kate looked around. Flowers were draped around the doorway and courtyard outside, pathways leading to manicured lawns and an outdoor pool. Nooks and crannies for quiet moments and wide spaces for group photos. The perfect spot for the perfect wedding.

"What did the paramedics say?" Kate chipped in. "Do they know what happened?"

Uncle Wallace's voice fell to a whisper "They have to run pathology tests, but they think it was the champagne."

"You mean Freddie choked?" Lucie asked. "That's terrible."

Uncle Wallace shook his head. "This was no accident, ladies. Freddie Granger was poisoned."

Kate's heart sank. Surely not? Who on earth would want to poison the jovial, friendly and universally popular Freddie Granger? Sure, his jokes were annoying, but they weren't that bad. Kate couldn't imagine that Freddie had any enemies at all.

"Remember the time Freddie rescued Mrs. Fitts' cat from the old oak tree?" she smiled. Freddie had been popular in the town since childhood. "He was only ten and he fell and broke his arm. He grew up nice too. I can't believe anyone would want to murder Freddie. There must be some mistake."

"Please, Kate, can you help me find out?" Uncle Wallace begged. "Without an explanation, Byron Manor is finished. I may as well board the place up now and give the bank the keys. I'm ruined. Your poor mother would turn in her grave."

Like a knife through her heart, Uncle Wallace got Kate right in her weak spot. Uncle Wallace was her mother's favourite brother, and she had even invested in Bryon Manor before she died. Kate knew her mother would want her to help Uncle Wally.

"Of course I'll help," Kate reassured him, patting his arm. "There's nothing to worry about, really. I'm sure there's a simple explanation."

A dead groom and no suspects wasn't simple at all, Kate thought to herself, but she didn't want to alarm poor old Wally further. The situation didn't look good. From what she had seen, Freddie and Moira had each taken a drink of their champagne, and a few minutes later Freddie had keeled over and died. Moira, on the other hand, was very much alive, and she was now sitting up and smiling at a handsome looking rugby player type who was fussing around her.

"Who's that guy with Moira?" Kate asked Lucie. "Do you know him?"

Lucie looked up. "Isn't that Harry something? Used to go out with Moira I think. Ages ago, when you were a rock chick."

Kate ignored the reference to her rock chick period, otherwise known as the lost years, when she had left Ewingsdale in search of love and adventure. Odd to have your ex-boyfriend at your wedding, Kate thought to herself, but then not everyone was like Kate. She preferred to keep exes in the past where they belonged, which Lucie said was part of her problem.

"You can't just shut things in a box and pretend they never happened, Kate. You need to deal with your issues before you can move on."

Kate thought that Lucie's touchy feely self-help approach to just about everything was only prolonging the agony of things she would rather forget. She was a much more practical sort, as her mother often commended her. And it had done her very well until now. Hadn't it?

She looked over to where Lachlan sat entranced by Selena the Fox and all of a sudden, Kate wasn't so sure.

Chapter 3

"Right," Kate ordered as she sprang into action. "I'm going to get to the bottom of this, before Uncle Wallace dies with a heart attack. I don't think he can handle the strain. Lucie, are you in?"

"Yes," chirped Lucie, fresh from swapping telephone numbers with a rather handsome guest who was ostensibly asking about a cupcake order but clearly had something not quite so innocent on his mind. Doe-eyed Lucie, with her silky brunette curls, sallow golden skin and the smile of an angel, was never short of suitors. And despite her innocent appearance she was pretty good at weeding out the jerks. She took no crap from guys with the result that she had men tripping over her from here to next week. And when she had had her fun with them, they would stay friends and those guys would do anything for her forever. Maybe that's why Moira had Harry at the wedding, Kate realised. Some people just had nice exes, unlike her. After her last relationship, she had her fingers burned. Singed. Scorched. That's not to say she wouldn't like a bit of fun every now and then. And someone like Lachlan would fit the bill very nicely.

"Okay," barked Kate. "Tell Lachlan and Selena to start feeding the guests. No-one can leave until the police have finished their inquiries so we may as well make the best of a bad situation. Who knows, if we can turn this around Uncle Wallace might be able to escape the bad publicity."

"Mmm, okay, sure," said Lucie, obviously dubious but humouring Kate anyway. She knew it wasn't worth riling her sister, not when she was in her groove. "So what are you going to do?"

"I'm going to speak to some of the guests and see if I can get to the bottom of this."

"Get to the bottom of what?" said Lachlan in that deep voice, sending shivers through Kate's core yet again.

"There's been a murder, Lachlan," Kate growled at him, "in case you hadn't noticed. The police are busy taking names and telephone numbers while the murderer is still on the loose. I'm just trying to take control of the situation before it gets even more out of hand."

"Oh, so we're under house arrest?" Selena gasped, raising her hand to her mouth. "How exciting!"

Kate rolled her eyes.

"Do you think we're safe?" continued Selena, closing in on Lachlan. "I mean, if there's a murderer on the loose, you'll have to protect me." She did that fluttery thing with her eyelashes again, making it look like something was stuck in her eye. Lachlan grinned, while Kate suppressed a snort.

"Sure, Selena, don't worry. I'll protect you girls." He turned and directed his next comment to Kate. "All of you."

His sparkling blue eyes seared her heart and Kate thought for a second that yes, he did like her. When they got this mess sorted out, maybe she would take him up on that offer of a date. Until then though, she had more pressing matters on her mind.

"I'll get this show on the road, shall we?" said Lachlan, taking charge. Kate smiled as Lachlan started ordering Lucie, Selena and the rest of the servers into action. Lachlan had been at the catering game longer than she had, and his company Truly Scrumptious was a slick operation. He had nailed the local market for high end quality catering with a trendy twist. His good looks and charm made him a winner with customers and he had the added cachet of the fame factor in his favour as well. It wasn't every day that a world famous hot and sexy surfer started a catering business so he had a few curiosity bookings to start with, but now his reputation in the catering market stood on its own merit. She knew the hospitality industry wasn't Lachlan's first choice as a business any more than it was hers, but since his leg injury in the shark attack, his sporting career was over. Partnering Sugar N' Spice with Truly Scrumptious for wedding catering was a brainwave of her mother's before she had gotten sick, but Kate sometimes wondered if her mum didn't have an ulterior motive as well.

"Catch a grip," Kate muttered to herself as she wandered out to the pool area. Drooling over a guy was not her thing. She really didn't know what had come over her.

~

"Oh Moira," said Kate, pulling the bride in for a hug. "I'm so sorry for your loss."

This was going to be all over the Ewingsdale Daily News tomorrow, and she wouldn't be surprised if it made the national news as well. Married and widowed in the same day, with a potential serial killer amongst the wedding party? It was tabloid heaven.

"Thanks, Kate," sniffed Moira into her tissue. "I wish I would wake up from this bad dream. This is the worst day of my life instead of the best. Hic."

Kate leaned back before Moira's champagne fuelled belch hit her right in the face. Moira was more than tipsy by this stage, but who could blame her? She wouldn't be having much fun on her wedding night now. The rumours must not be true about Moira being pregnant after all, thought Kate. Surely she wouldn't be drinking in that condition, would she?

Kate wasn't getting much sense out of Moira. "Think, Moira," urged Kate. "Go back through it all again and tell me what happened. There must be something else."

"Ive told you, Kate. We went straight from the church to here, apart from stopping off for a few photos along the way at the Old Steamboat Quay. Freddie used to take me courting there," Moira blushed. "It's where we had our first kiss. And now… wahhh," she wailed.

"Who was there?" said Kate, persisting with her line of questioning.

"Just me, Freddie, the limo driver and the photographer."

Kate made a mental note to speak to them both.

"And then we arrived here," Moira continued, "and spoke to everyone in the wedding line up. We had just got to the table when Freddie made the toast. Next thing I know, he's gone. Oh, my poor Freddie."

"The champagne, Moira," Kate pressed her. "You both had champagne from the same bottle, right?"

Moira looked confused. "Yes, I think so," she sobbed. "I don't know, I just drank it."

"Who gave you the champagne, can you remember who served it?"

Moira shook her head.

"Is there anything you can think of, any reason or anyone who might want to hurt Freddie?"

Moira, a little more composed now, shook her head again. "Everyone loved Freddie," Moira murmured. "Even my dad liked him in the end."

"What do you mean?" Kate asked, surprised.

"Well, dad didn't like Freddie at the start, you see," sniffed Moira. "He thought Freddie was a no-hoper who was only after me for my money. But dad never liked any of my boyfriend's anyway, except for Harry, so I didn't pay much notice. And once dad got to know Freddie, they got along just fine."

Kate made a few notes on her paper. Luis Sutton, Moira's father, wasn't the most popular man in town.

Now a successful businessman, he always maintained that he'd made his fortune in the mines, but there were whispers about the mines story being cover for a nefarious bootleg business and that he had dodgy friends in high places. Luis Sutton made out like butter wouldn't melt in his mouth, but there was something slimy about him that gave Kate the creeps. So Luis didn't like Freddie. Kate had a lightbulb moment.

"Is Luis still in the wine importing business, Moira?"

"Yes, I think so," Moira replied. "Why?"

"Oh, nothing," muttered Kate. If Luis's wine company had supplied the champagne, then she could have a lead. She made more notes on her pad.

Sucking her pen, she rummaged in her bag for the table plans so she could review the guest list. She knew most of the guests from around town, and Kate would have been surprised to find a villain amongst them. Unable to find her own copy, she went over to the board and unpinned the pages that were displayed for the guests to know where to sit.

"Who's Emma Krasnoff?" asked Kate, as she came to an unfamiliar name on the list.

"Emma's Freddie's ex," Moira explained. "Bless her. Sweet little thing, but it was never serious, not on Freddie's part. They kept in touch over the years, and I've met her a few times. She even visited and stayed at my dad's house last year. We just invited her to the wedding to be polite. Never expected her to attend. But hey, weddings are great places to meet men, are't they? Freddie figured he could fix her up with one of the guys and get her out of his hair. I think he felt a little guilty that she was still holding a candle for him or something."

Kate smiled. That would be just like Freddie.

Just then, an irate looking hunk strode through the French doors to where Kate and Moira sat by the pool in the shade of the trees.

"What the hell do you think you're doing?" he yelled at Kate, who was taken aback by his outburst. Unfazed, she glared right back at him. It was the man who had been fussing over Moira right after Freddie had died.

"And who, may I ask, are you?"

"Oh Harry," pleaded Moira. "Relax. Kate's only trying to help. She wants to try and find out who bumped Freddie off. And I just want to get out of here and mourn in peace. So why don't we try to help her so this nightmare can be over?"

"Hmmph," grunted the man, who extended his hand to Kate. "Harry Truman, at your service, Kate. If there's anything I can do to help, just ask."

"Thanks," Kate replied, "but I think I'm fine. If you'll just excuse us, I'd like to finish talking to Moira."

Harry folded his arms and stood his ground, his hulking shadow towering over the two women.

"I'd like you to finish talking to Moira too," he replied. "Can't you see the woman's distraught? Have you no feelings at all?"

Moira smiled a weak smile at Harry, who reached out and squeezed Moira's hand. "Come on Moira, let's get you out of here. I've had enough of this nonsense for one day."

And with that Harry led Moira away.

Kate watched them leave, Harry placing a tender arm around Moira's shoulders. It was a small gesture that belied a closeness inappropriate for a newly married woman. Kate scribbled on her notepad in capital letters and drew a circle around the name for good measure.

HARRY TRUMAN???

Chapter 4

"Hey Sugar," said a voice from behind the door, followed by a head belonging to a grinning Lachlan. "I thought you could do with these." The rest of his body appeared, carrying a tray with two full glasses of wine and several cupcakes.

"I bet you haven't eaten, have you?" he scolded, setting the tray down on the table and handing Kate a glass.

"I shouldn't really be drinking at work, but boy do I need this," said a grateful Kate, lifting the glass to her lips. The cool crisp taste of the ice cold chardonnay hit the back of her throat and she savoured the flavour seeping into her taste glands. The hit of the alcohol helped too.

"You're right, I'm starving," she mumbled at Lachlan, crumbs flying as she stuffed a bite of cupcake into her mouth. Once she'd inhaled two cupcakes and half a glass of wine she felt much better. Lachlan was staring at her throughout.

"So what's happening?" he asked. "Did you find out anything yet?"

Kate shrugged. "Not really. Poor Moira is so upset she wasn't much help at all. I don't think she knows what's hit her."

"Who's that guy she's with?" Lachlan inquired, settling back in the chair. It creaked under his muscular physique.

Kate had to drag her eyes away from the outline of his six pack under his snug white dress shirt to stop herself from drooling.

"Some guy called Harry Truman," Kate replied, her eyes narrowing. "He just went from the Incredible Hulk to Bruce Danner in the blink of an eye."

"Never heard of him," shrugged Lachlan, reaching for a cupcake. "But he's in there playing bodyguard to Moira right now. Won't let anyone near her. Hey, these cupcakes are good, Sugar." He winked at Kate. She couldn't be bothered arguing.

"I'd love to sit and chat all night, Lachlan, but I need to talk to a few more people." Kate stood up, brushing the crumbs off her skirt.

"Thanks for the wine." She took one last sip. "Oh, that reminds me, did Luis Sutton's Cloudy Vines supply the wine and champagne today, do you know?"

Lachlan shook his head. "No, Truly Scrumptious did. Luis ordered it himself. I did think it was strange when he has his own wine company, but if he wants to pay me instead, who was I to complain?"

"Mmm, okay," Kate replied, mulling that piece of information over. "Well one of us had better get back to work, so I'll see you later."

"Sure, Sugar," Lachlan laughed with another wink as Kate stalked off inside.

"How's it all going?" Kate whispered to Lucie who was walking around with a tray of cupcakes.

"It's fine, considering," Lucie relied. "And they really like the cupcakes. But Uncle Wallace is still really antsy and the cops don't seem to be getting anywhere. People aren't allowed to leave so it looks like the entire wedding party is going to have to stay here overnight. Or for as long as it takes."

"Well, if I have anything to do with it, that won't be much longer," Kate declared.

"Don't you think you should leave it to the police?" chirped Selena, in clipped tones. "I mean, it's not as if you're qualified or anything. Lachlan says you never finished university."

Kate could feel her temper rising up. Selena was such a bitch, but she wasn't going to be goaded into an argument. Why the hell was Lachlan talking to Selena about her anyway? That was so unprofessional. She would have to pull him up on that.

Deep breaths. And relax.

"Can you go around again with the cupcakes please, Selena?" Kate spoke at her sweetly. Her mother had always taught them that good manners cost nothing.

Looking around the room, most of the guests were seated. The band had been cancelled but canned music played in the background. A few shouts and roars from a couple of the tables signaled that some of the guests were getting stuck in at the free bar. Uncle Wallace had obviously decided it might make a bad situation better. She noticed Harry and Moira huddled together in a corner, Harry looking daggers at anyone who dared approach.

"Come on," Kate said, pulling Lucie by the elbow out of the main function room. "I need your help."

"Where are we going?" squealed Lucie. "Ow. Let me go!"

Kate didn't drop Lucie's arm until they were half way up the grand staircase that led to the guest rooms in the main Byron Manor house. There were other guest bungalows scattered throughout the grounds, but the Honeymoon Suite was in the main building. She looked behind her to make sure they weren't being followed and that no-one had seen them. The house was silent apart from the sound of their footsteps, the noise of the guests below now far away.

With another furtive look over her shoulder, Kate turned the handle of the Honeymoon Suite door and pushed.

Lucie followed her inside in disbelief, "You're going to be in so much trouble if you get caught! The cops will arrest you. Let's get out of here, quick," gasped Lucie.

"Ssh," whispered Kate. "If I go down we both go down so let's make sure we don't get rumbled, okay?" She started looking about the room. Rose petals were scattered on the bed, ready for the newlyweds first night as a married couple. Apparently, Housekeeping hadn't got the memo about the newly dead situation.

"What are you looking for?" hissed Lucie, following Kate's lead and picking up random things that were lying about the room. Moira's robe lay over a chair. There was hairbrush on the dressing table beside a jewellery box which lay open. A folded piece of blue notepaper on the table caught Kate's eye.

"I can't believe you're going to read that," accused Lucie. "A love letter from a dying man to his bride. That's gross."

Kate unfolded the paper, ignoring Lucie's protests. "He wasn't dying when he wrote it , was he?" she argued, scanning her gaze across the paper. Her eyes narrowed.

"What's wrong?" said Lucie.

"It's not a love note," Kate replied. Reading the note aloud she continued, "You know it's true, you just don't want to believe it. This wedding is a sham. Don't say I didn't warn you."

Lucie looked puzzled. "That's it? What the hell is that supposed to mean? Who's it from?"

"I have no idea," said Kate, folding the note twice and putting it in her pocket. "It's not signed. But let's get our asses out of here before we get arrested for tampering with the evidence."

They made it back down to the lobby without being spotted. At the bottom of the stairs, Kate hesitated. "Come on, let's go through the garden. There's people outside so if anyone asks, we can say we just went for a walk. Make sure to speak to someone so we have an alibi."

Lucie smirked at her sister. "Kate, you've been watching way too much Columbo."

Undeterred, Kate marched off leaving Lucie trailing in her wake. By the time Lucie caught up, Kate was standing under a pagoda talking to Luis Sutton and a petite woman who Lucie had never seen before.

"Hey," said Lucie sauntering up to the group with feigned nonchalance.

"Hey Lucie," Kate said, gesturing towards her companions. "You know Luis Sutton, don't you?" Lucie nodded and smiled at Luis. "And this is Emma Krasnoff," continued Kate. "Emma's a friend of Freddie." Lucie smiled again at the tiny young woman, a timid wisp of a thing with a cropped pixie haircut.

Luis and Emma didn't share Kate's exuberance at the meeting. Emma looked at the ground in silence, while Luis tapped his foot and pursed his lips as Kate spoke.

Awkward, but at least the sisters had their alibi.

"Well, nice seeing you guys!" Kate said in a cheery tone as she and Lucie left the pair, who exchanged a glance before resuming their conversation in hushed tones.

"That's Freddie's ex," Kate explained to Lucie as they walked away. "Moira was telling me about her. She seems nice, but I wonder how she knows Luis?"

"Well, you know Luis likes the ladies," Lucie offered.

"Lucie MacKenzie, I salute you," Kate said with a

grin. "Maybe that's who Freddie was going to set her up with?"

Kate grabbed her notebook out of her pocket and scribbled something down.

"Kate," said Lucie with a sigh, "I have no idea what you're talking about but I really need a drink."

And as Lucie headed for the bar, Kate set off on a hunch.

Chapter 5

The spike of the dart hit the bullseye with a pop. Kate winced at the power and precision with which it was thrown, and spoke up from her vantage point in the corner. "Hey Harry."

Harry turned around and viewed Kate with a weary smile. He lifted his pint from the table and took a slug. Wiping his mouth with his hand, he walked to the dartboard and pulled each of the darts out of the cork.

"Do you play?" Harry asked Kate, turning around and meeting her half way as she approached. He held out his hand with the darts.

Kate shook her head. "No thanks. I just wanted a quick word, if that's okay? I was told I would find you in here."

The dartboard was in a nook at the back of the small bar, which was empty apart from the two of them. Gnarled oak tables and leather club chairs were scattered about the space. The tiled floor gave the room an eerie echo and Kate had a sick feeling in her stomach at her close proximity to Harry.

"Go on, have a go," smiled Harry, holding the darts out to her again. Kate accepted, figuring that after Harry's sniper display, she was probably a safer keeper of potential deadly weapons. She aimed one after at the board on the wall and cringed as each one bounced and fell on the floor in turn.

Leaving the darts at a safe distance on the floor, she sat at a table opposite Harry, who had been watching her with a sad smile on his face.

"How's Moira?" Kate asked Harry, surveying his face as he replied. He was drawn, and Kate wondered if what she had assumed was hostility was something else. Harry buried his face in his palms before looking up again at Kate.

"Moira and I are old friends," Harry explained. "Between you and me, we used to date."

"So I gather," muttered Kate. Not only was Harry Moira's ex, he appeared to be a very possessive one at that.

"We stayed in touch over the years," sighed Harry, "and have remained close friends."

What was it with these people and their exes, thought Kate to herself. All very cosy indeed.

"So how did Freddie feel about that?" Kate asked, getting straight to the point.

"Moira loved Freddie, Kate, I can assure you of that," Harry retorted as he stood up from the table.

"And do you still love Moira?" Kate retorted, surprised by her own daring in the presence of such a formidable man.

Harry smiled at Kate. A cold smile, that didn't reach his eyes. "It's complicated, Kate, and it's also none of your business. You really should keep your pretty little nose to of things that don't concern you."

Harry pushed himself out of his chair and it scraped across the floor as he moved it back to step away from the table. "If you'll excuse me, this conversation is over. But of your information, and off the record? Yes, I care for Moira very much. And I would never do anything to hurt her."

Kate was left pondering Harry's words when Selena walked in. Her face was flushed as she rushed toward where Kate was seated.

"Have you found any clues yet?" gasped Selena, sitting in the chair just vacated by Harry. "Because there's something that you need to know!"

"Really? Kate replied with suspicion. She didn't trust Selena and she doubted that anything Selena could tell her would change her view of the case. She already had it pretty much sussed who the murderer was anyway.

She thought it only polite to hear Selena out. "Go on," offered Kate. "Only this had better be good, because I'm just on my way to speak to the police."

"Well," gasped Selena. "Will you tell them I helped you? The police I mean?"

"Sure," Kate offered. "So what's so important that you need to tell the police?"

"I've just overheard them talking. Moira and that man."

"I thought she was in bed."

"She was on her way upstairs," Selena explained.

"I was a little way behind. The concierge was allocating rooms and I wanted to make sure I got a good one."

Kate said nothing. That would be true, all right. Selena was always looking out for herself.

"Well anyway," Selena went on, "I was looking for my room when I heard crying and voices in the hallway. I waited, because I didn't want to interrupt a private conversation, you know? And it seemed important."

"So why didn't you just go away and leave them alone?" Kate snapped, tired now.

"Will you please listen?" hissed Selena. "So there was crying, and I couldn't hear it all, but she was saying something like 'You knew I loved him, why did you do it? It would have all been fine. We could have worked it out without anyone getting hurt.' So I figured they might be talking about Freddie."

Kate's ears pricked up. Maybe Selena was on to something after all. "Go on," she urged. "What else did they say?"

"And then the man said something like, "I don't know how it happened, I swear. But I will take care of it.' And then he said, 'I love you. Don't worry baby, everything will work out in the end.'"

"I knew it," Kate smirked. "And did you see them Selena, so you can testify it was definitely them—Moira and Harry?"

Selena looked at Kate with wide eyes.

"It was Moira, for sure. But who's Harry? The man she was talking to was that slimy old guy. Her dad."

Kate dropped her pen and raked her fingers through her hair.

"You're sure? It definitely wasn't Harry?" sighed Kate. Selena nodded vehemently and Kate believed her. If Selena thought she was going to get some of the glory for finding the killer, there was no way she would lie about something like this.

"Oh, okay, listen, thanks Selena," nodded Kate." I don't think we should go to the police yet. We probably need more proof. Can you keep this to yourself for now?"

Selena promised not to breathe a word, and as the clock chimed 10PM, Kate's weary legs claimed the stairs. Lucie was already asleep in the small but luxurious room they were sharing, and Kate tried not to wake her as she bumped about in the dark. She turned in for the night, still no nearer to knowing who had killed Freddie Granger. Lulled to sleep by the gentle sway of the trees in the light breeze outside, Kate dreamed of sexy surfers, bride and groom cake toppers, and deadly darts.

Chapter 6

"**I** pity your future husband," moaned Lucie, rubbing the crick in her neck. "You thrash about in bed like an octopus. I'm black and blue. And if you ever try to snuggle up to me like that again, I swear I will puke."

Kate raised an eyebrow at her sister. Unlike Lucie, she was surprisingly well rested and feeling hopeful about the day ahead. She was no closer to finding the murderer, but she knew the answer must be hiding in plain sight.

"Lucky I won't be getting married then, isn't it?" she snarled back at Lucie.

"Now, now," Lucie chuckled. "I'll remind you about that when Lachlan gets down on one knee, shall I?"

"He's got a dodgy knee, remember? Shark bite. Now will you quit with the Lachlan jokes and get dressed? The day anything happens with me and Lachlan Fitzpatrick will be a cold day in hell. Not after him talking about me behind my back to Selena."

"Did it ever occur to you," Lucie pointed out, "that Selena might be making it up? And everyone knows you quit university to run off with a rock star. It's not exactly a secret. If you've got a problem with Lachlan, why not just ask him what he said? Honestly, you should know better than to listen to Selena. She's a nasty piece of work."

Kate pondered what Selena had told her the previous night about Moira and Luis. She concluded that Selena was too dumb to make something like that up.

"Hmmph." Kate sulked, "I'm going downstairs to see if they need a hand in the kitchen. There are a lot of people to feed and I might be able to pick Lachlan's brains, see if he knows anything."

"Pick his brains? Is that what they're calling it these days?" laughed Lucie, before she was silenced by a pillow to the head.

Kate walked downstairs with a spring in her step and a smile on her face. She was a woman on a mission. Lucie was right. She should take control and scratch that itch she had for Lachlan. Her mind idled at the thought of sharing that cozy little bed with Lachlan rather than Lucie. It had been a long time since she had shared a bed with anyone.

Checking her reflection in the gilded mirror in the hallway, Kate fixed her hair before heading down the back stairs to the Manor kitchen. She had kind of hoped she would have run into Lachlan again last night, but after she had spoken to Selena there was no one else around. If she had to make up for lost time by slaving over a hot stove with him this morning instead, then that would make her very happy. And she wanted to ask him more about the champagne order as well.

Kate's heart raced as she flung herself through the swinging kitchen doors, ready to get her sleeves rolled up with Lachlan.

"Oh," Kate gasped, taking in the scene before her. "I'm, um, sorry, I…"

Lachlan lifted his head from a woman's lips and turned toward Kate, his eyes wide. The arms around his neck belonged to Selena, who was grinning at Kate like a Cheshire cat. Kate watched as Selena nuzzled into Lachlan's neck, staking her claim on her prize.

"Kate!" called Lachlan, pulling away from Selena. "Wait, please…. "

But Kate was already gone, the kitchen doors swinging behind her, tears blurring her eyes. She swore to herself that she would never entertain x-rated thoughts about that dumb ass sexy surfer ever again.

Chapter 7

"It's a bit early to be drinking, or is my watch wrong?" Kate asked Luis, who was propped up at the bar, nursing what looked like a whisky.

"Then what are you doing here?" Luis asked Kate with a wry smile.

"I went for a walk," shrugged Kate, pulling u a bar stool. "But I didn't get very far. It's like Fort Knox out there—police cars and crowd barriers to stop anyone getting out or in."

Word had travelled overnight, and paparazzi, news teams and TV crews were stationed around the perimeter of the Manor's grounds, trying to get a scoop on the story. A helicopter circled above them.

"I missed breakfast so I was hoping to grab a bar snack," admitted Kate.

"I'm sure that nice caterer would fix you something," sneered Luis. "I thought you two had a thing going on."

Kate glared at Luis, her colour rising. "I don't know where you got that idea. Absolutely not. No way, Jose." She shook her head from side to side, just to stress the point.

"It's okay, you don't have to convince me," remarked Luis, swirling his drink around in the glass.

"I'm no expert but I'd say there's something you're not admitting to."

"And what about you Luis? Is there something that you're not admitting to?"

Luis sighed. "Look, Kate, if you're trying to pin this murder on me you're barking up the wrong tree. Freddie wasn't a bad guy, considering some of the fellas that Moira has brought home over the years. I never liked the fact that he was a teacher, though. Poor as a bloody church mouse and no ambition. Oh yes, I can see why he'd be happy to laze around for half the year and spend my money. But Moira loved him, and that was good enough for me. I always thought Harry was a better match for her, but there you go. What does it matter what her old man thinks, eh? Cheers." He raised his glass to Kate and slugged down the last of the brown liquid. "I bet you never listened to your old man either, did you?"

"I might have, if he was ever around," Kate retorted." So what's the deal with Harry, then?"

"Harry loves Moira, always did. Don't tell the cops, but they had a fling while Moira and Freddie were engaged. Moira said it was a mistake, but I think Harry got his hopes up. At least Harry's not a leech, he's an established businessman. I told Moira to forget all about it and Freddie would never know. But Moira was riddled with guilt about Harry. And now she's riddled with guilt about Freddie."

"You mean because Harry killed Freddie?" Kate asked.

Luis raised an eyebrow at Kate. "Now, now Kate. I never said that Harry killed Freddie, did I? You're putting words in my mouth."

"Oh, silly me. You're right, sorry about that." Kate gave Luis a grateful smile. Of course Luis wouldn't want anyone to know that he had grassed Harry up. Unless he was trying to frame Harry because he was in some way implicated himself?

"Thanks Luis, I appreciate your help," Kate said, with a conspiratorial wink. "Oh, and just one more thing. Could you write down the name of that champagne for me please? I want to trace the source without having to ask Lachlan." She pushed a napkin and pen toward Luis, who wrote the name of the champagne vintage on the tissue paper with a flourish. Kate grabbed to napkin before he could change his mind. She wanted to check the handwriting against the note she had found in Moira's room.

"Oh, just one more thing. Do you mind me asking, why you didn't supply the champagne from Cloudy Vines?" Kate asked Luis as she stood to leave.

"Sure," Luis replied. "It was my daughter's wedding. I didn't want to get my hands dirty." Luis gestured to the bartender to fetch him another drink, as Kate scurried away.

On her way past the courtyard, she spied Moira and Harry in heated conversation, raised voices carrying in pockets through the air. Kate was fuming at the sight of Harry, arguing with Moira who was on the verge of tears.

"You should be ashamed of yourselves," Kate shouted as she marched toward them. "Do you think no-one would find out? That you were carrying on behind Freddie's back? That Harry killed Freddie to win you back for himself, Moira? How does that make you feel?"

Moira face paled at Kate's outburst, and she reached out in an attempt for support from Harry, before fainting in a crumpled heap at Kate's feet.

～

"I'm going to have to insist that you apologise to Mrs. Granger and Mr. Truman," said the police officer, shuffling his papers. "We have trained detectives on this case, Miss Mackenzie, and you're not helping matters by upsetting people."

"I'm sorry," mumbled Kate to Moira and Harry, who sat, hands entwined, in two armchairs opposite. The cops had made a makeshift office in the Manor's lounge, and had dragged the three of them in for questioning after the incident in the courtyard.

Much to Kate's dismay, the police didn't seem to be giving any weight to the evidence she had presented to them pointing to Harry as the murderer.

"Innocent until proven guilty," Detective Holmes had repeated until Kate was sick of hearing it. Her face flamed as she stomped out of the lounge, wondering how this day had gone so wrong.

"Well," said Uncle Wallace, who was flapping about in the lobby. "Did they arrest them?"

"Sorry, Uncle Wallace. The cops won't do anything."

Wallace's face fell, and Kate noticed he was shaky. Her mother's death had hit him hard too and now this.

"Ave you seen the TV crews outside?" he muttered. "I'm ruined."

"Don't worry," Kate promised. "I'll get to the bottom of this, Uncle Wallace, if it's the last thing I do in Ewingsdale."

"What do you mean? You're not leaving, are you?"

Kate thought of Lachlan and Selena, and hesitated for a moment. Seeing them together earlier had hurt her more than she knew was possible. Having to continue to work with Selena, and Lachlan, while those two were together… she didn't know if she could do it. She imagined her mother, telling her off for being so silly. No, whatever happened between those two lovebirds wasn't going to determine her future. Her mother would want her to stay in Ewingsdale and carry on with Sugar N' Spice. If she could only muster a fraction of the strength of character that her mother had shown throughout her life, she would be doing well. She wasn't brought up to be a quitter.

"Don't worry, Uncle Wallace." Kate gave the shaky man a hug. "I'm not going anywhere."

Chapter 8

"I know they're here somewhere," Kate muttered to herself later that evening, rummaging in her bag. The afternoon had passed without incident, and she had successfully managed to avoid Lachlan and Selena. After helping Uncle Wallace organise a game of charades for all the guests after dinner, Kate finally had a chance to devote herself to the case in hand.

"What are you looking for?" Lucie asked, sitting on the bed.

"My glasses," Kate said, tipping the entire contents of her bag on top of the bed. "Here, take this." She thrust the napkin at Lucie and pulled her glasses on. "Right, let's compare the writing on the napkin to the note from Moira's room."

Kate opened the blue notepaper and handed it to Lucie, before another document from her bag caught her eye. It was the table plan from the wedding planner that she had been looking for the day before.

Excitement flooded through her as she scanned the document. She waved it at Lucie in glee.

"They don't match," Lucie said flinging the napkin and notepaper back to Kate. "Whoever wrote the note, it wasn't Luis."

"That doesn't matter," Kate triumphed, her eyes

shining. "Here look at this." She thrust the table plan at Lucie who viewed it with confusion.

"It's the table plan. So what?"

"They changed it," gasped Kate, pointing at the seating layout for the top table. Don't you see?"

"Um, no?"

"On this table plan, Moira was supposed to be on Freddie's right, see? And Freddie was on Moira's left."

"Okay… " hesitated Lucie. "And the point is?"

"For some reason, at the last minute they switched. On the wedding day, the bride and groom were sitting the other way round. The poisoned champagne was at Moira's place setting, but Freddie drank it by mistake. Do you get it now?"

"Oh my God. The poisoned champagne was for Moira, not Freddie?"

"Exactly. So the murderer can't be Moira or Harry after all. And whoever was gunning for Moira could still be trying to get her. We have to warn her before it's too late!"

"You've just accused her of conspiring to kill her husband," Lucie pointed out. "Do you really think she's going to listen to anything you say?"

"No," Kate agreed. "You're right. Moira and Harry won't listen to me. But there's one person who can convince them."

"Who?" Lucie asked, but Kate had already gone.

~

"Please Luis, open up. It's really important."

The door opened a crack and Luis peered out.

"What the hell do you want, Kate? It's late and I'm kind of busy right now."

Busy, huh? Did Luis have someone in there?

Kate put her foot in the crack of the door so Luis couldn't close it. Unless he wanted to crush her foot to smithereens. He let out an exasperated sigh and unhooked the chain on the back of the door.

"Two minutes. Kate. That's all I've got."

"Why the high security?" Kate quizzed him when he finally opened the door. He was wearing a robe, and a strong smell of cologne permeated the air. "Did I interrupt something, Luis?"

"To be honest, Kate, I'm not feeling very well just now," Luis insisted. "I really need to go to bed. I would like you to leave."

There was something going on with Luis, Kate felt it in her gut. Turning on her heel she checked the bathroom, but there was no-one there. What was Luis up to?

Returning to the main suite, she saw it. A sheet of notepaper on the coffee table, in a familiar shade of blue. Before Luis could react, she had stalked over and grabbed it and started to read. Her eyes nearly popped out of her head.

Luis made a grab for the sheet of paper, but Kate waved it out of his reach.

"Ah, sorry, Luis. I didn't realise you were expecting company. Is this from your lover? It's kind of kinky," laughed Kate. "I mean, it's no wonder you're primed and ready for action. The things this woman wants to do to you, some men could only dream of. She's got the hots for you, that's for sure. There's just one problem."

Kate paused, pulling out the original folded sheet of blue notepaper from her bag. "I think your lover is actually a murderer. And they were trying to kill Moira, not Freddie. So are you going to tell me who it is?"

"What?" muttered Luis, comparing the two sheets of paper. "Now it all makes sense. That crazy psycho little bitch."

"And that would be who, exactly?"

"Emma bloody Krasnoff."

Kate rushed down the hallway toward the lift, eager to get to Emma's room before the cops, who Luis was calling right at that moment. There was a squad of them stationed downstairs, so it was unlikely Emma would get away, but Kate wanted to see the arrest with her own eyes. As she rounded the corner she slammed smack into a wall of muscle, and peeled her eyes upward to stare into pools as blue as Byron Bay.

Two strong arms reached around her waist to steady her.

"Um, sorry," Kate gulped, trying to figure out whether this was a stroke of unbelievably good luck or bad. She tried to get away from his grasp, but Lachlan wasn't letting her go anywhere.

"Ah, Sugar," he teased, his eyes dancing. "I've been looking for you all day. Have you been avoiding me?"

"I thought you'd be busy with your bit of fluff," Kate said with a stomp.

"Did you just stomp your foot at me?" Lachlan tutted. "Temper, Sugar."

Kate was getting riled, while Lachlan seemed to be enjoying this.

"Selena?" she hissed. "The woman you spent last night with? Or are there so many women that you can't remember?"

"Are you jealous, Kate?" Lachlan tipped her chin up with one hand to look at him, his tone turning serious.

"Of course not," mumbled Kate, shaking her head away. "Why would I be jealous? You can sleep with whoever you like, I don't care."

Lachlan leaned his head back and roared with laughter. "You must be joking," he said shaking his head. "Selena grabbed me in the kitchen this morning out of the blue. The phone rang before you came in and she said it was Lucie. Selena must have known you were on your way down and you walked into her little flytrap. I was wondering why she suddenly grabbed me like that but I can assure you it was entirely innocent, ma'am."

"You were kissing her, Lachlan! I saw you with my own eyes."

"Yes, well technically I was," admitted Lachlan, with a sheepish grin. "But I can assure you, it wasn't my idea. I'm very sorry for kissing Selena, but have you any idea how hard it is to stop kissing someone once you get started?"

"You're impossible," said Kate stomping her foot again, just as Lachlan leaned in. He pulled her close and she felt herself melt into his embrace, willing him not to stop. Closer, closer, until his lips were millimeters from hers.

"See what I mean?" he whispered. "Once you start you won't want to stop."

Kate had a suspicion that in this instance, Lachlan was probably right, and seeing as she was on her way to nab a murderer, his timing was lousy. Besides, she wasn't going to fall into his arms like some floozy. Although, boy was she tempted. Wriggling out of his grasp, she pulled away.

"I've got to go," she panted, catching her breath, and leaving Lachlan scratching his head in amusement as she bolted on past.

Chapter 9

"Thank you so much, Kate," said Uncle Wallace, kissing Lucie and then hugging Kate. You've not only saved my business, you've put Byron Manor on the map. We're booked out for the next two years!" Uncle Wallace scratched his head and let out a chuckle.

"Everything happens for a reason," Kate smiled, as she watched the police lead a handcuffed Emma Krasnoff outside. The lobby was full of wedding guests checking out and getting ready to leave.

"There's just something I need to do, Uncle Wallace," said Kate excusing herself and walking over to where Moira and Harry stood by the front steps.

"I'd like to apologise again, Moira," Kate offered, approaching the pair with caution. "And you too, Harry. I hope you can forgive me. I never meant to cause you any more distress. I just thought…"

"It's okay, Kate," beamed Moira, gazing adoringly into Harry's eyes. "If it wasn't for you I'd never have found out that Freddie was a cheating love rat. When I got that note before the wedding I thought it was someone who knew about me and Harry. I had no idea that Freddie had been carrying on with Emma all along. I would have lived in guilt for the rest of my life, after my affair with Harry, with the finger being pointed at us. We all make mistakes and I've forgiven poor Freddie for what he did. Emma will have to pay the price for the rest of her life. Now I've got Harry to look after me, I think my future could be better than I ever thought I deserved. Freddie and I should never have gotten married in the first place." A silent tear trickled down Moira's cheek, which Harry reached out to gently wipe away.

"Goodbye, Kate, and thank you," said Harry, with a gruff nod. He led Moira through the doorway, and Kate heard shouts from the press outside as Moira and Harry exited the building. Harry shielded Moira through the mob before they drove off with a police escort.

A cough alerted Kate to a man who had stepped up beside her.

"I'd like to thank you, too," Detective Holmes muttered, extending his hand to Kate who accepted his handshake. "Emma Krasnoff will be behind bars for a long time, and her next victim can sleep sound in his bed for years to come."

"Next victim?"

"Turns out Emma was setting Luis Sutton up for Freddie's murder. When her plan to kill Moira backfired, she needed to pin the blame on someone else, and quick. After her little fling with Luis last year, she planned to seduce him again and plant the poison in his room. When you went to talk to Luis earlier, he was waiting for Emma, to consummate their little tryst. We've extracted a full confession and don't expect any problems during the prosecution. Miss Krasnoff is a very disturbed young lady."

"Lucky for me you arrived when you did," said Luis, walking up to Kate and the detective. "Otherwise I could have ended up in jail. Or worse. Thank you Kate, I will always be indebted to you."

Coming from Luis, Kate appreciated his praise was a big deal. She was delighted that things had worked out for everyone, even though they had never figured out who had served the poisoned glass of champagne. That was something that she might never know.

As Luis and the detective moved away, Lucie arrived with their bags.

"Where's Selena?" Kate asked her sister, realising that they would probably have to give her errant employee a ride home.

"She's already got a ride," giggled Lucie, pointing at Luis who stood with his arm around Selena on the steps outside.

Selena was beaming for the cameras and twirling her hair round her finger as Luis spoke. "I'm indebted to Miss Kate MacKenzie forever," Luis told the waiting crowd, "and she will be receiving a Cloudy Vines delivery box with my compliments every month for the rest of her life."

Kate chuckled to herself. Good old Luis, never one to miss a marketing opportunity. And free wine for life was something that she wouldn't be turning down either.

With one last glance around, Kate bent down and lifted her bag.

"Looking for someone?" Lucie quizzed her with a raised eyebrow.

Kate glared at her sister and took a deep breath, steeling herself for the waiting paparazzi. Even so, it was a shock when they stepped into the glare of flash-bulbs, the shouting started, and several large micro-phones on sticks were shoved in her face.

"Is it true, Miss Mackenzie, that you are dating three times World Surfing Champion and Aussie leg-end, Lachlan Fitzpatrick?"

Kate was so taken by surprise by the furor that she wobbled. Up until now it had been pure adrenaline that had kept her going over the past few days. But now it had all caught up with her.

Grabbing Lucie's arm for support, she shielded her eyes with the back of her hand, looking for an out.

"No comment!" came the deep timbre of his voice from behind her. A strong arm in the small of her back steadied her just where she needed it.

"It's okay, Sugar, I've got you," his voice whis-pered in her ear, as he pushed the reporters out of the way and swept a path through the throng for Kate and Lucie. Several persistent reporters chased after them to where the Truly Scrumptious and Sugar N' Spice vans were parked.

"Are you confirming, Mr. Fitzpatrick, that you and Miss Mackenzie are an item?"

Lachlan stared at Kate, who stared right back. Her face flamed as the question hung in the air, the reporters waiting for an answer. Lachlan reached out for Kate and pulled her close. She sank into his chest in relief, stealing his warmth, and closed her eyes.

Holding her tight, Lachlan reached out and pushed the camera lenses away.

"No comment," he whispered, burying his head in her hair.

Deadly Liaisons

Chapter 1

Katherine MacKenzie took a look around the room and wiped her forehead with the back of her hand. Six plastic tables, it took six entire tables stacked four rows high to make enough room for the finished product. As the new owner of the Sugar and Spice Cupcakery, she was quite proud of herself for overseeing and completing their biggest order to date! Helping Hands, an organization centered around helping the homeless find new jobs and integrate back into society, was hosting its annual benefit gala and after Kate's...or rather Kate's late mother's...cupcakery interview landed on the front page of the second-largest paper in New South Wales, the owner of Helping Hands was eager to give them a try.

Kate's first thought after throwing the piping bag into the trash and chucking the tip into the sink basin was that she would never again give a customer such a steep discount for a large order. They would still turn quite the profit from these babies, but there was in no way reason for such a large discount. Her back ached more than ever after finishing a round of cupcakes, and half of her help had bailed on her once eleven o'clock rolled around tonight. She glanced at the clock over the pass-through and sighed when she noticed that it read two in the morning. At least they were all completed, though she'd have to give Lachlan and herself a bonus for staying later than everyone else. Maybe just a dinner date would do it, she thought. That would really chap Selena's hide, and Kate had half a mind to do it just for that reason.

Lachlan was the owner of Truly Scrumptious Catering Co. and had partnered with Kate's cupcake company to both bring in more orders, and then to help fulfill those orders. It was really a win-win for both of them, as Lachlan was born to be in the catering business and had all the business sense of a Fortune 500 CEO wrapped up in an ex-pro surfer's amazing body.

He was the best thing to ever happen to Kate, he complimented her wit and kept her blood flowing through constant pestering and borderline flirting, and he handled most of the business side of things such as emails and correspondences. It was something he was happy to do, and something Kate gladly handed over to him as part of his responsibilities in the partnership. She was smart as a whip, but she often felt scatterbrained and incompetent on the business end of things. Her scatterbrained nature meant that she often became overwhelmed, but it was amazing as far as creativity goes. There was no question she was great at her job. Her creations could not be topped.

To Kate, the whole creative process was a wonderful journey. From coming up with the design for the customer, to practicing it and making sure she could actually pull it off, to creating dozens, and sometimes hundreds, of duplicates. That was her favorite part. Making sure that each cupcake looked nearly identical to its brother was a soothing balm to her mind, and it quieted her soul in a way that nothing else could.

Lachlan swung around the corner and pulled the thick black trash bag out of the large trash can near the far table. Careful not to bump it, he lifted the bag with ease, accentuating his muscles. Kate watched his delicious arms press against his t-shirt, and he caught her staring.

"Enjoying the view, Sugar?" He raised his eyebrows twice in quick succession and the color drained from her face.

"You wish," she said, spinning around to wash the food coloring from her fingertips.

"There's no getting that off, love. I don't know why you even try," Lachlan called on his way to the parking lot.

Kate turned to watch him walk out the door without saying anything and smiled. The man sure knew how to make a batter-covered apron do his bidding.

"How about you let me do the last walk? You can get some rest, you look tired." He grinned out the side of his mouth and his eyes sparkled.

"You know that's not really the nicest thing to say to a lady," Kate replied, switching off the faucet and drying her hands on her own, dirty apron. One more walk-through would complete preparations for the gala, and Kate always wanted to do that herself.

"You know I can't let you do that, sorry. But thanks for offering…I'm not trying to be a snooty butt, I just like to see them once more to make sure we…" as he held his fingers up to her mouth but didn't touch them. "And you smell like trash, go wash up."

"Yes ma'am. At least let me stay with you while you do it? Then I can walk you out."

"Fair enough," she admitted. With purpose, she walked slowly through the tables, checking to make sure that the Helping Hands company logo was correct and centered on each and every cupcake. Lachlan was nothing if not a gentleman; she had to admit, even if he teased her endlessly.

"18…..24…." Lachlan called out over the rushing water as he washed up.

"Not funny," she yelled back at him.

A half hour later and she was blissfully under her covers at home and thankful she had a job that could wear her out once in a while. She rolled over to turn out the light, but not before her phone buzzed under her pillow.

"You make it home okay?"

It was a text from Lachlan, his chivalry made her smile like a schoolgirl.

"Sure did, hope you did too." Kate reached over and pulled the chain on her bedside lamp.

"I did, see you tomorrow, Boss."

Chapter 2

The dining hall was busy the next afternoon; Kate quickly surveyed the place from the huge entry doors to make sure the cake tables had been set up according to plan.

"Already checked, Sugar. They're right where they're supposed to be." Lachlan touched her back as he leaned over her shoulder and looked over the crowd. The sensation sent chills up her spine. This feeling, she expected, because it happened every time he touched her. This time, though, he left his hand on her back while they looked around the room and this made her ears ring.

"They're already eating," Kate whispered. "I thought dinner was supposed to be, you know…at dinner time."

"Oh no," he laughed. "Fancy people eat earlier than the peasants. What's going on over there?" Lachlan pointed in front of Kate and turned her face toward the front corner of the room. The delicate touch of his hand on her chin felt sweet and made her knees wobble a bit.

In the front corner sat Bertie Florsheim, a well-known man in town, generally disliked by a number of people. Not the least of which was his own daughter, Rachel Bloomingdale. A lifetime ago, Bertie left Rachel for dead as a young girl. Rachel, of course, never got over it. She hated her father, and so did her husband, Ian Bloomingdale.

About the only thing that Bertie had going for him, other than a full head of hair, was his fortune. He was very wealthy, and Rachel stood to inherit a tidy sum upon his death. A death, she always fantasized, that would come sooner rather than later. Everyone in town knew that Bertie was only here to make amends for Rachel's tumultuous childhood, and he did a piss-poor job of trying to hide it. He would attend this evening's function in order to donate a large amount of money to his daughter and her husband's ministry foundation, Helping Hands. It was probably the only reason he was allowed in the door.

It appeared that Bertie and his son-in-law were arguing about something, and Ian Bloomingdale was perched delicately on the edge of this seat, seemingly ready to deck his father-in-law. Kate rolled her eyes and pushed Lachlan out into the foyer.

"Let's get the cupcakes in here. We can use the side door."

Kate's assistant, Selena Fox, bustled in the front entrance just in time to help unload, though Kate knew that would never happen. The girl, a gorgeous young woman in her early twenties, pranced toward them in her black pumps and perfect hair. Her eyes remained fixed on Lachlan, who clearly admired her attention to detail in getting ready before the function. No doubt it was done only to impress him. The truth was, Lachlan could barely stand Selena's personality, but he enjoyed how it bothered Kate when he paid attention to her, so he made a point to say how nice she looked. Kate rolled her eyes and walked toward the door. She heard Lachlan chuckle behind her.

"What…I would have said your hair looked nice too if you'd done anything different with it. In fact it does look nice, as per the norm." He reached up and ruffled the pencil holding Kate's work-bun in place and a few strands fell around her face.

"You know she left early last night so she could get started on that get up. If I hadn't stayed up and finished the job with you, I could look like that too."

Lachlan smiled widely; he loved it when she showed her jealous side. "In all seriousness, though, it must be exhausting."

Kate grinned and opened the back of the truck, hundreds of cupcakes smiling back at her.

"Kate!! It's happened again come quickly!" Selena burst out the front doors and grabbed Kate by the hand. Dragged up the front steps by a woman half her age and in three inch heels, Kate tripped several times, refusing to even ask what was going on lest she have to listen to Selena drivel on about table placement. Lachlan trailed behind them, which is probably why Selena kept turning around and then fixing her hair as they ran.

When Kate reached the doors leading from the foyer to the dining hall, though, a familiar chill ran down the back of her neck. This couldn't be happening again. No one had even eaten a cupcake yet. Selena pulled at her wrist and dragged her straight to the front of the room. Kate swallowed hard the lump in her throat and pulled her hand free from Selena's. Everyone at Bertie's table were standing up, some of them still had forks in their hands, all covering their mouths. Ian was not to be excluded, standing over his father in law's body, in a heap on the floor.

Lachlan pulled up just behind Kate and let out a gasp. "Oh no, what happened?! Is he…"

"He's dead!" Screeched a woman from another table, bringing her friends to gather around the body. "Someone call the police!" She reached quickly for her mobile phone and began dialing it herself.

Kate dropped into a chair and took in the situation, making note of everyone's reaction to something that had clearly only happened a few moments ago. It was lucky Selena brought her in immediately, as the people's faces would tell her more than witness statements could ever tell police. In this moment, this moment of shock, a face couldn't lie.

Why does trouble seem to follow me? Kate thought to herself. She quickly scanned the room for Rachel, as the girl had the most motive of anyone to want her father dead. Surprisingly, she was standing in the corner with a worried look on her face. Kate made a note of it; she looked more surprised than pleased, merely shaking her head back and forth with tears streaming down her face. Kate knew she wasn't sad that her father was dead, but the particular look in her eyes and the incessant nail biting she'd suddenly taken up had Kate worried and she wanted to figure out what it meant.

Remembering the success of the last case she'd helped solve, Kate wanted to try her hand at helping with this one as well. After all, she knew that Sugar and Spice had nothing to do with it, but it would certainly be her head on a platter if she didn't figure out who it was before the press got a hold of the story. Once her nerves calmed, she brought the front of her shirt up to pat the sweat from her brow. When she opened her eyes, Lachlan took a seat next to her and set a tall glass of ice water down between them.

"Here you go, love. You look like you're about to go into shock, settle yourself a bit." He placed his hand on hers and she quickly recoiled it and reached for the glass. He was charming, no doubt, and was obviously genuinely concerned about her, but she didn't have time to pay attention to his flirting if she was going to solve this case. He would just have to wait. She gave him a weak smile and nodded her thanks for the water. Lachlan sighed and patted her on the shoulder before he left to talk to Ian. Selena trailed close behind him with a glass in her hand, eager to be there when he needed something.

Chapter 3

Although Kate knew who Rachel was, Rachel did not in fact know Kate. She used this to her advantage once the police arrived on the scene, and made her way over to Rachel to ask her some questions under the guise of being a reporter. She offered Rachel her glass of water, the poor girl looked like she was about to pass out. Rachel accepted and guzzled it down nervously.

"So, Rachel, you probably haven't had time to talk to the police yet, and this is all off the record until official statements have been given. I just wanted to ask you a few questions if that's okay with you, don't answer anything you're not comfortable with, okay?" Kate straightened her shirt over her jeans; thankful she hadn't put on an apron yet as it would give her away.

"Where's your notepad if you don't mind me asking?" Rachel's eyes darted around the room as though she were looking for someone.

"Oh…well it's off the record, so legally I can't write it down. Also I have an excellent memory. Where were you sitting, if I may, during the last half hour or so?" Kate tried to fix her face in a fashion that hopefully said reporter to everyone looking at her, and hoped Selena or Lachlan wouldn't come and ruin her disguise before she had a chance to get a read on Rachel.

Rachel pointed and spoke softly. "With my husband" She lifted her long arm and held it in the air long after she spoke, her eyes settling on the body of her father on the floor. The forensics team was snapping pictures and asking people to move to the back of the room, but when Ian caught his wife's eye he rushed over.

"Hun...honey. Are you okay? Who's this..." He was visibly shaken, but concern for his wife overshadowed it.

"Reporter," she mumbled. He looked at Kate and then back to his wife, rubbing large circles on her back to calm her down. Rachel started to weep a bit and took to rubbing her hands together in front of her.

"It's okay Miss—what did you say your last name was?"

"Bloomingdale," Ian answered. "I can answer your questions if you like."

"No, I'd really like to ask Mrs. Bloomingdale a few questions." Ian nodded at his wife as Kate spoke.

"It's okay," he told her. "Go ahead and tell them whatever you like. You have nothing to hide. Your father was awful."

Rachel went into a short history of her relationship with her father, most of which made Kate cringe and want to cry, herself. The poor girl didn't have the innocence of childhood that Kate had enjoyed, and it made her sad. No wonder someone wanted to kill Bertie. He was a terrible person!

"I wouldn't hurt him, though. Not really," Rachel concluded quietly. "It'll come out, no doubt, in the news...but we are poorer than we let on, Miss. But the only money I was ever going to receive from my dad was my inheritance money. While that is a decent amount, it's certainly not enough to murder him over. No way"

"I believe you, Rachel." Kate gave her a quick pat on the shoulder and thanked them both for their time before setting off to find her sister. Lucie always knew what to do.

Kate searched the crowd for her sister, peering over the tops of people's heads, looking for the gorgeous one of the family. The level-headed, less scatter-brained sister. Making her way around the edges of the room, she spotted Lachlan and Selena in some sort of conversation that looked to be a little more intimate than Kate would have expected. It made Kate uncomfortable, especially since Lucie always insisted that he only had eyes for Kate. She waved thoughts of Lachlan and Selena to the side and walked faster.

Outside, on the balcony overlooking the courtyard of the building, Kate spotted Rachel and another man. They were being even more intimate than Lachlan and Selena were, and it was cause for alarm. A quick scan of the room inside told her that Rachel's husband was deep in conversation with a police officer, and nowhere near close enough to catch his wife locking lips with another man. Seeing the blatant disrespect for the situation at hand, let alone respect for an entire marriage, Kate shuddered. It made her sick to think anyone could cheat on their spouse, but at your father's murder scene? That was just plain cause for concern.

Kate almost went to confront the two lovers, but remembered what it was like when she confronted Moira and Harry. She shook her head and logged the act away for later. Lachlan caught her eye from across the room and signaled for her. He then put his hands to his throat and made a strange face with his eyes closed, followed by pretending to spoon food into his mouth from an imaginary bowl in his hands. Kate cocked her head to the side for a moment, and he repeated the movements. "Oh no!" she said aloud. He's been poisoned!

Chapter 4

Kate decided to check the kitchen out, since she was told that Bertie Florsheim was poisoned by his dinner this evening, and made her way through the crowd, thankful that it wasn't that cupcakes that did him in. When she rounded the back of the room, she spotted Ian Bloomingdale in the far corner with another man, someone she'd never seen before. The two of them were standing quite close to each other and if Kate's movie watching days had taught her anything at all, they appeared to be doing some kind of illegal deal. When their eyes weren't locked on each other's hands and mobile phones, they were darting around the room looking to see if anyone was listening in to their conversation. Kate quickly pulled out her own phone and did a search of the name Ian Bloomingdale. She gasped and covered her mouth. He had been arrested before and imprisoned for fraud and assault.

With this knowledge, Kate's first assumption was that Ian was after his wife's inheritance. She cleared the screen on her phone and deleted the history before slipping it into her back pocket. In the kitchen, she was quite disappointed to find that the only person in the room available for questioning was Lachlan. Not that that was a huge letdown in itself, but it certainly wouldn't help her with the case.

Lachlan offered her a drink of some of the champagne he'd found for later in the event, and Kate gladly accepted. It would take the edge off of the afternoon, and she couldn't resist such a handsome man offering her a drink. The pair stood quietly for a few moments, watching through the small window in the kitchen door as everyone bustled around in the main room.

Kate turned to Lachlan and rubbed her glass on her lips as she spoke, deep in thought. "What do you know about Ian, Lachlan?"

He turned to her and thought for a moment. "Not much, actually. He's generally a good guy, I mean, we went to college together and ran in the same group for ages but kind of lost touch after we graduated. ...'Cause I was always at the beach, of course." He grinned and her knees buckled a bit, just as they always did when he did that thing with the corner of his mouth.

"Yes, yes," she said sarcastically. "Big time surfer, we know. But seriously, that's all you can say about the guy? Didn't he look like he had a bad side or something? Think hard....could you picture him like going into a life of crime? Be creative...."

"Are you serious? No—I would never suspect he would go into a life of crime." He mocked her, and though it stung, she knew how to remedy it quickly.

"What about this, then?" she asked, pulling up his name on her phone again and holding it in front of Lachlan's face.

He scanned the article for a moment, taking her

hand in his to manipulate the content on the small screen. His fingertips felt nice on hers and she smiled where he couldn't see it. The more he read, the more upset he seemed to get, and Kate wasn't sure why. His brows came together in a frown and when he was finished reading, he looked up at her.

"This is ridiculous. This isn't the same guy."

"That's his picture, Lachlan. Why would you even--? You don't believe I made that up, do you?"

"Listen I don't know where you found this, but the guy I used to know wouldn't do anything like fraud, and even if he did he wouldn't have assaulted anyone." Lachlan was downright mad, now.

It didn't feel nice, but the fact that she was getting a reaction at all may just point her in the right direction for the case. After all, with her, it was all about how she felt about things and people....that's usually what helped her figure things out. It helped in dealing with customers and diffusing possible arguments or set-backs in business, and it helped her solve the last case she helped out with.

"I'm sorry," she said, putting her hand to her chest. "Are you mad at me??"

"Yeah kinda," he admitted. "I just don't see how you can assume that some guy, who you don't even know by the way, is at fault for an actual murder. That's a little far-fetched, even for you." He took a deep swig from his glass and set it forcefully in the sink.

"Well I'm sorry – but what else am I supposed to do

when I see him making creepy faces in the corner with some guy that looks like he just busted out of prison!"

Lachlan laughed. She'd always loved his laugh, but this infuriated her. He was laughing AT her this time, and it didn't feel nearly as nice.

"What's so funny?! I did! I did see that..." She dragged him to the little window in the kitchen door and pushed him up to the glass. "Look, right over there in the cor—"

"I don't see anything, Sugar."

"Okay stop calling me that, and they were just there. I promise." Kate felt her cheeks redden in embarrassment. "I swear they were," she whispered to herself, looking for them among the crowd of people.

"You're ridiculous," Lachlan muttered, grabbing her bicep. He spun Kate toward him and pulled her in to a kiss. It was sweet, but forceful, and so lovely. Kate gave in for a few moments, then pulled away and flipped her hair over her shoulder. She wouldn't stand for being made fun of and then kissed, it just wouldn't do. Plus this nonsense would get in the way of having the case be resolved and everyone would be cooped up here for the whole day. She spun on her heel and marched through the kitchen door and into the main room. Flustered and red-faced, she looked for her sister.

Chapter 5

Where are you??

Kate texted Lucie, unable to find her, and her sister quickly replied that she was in the restroom, but that she'd been trying to stay out of the way all afternoon. Once everything went down...or rather, once Bertie went down, she pulled back to watch how the whole thing played out. That was Lucie for you. She was similar to Kate in that she always wanted to know why and how things happened, but where they differed was that Kate would actually do something about it. Even as a child she couldn't let arguments go unresolved, and would often get sent to time out for trying to solve their parent's spats as well. Lucie always thought it was funny, and made a habit of warning Kate to stay out of things. But she never could. If something was in her power to solve, she just had to try.

"Fine, meet me in the foyer. We need to talk."

"Oh, Kate. Stay out of it, please. You know what these things to do you. You'll become obsessed with trying to solve it before the police can. Just let them do their job, sis..."

Kate didn't respond, slipping the mobile phone into her pocket again. She needed to think. Outside the main room in the foyer, there was a pretty little church pew nestled along the side wall and overlooking the front steps. She could see them outside the large glass doors that framed the whole front of the church. It was a beautiful location for an event, she thought to herself. Certainly wouldn't do for a murder, though.

Crossing her legs, she leaned back in the pew and rubbed her temples. After a few minutes, assuming that Lucie would be a few more minutes in the restroom, she ducked her head down between her knees to stretch her back, just like a child would do when they're bored. To her surprise, it was very relaxing—until that moment when she opened her eyes, that is.

Under her nose when she opened her eyes was a briefcase, tucked quite neatly under the pew so that it would be noticed. Directly underneath the handle of the case was a beautiful insignia, and the name Bertie Florsheim underneath it in, an engraved copy of Bertie's own script. Kate craned her head up and looked around, then yanked the case out from underneath her seat to open it up. Inside was a cheque made out to one Hugo Armstrong in the amount of one hundred thousand dollars.

Kate gasped. She had seen plenty of large cheques made out for large amounts, but never one quite that large. She tucked the cheque into her pocket and stood up just as Lachlan burst through the double doors into the foyer. Perfect timing.

"Listen, Kate," he blurted out, rushing up to her and placing one large hand on each shoulder. "I don't think it would be such a good idea."

Kate looked at his eyes, confused. Was he not here to talk about the case?

Lachlan shook his head and tried to sort his thoughts in a hurry. "I just don't think it's the best thing for us to start something right now, y'know?" His face softened, as if she should understand what he meant by this declaration.

"I didn't know we were" her voice trailed off; searching for the words he was looking for.

"Well, yeah. I mean it would be great and all but I don't know if it's the most professional thing for us to start a relationship."

Kate just shook her head back and forth, her brows furrowed. What was she to say to this?? Would he always want to NOT date her? And why was he even thinking about dating at a time like this, anyway?

"The kiss," she whispered almost as a question. "I didn't realize it meant anything more than a silly kiss."

Lachlan looked offended. "'Course it did."

Speechless, Kate thumbed the folded cheque in her pocket, completely at a loss of what to say.

"Okay, then. That's settled." Lachlan patted his hands on his pants twice and walked out of the foyer, leaving a baffled Kate in his wake. Someone exited the front men's room which broke her concentration for a moment. She noticed that he was wearing a long, white chef's coat and had a dish towel stuck into his belt. Kate raised her arms and flagged him down.

"Excuse me!"

He stopped quickly and turned to her, his face as pleasant as she'd ever seen on a gentleman. He looked kind, but timid. "Yes ma'am?"

"I—I'm sure you've already been questioned by the police, but would you mind just telling me quickly if you've seen anyone in the kitchen this morning that looked like she maybe didn't belong?" It was a long shot, but worth a try.

"I'm sorry, she?" he asked, puzzled.

"Oh, well. I mean anyone, really. Could be a she…"

"Well yes I did, actually."

I knew it! Kate thought. Rachel was in there, probably helping carrying out the murder so she and Ian could split all the money…but where does that other guy fit in?

"Your assistant," the chef said.

Kate stopped mid-thought. "Excuse me??"

"Yes, your assistant. What's her name? Something with an S?"

"S-Selena?" Kate asked.

The man snapped his fingers and pointed toward Kate's face. "Yes, that's the one! She was in there messing with some of the dishes for the head table. I wasn't really sure what she was doing, but she left right away and nothing about the plates looked any different, so I didn't think anything of it. She kind of just looked like….well, like she wanted to see what the food looked like. She mumbled something about it being so fancy, then giggled, and scampered off."

"Are you sure it was my assistant?"

"The attractive one, yes ma'am."

Kate rolled her eyes, Selena wasn't that pretty. She shouldn't have been at the gala before me…not for any reason. What in the world was she doing here before their food was even served? As far I knew she's spent all morning getting ready so she could make a grand entrance.

Chapter 6

Kate thanked the chef and sent him on his way. Lucie came strolling through the doors about that time, and Kate rushed to embrace her.

"What's gotten into you, sis?" Lucie hugged her sister and best friend tightly, then pulled her away to make sure she was alright. "Solve the murder yet?"

"Not hardly!" Kate exclaimed. "Guess who was here messing with the food earlier today? For the head table, no less!"

Lucie opened her mouth but didn't say anything. She just shook her head and shrugged her delicate shoulders.

"Selena."

Lucie laughed. It was a knowing sort of cackle, the kind one would usually use to signal an "I told you so" was on its way. "Seriously??"

"Yes! What in the world would she be doing here at all? Let alone so early…" Kate put her hand to her forehead and her eyes darted around the room. "Let alone messing with the food for the head table!?" This was no good. There hadn't been any reason to suspect that the murder could be tied to the Cupcakery…and now this. This would be terrible for business, and probably terrible for whatever Lachlan had had on his mind a few moments ago. That would be water under the bridge compared to the news that Selena could somehow be involved in all of this.

"Duh, sis. I told you that girl's no good! She's a snake in sheep's clothing. And by sheep I mean Prada and Marc Jacobs." Lucie shook her head again and put her hands up between them to dismiss whatever remark she was about to utter. "No, no. Just no. She's no good. Go find her."

"What am I going to do? What is the responsible thing to do, here?" Her breath picked up and she to concentrate on not hyperventilating. Her mother had worked her entire retirement years building Sugar N Spice into the behemoth it was today, and the stupid assistant baby she'd hired to help with the transition was going to go and screw the whole thing up. Not only would this ruin her own life, and possibly love life as well, but it would also taint the legacy of her mother. And THAT was no laughing matter; it made Kate's blood boil.

"Lucie, will you go find Selena for me and ask her to meet me in the kitchen please? I'm going to run one quick errand and then I'll be in there. I—I just can't stand to look at her face right now and I'm afraid she'll run if we spook her. She's too young and dumb to know what's good for her, so just trick her into going into the kitchen for me please. I swear I'll be right there…"

With that, Kate gave no space for her sister to interject or refuse. She just pushed past her and through the double doors into the main room. The first few guests she approached didn't know who Hugo Armstrong was, but her request with the fourth gentleman she inquired upon gave way to a very obvious finger pointing session that had him easily picked out of the crowd. Kate thanked the gentleman and went for him. Someone who had a hundred thousand dollar check waiting on them in the foyer should not be so casually mingling with the other party/murder guests.

Chapter 7

When approached about the cheque, Hugo looked legitimately astonished that such a thing would be an issue. He nearly laughed at Kate's assumed suspicion, assuring her that it was probably just a cheque from Bertie to himself to settle an old debt, and that it was nothing to be concerned about it. It was obvious to Kate that he was lying, however, and she had to switch tactics, clearly this guy could not be startled with just presenting the suspicious cheque to him…Kate thought for a moment.

"You know I'm not stupid, right, sir? This handwriting doesn't match Bertie's handwriting. There was no settling of any debt, someone other than Bertie wrote this cheque to you and put it in his briefcase. Why would someone do that, would you say?" Kate tapped the cheque on the table in front of him, but Hugo never batted an eye. He too, changed tactics.

Leaning forward so that he could whisper softly into her face, his breath warm on her cheeks. He spoke as if he had a secret and would bless her with his knowledge. "You know Gerald has many crime connections…maybe he did it?" He shrugged his shoulder nonchalantly before leaning back in his chair as though he had nothing to hide.

Unable to do anything further with someone bold enough to give her the runaround, she headed to the restroom, flustered. And why shouldn't he give her the runaround? She was just an amateur sleuth, he would be saving his more efficient lying for the policemen, surely. The door of the ladies bathroom slammed against the back wall, and Kate gasped, though not at the sound. At her feet lay Rachel. She was in a prone position on the bathroom floor and was completely motionless. In a panic, Kate dropped to her feet, afraid that Rachel was dead. It took a moment to get her wrist out from under her, and even when she did, Kate couldn't find a pulse. That was no surprise to her, since she'd never tried to take someone's pulse before. Instead she took to trying to roll Rachel's body over.

I'm pretty sure the last thing you're supposed to do with an injured or dead person is try to move them around, Kate, she said to herself. It was more of an instinct, anyway. Unthinkingly, Kate twisted Rachel's head toward her and saw that she was, in fact, still breathing. Her face, though, was badly battered and bloody.

"Oh my God, Rachel. What happened to you??" she whispered, but there was no answer. Not even a whimper. Gently laying Rachel's head back down on the ground, Kate stood up and ran out of the bathroom.

"Anyone! Please! Get a medical team to the ladies bathroom and someone find Ian, NOW!" Ian came out into the foyer at the same time asking if Kate had seen Gerald, reporting that he was nowhere to bed found.

Your stupid brother probably did Rachel in, you creep. I'm not interested in hearing your voice at the moment. Kate merely pointed to eh restroom, then walked over and opened the door, her eyes never leaving Ian's. When Ian saw Rachel lying there on the floor, he shrieked in a manner she had never heard coming from a man and fell to the floor. Ian threw his body over Rachel's and his voice was panicked.

"Rachel, Rachel, honey please...no no..."

Watching him fawn over his wife reminded her of Lachlan, strangely, and she imagined his strong arms cradling her small body in a time of need. A pang of sadness hit her chest and she walked out of the bathroom and let the door close, the medical team already rushing toward her. On a whim, she made her way upstairs in search of the cloakroom. Maybe there was a clue in the guests belongings? When she found it, she jimmied the lock and snuck inside. Next to a piece of cardstock that read GERALD on it, Kate found an open laptop with a message reading "Meet me at the top of the building." For about two whole seconds, Kate considered telling the police and letting them handle it. But the way they usually behaved with these things, that would likely not go well, so she climbed the stairwell and found the room mentioned at the end of the email.

Chapter 8

The moment she opened the door, someone grabbed her arms and threw her into a chair, tying her wrists and ankles to it tightly. "What the hell, Gerald?!" someone asked behind her.

"Collateral damage," Gerald quipped.

A moment later, Ian burst through the door and pushed Gerald as hard as he could, giving a swift kick to his gut after he hit the floor. Ian quickly made sense of the knots confining Kate and freed her with ease. "What's going on in here??" he demanded.

"I'm waiting for my money from Hugo," Gerald answered, spitting blood onto the carpet as he brought himself to his feet. Confused, Kate turned toward Gerald.

"But...but Hugo said YOU were the one framing him, and were probably stealing Bertie's money.

Gerald threw his head back in laughter. "Ha! Why would I need Bertie's money? Hugo himself is the one who owes me half a million."

The four of them ran downstairs, where Rachel was being loaded onto a gurney. Surprisingly, she was conscious and talking to the medical staff while they filled out her paperwork. Ian ran over to her and grabbed her hands.

"Hun! You're awake, thank God. What's this about a cheque, honey?" he asked, watching the medical staff start to pile her things onto the cart, prepping to load her into the ambulance. Rachel's bottom lip quivered and Kate stepped toward the emergency cart, placing her hand on Rachel's leg.

"Rachel, the cheque. Tell us quickly, please."

"I'm so sorry," she cried, burying her face in her hands. Ian sat down on the side of the cart and took her into his arms. She pushed her hair back and looked at Ian. "I asked my father for money before his death, in order to save you from your debt to Hugo. I wanted to clear you of it. I'm so sorry….I didn't mean for anything bad to happen, you have to believe me…"

Kate and Ian looked at each other, then to Gerald. The man stepped closer to them and explained that Ian had no debt, and that it was Hugo who actually owed him money.

"Oh my God," Rachel explained, bursting in a fresh bout of tears. "You wouldn't believe what I was doing…I thought you were in debt…I thought…."

Ian picked her face up in his hands and pulled her close to him.

"No matter how bad it was, I already forgive you. Please tell me what you did."

Rachel took a moment, and spoke slowly when she was ready. "I was going to have my father killed, to settle the debt with my inheritance. But I couldn't go through with it for obvious reasons. It's just an awful thing to do. I just love you so much, and I thought you had the debt and was willing to do whatever I needed to take care of it. And that's really the only access to a large amount of money I had. I'm so sorry."

Kate patted Rachel on the leg and nodded to Ian, who shooed her away with his free hand. She grabbed two police officers by the hand and scrambled to find Hugo, who was trying to escape through a window. By spilling the evidence quickly and loudly while also helping to pull his large body back through the window, she got Hugo to confess that he poisoned Bertie to gain access to Rachel's inheritance…in order to settle his debt with Gerald.

Impressed with Kate's findings and quick action, the policemen strapping the handcuffs onto Hugo commended her for her actions. She was quite impressed with herself, too, as a matter of fact. A while later, Lachlan and Kate had a chance to catch up while everyone was being released by the policemen, assuming they had already given their statements. It would appear that none of them were on house arrest any longer. The pair apologized to each other for being so strange and hasty. They also both decided that they would like to pursue something in the form of a relationship, because they obviously had chemistry. And when Lachlan said the word chemistry, Kate's knees buckled again. Whatever it would be, they agreed, they would take it slow.

"So Rachel told Ian of her affair, by the way," Lachlan said, sliding up onto the counter and stroking Kate's hair gently.

"Oh yeah?" she asked. "And how'd THAT go?"

"About as well as you'd think it would."

They shook their heads and Kate leaned over onto his shoulder. It felt like just the right thing to do, not too personal, but a small nod to the fact that they were finally both admitting they had feelings for one another. It was enough for now.

Deadly Soiree

Chapter 1

I really couldn't believe how lucky I had become! The Sugar N Spice Cupcake Company had a big sales milestone and it was nearing the holidays! I really had not suspected us to have such a great sales season and yet so soon. We were on a roll, like a cinnamon roll and I hoped that this tasty good fortune would last.

Currently, we were prepping for a big knees up party for a tech company called Zuber. Our point of contact in the company, Emma White, had placed a rush order and that's what Lachlan and I were doing now – rushing around to finish this massive batch of cupcakes before the party on Sunday.

My back could've easily started aching from all the time Lachlan and I spent making those cupcakes for the celebration party. I was no stranger to working hard but wow! Sometimes it really is surprising just how much effort goes into making such a tiny product! But people did seem to like our cupcakes and our reputation was growing.

Cupcake tins were neatly arrayed in a little stack but mixing bowls were everywhere! There were quite a few spoons, spatulas, food processor beaters and other tools that needed to be cleaned resting in the sink. Baking was a messy business but oddly satisfying at the same time.

Fortunately for me, I had an eager helper in Lachlan by my side. When he was in the zone, he would move like a gazelle from one part of the kitchen to the other without breaking a sweat. Okay, maybe a little bit of a sweat and there was the occasion that I took a few seconds to admire his well-built and muscular frame.

Selena was nowhere to be found but I can't say that entirely surprised me. I wasn't exactly sorry not to see her here as she would be too busy trying to flirt with Lachlan or any other handsome guy in the business than to do work. My mother had hired Selena as her assistant before she died and out of loyalty to my mum I kept her on board.

I really didn't know what it was with Selena. If I had something better she had to have it! If Lachlan and I flirted, Selena had to force her way on in or to get his attention. It was like the bratty and jealous girlfriend that I never had. So far I had been successful in keeping Selena at bay by giving her extra work to do or something to keep her busy.

"And done! Whew, that was a lot of work, Sugar!" Lachlan said to me.

I smiled and nodded. "It's worth it, though."

"Did you ever think we'd make it this far?"

"What do you mean?"

Lachlan gestured around the kitchen with a sweeping move of his arm. "All this! Did you think we'd ever reach such a milestone" Lachlan commented looking around the kitchen and reminiscing about our business.

"I always hoped we would," I admitted. "Though I wish Mum would be here to have seen it."

"I imagine she is somewhere and she's happy about what you've done."

I nodded a little and went to the sink to pour myself a glass of water. I hadn't realized how hot I was until I was done. I avoided making that comment out loud as it would have been very easy to make a joke about Lachlan's appearance.

"I hope so. It was a lot of work and so close to the holidays!"

"That could be a good sign! Think about it, Christmas cupcakes! I think those would be a hit."

"Maybe sometime in the future," I said. "I don't want to think about all those cupcakes after the work that we did!"

Lachlan laughed loudly at my words. "I suppose not. Tomorrow we can go about decorating the cupcakes as they need tonight to cool."

"Hopefully Selena will be there," I mumbled.

"Pardon, Sugar?"

"Oh? Nothing," I lied and gave him a sweet smile. "Well, we better start cleaning the kitchen before it gets too messy in here."

"I'll take the trash out," Lachlan volunteered. I certainly wasn't going to complain about that as it also gave me the opportunity to admire his muscular body as he worked away.

Chapter 2

Lachlan, true to his word, was up bright and early to help me with decorating each cupcake. We decided on cheerful colors that would grab the attention of viewers in hopes they would remember the Sugar N Spice Cupcakery better. In the beginning, we flopped between pastels and even Christmas colors before deciding to settle on some pretty and bold colors to make the cupcakes pop.

We already had some white frosting which Lachlan took advantage of and began to frost what would be the white cupcakes. The colors in the frosting were always fun to mix. It was exciting to try to mix up different colors to see what you would end up with. This time, however, it had to be all about business. Playing around with colors would have to wait for another time.

"Hello, Lachlan," Selena's voice purred. A flirtatious smile tugged at the corners of her mouth.

I resisted the urge to roll my eyes so hard they would fall out of their sockets at her toying with Lachlan.

"Selena, could you bring the little signs that read 'Sugar N Spice Cupcakery' out of the pantry, please?" I asked.

Selena looked a little irritated to be pulled away from her flirting. She walked over to the pantry, her hips swaying from side to side hoping Lachlan was fixated on her posterior and brought the little signs out that would be placed on the cupcakes. I really couldn't think of why she'd be so testy about doing something like this. She was employee but perhaps more than likely it was because her catwalk stride of seduction was totally missed by Lachlan. I smiled as I chalked another one up for the good girls.

Lachlan slipped past her carrying a large tray which made her smile again. He tore open one of the bags and carefully placed each little sign dead center in the middle of each frosted cupcake. I noticed him look up at Selena, "Would you like to help?"

His question surprised the both of us. We certainly hadn't expected that! I had expected Selena to run off somewhere rather than do something to help us out.

"What do I do?" Selena asked.

"Put one of these little signs in the center of each cupcake. You have to be very gentle and careful so you don't ruin the work I put into frosting these. Isn't that right, Kate?"

"Of course! We don't want to ruin Lachlan's work, after all!" I said a bit too loudly.

"I don't suppose you could show me the proper way, Lachlan," Selena flirted. "Just like Kate said. I don't want to ruin all your hard work."

Lachlan burst out laughing. "Show you how to decorate a cup cake? This is stuff we learned as kids! Just place it in the center and move on to the next one. Easy as that."

I had to work hard not to laugh at Lachlan's misunderstanding. Either he didn't get the subtle flirting or he was being deliberately obtuse. Either way, I was fine by that. The less flirty behavior from either of them, the better. We had a job to do...and it didn't involve making goo goo eyes over the cupcake frosting.

Lachlan and I had a bit of an understanding now. Not in so many words and not really out in the open but still...it was a start. I was glad to see that he was now immune to Selena's flirting. It will would make all aspects of our growing professional and personal relationship that much sweeter.

Chapter 3

I felt practically like a church pastor handing out wafers to the people coming up for their cupcakes inside the hotel building. It was both a giddy and kind of nervous feeling. I was glad so many people were enjoying them and still hoped that there were enough to go around. Wouldn't that be something if we ran out? I knew we were growing in popularity, but this long line at the cupcake table was the best sign yet.

Someone brought in a large tank of hot apple cider that could be distributed through a nozzle at the end. It was like one of those big sport's coolers you find but pink colored and hot to the touch. Currently, it rested on top of a table with plenty of folded cloth beneath it to avoid damaging the table. There were white mugs with red lettering next to it. As I got closer, I noticed the red lettering were people's names. We all had personalized holiday mugs. I found mine and Lachlan's and poured apple cider into each. Lachlan smiled when he saw me heading toward him with the steaming cup of cider.

"You read my mind, Sugar."

I handed over his mug. "To a job well done."

We clinked mugs. "And too many more."

People around us sipped at their hot apple cider and enjoyed pleasant conversations; mostly small talk. It was a little intimidating being in the middle of a party for such a heavy hitter in the tech world like Zuber but I enjoyed rubbing shoulders with the elite. Tomorrow, if we were lucky, a magazine would interview Emma White and she'd mention the catering by Sugar N Spice. Now that would be the icing on the cake!

Lachlan and I both turned when we heard the sound of someone choking. At first, I thought it was a case of hot apple cider down the wrong pipe, but the person continued to splutter and gasp with no relief in sight. I felt the color drain from my face as I recognized Emma White.

"Emma? Emma, are you alright?" A man patted her on the back. She shook her head, grasping at his jacket lapels as she continued to splutter and gasp.

"Give her some air!" someone in the crowded party called.

"No, no, someone should call an ambulance!" Another voice said.

Lachlan was the first to take charge. He sprinted to the nearest phone, dialed, and started talking rapidly to the operator. I watched in horror as Emma's body began to collapse. She would have fallen flat on her face had it not been for people who grabbed her and carefully laid her on the floor. There was a small circular crowd around Emma who, by now, had stopped making any noise. Was she breathing? Was she even alive? I was rather afraid to ask.

Everyone looked toward the door as the police scurried inside the building followed by two paramedics. One of the ambulance officers crouched down and felt for a pulse before quietly saying "She's dead."

"But…how is that even possible?" Someone murmured.

"We have to leave that to the coroner," the ambulance officer said. The police herded everyone away from the room – now a crime scene – and put the hotel and everyone in it on lockdown. Lachlan and I ended up in the kitchen. I toyed with the idea of baking since it usually calmed me down but I doubted even baking could erase the sight of Emma White gasping for her last breath.

Lachlan watched me from across the room. "I don't know how this could have happened. Was Emma sick?"

"I have no idea," I admitted.

"Maybe she had an allergic reaction to something in the apple cider?"

I raised an eyebrow. Surely Lachlan didn't think someone set out to intentionally murder her! Who would do such a horrible thing? I didn't know Emma well and I certainly didn't know of any enemies that she could possibly have. She was a senior executive at Zuber. Did that somehow put a target on her back?

An older man stepped into the kitchen. He was dressed in a nice suit with his hair brushed back. "Good evening," he said very formally. "Do you have any ideas about what happened with Ms. White?"

"Only what we saw and what the police told us," I said. I couldn't say, why, but I didn't exactly trust this guy. Something about him just seemed rather strange.

He wiped at his brow with a linen handkerchief. "I am the owner of this hotel and this death will cast a very negative light on my business."

"But, but it's not your fault that someone—"

He was quick to cut me off. "I know who you are and I know of your part time sleuthing you have done in the past. I'm merely suggesting that you help me like you helped those other business owners."

I didn't like where this was going. "We don't even know if this was a murder! It could have been an accidental death or an allergic reaction for all we know."

"That may be, but I expect you to solve this possible crime and in quick time." He paused and gave me a hard look. "If you don't, I will make sure I put Sugar N Spice Cupcakery out of business."

My heart skipped a beat. I could lose everything that my mother worked so hard for over someone's threat! I didn't know how he planned to follow through on his promise, but I didn't want to test the waters either. "Are you blackmailing me?"

"Think of it as an incentive to solve the crime. Are we understood?"

"Yes," I said reluctantly.

"Are you going to help solve the crime and clear up this mess?" He spoke to me as one would when scolding a child.

"Yes."

"Good girl."

Chapter 4

I was trapped between a rock and a hard place. Solve this crime or else. I didn't want to even think of the "or else" – especially now after Sugar N Spice was growing in popularity. I would have to start at the most likely culprit. Usually that was a boyfriend or husband. Once he was cleared (if he was cleared) I could move on and investigate others. I asked around till I found out Emma's boyfriend was Scott Zubinsky.

"Zubinsky," I murmured. "How do I know that name?"

"Try he's the founder of Zuber," Lachlan said. "Emma was dating her boss."

"I need to talk to him before he lawyers up." I looked around the crowded reception room. Some people had tried to keep the party going despite Emma's death. I suppose they figured if we're not going anywhere, we might as well enjoy ourselves.

"What can I do to help?" Lachlan asked.

"Just be charming and try to get people talking if you can," I said. "We need to find everything out we can about Emma in as little time as possible."

"Charming is my middle name," he said with a cheeky smile.

I rolled my eyes – it was my favorite comeback to any of his cheesy lines – but Lachlan just stared with innocence. I could count on him. That was important.

I was about to go find Zubinsky when I felt a hand on my arm. This simple action took me by surprise and I practically jumped out of my skin. I whirled around to see my sister Lucie; a troubled look on her face.

"Where are you going, Kate?" she asked.

I looked around to make sure no one was paying attention to our conversation. "I need to talk to Zubinsky," I said. "The owner of the hotel wants this case solved, by me, or else."

"Or else what?"

"Or else all of us will be out of a job," I said. "Just let me go, Lucie. I won't be long. The sooner I figure out what really happened to Emma and by whom, the better."

I pulled my arm away gently enough to get Lucie to let go of me. She did let me go and I made a B-line for Scott Zubinsky before anyone else could stop me. He was sitting bent over in a chair with his head in his hands. Occasionally he would take a deep breath between rapid and shallow breaths like he was trying to not start crying or, maybe, like he was trying to stop crying. Poor guy. I felt bad about questioning him so soon after his girlfriend's death but I needed to do it. The future of my business depended on it.

"Mr. Zubinsky?" I asked despite already knowing the answer.

Slowly he lifted his head to look up at me. "Yes?"

"I'm Kate the, uh, the cupcake caterer. I was wondering if I could ask you some questions?"

"About what?" Scott asked apprehensively. "The food is fine."

"I wanted to ask you about Emma and what happened. Can you tell me if anyone wanted to hurt her?"

"No…" Scott shook his head. "No."

"Was Emma worried about anything?"

"No!" Scott pounded his fists against his knees but didn't react to any pain he may have felt. "I said no! I don't know who did it! Who keeps on asking about this? Do you think that I did it, you stupid girl? I didn't! Why don't you look at any of those morons?"

He gestured wildly with his arms to the crowd who were watching him in stunned silence. "I don't know who could have done it!"

I was about to try to say something to calm him down when Lucie scurried to my side. "Let me…" she said and approached Scott as if he were a wounded animal. "Scott, no one is blaming you."

Scott spoke quietly with Lucie and I couldn't hear all of their words. Finally he nodded and once again placed his head in his hands. So much for any clues he could have given me. I was still standing on square one.

Chapter 5

As Lucie continued to speak calmly to Scott, I took the opportunity to roam around the hotel. Privately, I hoped I would be able to find some sort of evidence to shut this murder case very quickly. I still hoped it was a terrible tragedy that caused Emma's death, as a coroner's report would take time. Time that I didn't have.

I found a man sitting in an empty conference room. He was leaning hard against a table. He looked as if he were in desperate need of a strong drink. I couldn't entirely blame him for that. I felt the same way, and I only knew Emma as the lady who booked me to cater the party.

"Horrible night, huh?" I said cautiously in case he went off at me like Scott did.

He looked up at me and gave a long sigh. "One hell of a night. I can't believe she's gone. Who would do such a thing?"

"You think it was murder?"

"Emma was in good health! She had no explainable reason to suddenly become sick and die like that! She didn't deserve to die like that," he said quieter as if he was talking to himself.

"What's your relation to Emma?" I asked, hoping it

didn't seem like too personal of a question. I couldn't solve anything if no one was willing to talk to me.

He smiled a little. "I was her 'plus one' to the party. She said to me 'Tom Rochester, how would you like to come with me to swank party being put on by a high rolling tech company?' She said it would be fun. Some fun, huh?" I nodded sympathetically.

"Do you think she invited me because she felt sorry for me?" Thankfully he was in a chatty mood. I hoped everyone was this forthcoming.

"What do you mean?"

Tom shook his head. "I've been in love with her since we were kids. I never had the nerve to act on it but I suspect some part of her knew. Even though she was dating Scott, I still held a torch for her."

"Do you think anyone might've wanted to harm her?" I asked.

He shook his head again. "No. I don't believe Emma had any enemies. I've certainly never heard anyone wanting to hurt her. That's what makes tonight even more shocking."

I did feel sorry for him. I really did. What he had witnessed and gone through could not have been easy for anybody. Yet, and as much as I felt bad about it, he was still a suspect and I would need to treat him as such.

"I'll give you some space," I said quickly in the most sympathetic way possible.

"Well…thanks for listening to me at least. You're the first one to do so."

I managed a small smile before departing the conference room with plans on making my way to the reception room. I almost felt obligated to book a room for the night so that hotel manager didn't feel like I was trying to run away. His threat did loom deep and hard on my mind. I wasn't about to tempt fate by calling his bluff on his actions.

Coming around a corner, I saw an older, well-dressed man with a younger woman who was wearing a brightly colored dress showing more curves than a racetrack. Like a road with bends, she looked dangerous. I noticed they seemed remarkably calm for having just witnessed an innocent person's death. Too calm and comfortable for my liking.

Turning around, I pretended to be enthralled with a painting on the wall as the two spoke within hearing range.

"You've done good work while you've been in town, Claude," the woman said.

"Thank you, Marbella. Getting here, now, that was the real bitch."

"I do need to pay you for all the hard work you've done."

"And you shall!"

I heard the two of them share a chuckle before leaving the reception area.

Good work? Getting paid? For what? It immediately sent up a red flag for me, yet I knew I couldn't jump the gun just yet. At least not without any form of solid evidence against them.

Remembering I had to still book that room, I hurried around the reception desk and paid for a night. I still wasn't ready to give up on finding out what really happened to Emma, but at least I had a room to stay in tonight.

There was one last person I wanted to visit and ask a few questions to tonight--a man by the name of Nelson Zubinsky. I did not know much of him since he rarely made the papers, unlike his ultra-successful brother Scott, but he still might know something of use. Now, where was he? He couldn't have gotten very far, especially since we were all on lockdown. Nelson was in the hotel somewhere and I intended to find him.

"Is Nelson with Scott?" I overheard a party guest ask another.

"No, I heard he was at the hotel's tennis court," the other guest answered. "I'd get some fresh air too if I were him. Tragic business with Emma. Just tragic."

At the tennis court? Shouldn't he be helping to comfort his brother instead of playing a set in the heat? Strange behavior or not, I still needed to ask him some questions. I made my way down to the tennis court. I waited in the shadows and watched as he hit tennis balls alone. One ball bounced off the net and rolled in my direction. Naturally, I bent down and picked it up.

Nelson looked to me, raised his racket, and gave me a sheepish smile. "A little help please?"

"Sure," I said, "But can I ask you some questions first?"

This seemed to confuse him. "What about?"

"About your brother and your relationship with him."

Nelson rolled his eyes dramatically at my words. "Oh, not this again! I really wish people would stop questioning my love for my brother! Just because he has been so successful it doesn't mean that I hate him or want bad things to happen."

"Can you elaborate for me?"

"People wrongfully assume that just because Scott was successful in all of his tech adventures and I wasn't that it must mean that I'm jealous of him. I'm not jealous! I've always supported him in his tech ventures! Some people, huh?"

"Yeah, some people," I agreed.

"Are you familiar with Claude Rochester?" Nelson suddenly asked. He pointed his racket at me which made me feel rather put on the spot.

"Uh, no, I can't say I'm familiar with that name." I didn't add that I just overheard a very interesting conversation between Claude and Marbella in the lobby. The more information Nelson gave me willingly, without prompting, the better.

"Yeah, well he's been lying low lately. Claude Rochester is Tom Rochester's uncle and he's in desperate, and I mean desperate, need of money right now," Nelson said. "Something about losing a job. Anyway, I wouldn't put it past Claude to try to extort or blackmail money out of Scott. You can't really trust Claude and people get desperate when money is on the line if you know what I mean."

"They do say money is the root of all evil," I said.

"It does make you think. Anyway, I need to get back to my practice so if you'll excuse me…"

"Yes, of course." I had more than enough to go off of from my brief talk with Nelson. "Thanks for taking the time to talk to me."

Nelson saluted me with his tennis racket once I tossed his tennis ball back to him. He got back to his practice almost immediately and I headed back to the hotel.

The moment I entered the hotel doors I wanted to find Lachlan to tell him what I found out. Usually I bounced ideas off of Lucie but, for some reason, it was Lachlan I thought of tonight. It took some searching but I finally found him, head in hand, nursing a drink at a table in the corner. He looked up when he heard my heels clicking across the tile floor. The look on his face didn't exactly say 'I'm happy to see you.' More 'Get away from me' than anything else.

"What's wrong?" I sat down at his table. I saw he had a second drink sitting at the table. I don't know if that was for me or a double for him, but I drank it anyway. "You look…distant."

"I feel like I'm struggling," he said grudgingly.

"Struggling with what happened to the victim?" I asked. "We all are. Everyone keeps repeating she had no enemies and now we're all on lockdown till the police interview everyone."

Lachlan shook his head. "No. No, I'm not struggling with what happened to Emma."

"Then what is it?"

"I'm struggling with us." He gestured at the small space between us. "I'm struggling with our relationship if that's what you can even call it. I'm patient, Kate, but I'm not a saint. You need to decide what you want or I might not be around."

Two ultimatums in one day. I gulped hard. I felt a pain spread through my chest at his words. We may not be moving toward an 'us' at a rapid pace, but we were still moving.

"What are you saying?" I swallowed around the lump forming in my heart.

"You like solving mysteries." Lachlan stood and headed for the stairs leading up to the guest rooms. "You figure it out, Kate."

Chapter 6

I was lying in my bed half-awake when I heard a hor-rible sound. I quickly sat straight up, trying to identi-fy the sound. Someone was screaming. Not good! Not good at all!

I threw on some very basic clothes so I wouldn't be marching out into the hallway in just my pajamas, and went to investigate what happened to cause all this lat-est chaos. I cracked my door open and peered into the hall. After the day we had yesterday, I was expecting some sort of stampede but, instead, the hallway was relatively clear. I saw someone disappear around the corner. I followed them and soon found a crowd gath-ered near the open door of one of the rooms. I managed to worm my way through the crowd and get as close to the doorway as I could manage.

"What happened?" I asked.

The hotel manager—Mr. Ultimatum -- was the first one to look over at me. "Tom Rochester is dead."

He moved aside so I could see a body lying face down on the bed. Tom was sprawled across the bed with his arms stretched out and his legs straight. It was almost a Christ like pose. I wondered if the pose was in-tentional or if he had been placed that way after death?

"Did he do himself in?" A voice in the crowd asked.

The hotel manager's face flushed with what I assumed was embarrassment combined with anger.

"All of you! Leave! Go back to your rooms, get breakfast, whatever! Just go away!"

After he was satisfied with his yelling and the crowd dispersed, he looked over at me. "Still here?"

"Still trying to solve the task you gave me," I said. "Tom was part of it and now he's dead."

"At least there's no blood. The maid will be happy for that," the manager said callously. "Less clean up."

"Was it an accident?" I asked. "Suicide? Another suspicious death?" There were far too many questions and not enough answers.

The hotel manager handed me a note. I didn't feel all together touching possible evidence before the police got their hands on it, but it could be important to finding out what happened to Emma. I hastily read it before I lost my chance for good.

I cannot go on without Emma. She was the love of my life and now that she is dead I have nothing more to live for. I have been thinking about harming myself and even killing myself for a while now. Soon I shall be reunited with Emma.

"The police have already been called and are probably getting even more calls by now," the hotel manager said when I looked up with the unasked question hanging on my lips. "A suicide in here of all places! As if my business wasn't suffering already from the Emma incident, now Tom goes and does himself in my hotel. Some people…"

He left abruptly and I was alone with Tom's body, his suicide note still clutched in my hand. I had seen death before, I had seen horrors before, I had even helped solve mysteries before, but this was somehow different. Two murders within twenty four hours. I don't think I'm prepared for this. My muscles tightened up as a wave of stress and frustration hit me. Everything was wrong!

Lachlan and I weren't on good terms relationship wise, I was no closer to solving Emma's murder when faced with a second murder, and the hotel manager's threats were getting to me. As a child I would break out in a rash almost every exam time. Here I was scratching myself through my top feverishly. My mother said I was a perfectionist. I just think I'm a stress head.

I thought of Lachlan. I wanted to see him, yet didn't want to see him at the same time. It felt like an "I want you here now go away" sort of thing. There had always been a strange push and pull to our relationship but now it seemed amplified. I set Tom's suicide note on the bed before turning and walking down the hall toward Lachlan's room. I needed to talk to him – even if I didn't know what I wanted to say.

I knocked on Lachlan's door. No answer. Maybe he was asleep. I listened closely for any sounds of life and, to my surprise, heard a light giggle. It was too high pitched to be his. Maybe he was watching TV and didn't hear me knock.

"Lachlan, are you in there?" I knocked again.

Still no answer.

Frowning, I knocked harder. When there was still no answer, I decided to take matters into my own hands and open the door. It was something I quickly regretted once I saw the scene before me.

"Lachlan! Selena!"

Lachlan and Selena were lying in bed. Lachlan was clearly drunk as his face was flushed and his eyes bloodshot. Selena, however, appeared to be sober as a judge.

They were both fully clothed so it had not gone beyond any type of flirting and teasing, but I was still angry and so very hurt! How could they? How could he? What was all this "I'm patient" if he was going to jump in bed with Selena right after?

"Kate, it's not like that—" Lachlan began.

"Save it, you—you! I've got eyes!" Before I could say anything else or give them the gratification of seeing me cry, I spun on my heel and slammed the door behind me with such force the entire wall shook.

As I hurried away, it felt like my heart was literally breaking in two. I thought Lachlan and I had an understanding. We seemed to at least but then, every time we made any sort of progress, Selena showed up to completely undo it. I had a mind to fire her. I would if I didn't think I owed it to Mum to keep her on. At any rate, my mind was in no place for solving this case. How could I solve one murder let alone two, feeling the way that I did? I would have to risk the hotel manager's wrath and threats. I couldn't solve it. So long Sugar N Spice.

It didn't take me long to find the hotel manager behind the front desk. "Well?" he asked impatiently. "What do you have for me?"

I shook my head as I struggled to force back the tears that threatened to flow. "I can't do it. I can't go on with this case. You'll have to leave it to the police."

"You can't do that!"

"Why not? They're more equipped and trained in this sort of thing. I'm just an amateur."

"The police are dedicating too much time to Scott Zubinsky," the manager said. It was a detail I didn't realize until he told me. "They can't see beyond him as their number one suspect. Now I have two deaths on my property in less than twenty four hours. Unless the crime is solved, this hotel will be ruined."

I almost said "then let it be ruined" but somehow I was able to hold that bitter comment back.

The hotel manager glared at me. "Don't forget our 'agreement'. If you don't solve this case, I'll be driving you out of business! If I'm going down, I'm taking you with me."

It wasn't fair, it wasn't right, but I had no other choice. I would have to solve this case or everything Mum worked on would be for nothing. I just hoped I would survive the case.

Chapter 7

My latest search for Scott was fairly unsuccessful until I found a uniformed police officer.

"Excuse me, do you know where Scott Zubinsky is?"

The police officer eyed me suspiciously. "Why?"

"We grew up together," I lied easily. "I wanted to pay my respects and see if I could do anything to help calm him down."

"You can speak to him later. He's quite agitated right now."

I watched the police officer walk away. If I trailed far enough behind him, I could probably find out where they were keeping Scott. The sneaking about lead me to a room that was down the hall and to the right. I could hear Nelson Zubinsky's angry voice all the way into the hall. He wasn't even trying to be quiet or keep his voice down.

"Dad always preferred you!" Nelson said angrily. "I had potential to become a tennis star but nooooooo! Dad had to prefer the perfect Scott Zubinsky!"

I felt my jaw drop open at the angry words. Was Nelson serious? What could have possibly brought on such hateful and angry words?

"It's not like that!" Scott protested.

"It's exactly like that! I had so much potential but I was ignored for you! You were always perfect! You could do no wrong! Dad's preference for you cost me my tennis career."

Could Nelson be behind Emma's death? Could he have murdered his brother's girlfriend as a way to get back at him for a lifetime of being overlooked? I didn't know for sure, but I intended to find out.

I was preparing to make my escape before the Zubinsky brothers could find me ears dropping outside of the hotel room and sneak to the area of the hotel where Emma was staying in case something was overlooked in her room when someone grabbed my arm. I spun around, biting back a scream, as flight or fight kicked in. Lucie held up her hands to ward off any sort of attack.

"Hey, hey, calm down. It's just me."

"You really need to stop sneaking up on me like that." I put a hand over my racing heart.

Lucie held her hands up in a gesture of surrender. "Listen, I didn't mean to scare you, but, I have some important news and a theory I think you need to hear."

"About Nelson Zubinsky? I already have my suspicions about him."

Lucie shook her head. "No, not him."

"Then who? " I forked both hands through my hair. "Who else could have done it or even have motive? He's angry at his brother…Angry enough to do something drastic."

Lucie took in a deep breath before saying: "I think Selena is involved."

"Selena?" I looked at Lucie skeptically. "Sure, I'm not her biggest fan or anything, but I don't think she'd murder anyone."

"I don't have any evidence but I saw Selena flirting with the kitchen staff," she said.

"That doesn't mean anything," I said. "Selena flirts with any male that is breathing."

"But she could've gotten near the apple cider," Lucie insisted. "I know she was in the kitchen at the time of the murder."

I folded my arms across my chest. "So you think Selena was able to poison just one cup of apple cider and that cup magically fell into Emma's hands? Do we even know if she has any connection to Emma? Lucie, I love you, but pinning a murder on Selena just because she was flirting with some kitchen staff is farfetched."

"Unless you saw someone give Emma her cup of cider, it's still possible!" Lucie insisted.

"Selena could've been given the poison by someone and put it in Emma's cup. It wouldn't surprise me if she's not above bribery."

I shook my head. "I don't want to have anything to do with Selena or Lachlan!"

She looked surprised at my words and jerked her head back. "Lachlan? Who mentioned Lachlan?"

"It's—" I waved my hand to wish away my thoughts and words. "It's nothing. Really! Don't worry about it!"

"Wait, did something happen between Selena and Lachlan?"

Facing my feelings is not something I'm good at. Facing the fact that Selena and Lachlan might have something going on is definitely not something I'm good at. To get myself out of this conversation as quickly as possible, I said "Not now, Lucie, okay? I have some investigating to do."

"Kate!" she called after me but I was already gone. I practically ran up the stairs and through the twisting hallways till I came to Scott and Emma's room.

The door knob was cold to the touch suggesting that no one had been inside for quite a while. This convenient little fact would certainly work in my favor. It meant no one was inside recently to mess up any possible evidence. I turned the knob and heard it open with a dull click. Taking a deep breath, I stepped into the room not knowing what to expect or what I would find inside.

Chapter 8

To my surprise and relief, the room looked relatively untouched aside from the small mess here and there. Clearly 'everything in its place' had not been applied. Still, I could work with this as, other than the messiness around me, the room looked relatively untouched. No one had ransacked the room in a desperate search for any sort of evidence.

I started with the closet which was closest to the door. There was nothing in there other than expensive looking clothing that hung from hangers. I felt like a pick pocket when I stuck my hand into the pockets of each piece of clothing to see if I could find anything. To my relief and disappointment, there was nothing in the first few pairs of clothes. It wasn't until I reached a fancy looking skirt that I found something.

My fingers touched a crumpled up piece of paper that I had first assumed was a receipt until I opened it.

I'm coming for you next! You better watch your back, Emma.

It was unsigned yet there was something oddly familiar about it. Who wanted to hurt her and why? What motivation did they have?

Turning away from the closet, I began to rummage through the rest of the room.

I opened up one drawer in the chest of drawers and then another. The first drawer had nothing but socks and underwear in it. The second drawer was much more interesting. I found a heavy smartphone case. When I opened the case, I was surprised to see there was no smart phone inside!

Instead there were several small vials of liquid. They were not labeled but I knew the odds that they were filled with something that could kill a person. It worried me that there was more than one case. Who else were they planning to make sick or even kill? I quickly pocketed my newfound evidence and hurried out of the room, shutting the door behind me.

～

Acting as casual as I could under the circumstances, I walked downstairs. I caught a glimpse of Marbella and Claude Rochester in the laundry room. I walked down the steps as quietly as I could, hoping to hear something that could possibly help with the case. For the life of me I couldn't make out much of their conversation.

Claude looked up suddenly and locked eyes with me. His face went white before he turned and made a break for it. Why did he run away? Did he have something to hide? Marbella, on the other hand, looked like a deer in the headlights. She wasn't going anywhere. I decided to use that to my advantage.

"Marbella, hi!" I said in a forced cheerful voice.

She looked stunned, as if I had slapped her. "Uh, hi," she squeaked.

"Crazy party, huh?" I continued in the same overly cheerful voice. "Why don't we sit and chat a bit?"

"Uh, about what?" She hesitated when I sat in a small couch next to the laundry room. I pulled her down beside me.

No use beating around the bush. I decided to cut to the chase. "I'm investigating Emma's murder and I wondered if you knew anything about it. Even details you think are small might be significant."

Marbella's face went white. "Do you think I had something to do with it?"

"Why would you say that?" I asked. "Did you have something to do with it? Or know who did?"

"What? No! It wasn't me! I swear it wasn't me!" Marbella was babbling so fast it was hard to decipher what she was saying. "I didn't kill them!"

"Then who did?" I demanded.

"I don't know! I swear on my mother's life I don't know!"

Either Marbella was the best actress in the world or she was truly innocent. She was even fidgeting with shifting her weight from side to side and her arms trembled. Her eyes were wide and she kept shaking her head as she projected her innocence in the case. I knew I would have to change my line of questioning if I hoped to get answers.

"Why did Claude Rochester run?"

Marbella sighed and her shoulders slumped. "I've been stealing goods from Claude to sell. I need the money and I've done bad things in my life but I've never killed anyone! I swear it!"

It all made sense to me now! Marbella was so scared because she knew if the crime were pinned on her, the news about the theft would come out which meant more jail time. She had no reason to lie about the murder when she was telling me the truth about her stealing. While her story was shocking, I did believe her. That left me with only two suspects.

"You won't tell anyone, will you?" Marbella asked. "About the stealing, I mean?"

I thought a minute before shaking my head. "That's between you, Claude, and the police."

Chapter 9

With just two suspects left, I decided to see where Scott was. I remembered someone mentioning he was in the 'sick room' which was sort of the hotel's version of a hospital room. Maybe his nerves finally gave out and he needed treatment.

I knocked on the sick room door before poking my head in. "Scott Zubinsky? I'm Kate. Do you remember me?"

He looked up at me. "What do you want? Haven't you done enough damage already questioning everyone at the party…questioning me. I just want to grieve. Leave me alone."

I stepped inside the room. "I wanted to apologize for my initial behavior earlier. It was wrong of me to behave in such a way."

Scott waved the hand that had been resting on his thigh, "Don't worry about it. It's been a rough time for all of us lately."

"How are you feeling?"

Scott smiled a wry smile, "I've been better."

I motioned at the chair next to him before sitting down. "I found something rather odd that I'd like to talk to you about. I was looking around and found some vials with liquid in them. I think they might be poison."

Scott's eyebrows went up at my words. "Poison? Where did you find it?"

"I found the vials in a smart phone box," I said. "Does that mean anything to you?"

Scott thought for a moment before nodding slowly. "I gave my brother a full set of gadgets including a smart phone and a smart phone box. He mentioned in passing that he needed one and I was hoping that it would help smooth things over between us. Nelson and I have always fought and he feels like our father favored me over him. Nelson blames me for him not being able to pursue his tennis career." Scott shook his head, remembering.

"He was jealous of my business. He fails to see that Dad loved both of us! I wish he would let go of his jealousy."

"Do you think that jealousy would be enough to cause him to try to murder someone?" I asked.

"Nelson was always one to use words – mean, nasty, hurtful words – but still just words. I don't think he'd go as far as murder."

"Jealousy makes people do things that may seem out of character for them," I said.

"Yes, but why target Emma when his real jealousy was toward me?"

If Nelson really wanted to hurt Scott, Emma would be the most likely target. Scott would fall like a house of cards. Nelson would be left to claim victory. That alone was enough for me to suspect a very jealous and vengeful Nelson was Emma's killer.

If Nelson was indeed Emma's killer, it also led Tom to take his own life. It was possible Scott would also blame himself for Tom's death too. I didn't think Nelson planned it that way, but I suspected he would capitalize on the fallout as much as possible.

Chapter 10

Before I could confront Nelson about Emma's murder, I needed some back up. If he confessed when it was just me in the room, it would be my word versus his. I needed another witness. I felt a little evil asking the hotel manager to hide and wait for a confession but he's the one who wanted me to solve the murder no matter what. That meant he could help me out.

"You think you know who was involved in the murder?" he asked eagerly when I brought up the suggestion of a sting operation.

"I do," I said. "I want you to come with me as my witness."

"I'll do more than that! I'll arrest him myself!"

"We need a confession first."

He wilted ever so slightly but nodded. "Then let's go get that confession."

We found Nelson on the tennis courts practicing his game. How could he be so calm at a time like this? How could he pretend like two people didn't just die? It made no sense!

"Come to watch me play?" Nelson asked when he noticed me watching him.

"No, I wanted to talk to you about Emma again."

"What about her?" he asked. "Did you find her killer yet?"

"I believe so."

Nelson turned away and acted as if he were about to swing his racket in a mock serve. "Yeah? Who?"

"You," I said.

"Me?" Nelson laughed.

"Yes, you! Oh, come off it! I know about the smart phone box and the vials, Nelson. What are they? Full of poison?"

Nelson lowered his racket and looked at me. "Will finding out the answer make you feel all grown up? Do you want to know the truth?" I waited, holding my breath, before he answered.

"Yeah, I did it."

I suddenly felt dizzy. I grabbed at the tennis net to keep myself from falling. "Why?"

He rolled his eyes dramatically. "Because precious little Scott was always the chosen child! The loved child! The perfect child! I could never live up to him! I was always in his shadow! So yeah, I did it! I did it to hurt him and to take away something he cared about just as he did to me! An eye for an eye! He deserved it for all that he did to me!"

I felt my blood grow cold at what he said. He may have his grievances with Scott, but that did not mean that an innocent person had to die! It didn't mean that two innocent people had to die!

"Did you kill Tom, too?" I asked.

"No, that was all his doing. He was too wrapped up in Scott's precious little Emma to live without her."

The hotel manager must have followed through with his side of the plan because the police swarmed the tennis court. They led Nelson away. Because of his out of control jealousy, two people lost their lives.

Bringing justice for Emma did help me feel a little bit better, but I still felt a strong ache. Lachlan and Selena were still around somewhere, maybe even partying and enjoying themselves without a care or worry in the world. I didn't want to be around either of them right now. I did want to be around Lucie, though. I wandered back to the hotel searching for my sister. When I found her, I was hoping for a smile or some sort of comforting gesture. Instead, she gave me a frown and an angry look.

"Lucie, I need to talk to you about Selena and Lachlan."

"Well, I don't want to so go talk to yourself!"

I took a step back. "Lucie, please…"

"No! You were incredibly hurtful earlier and as you didn't want to listen to me then, why should you listen to me now? I'm not some sort of toy that you can pull off the shelf when you want my attention!"

I watched as she turned and stormed away. We fought before—what siblings hadn't?-- but never quite like this. I wanted her, I needed her, and she rejected me. Sugar N Spice was successful, but at what price?

Losing my sister was not the price I expected to pay. Without her, I was completely alone in the world.

With my head down, trying to see through the sudden blur of tears, I left the hotel and found my way to my car. An ache of loneliness and sadness stabbed me with each breath and every beat of my heart. The victory was not worth this painful defeat.

Deadly Birthday

Chapter 1

A vacation….a vacation. I'm just going to pretend like this is a little getaway, Kate thought to herself on the drive. The trip up to Byron Bay was one of the prettiest drives she'd taken in some time, and getting out of city was good for the soul, she'd heard. Plus, she got to stare at the back of Lachlan Fitzpatrick's truck the whole way there. It wasn't as nice as staring at him, but close enough. Lachlan owned the Truly Scrumptious Catering Company, which made him even sexier than he already was. A man after Kate's own entrepreneurial heart.

Sugar N Spice partnered with Truly Scrumptious in order to increase the bookings for both companies, a tactic that had worked like a charm. Kate and Lachlan worked with each other more and more every month. Just in front of Lachlan's truck was the awful Selena Fox, the evil assistant Kate's mother had hired for the Sugar N Spice Cupcakery before she passed away. Evil was a stretch, of course, as Selena could do no one any real harm, but the girl tried Kate's every nerve. She was incompetent at customer service, and really only lived to be the center of attention. The center of Lachlan's attention, if she had it her way. Goodness that girl was incorrigible.

Kate tried not to think of her mother too much, when she did it made her incredibly sad. Sad to think of how much she would change about the company...namely, Selena's existence there...if she weren't so set on honoring her late mother's final hire. She saw herself as amazing, and a go-getter, confident and capable, but something always seemed to happen at her events that set her back a bit. There had been more than one occasion where people were murdered at events that she was catering, and somehow Kate always managed to help the police figure out who was behind it. Surely, though....surely trouble couldn't follow her all the way to Byron Bay?

Lachlan made a sharp left turn and took them through a small road that lead toward the water. There was no mistaking Byron Bay when you say it. It was the up-and-coming crowd's favorite place to throw a party and this evening was no exception! The Sugar N Spice crew was bringing carefully crafted gourmet cupcakes at the special request of tonight's birthday girl, Chelsea Gibson. Chelsea would be celebrating her twenty-first birthday tonight...no doubt with a gaggle of annoying wealthy youngsters flocking around her. Kate had the pleasure of talking to Chelsea and her mother on the phone for three of the last four weeks, ensuring that everything would be perfect for the cupcakes for their big event. Surely they weren't that overly dramatic about everything on the event list, because she sure felt sorry for the party planner if that was the case!

The bright green of the grass backed up against the clear blue sky and perfect water was just what Kate needed to see before she got to the venue. Although she was fairly confident that there would be no murder in this beautiful part of Australia tonight, she was extremely confident that there would be some drama with that many young people at a beachfront twenty-first birthday party. Her phone buzzed in the seat next to her, it was her younger sister Lucie.

"Hey there, Kates! I'm not far behind you...just get started without me. How's looking at Lachlan's backside going" she teased.

"Very funny, Lucie. And just fine, thank you." Kate smirked into the phone, watching Lachlan's tan arm hang out the side of his truck window, catching the breeze.

"Okay so remember not to nag the she-devil until I get there. You know how you get, and Serena is not actually the terrible beast you make her out to be. And I have all the forms with me so don't worry about that, I'll get them all signed when I get there and you won't even have to think about them. They prepaid, right?"

"Yes," Kate's eyes rolled heavily. "They prepaid six months ago. Who does that? For a birthday??"

"I know, it's not like she's a hundred or any cool number. Oh well, she probably won't even remember tonight...do you remember what we did when you turned twenty one?"

"Nothing," Kate said flatly.

"That's right, and it was glorious. This is going to be ridiculous," Lucie giggled and made a kissing sound before hanging up.

Chapter 2

The hotel that was chosen for Chelsea Gibson's birthday party was not to be matched. It was touted as the only beach front even property in the area...the only place you could actually party and eat that close to the water. And it was breathtaking.

It must have cost a fortune to reserve this, Kate thought as she pulled into a parking spot. The birthday girl, so she'd heard, had a beach house rented all to herself that wasn't too far away, but her guests were all staying at the spa resort that hosted the party. Why anyone would want their own private beach house that was a fifteen minute walk away from where all their friends were staying was beyond Kate, but apparently that was something that fancy people liked to do. The beach house was definitely on her list of places to check out before she left for the evening, though, because from the way Chelsea's mother was absentmindedly describing it on the phone one of the thousand times she had called, it sounded divine.

Kate picked up her laptop bag that carried her recordkeeping and datebook devices out of the front seat and went to meet Lachlan so they could find the parents and get everything situated before the festivities. When she reached his truck, he was stretching his messenger bag over his broad shoulders, leaving plenty of room for being appreciated from a distance before he turned around.

"So, let's go find Mr. and Mrs. Fancypants," Kate chimed, startling him.

"Good Lord, woman. You scared me. Enjoy the view?" he joked, one eyebrow raised.

"Maybe," Kate answered, sounding almost bored and nudging him in the arm before trotting up the resort steps. "Wow, this place is amazing."

"Yeahhhh.....I don't' think......"

When they got to the top of the long, whitewashed wooden staircase, Kate's jaw dropped. Everything was twinkling already, and it wasn't even sundown! There were white lights on every single surface imaginable, and white and cream colored roses everywhere. Lachlan let out a long whistle.

"Give me a tent and a good view any day, it would beat this. This is nuts."

By the time the two were done making their rounds and finding out where the kitchen was, and where their respective goodies were supposed to be set up, they still hadn't seen one adult. There were teenagers and young twenty-somethings running around everywhere...and many of them looked like they were already getting the party started in one way or another.

"Ummmm....where's the grown-ups?" Kate asked a passing party-goer. The young man just scoffed and walked away, adjusting his sunglasses.

"Oh. My. GOD." It was a screech from the far corner of the dining hall. "Would you please shut up about Trey. I am not sleeping with him, Gi. Now please go relax somewhere else." The young girl made air-quotes around the word relax, and Kate and Lachlan looked at each other. The twang of that screech sounded a bit familiar to both of them so Lachlan ventured a guess and strode across the hall.

"Chelsea?" he asked, long arm extended in a friendly handshake.

The girl, long blonde hair and big in all the expected places, spun on her heels and immediately flashed a smile that looked like a million bucks. "Why yes, yes I am. And who are you?" She took his hand gingerly and giggled, casting a glance toward Kate and immediately looking defeated. Kate flipped her hair over her shoulder a bit and stepped around Lachlan.

"We're here with your food and cupcakes," she said boldly, holding out her own hand so that Lachlan's could be released.

"Oh goodie!" Chelsea jumped up and down, which was something that it looked like she probably did a lot of, as she seemed to be easily amused by everything. "Okay, okay. Just put them wherever you people put things and come have a drink before the cake gets wheeled out."

Kate and Lachlan cast each other a hard, unapprovingly glare and chuckled quietly. Lachlan winked at her before he looked away, which made her heart skip a little. "So," he asked. "Where are the adults?"

"What adults?!" Chelsea cackled. "There's no adults here..." She burst into laughter for some unknown reason. "...unless of course you mean ME! Because I'm an adult now!" She giggled again and ran off in the direction of some boy that was waving at her, but quickly glanced back at Kate. "Mommy already paid for everything so just have a good time!"

"Oh, puke," Lachlan said almost to himself before adjusting his bag and heading to the kitchen to get set up. Kate sent him a fake salute and headed out to her car to get the cupcakes. Lucie was coming up the big staircase just then, and Selena was of course nowhere to be found. Though her car seemed to have parked itself somehow. How could she be missing already?

"Hey!" Lucie gasped. "Hey!! They're about to do the cake!" The poor girl was trotting up several stairs at once.

"What?!" Kate yelled? "But I just....but she...." she scanned the horizon and noticed a leggy blonde in a tiny jean romper waving her arms and shouting.

"I dunno," Lucie said, exasperated. "I passed someone asking me if I was the cake lady...apparently whoever the birthday girl is is already demanding that the cake be brought out. She sounds hideous--"

Kate pointed, without a second thought, toward Chelsea down on the beach. Lucie rolled her eyes. "Figures. Well, go alert the main cake lady."

Not ten minutes later, everyone was gathered in the

dining hall, where appetizers still had not been served yet, and was singing happy birthday to the star of the evening. Someone had carried over a princess tiara and set it atop her head gingerly, and she giggled and acted surprised.

"If I had to guess…" Kate whispered into Lachlan's ear as they watched.

"She probably made her friend make it for her?" he asked.

As the last notes of the song faded, a tall boy that planted a kiss on Chelsea's lips began cutting the cake and passing it out. Two or three people were handed plates, and Kate had turned to tell Lucie that she'd better make her a princess tiara for her next birthday, but only moments later there was shouting from every corner of the room. People began moving quickly back and forth, excitedly trying to see what all the commotion was suddenly about. Lachlan jutted his hand out toward Kate and she grabbed it. With the other hand, he was quickly pulling a chair over in front of her. She stepped up onto it and used his shoulder for balance.

The blood ran from her knees and they wobbled on the folding chair. "What is it??" Lachlan asked. She looked down at him and shook her head, unable to believe it.

"I can't….I can't……" Her eyes were wide and he could see the shock had her tongue-tied.

He picked her up and set her down gently, climbing up into the chair himself. "Oh my god."

Chapter 3

Kate put her head in her hands. The police had already come, and some of them were already headed back to the station with squad cars full of under aged drinkers. She must be jinxed, to have this follow her all the way out here. Lucie had her convinced that it was just small town drama that had caused so many horrible things surrounding them, but now it was clear. Kate was a beacon for murder! The police chief trotted off toward the beach, away from her, having just asked for her help. Of course she would help. Kate had already proven to be invaluable on so many other cases, it would be rude for her not to help. Plus, she herself was technically still a suspect so it wasn't like she could go anywhere until they figured it out. Lucie rubbed her back lightly, unphased by the events. Lucie remained unphased most of the time, and was the calm to Kate's storm.

"Okay so what do we know," Lucie asked, her hand still on her sister's back. "You always know what to listen for, what did YOU hear when he was talking?"

Kate brushed the hair out of her face and wiped her eyes. She wasn't crying because people were dead, although that was very sad for their families. She was sad because this sort of thing always seemed to happen, and it rocked her to her core. "I can't even…" she muttered into her palms.

"No." Lucie scolded her flatly. "You've had your five minutes of this always happens to me, not it's time to get to work. This has nothing to do with you and you know it."

Kate sniffled again, looking up to see if she could see where Lachlan or Selena had run off to.

"I mean, it," Lucie demanded, flicking her sister in the forehead. "Quit your whining and figure this out."

Kate was dumbfounded as usual by her sister's ability to compartmentalize a dire situation, but as usual….she was right. This had nothing to do with her, and the sooner they figured out what was going on, the sooner they could all go home. Or have that drink she should've had before this mess.

"He said, I think, that two are dead. And I think they're both boys, is that right?" she asked, retracing what the officer had just told her.

"Yes, that's right. Now who did it?" Lucie joked.

"I don't know how you can be so lighthearted, you're awful. But that's not how it works. Who were the boys? And where the hell are all the grownups?" Kate said, annoyed.

"Yeah I don't know….and Trey something. Also Connor something."

"No," Kate corrected, rubbing the mascara from under her eyes with her shirt sleeve. "Connor is Chelsea's boyfriend. It's Zac Wilde."

"Oh yes! The douchey son of the oil tycoon. I've heard all about him from that girl over there. Mainly just that he's a jerk." Lucie pointed across the beach. "That's his girlfriend. I heard her talking to the police. She was defending him when one of her friends was trying to tell one of the officers what a jerk he was to her."

"We'll start there, c'mon." Kate grabbed her sister's hand and pulled her up off the boulder they were perching on. "I'll talk to that girl, did you catch her name?" Lucie shook her head. "Okay you go see if you can conveniently overhear anything near the birthday girl. I am not about to try my hand at her yet, we should wait until she calms down a bit. Although it does look like she's loving all the attention." Chelsea was surrounded by nearly everyone at the party while she was trying to talk to the police. This part of the story wasn't about her, but she sure was trying to make it that way, asking people to bring her water and asking the police to repeat things. Kate strolled by her without being noticed and went to talk to Gianna, the friend she'd seen Chelsea arguing with upon arrival.

"Okay," she whispered to her sister before they split up. "Two dead, immediately after eating a slice of the birthday cake. We're on a mission, because if we don't figure this out soon, they're going to start wondering if the food people had something to do with it….and that's not a point I would like to get to. By the way have you seen Lachlan?" Lucie shook her head and ran over toward the crowd surrounding Chelsea.

Kate didn't get much out of Gianna besides her name, and a general impression that she was off a bit. While she seemed to be in with the main group, it almost seemed as if she didn't belong there. Apparently, Chelsea and Connor had been dating a long time, but Connor was abusive. That much she gathered from Gianna, but the girl seemed uninterested and was hard to get a read on. When Kate motioned to Lucie, the two met back at the same boulder.

"Tell me what she said," Lucie said immediately. "Oh and I brought you this." She handed Kate a cold soda, as everyone surrounding Chelsea was being handed things whether they wanted them or not.

"I didn't really get much out of her, actually. She seemed kind of strange. But I'm pretty sure she's only IN this crowd because she's that rich kid's girlfriend."

"Oh, absolutely!" Lucie interrupted. "And Gianna was high, by the way, not weird. Chelsea told me that." She then blathered on for a full five minutes, almost sounding like a young beach party-goer herself from time to time, waving her hands and really getting into the stories. Evidently Gianna had a drug problem, and had been the high the entire day, something that Chelsea didn't approve of. Kate had a hard time believing there was anything that Chelsea didn't approve of.

"Okay, but what about that other girl next to you. The one that kind of looks like Gianna.....in the short burgundy dress??"

"Oh THAT's Alexis," Lucie said ridiculously. "Sorry…..I mean that's Alexis. Chelsea says she's the jealous type and it's because she's the poorest person in the group. She actually said that the girl is lucky to be able to hang around them….though she was sure that would change now that her rich boyfriend was dead. I mean who says stuff like that?!"

"Gross. Okay. So Alexis was dating Trey, the other victim?"

"Engaged, actually. She stands to receive quite the inheritance from his passing."

"Seems like a good motive," Kate thought aloud. Lucie nodded.

Chapter 4

About a half hour later, when the sun was just start-ing to set and the colors over the bay started to soften, Kate walked down to the beach again to find Chelsea smoking a cigarette by the bonfire with two of her friends. Where they had found someone to allow them to make a bonfire during a murder investigation Kate would never understand, but she had her doubts that anyone told these people "no" about anything. Kate recognized Chelsea's two friends once her feet hit the sand, it was the two that were wearing similar dresses. They both had long, flowy brown hair that made them look like bohemian beach princesses. And at ordinary glance, you wouldn't necessarily think that they were much different. Alexis, the odd girl out because of her financial status, and Gianna, the odd girl out because of her drug issue. And Chelsea, the dramatic birthday girl. It was still anyone's guess as to who murdered the two young men.

"Hi, girls. Can I get you anything? I know it's get-ting late, but I heard that the constable just finished booking all the under aged drinkers so that's good? It means you've thrown quite the shindig, Chelsea......" She wasn't really sure what to say. Not because she was uncomfortable on a crime scene, for goodness sake she'd been to plenty of them by now. It was because the vibe that the young crowd put out was so surreal. It was almost as if some of them weren't very affected by their friends' deaths. Alexis, for example, didn't really seem all that phased that her fiancé had just died in front of at least a hundred people on the beach. Gianna, to her left, was twisting her hair into little braids and then undoing them. They seemed downright bored. And the pair of them were already over Chelsea's antics, which in turned had calmed the birthday girl down a bit. She pulled on her cigarette and looked out onto the water.

"You know, I think Gianna's really out of it…" Chelsea declared where only Kate could hear her. She leaned down to rest her elbows on her knees and flick her cigarette onto the sand. "I doubt that has anything to do with it, but you never know."

Kate pulled her cell phone out of the back pocket of her slacks and texted the police chief. Against her better judgement, she suggested that Gianna's belongings be checked for any evidence, just in case. Not long after she sent the text, two officers came down and escorted Gianna back toward the dining hall. When she came back, she was livid and demanded to know who made the suggestion for her things to be trifled with. Kate said nothing, and felt bad for causing trouble. Surely they would have confiscated whatever she had in her purse….which would likely make it a long night for all of them. Moments later, Gianna saw that Chelsea was hiding a conversation she was having on her phone, and assumed that it had something to do with her bags being searched. This caused an uproar the likes of which you would only expect to see on television, and within moments there was screaming and name-calling. Kate didn't recognize half of what Gianna was calling her friends, but it all sounded bad, so she took the opportunity to try and find the beach house that Chelsea had rented for the night.

The police chief had ordered everyone to stay close, but she figured that a brief hike up the road wouldn't do anyone any harm, especially since, at this point, she was still helping to solve the case. Although no one had seen Lachlan since he hopped off the chair at the scene of the crime, which really bothered her. She wasn't above suspecting that he had something to do with it at this point, because what other reason would there be for him to disappear?? It was no matter, Lachlan or not, she had a job to do. Her phone screen showed that she had plenty of battery left for a night of investigation, so she sent her sister a quick text to let her know her whereabouts and hiked up the hill behind the resort property. Surely the house wouldn't be too hard to find, it was apparently one of the only properties around the area, and was recently renovated to a point that made it stand out against its beautiful, natural background. Not five minutes into her hike and she spotted it. Boy did it stand out! The place was a tiny, shining beacon of glamour, and for the moment looked utterly uninhabited. Perfect for investigating.

Luckily, as she expected amongst rich people who were basically on a mini vacation for a birthday party, the door was unlocked. She really hated having to jim-my her way into places, so she was thankful for that. Chelsea and Connor were both staying at this house, she'd been told by the mother, months before. Why anyone would tell a cupcakery owner their family's personal business was beyond her, but they were noth-ing if not an odd, wealthy family of oversharers. Inside the room, the trash can had been kicked over and there were scraps of paper littered all over the floor. They all looked like they were from the same piece of paper…. Kate nudged a few of them around on the floor with her toe. Sure enough! She squatted down and quickly pieced the puzzle together as best as she could and re-alized that she was looking at parts of a love letter from Zac, the wealthy victim and the boyfriend of Gianna, to Chelsea!

Surely this means…

Kate frantically tried to piece the rest of the letter together but she was stopped by shouting in the dis-tance. With a wave of her hands across the floor, the pieces of paper were scattered again, and Kate ran to the nearest closet. The door was heavy, for a closet door, with bamboo slats angled closely together. She couldn't quite see out of them, but it was at least light enough inside that she wouldn't fall over anything. The shouting eventually made it into the house, and Kate peered through a crack in the wood. She recognized Chelsea's voice, but couldn't place the male's. Whoev-er he was he was very upset, and Chelsea was pleading with him to try and understand something. She could see her pulling at the arm of whoever she was arguing with, and when he turned around Kate saw that it was the boy who was cutting the birthday cake.

Connor!

Her boyfriend, Connor, was rejecting her affections and accusing her of cheating on him. His voice raised almost shrilly and he started picking things up and throwing them. First the vase on the table, then a piece of the vase that landed on the counter, and next an oversized pepper grinder that looked like it cost more than it should. That would explain the trash can that was knocked over when I got here, sheesh... Kate thought to herself. The hairs on the back of her neck were starting to stand up and she nearly stepped in, fearing for Chelsea's safety. Kate placed her hand in front of her face to open the closet door as Connor stomped down the front stairs and into the night. Chelsea followed behind him, not bothering to close the door. Kate waited a few minutes and followed after them, before anything else happened in there.

Gianna stood nimbly by the staircase, her burgundy skirt blowing lightly behind her in the breeze. Her elbows rested on the railing and her hands were folded softly in front of her, the lines on her face were relaxed. Her posture struck Kate as out of place for a day when her love had just passed away. With as much noise as would have startled a normal person, Kate tromped down a small hill and came up behind her. Gianna was not startled, however. She barely moved.

"Hey there," Kate started. "How are you feeling?"

"Pretty good," Gianna said, her eyes never leaving the horizon. "I just love watching it get darker and darker. It's so pretty to watch how the evening starts to light things up. She was right, too. The twinkle lights that wrapped around every surface of the party were now in their full majesty reflected on the water. It was definitely a pretty sight, but seemed an odd one to be appreciating at a time like this. Wasn't she sad?

"Gianna, listen. I don't mean to be rude at all…. but why do you seem so relaxed?" Kate assumed it was from the drugs she'd been hearing about all night.

"That is kind of a rude question, considering we just met. But I'm an open book now I guess. A couple of my friends have already been talking about it so word is gonna get out...I do stand to inherit some expensive belongings that are worth quite a bit of money now that Zac is gone." She didn't even flinch when she said it, which creeped Kate out, but then made her sad. How sad that he wasn't missed by his hot mess of a girlfriend. This bit of info, she would definitely be reporting to the police. She should at least be a prime suspect.

Out of the corner of her eye, Kate spotted Lucie, who was waving frantically from the beach for her to come. Kate politely excused herself, and ran down to her sister, who looked very serious about something. "I think Serena is behind this," she said.

Shocked, Kate stepped back. "No way. There's no way. I'm actually pretty disgusted that you are even saying this."

"No, I'm serious. Just listen--"

"Actually I'm not going to do that. I'm going to go report something I learned to the police and then follow up with someone about it." Kate spun on her heels and left her sister standing in the sand, stunned from being ignored.

Chapter 5

The detective was really pleased to hear about the new lead on a suspect, hoping to get things wrapped up sooner rather than later. When he texted back, he reminded Kate to eat something. He said he always reminded his new detectives and officers to eat something after a long day on a case like this, and she wasn't any different. A low grumble of her stomach agreed with his suggestion. Kate headed toward the kitchen to grab something to eat. Alarmingly, she had no qualms about eating something at a crime scene where several people had been poisoned recently. Although she still could seem to find Lachlan, she was fairly certain that the poison was isolated to the cake and the meat tray he'd brought would most likely be fine. A handful of meat and cheese wrapped up in a napkin, and she was ready to go find Gianna.

That proved easier said than done, because the girl seemed to have vanished. Kate looked everywhere; she even considered giving a quick call to Lucie to see if she knew where the girl was but changed her mind. It wasn't like Lucie to suggest something so ridiculous and close to home, and the words were stinging more and more as they sank in. Surely no one on her team was capable of killing another person....surely?

Tossing the napkin into the trash bin outside the restroom door, Kate checked the last ladies bathroom she knew of, way down at the cabana near the hot tub. She was immediately rewarded with an end to her quest, but not the one she was hoping for. Gianna, still in her flowy dress and pretty hair and still with a look of ease on her face, was sprawled out on the floor completely still. Kate dropped to her knees beside her body and checked for a pulse, careful not to move anything. Nothing. Two boys dead and now Gianna.

There was no way, Kate thought, that Gianna would have poisoned herself and therefore couldn't be the killer. The girl was so pleased that she was going to receive some valuables that she literally looked peaceful--at the scene of a murder! There was her suspect to question, dead on the bathroom floor. And what she originally assumed, from the doorway, was maybe an overdose, turned out to be something more grim. There were bits of turquoise and coral icing stuck to Gianna's lips, and small cake crumbs nestled into the folds of her dress and clinging to her hair. Quickly texting the police about another body, she walked briskly out into the open in case whoever poisoned Gianna was still close by.

Just as she was sliding her cell phone back into her slacks, Kate heard a familiar voice behind her. It was Selena. She looked as perfectly put together as the moment she got here, and though there was sure to be an explanation for that that involved laziness and staying in the air conditioning, Kate didn't want to hear it. She turned to walk away without speaking but Selena trotted up closer, effortlessly gaining ground even in her three inch heels.

"Wait up! I have a message from the detective." Selena shouted, though she was close enough not to. "That cute guy in uniform over there just told me that they're shutting the place down for the night. They don't seem too hip on the young people here," Selena adjusted her skirt and threw her hair behind her shoulders like a shampoo commercial. "But he seemed to like me alright," she smiled.

"Yeah I'll bet," Kate muttered. "Okay so what does shutting the place down look like?"

"Okay so everyone that hasn't already been taken to the station, everyone that is left here, has two options. Including us. They can either stay the night in a holding cell, downtown. Or they can hunker down in the beach house for the night with some officers stationed there." Selena looked shyly over her shoulder to see if the officer was still looking in her direction. Newsflash, he was.

"Anyway," she continued. "You and I and Lachlan, wherever he is, are supposed to help inform everyone."

While it was comforting that she didn't know where Lachlan was, either, it was starting to become a bit worrisome that she had seen more of these intolerable teens and young adults than she had seen the people she came with. She was also starting to worry a bit that even if he wasn't involved in a long-running poisoning conspiracy, that maybe he was a victim, himself. Figuring out how all of these murders were connected would put her mind at ease, because that may help her to pinpoint the ultimate goal of the killer, and possibly anticipate who might be the next intended victim.

"Okay, I don't really want to see anyone right now. Not you, not Lachlan. He could be part of all this. Hell, even Lucie could be the killer for all I know. Just go get some sleep and I'll see you in the morning."

The lack of sleep was really starting to mess with her head, so she went against her better judgement and decided not to be irritated with Selena for the rest of the evening and to instead simply try and get a good night's rest. There was no way to operate at her best with sleep pulling at her system, and it was getting so late that even the beauty of the beach was wearing thin. Looking around outdoors, she could tell no one had heard about Gianna yet, which was probably a good thing. Two officers were walking swiftly toward the direction of the cabana restroom, and everyone else seemed to be gathering up their things and heading for the beach house that Connor and Chelsea had rented for the night. What perfect timing. One of the officers looked back toward Kate when he passed, not too far away, and gave her a nod thanking her for her help. She quietly nodded back where Selena couldn't see and instructed her assistant to continue gathering everyone up.

"Do you know where the beach house is?" she asked Selena.

"No, I've been in the office in the back of the kitchen most of the evening."

Well that explained her whereabouts, but there was no telling what she was doing back there. If she asked, Selena would probably either bore her with a story of laziness, or lie if she really had anything to cover up, so there was no use bothering with it before morning. Kate gave simple instructions of where to locate the beach house, and told Selena not to become too distracted with her surroundings, as she knew the glitz and glamour of the place would likely keep her up for hours.

Kate chose to sleep on the couch nestled on the back porch at the beach house, because that was just about the only place that didn't have someone on it. How this comfy-looking couch went unnoticed was beyond her, but she was very thankful for a place to rest that was big enough for a whole person, and also to have the privacy of the back porch to sleep. While it still bothered her endlessly that she hadn't seen Lachlan yet, she tried not to let it keep her from drifting off. After all, she hadn't really looked for him, per say, so they may have just barely missed each other all evening. While she was falling asleep, she chose to imagine that he was at different places at different times and was working just as hard as everyone else to help solve the murders.

Chapter 6

In the morning, Kate awoke in a way that she had never woken before. On the porch of a secluded beach house on Byron Bay, surrounded by more pillows on the outdoor furniture than she'd ever had on a real bed, with the sound of the water in the background. On any other day, for any other occasion, it probably would have been wonderful. As it were, she was a bit sore from sleeping so hard in one position, and her mind was immediately filled with all the details from the day before. But she took a moment to at least breathe before opening her eyes. As soon as she did, her phone made a sound under her pillow. It was the sound that signaled she had just missed a message.

The message was from Alexis. It took her a moment to remember giving her number out to all of the kids on the beach, but it came to her. She didn't really think any of them would use it, though.

This is Alexis. Chelsea is hiding something. Don't tell anyone I sent this to you.

Alexis was Trey's girlfriend, one of the first victims. Kate hadn't gotten a really good feel for her other than she reminded her of a poor version of Gianna. They even looked a bit like sisters. But she did remember that Alexis was only in the group because of her wealthy boyfriend, and Kate wondered if anyone around here was actually friends. Hoping not to here simply a bunch of teenaged back and forth, and maybe get something meaty that she could actually use, she texted Alexis to meet her out on the back porch. A quick trip to the bathroom proved that not many people were up yet, and she imagined the people strewn in every corner of the beach house to be something like what a college drinking party to look like. Everyone looked ragged and like they were in a pretty good sleep from what she could tell. Kate quickly got a glass of water and headed back out onto the porch to wait for Alexis and see what bit of news she had to offer. Luckily, she didn't have to wait very long.

Alexis had somehow managed to change clothes, probably borrowing something of Chelsea's, and looked freshly showered. And just like she imagined, Alexis went right into chatting wildly like a gossipy teen, which hurt Kate's head so early in the morning but she did try to keep up. Apparently Chelsea had an affair with both of the victims, Trey and Zac. Why this girl would be telling her that someone else had slept with her boyfriend she had no idea that seemed strange to her. And Alexis didn't really seem terribly offended, maybe they all slept together like a soap opera. Either way, it was still too early for Kate to try and figure out the how's and why's of being a rich young person. While Alexis painted the picture of Chelsea sleeping around, it fit well with her description of Connor. She described him as a very jealous boyfriend who was easily sent into a rage, something that Kate could verify heartily.

Alexis was obviously trying to create a story here where Connor was the killer, wiping out the two people who had been intimate with his girlfriend. But she was a little too eager in her telling. So much so that she let slip the fact that she stood to inherit a lot of money from Trey's death. She looked downright surprised when she said it out loud and tried to play it off, but it made Kate wonder if she was trying to hide her own guilt.

Kate pretended to blindly accept everything Alexis had to say, partly to log that information away and then make her own discoveries and assessments as only she could, but also because the girl seriously made her head hurt and she wanted to space to think. As soon as Alexis left to go inside, Lucie came walking up around the outside of the porch, angry tears welling up in her eyes. She wasn't in eyesight two seconds before she burst into a fit.

"How dare you?!" she raged.

Taken aback, Kate searched for something she'd done wrong in the last twenty four hours. "What what?? What did I do?"

"I heard everything you said to Selena yesterday, you said that even I could be behind these murders. How DARE you?!"

"Lucie….please. You can't possibly think I was--"

"I'll tell you what I think. I think Selena is your least favorite person on the entire planet and you told

HER of all people that I could be killing people. What kind of sister says that!"

"Calm down, Lucie. I didn't mean that."

Without saying another word, Lucie turned around and stomped off, which made Kate well up with her own tears, and they poured easily down her face and into her mug. They were the hot tears of embarrassment, she had not meant to hurt her sister, but the exhaustion from yesterday was just too much for anyone to make sense of at that point. Surely she would understand that.

Just then, the screen door to the back porch frightened Kate when it slammed shut. There, in all the glory of a man who had spent the night on a camping trip, worn and weathered and probably smelly from the looks of it, was Lachlan.

"I heard...I heard her yelling and came out to see what it was about. Are you alright?"

Kate was dumbfounded. Dumbfounded that he was even standing there, much less trying to console her. "Where in the hell have you been?!" she asked, pulling away from his arm that he tried to wrap around her.

"Working," he said flatly. "Isn't that what you've been doing? Good God woman, I haven't even showered since yesterday, what is the matter with you?"

"The matter with me...if you must know...is that I haven't seen you at all since this started. And now you show up at the most opportune time for you to be chivalrous, I mean come on. Doesn't that seem a little weird to you?"

"Um, no. I does not, in fact. Where have you been, all this time?"

She didn't even answer him. No way was he going to turn this around on her. Kate knew where she had been, and what she'd been doing. And that was all that mattered. At this point, everyone was a suspect. "Leave," she said, extending her arm toward the door. "I don't want to talk to anyone now, I have to call the Constable."

Lachlan may have made a face, he may have even thrown a hand gesture or two in the air, she didn't look in his direction so it didn't matter.

Chapter 7

K ate was so upset she could barely see straight. Part of that was probably due to not having a proper night's sleep, and partly because at this point in her day? She should be waking up to a nice cup of tea in her own house, not stranded in some beach paradise trying to figure catch a murderer. She wiped the angry tears from her eyes and pulled out her phone. Contacting the Constable and getting back to business was going to be the only way to distract her. And the quicker she helped figure this thing out, the quicker she could go home. Probably, she thought, the best thing to do this morning is to go talk to Chelsea. I'd like to find out what her reaction is when I tell her I know about the cheating that's been going on!

With a plan in mind, Kate freshened up in the restroom with what she could only imagine were the deodorants and soaps that were set out for the beach house guests. Either way, she smelled divine all of a sudden. The Constable picked up on the second ring, and immediately asked if she had any news. Kate told him of her plan to speak with Chelsea, operating only on what Alexis had told her this morning. He seemed fine with that, and thanked her for her help.

"It would probably be better for a lady to handle

those kinds of questions, anyway. Our boys seem to be given the runaround with those sorts of conversations," he said before hanging up.

There was always a pep in her step when she was in the groove and helping the police, and luckily for everyone here, she did her best work when she was upset. Set on a new mission to get this figured out by lunchtime, she practically ran down the steps and into the trees toward the beach. Down those same steps that she had just jumped down the night before after hearing that terrible altercation between Chelsea and Connor.

I don't know what kind of messed up relationship that is, but it sounds like it was bound for trouble no matter what.

Connor stomped past her, from the direction of the house and walked toward the beach in an angry plodding fashion. He sort of startled her, and Kate wondered how many people he had snuck up on his lifetime, while also being upset. The guy was downright intimidating. His broad shoulders, while to some might seem attractive, were not so much so when they were all pulled up in anger. And Chelsea wasn't a really big girl, why would she cheat on him so much and poke the bear, so to speak? He could easily hurt her. Connor kept checking his phone while he walked, not paying attention to where he was going because he tripped several times and nearly fell. Kate assumed that he was probably in search of Chelsea. He veered to the right, going up toward the dining hall, as soon as the trees cleared, never looking up from his phone. Luckily, Kate spotted

Chelsea near a pop up tent that was nestled behind the bonfire. She hadn't even noticed it was there before, and Chelsea was sitting on a tiny bench near the canvas flaps, almost out of sight.

Trying not to be noticed, she kept an eye on Connor, who trudged right up the white steps and into the dining hall without missing a beat. Kate broke away from the trees and headed down onto the beach where Chelsea sat with her head in her hands. The last time she tried to just go based off of what someone told her, Gianna ended up really upset that her things were being gone through without permission, so this time Kate thought it would be better to simply ask Chelsea what was bothering her.

Kate tried not to startle her, and cleared her throat loudly before sliding onto the bench next to her. When Chelsea looked up to see who it was, her eyes were wet and one side of her face looked a little red. Almost like she'd been struck.

"What's the matter, hun??" Kate pressed.

"Connor. He's just...he didn't mean anything by it." she answered, looking away. Her pretty blonde hair blew behind her, and Kate wondered how anyone who seemed to have everything they needed could be in such a terrible place and in an unhealthy relationship.

"Didn't mean what, Chelsea. Did he hurt you?"

Chelsea's phone buzzed on the bench next to her. She picked it up to look at it, grunted, and set it back down between them. She looked Kate in the eye and then back at her phone, as if to say See?

"He's really upset that I ran off this morning, he's wanting to know where I am." She looked up toward the dining hall; Kate assumed she knew he was in there. "He can just wander around for a while and cool off for all I care." A tear dripped down one of her cheeks, and it surprised her. "Can you excuse me for a sec? I gotta freshen up, he doesn't like when I cry."

Kate looked down at the bench. She had left her phone. Without a thought, she scrolled once through the list of people Chelsea had texted, and saw Alexis's name as the second contact. It said I didn't think he would find out. Kate clicked on it and glanced back toward the cabana restroom where Chelsea had gone. What she saw was a very long string of romantic messages between Chelsea and Alexis, some that were so intimate they made Kate blush harder than she had in a long time. And that's when she figured it out...Chelsea would flirt with anyone. And everyone, apparently! This poor girl must have been starved for attention, although she didn't know how that was possible with the way her mother gushed about her on the phone to a total stranger over the last six months. When Chelsea emerged from the restroom, Kate exited the text thread and clicked the phone so that it shut off. As she walked across the beach toward Kate, she wondered if this was possibly the killer coming toward her. Chelsea obviously slept with people to gain attention and approval, could she have murdered Trey and Zac because they ultimately didn't want to be with her? The thought gave Kate chills and she scooted over six inches or so to put some space between them as Chelsea sat down.

Chapter 8

In her hands, Kate's phone also buzzed several times while she finished talking to Chelsea, but she knew who it was, so she didn't even look down at it. With a flick of her index finger, she silenced it after Chelsea took notice of it. They finished their conversation, which wasn't too hard to do when talking to Chelsea. All one had to do was go silent for a little while and she got bored and looked for entertainment elsewhere. Once the girl had left, she scrolled through some text messages from the police chief. He wanted desperately to know if she had any new leads, apparently the people in the holding cell were driving him crazy with their ridiculous requests. They kept asking his deputies for insane things like silk pajamas and cashmere blankets. She messaged him quickly that she was on her way back to talk to Connor, but requested that an officer go with her. He promised to have someone waiting at the beach house for her when she got there. On her way up to the house, however, she found Connor and Alexis arguing near where the trees met the beach. He had her backed up against a tree, towering over her and yelling just loud enough at her that no one was alerted.

Alexis looked afraid, and Kate was unsure of what to do. With the two of them standing where they were,

Kate wouldn't be spotted until she made a move either up or down the small hill, and she waited for a sign to move forward. There wasn't really anything around her that could be used to hurl at Connor, or even to distract him. The only weapon-type object she had near her was her cell phone. And that wouldn't do much good being lobbed at someone's head. Especially someone that size, it would likely only anger him more. She froze with her phone in her hand. He didn't look like he was going to hit Alexis at first, so Kate tried to think about the best plan of action. Yelling would only capture his attention for a moment, but if that moment was long enough for Alexis to get away then maybe it would be worth it. But then he did it. Connor pulled his arm back and balled up his fist in an unmistakable manner and Kate screamed before thinking about it.

"Hey!!"

It was louder than it needed to be and Connor jumped a little. When he turned around to see who it was, she didn't recognize his face. She'd barely seen his face at all, because she'd mostly seen him walking away in a huff, but this did not look like the face of the boy cutting the birthday cake yesterday. It looked like the crazed boyfriend that was arguing in the beach house, though, and that boy scared the daylights out of Kate. His eyes were so red that Kate wondered if he was on something. The way his shoulders moved when he turned around frightened her, but she was certain that if she screamed louder that someone from the house would hear her. An officer, even...maybe. Connor left his arm in the air and turned all the way around to face Kate, breathing through his mouth like an animal. She thought it was strange that he just left his arm in the air like that, but it didn't make much of a difference for her being able to move her legs. They wouldn't budge.

Cleverly, she flipped her phone unlocked and pretended to dial a number and then brought the phone up to her face slowly, hoping it looked intentional and convincing. That was a bad idea. It was the straw that broke the camel's back....or however you want to think about it. That one move sent him reeling toward her, his legs moved like a bull, digging into the ground in an unnatural way. Before she could scream, he had a huge hand at her throat. With ease, he picked her up off the ground by her neck, which was only made less painful by the fact that she grabbed his wrist with both hands and held on for dear life. Her legs dangled and Kate really wished she had actually called someone. Or screamed.

Connor opened his mouth to speak, rage filling his eyes. But just when he was clamping down on her throat, preparing to speak, there was a loud bang and his head jolted foreword. Kate clumsily fell to the ground, grasping her neck to feel if anything was broken. Would she even be able to tell if anything was broken?? When she looked up and her eyes settled on focusing properly, she saw her sister standing over the unconscious body of Connor, their largest cake pan in her hand.

"Is he....is he unconscious or dead??" she asked warily, scooting backward on the ground away from him. Quickly, she dialed the Constable's number. She tried to yell for help but it hurt too bad to use her voice that much so she settled for finding comfort in the ringing on the telephone, confident he would pick up soon.

"I don't know, that was our heaviest one. I used the ceramic," Lucie said with a smile. "I've never done that before, that was pretty amazing!"

"Settle down there, boss. You could have killed him."

"Um, yeah?? But he was about to kill YOU! Anyway I think I cracked this pan." Lucie tossed the pan next to her on the ground and kicked Connor's ribs with her foot before stepping over him to pick her sister up off the ground. "Are you okay?? Is there a medic nearby? Can you swallow? Does it hurt?"

Kate just nodded that she was fine and handed the phone to Lucie, waving the phone in front of her so she could see the caller ID, first. Lucie nodded, put the phone to her ear, and told the Constable what had happened while she helped Kate to the house. Two officers were already running down the back steps toward Connor. They took one look at the cake pan and one look at Lucie, who simply shrugged her shoulders and kept talking on the phone. Alexis had run over to the back steps and was crying. Kate turned back as the police were pulling Connor up off of the ground. They were trying to make him explain himself but he was still delirious.

"Are you alright?" Kate asked Alexis, sitting down beside her. Lucie nodded to Kate to make sure she was okay and went inside, still talking to the police on the phone. Alexis gushed. Surprisingly, she broke down and confessed that there was more to it than Chelsea's rough past. She knew about Connor's plot to get rid of anyone who got close to Chelsea, because he was really getting fed up with all the extra attention she was getting. And he knew how to snoop on her phone so he already knew that she was sleeping with them occasionally, and it enraged him.

"Why didn't you tell the police?" Kate had to ask the obvious question, though she knew the answer would probably annoy and disgust her.

"Honestly," Alexis hesitated, then her shoulders slumped forward. "I didn't want to tell them because I wanted Zac's inheritance money."

Kate placed a hand on her back, and within the hour, she was being placed under arrest for aiding a murder.

Chapter 9

"I think," the Constable said, "that you should be
the one to question Connor. I'm making you an
official consultant, so it's all legal and everything. But-
-would you mind?"

Connor wasn't so scary now that he was handcuffed
to a table and prepared for questioning, complete with
an armed officer standing behind him. Kate opted to
stand across the table from him, not because it made
her feel important or threatening, but because she was
so disgusted to be near him. She asked her questions
and tried to charm the answers out of him the best she
could, and between her and the officer standing behind
him, the full story went on record. He admitted to killing Zac and Trey on purpose.

"Nobody needs to be sharing what I have. This isn't
kindergarten." His voice was cold and unfeeling.

"And how about Gianna? What did she have to do
with all of this? Was she sleeping with Chelsea too? Or
did you sleep with her, perhaps…"

Connor laughed. "I wouldn't touch her with a ten
foot pole. Believe it or not," he leaned forward in his
chair. "I only have eyes for Chelsea. It's just that she
gets distracted sometimes when she's bored."

"So then why is Gianna on our victim's list?" she
asked.

"Honestly, I just thought she was Alexis. It was a simple mistake."

Kate's ears and the back of her neck grew hot. "An innocent girl is dead because you made a simple mistake."

Connor threw his head back. "Oh I would go that far, I wouldn't exactly call her innocent. But anyway it was actually an accident." A few moments later he was taken away by the police to be fingerprinted, a distraught Chelsea hot on his heels promising to remain loyal to him. Kate shuddered, hoping that somehow the girl would get some help.

Lachlan slipped in next to Kate in the hallway after questioning. He apologized for not being around where she could see him the day before, and tried to make amends even though it sounded like he didn't quite know what he was apologizing for at times. She nodded her head a lot, signaling that she heard what he was saying, but she wasn't ready to forgive him. Being absent that long was a Selena-type move, and she expected more from him. Lucie and she, of course, moved past their incident quickly, because that's the way they are. The team comes first, and they both knew that.

Kate stopped the police in the hallway as they dragged Connor toward the room with the holding cells.

"I almost forgot to ask," she said to him. "How did you do it? How did you poison the cake??"

But Connor said nothing. He simply smiled as he was dragged away.

Deadly Finale

Chapter 1

The bell on the door of Lachlan's industrial kitchen wouldn't ring if Kate opened it just so...and today she was extra careful not to let it jingle. She stood there and watched for a few minutes as Lachlan swayed back and forth in the kitchen, his headphones drowning out the world. She always used to love watching him work, and his being so handsome and charming always made it easy to be around him during the busy season. Today, though, it wasn't quite as mesmerizing as usual. There was just no getting around the thoughts that had been swarming through her head the last couple of weeks. And if she were honest with herself, all of these thoughts started a couple of months ago with the second murder. Now, after everything she'd been through, it would be foolish of her to think that someone on her team wasn't behind it all. What other explanation could there be? Trouble and murder seemed to follow her everywhere, and that kind of coincidence, well she just couldn't make it right in her head that it was all coincidence. It couldn't be...the universe wasn't that smart.

No, the universe was haphazard and unpredictable. This was more like the work of a serial killer than some random, happenstance murders, and that was a problem. Because even though it seemed to everyone else like the murders were unrelated, Kate Mackenzie knew it was something much more grim. It was likely the work of one or two people, and she resigned herself to finding out who that was. She looked around the kitchen, neat and tidy as it always was while Lachlan was working. He was such a neat freak and she loved that about him. It always seemed to say a little something extra special about him, like he took himself and his work very seriously, and Kate admired that very much. Right now, though, all she could think was that there weren't many people on her team, and that left Lachlan as a prime suspect in a long string of murders. The police would catch on soon enough, and probably try to pin it on someone at her cupcakery or Lachlan's company, so she had no time to waste in figuring it out before they started poking their noses around.

Lachlan was humming something, and Kate recognized the tune. He always hummed along to the same soundtrack when he made one particular dish because it was his favorite thing to make. Malpua, she whispered to herself, certain he wouldn't hear. Now she understood the extra pep in his step. This was a dish his mother always made at Christmastime, and it usually meant he was in a good mood. The smell was divine, and Kate made her way over toward him, careful not to startle him. He jumped anyway as she rounded the large silver workspace.

"It smells amazing," she mouthed, pointing to her nose since he wouldn't be able to hear her. He immediately pulled at his earphones, freeing them from his ears and draping them around his neck.

"You scared me!" he admitted with a grin. That grin. It was a smirk that could melt any girl's knees, and Kate almost always felt lucky enough to be on the other end of it. Today, though, it was bittersweet, because he was still a prime suspect in all of the murders over the last few months and she was there only to get details that would lead to capturing the mastermind behind them. She dipped her first finger into the bowl of fruit glaze in front of her and licked it clean. Of course, it wouldn't hurt to enjoy the sweeter side of life while she did her amateur sleuthing.

"So what do you think will happen this time?" she asked. There was no point in beating around the bush if she was going to figure this out before the police did.

Lachlan didn't even look up from the malpua batter he was pouring out. "What do you mean? These are going to be perfect…" He had that look in his eye that she loved so much, intensely focused on what he was doing, aiming for perfection. And from the way the batter sizzled a little in the pan, she was certain it would result in something fairly close to perfect.

"I mean, something always happens at our events. Something bad. It's like our new thing, just wondering what your take was on it since we haven't ever really just had a chat about it."

"Well," he said, still staring at the pan. "I think that it won't happen again. At least that's what I've been hoping for since the beach party." He sighed heavily; it looked as though he was affected by all this, after all. His shoulders dropped and he looked more vulnerable than Kate had ever seen him.

"Honestly," Kate shrugged. "I've pretty much given up on not having trouble follow us at this point. Now I'm ready to watch for it."

Lachlan turned to her, his eyebrow raised. "Oh yeah?"

Kate nodded, stuck her finger into the bowl of glaze one more time for a taste test, and walked out the door without another word.

Chapter 2

Back at her cupcakery, Kate pulled out an old binder and ripped out all the pages that had writing on them. On the first, new page, she wrote a list of all the events that there had been a murder in the last year. There were so many that she squirmed on her barstool, and pulled her phone from her pocket. In the notes section on her phone, she made a new page for each of the events, and began making as many notes as she could on each one. She originally planned to do it all in the binder, but with the things she had seen while helping the police? That could be easily found, accessed, and used against her. So she decided, instead, to put a lock on her phone and use it for notes. Somehow, she would find out what the connection to all the murders was... there had to be something.

At the top of the first page in her phone, she typed the names of the people she worked with on a regular basis: Lachlan, Selena, and Lucie. Hopefully none of them had anything to do with it, but she wasn't going to leave any stone unturned. She spent about an hour, hunched over her work counter space on the barstool, trying to think of as many details as she could. Eventually her eyes became tired and she switched over to her work email to confirm the details of this weekend's event: A posh wedding for some high-end clientele.

When she got the heebie-jeebies on the phone after speaking with the dad, she looked up the family on the internet and discovered that they might be loosely tied to organized crime. There was no mention of details on any news websites, just that they always seemed to be under watch. Kate had seen enough television to know that in a case like this, it was best to just perform the service that was requested, and then be on your way. In this case, the service was cupcakes shaped like roses on top and malpua for the sweet main course.

When Saturday evening rolled around, Kate decided to go all out. A nice wedding was a good excuse to be a little sassy, so she put on her favorite little black dress and did her hair and makeup with a little extra pizazz. The venue was your typical wedding venue, and all the usual niceties surrounded Kate's team as they unloaded their trucks. The flowers at this event, however, were something to write home about. Someone had handmade and arbor to be placed outside the front door, and the entire thing was covered in wisteria. The purple flowers hanging from it were the prettiest thing Kate had ever seen, and she made a point to go out the front door instead of the servant's entrance whenever she could.

"Selena!" Kate shouted, since the first two times her name was called didn't seem to register. Selena was leaned against the far wall talking to someone. From the immediate looks of things, Kate wasn't impressed, and thought her assistant could certainly do better at this event. Still shorter than Kate even in heels, Selena skulked over toward her, begrudgingly.

"Yes, master?"

"Still not funny. Who was that you were talking to?" Kate asked.

"Isn't he cute?! He has the most divine name. Julius Diamond." She let it roll off of her tongue like butter, quite enamored with herself.

"No, he looks gross. Now can you please get the rest of the cake stands out of the truck? I had to grab all the extras we had, so some of them might be dusty. Make sure they're all wiped off before you set them on the main table, please."

Selena didn't technically roll her eyes, but Kate could tell she meant it. It didn't matter; every sour look was going to be jotted down in her phone's notes section for later. Kate checked her hair in one of the mirrored pillars in the dining hall and went to find the Matron of Honor. She'd never met the mother of the bride before, who was no doubt footing the bill for all of this, but Lola Kumar had come in with the bride-to-be months ago to place the cupcake order. Kate was pretty sure she would recognize her, and Lola would most likely be somewhere near the bride right about now.

It didn't take long for her to find all the girls in the wedding party laughing and carrying on in the room behind the stage. It was a small room, almost too small to hold them all, and they were boisterous enough to fill an auditorium. The sound of them laughing and half-singing on their friend's wedding day was music to Kate's ears. She, too, hoped to hear that someday. Pushing the door open just enough to get her head in, Kate waved to Lola, who was already dressed and ready to go.

Tall and confident, Kate immediately took to Lola.

She was beautiful in an in-your-face type of way, but didn't make a big deal out of it. The type of person that didn't need even the slightest bit of makeup. The day she came into the shop to place the wedding order, Lola had introduced herself as the groom's best friend. Every story was "Blake this…" and "Blake that…." and "When Blake was younger he really loved….." Kate wondered why Blake hadn't chosen Lola to marry, and imagined some magical creature as the bride, someone even stronger and more beautiful than Lola. Kate peered over at the bride before they left the dressing area, and she wasn't immediately enamored with her. Small in frame, the bride looked positively frail next to everyone in the room. Kate shrugged, because sometimes the quietest and most non-intrusive people can be the loveliest, and also because it was none of her business.

As the pair walked back toward the dining hall, both of their shoes clacking on the hard, marble floor like a couple of girls at the prom, they passed the groom. Lola's eyes lit up, and Blake looked happy to see her as well, though maybe not quite in the same way. Lola grabbed him by the arm and spun him toward Kate.

"This is him! The lovely groom." Lola's face was lit up like a child at Christmas, though if she weren't mistaken there was some pain behind those eyes.

"Ah I see you've met my best mate in the world," Blake crooned. There was a definite love in his voice. "Lola is the best person you'll ever meet, and also the most helpful?" he said with one eyebrow raised. He then looked down toward his chest and back up at her with a grin. Lola threw her head back in flirtatious laughter and re-folded his pocket square before tucking it expertly into his jacket pocket. It looked almost the same to Kate, but she was no expert. Blake kissed her hand and jogged off down the hall.

Lola rolled her eyes. "I'm sure Ruma knows how to do it, too. And if not, then I'll have to teach her. Because if you're going to marry in to that family, you'd best know how to dress properly!"

"Ruma?" Kate asked.

"The bride, oh my goodness I didn't realize I hadn't mentioned her name. She's quite lovely."

"Yes, when you placed the order you put everything under Blake's name, and I honestly hadn't even thought to ask!" she laughed. "No matter, I'll remember it for tonight and then I'm off to learn someone else's name next weekend." The two girls giggled and locked arms for the rest of the trip to the dining hall. It was nice to have someone so easy to talk to about absolutely nothing. Well, someone besides Lucie, no one could ever take her sister's place. But Kate made a vow to try and make at least one more female friend this year, and to really spend time fostering that relationship. Maybe she should start with someone she already knew, but that thought wasn't in her head very long before she chuckled to herself. Maybe I should start with Selena! The thought tickled her, and then made her cringe a little.

Chapter 3

Lola showed Kate to the guesthouse behind the venue, which was where the bride and groom would spend their first night as a married couple before leaving for their honeymoon the next day. That was really smart, Kate thought. This particular wedding ceremony was being held rather late in the evening, and to leave right away for a honeymoon would mean a drive and a flight in the middle of the night. These people had enough money; their honeymoon would almost definitely include a really long flight somewhere. It was in this guesthouse out back, really more of glorified barn by the looks of it, is where Kate set up a small serving next to the bed for the new couple. There would be an assortment of cupcakes on their nicest silver serving piece, a beautiful stand with an ornate domed lid that held only four cupcakes. These were a special gift from Lola to her best friend and his new wife, and Kate thought the idea was lovely. Though she couldn't help but think, while placing the doilies carefully on the tray, that these cupcakes very well might spell disaster for one of the couple later in the night. The thought made the hairs on the back of her neck stand up.

At the ceremony only an hour later, the bride emerged in the most intricate dress Kate had ever seen, and every moment after that was just as beautiful as the thing before it. Even the guests were beautiful. They all smelled of money, all the women had expensive-looking jewelry, and everyone had their eyes glued to the bride.

Everyone except for Lola.

The poor girl looked like she might cry through the whole thing. Later in the evening, she penned a beautiful speech, mostly directed toward the groom, naturally. And it had everyone in tears. The whole evening, though, Blake never took his eyes off of his bride. Even when Lola snuck in a dance with him, he spent most of the dance scanning the room for his new bride. When they caught each other's eye, they would do some sort of private wink that seemed very romantic to Kate. Once dinner was brought out, Kate was famished. The entire few months leading up to the wedding she had been looking forward to Lachlan's malpua stealing the show at this wedding, and it did just that. The presentation was one of his best, and every plate looked like a magazine spread.

Lola clinked her glass with a spoon and cleared her throat. "Before we eat this…….amazing malpua, my goodness this is a pretty one…..I'd like to make one more toast to the happy couple. May you really," she swallowed hard as though it hurt her to say. "Really be happy forever."

There was a steady round of Here here! And a melody of clinking glasses around the room as everyone threw back more champagne. The bride grinned from ear to ear and kissed her new husband before cutting into her malpua. Not two minutes later, she pulled at her throat and slumped over onto the table, and Kate's heart felt like it dropped into the bottom of her stomach. Not. Again.

There was a flurry of commotion unlike any of the other murders. Obscenities were thrown around, people were being shoved out of the way, and Blake would not leave his Ruma's side no matter how much the police pulled at him. He was sobbing and not hearing anything around him, even though his father was yelling something at the back of his head and shaking his fist. Kate looked everywhere for her team so that she could document their first reactions to the tragedy and study them. She saw the Chief of police come through the front door not thirty minutes after the bride had died, and he gave her a side glance that seemed to say they had something to discuss later. And it didn't look like something Kate was going to want to discuss, so she took this as her cue to hurry and catch the murderer. On the other side of the room, Selena was slinking off with the man she'd been talking to earlier….Julius something….and Kate set her mind on finding Lachlan, first. Selena would no doubt be making unladylike decisions off in the bathroom somewhere while everything was going on, so Kate would deal with her later. Lachlan, however, is the one whose main dish had just been poisoned, and she wanted to see his face.

When she found him, he was talking to an officer in the kitchen in a very animated manner. He was clearly upset that the officer was being so candid about the notes being jotted down, and Lachlan was trying to explain every minute detail of how he made the dish and who could have possibly come in contact with it.

"It's not like this is a major make-ahead meal?!" he was screaming. "I literally just whip it up on the spot and it's served minutes later. There's not a lot of time for antics?! I think you should be looking OUT THERE for whoever did this!" He was pointing aggressively and the officer simply nodded at him and left the room.

"You were right, Kates!" He'd seen her come in and turned his voice toward her. "This follows us wherever we go! I tried my hardest not to play into all your notions, but you're right."

Kate just watched him talk. She'd known this man for years, admired him almost the entire time, and now she was watching his face to see if he was lying. His neck was red and there were veins popping out of it. From the looks of it, her amateur sleuthing would tell her that he was genuinely upset. Her woman's intuition also leaned toward him telling the truth, but it was too early to tell and she had a lot of work to do. Kate flipped her phone screen open and furiously typed in Lachlan's initial reaction. He looked perplexed and she waved her hand flippantly at him to say Don't worry about it.

"We'll figure it out," she said matter-of-factly. "Ready to get to work?"

"Yes ma'am," he said, a stern look in his eye. "What do you want me to do?"

"Go find Serena and bring her to me. She's off with some guy."

"Naturally," Lachlan rolled his eyes. "You know, I used to think she had a crush on me, and then I realized she has a crush on herself. I'll go find her."

Chapter 4

Selena showed up about the time Kate had given up on finding her.

"Lachlan said you were looking for me?" She seemed out of breath, which Kate had never seen.

"Yeah, absolutely. I wanted to know if you'd be willing to help the police again for me?"

Selena sighed. "I'm sorry," Kate stated. "Was there something more pressing you had to do?"

"Well I just don't understand why we have to keep butting in on police business." She twirled her hair in her fingertips. "I'm not getting paid any more than any of these guests are??" She motioned toward the noisy crowd. "So why can't I just go relax somewhere and wait for it to blow over?"

Well I made a mental note of your nonchalance, Selena…

"For your information, the police are starting to think that one of us is in on these murders, so it's in your best interest to help us catch whoever is behind this." Kate took several steps forward toward her assistant until she was standing directly in front of her. "Also, you were paid to be here tonight, anyway, and they are not. It won't hurt you to put in a little overtime at a place where you are a suspect for murder."

Selena's eyes widened. "Okay, well, the officer over there...the cute one...said that everyone is to stay in the guest barn tonight since it's so late. And that they're sending fresh recruits in the morning, but leaving two officers for guard duty overnight."

Without a word, Kate walked off. Stopping at the doorway, she turned back toward Selena and gave her instructions that would take at least an hour to keep her busy. "Offer every single person in here, guest and officer, if they would like something to drink. Then come find me." It went on for another two hours like that, Kate giving Selena odd jobs that would not only assist her but also just keep her busy. And each time she was given an instruction, Kate would make a note of Selena's response. A couple of times, she found her talking to that Julius fellow, but it looked like he was busy with his own thing so he was barely entertained by her. From speaking to different guests, Kate found out that Julius Diamond was one of the right hand men of Blake's father in the crime scene. He was very effective at what he did, whatever that was, Kate hadn't discovered that bit yet.

Everyone retired to the beach house at about two in the morning, and for once Kate slept like a baby. It seemed being determined helped her rest better! In the morning, she found Blake for questioning, and the poor guy looked ragged. They sat on the stage in the main hall and let their legs dangle over the side while they spoke. He was a lovely man, she discovered after half an hour in his presence. When he spoke, there was always kindness in his voice.

"You seem really clever," he said at one point. "Very smart...you're going to solve this." And then his voice began to tremble. "You know my father never liked her, right?"

Kate's curiosity piqued, and she shook her head silently.

"Well, it's not that he thought she was bad, he just never saw her as good enough. For me...for our family." He trailed off and his big brown eyes wandered. Kate put her hand on his back and patted him softly, thanking him for his help.

"I promise I'll figure it out," she said, standing. "I always do."

Blake's head fell into his hands and Kate left him sitting there on the stage. Lola and some commanding young gentleman were deep in conversation at one of the small side tables, both leaned in toward the middle of the table. Lola looked as though she'd been crying all night, and she seemed to be pleading with him about something. As Kate neared them, she could see the man's face come into view. He was very handsome, but his face was scrunched up in anger and he was yelling at her under his breath. When they saw her coming, Lola used the hem of her long dress to dry her eyes and turned to Kate with her best smile.

"Hi, Kate. This is Nazim." The young man cleared his throat and extended his hand, though he didn't bother to smile.

Kate shook the gentleman's hand and folded her arms across her chest before squatting down next to Lola. "Are you okay?" she asked.

Nazim scoffed and rose from his seat. "Excuse me," he said gruffly.

"No, no." Lola rose from her seat forcefully, her voice quivering. "I'm actually just going."

Nazim glared at her and breathed heavily through his nose. "You have some nerve!" His fist began balling up at his side and the veins in his forearm began to show. He let out a quick, hard breath that sounded too primal for Kate's comfort, and stormed off without another word. The tears welled up in Lola's eyes and without so much as a glance toward Kate, she swallowed hard and stomped off, as well, but threw something into the garbage bin on her way toward the exit. Kate saw her wiping furiously at her eyes as she walked and wished she knew what to say to make it better.

When the coast was clear, Kate ran to the trash bin to see what she'd tossed away, and she discovered that it was a handful of crumpled up photos. And they were pictures of something she'd almost expected to find. In her hands were five pictures of Lola and Blake together. With a somber heart, Kate added both Lola and Nazim to the suspect list. Lola may have killed Ruma to have Blake for her own, while Nazim may have killed her to get revenge on Blake for something. He seemed pretty upset about something, and she was determined to find out why he hated the groom so much.

Chapter 5

Kate shoved the pictures into her bra and went to find Blake's father, the man who was yelling at him at the scene of the crime. Who does that?! Kate thought. But she remembered reading that people sometimes have very strange responses to trauma, so she would hold her judgement for a while. It wasn't long before she heard him.

A tall, dark-haired man in his fifties with a strong jaw and a weathered face leaned on the bar. He looked like Cary Grant. Even though no one had been allowed to leave last night, he was somehow standing there in a clean, pressed suit. The white of his shirt that was showing was bright and stiff and it looked as though his cufflinks had been recently polished. She didn't even normally notice things like this, but the man looked like he was straight out of a movie. Intimidating was the only word she could grasp for me. He hadn't notice her yet, but seemed to be scanning the room for someone. The hostess walked up behind him, got his attention very quietly, and seated him for the brunch service. Blake was nowhere to be see, so Kate thought this was a good time to question his father, but before she can introduce herself Blake's father was interrupted by none other than Nazim. The two immediately began arguing about something, and though they weren't quiet about it, no one looked at them. The family's right hand man, Julius Diamond popped up out of nowhere and swooped in behind Blake's father to escort Nazim away from the table. On his way out, with one of Nazim's arms behind his back, Julius's wallet slipped out of his hand and fell onto the floor. He must have been holding it right before he swooped in to save brunch service.

Kate walked briskly behind one of the morning waitresses and leaned down to snatch up the wallet, tucking it under her arm and out of sight. A few quick turns down the hallway and she was successfully holed up in the venue's office. Surely they wouldn't mind her using one of the computers, after all, she was still helping out with official police business! With not much more knowledge than she had garnered from television police shows, she worked her way around the internet in search of information on Julius Diamond, which proved pretty successful with the goodies she found in his wallet. Kate came across a lot of articles, mostly about organized crime and his connections with the Wendell family. Apparently Blake's father's name was Eddie, short for Edison, a bit of information that she planned to use later.

There were even two articles from obscure blogs about how Eddie Wendell was a very prejudice man who did not approve of Ruma and Blake's marriage. The second article seemed to be a lot of hearsay, but strongly suggested that Mr. Wendell didn't think Ruma was good enough for their family, and especially not for his son. Careful not to be gone too long with a dangerous man's missing wallet, Kate cleared everything off of the computer that she could and slipped back into the dining hall to return it and find something to eat. She dropped it somewhere that wasn't really near where Julius dropped it, but it was near enough to a corner and a large plant that hopefully no one would see her place it on the floor. After a quick couple of steps toward the hostess stand and she spotted Lucie at a table, unfolding a menu.

"Ah, I'm with her," Kate whispered to the hostess when she returned to her post. And she trotted over to her sister without waiting for the girl to escort her. "What did you order me?"

"GOODness! You startled me. Oh my gosh, sit down I have something to tell you!" Lucie unfolded the menu in front of them and waved the waitress away when she came over. The girl looked confused, but did as was hastily requested.

"Wow, Lucie....you know we look pretty suspicious back here--"

"Oh shush. Now listen, I know you don't like when I say this, but I REALLY want you to listen to me this time. Selena is behind all this somehow, and before you make that face, hear what I have to say. Consider the fact that she and Lachlan are the only ones who seem to always be in the kitchen. I know you probably think she's too dumb and vain to do anything terrible, but if you think about it as long and hard as I have, you may just start to make a couple of connections on your own that I'm not even seeing."

Kate sighed. "I actually have been thinking about it, yes." Lucie looked surprised but pleased. "At this point I'm not ruling anyone out. Except you and me, stop looking at me like that. I'm sorry I hurt your feelings last time, love you more than anything and you know that."

"You've been under a lot of pressure lately, and I respect that you didn't want to believe someone you knew was capable of being bad. But thanks for at least considering it." Lucie said.

"Yeah, I've been making a lot of notes." Kate looked around, and noticed that Eddie Wendell had caught her eyes with his for a brief moment. "I would show you the notes but I don't think now is the time or place to do it."

"Just show me, I'll read them quickly."

But Kate refused; she didn't want to explain what she'd learned about the Wendell family with its head member sitting a few tables away trying to enjoy brunch. And there was no telling where Julius Diamond was, either.

"Fine, I'll go figure it out myself. I'm gonna find Selena and drag her out here by her hair." Kate pushed her chair back so hard it nearly fell over.

"No, PLEASE." Kate pulled at Lucie's arm gently, but desperately. She didn't want any attention being drawn to them, and her sister was certainly drawing attention. Lucie didn't listen, however, and stormed off without ordering any food. The urge to look toward Eddie Wendell was enormous, but instead Kate unfolded the menu and pretended to decide what to order for brunch. From behind the folded paper, Kate spotted Julius walking through the hallway, seemingly consoling Lola about something. It was far too risky to get up now, and risk setting off the suspicions of Eddie Wendell, so she simply ordered an omelet and ate it as quickly as she could, scrolling through her phone to look busy, and never once looked up.

Chapter 6

With no real leads, Kate decided to start back at the beginning, with Blake. This made sense partly because all of his kind words boosted her confidence in finding his bride's killer. And partly because she wasn't sure where else to turn. Luckily, Blake was exiting the men's restroom and she waved him down.

"Oh good, I have something to show you," he said, handing Kate his cell phone.

"Oh my goodness, Blake, have you shown these to anyone else??" Kate scrolled through the string of texts from Nazim to himself. Every one of them was threatening in nature. And not in a sly sort of way, they were very explicitly threatening.

"I haven't shown a soul. Wondered what you would think, should I show them to the police?" She thought it was really nice that he wanted her honest opinion before proceeding, it made her feel needed and validated, yet she really wasn't sure what to tell him. After all, Kate still wasn't convinced that Nazim was the killer.

"Honestly, I would. But give me like an hour, first. Is that alright?"

Blake's face was serious, and he nodded once in agreement. Kate left his side with her mind reeling about Nazim, wondering what kind of person he really was. Maybe she could look up information online about him, too? It probably wouldn't hurt...

Selena rounded the corner a little too quickly and bumped into Kate's shoulder.

"Oh, hey boss." Kate always hated when Selena said boss like that. "I heard there was something weird going on in Lucie's room, you might wanna go check that out." Selena winked at her and walked off. The nerve of that girl! Who winks at a murder scene? It just seemed absurd.

Either way, Kate went up to the room Lucie had gotten at the hotel the night before. There weren't many rooms to be had, but Lucie had the foresight to reserve one just in case. Now that she thought about it, that seemed like an oddly perceptive thing to do. When Kate arrived at the room, the door was almost closed....but not quiet. She was able to push it open easily. Nothing looked immediately out of place as Kate went around the room. On the second queen-sized bed, though, there was a small vial with some liquid in it that was tucked up underneath the pillow. It was wedged in there to where it was almost unnoticeable. Kate really wanted to open the vial, but if the contents of it were at all poison, even smelling it could make her very ill, so she didn't.

There was no way Lucie could be responsible for a murder, but especially not one related to a family who was involved in organized crime. Lucie was a lot of things, but incredibly stupid wasn't on that list. So not only would she not get involved with anything surrounding this family, but she also would not be careless enough to leave a bottle of poison lying around in an open hotel room that her name was attached to. That was too many obvious mistakes for someone as smart as her sister to make. No, the connection to the vial had to be solely with Selena. And Kate's mind swirled with new possibilities for solving the case.

Downstairs, the vial safely inside her palm and also delicately inside her dress pocket, Kate overheard some police officers at the bottom of the stairs. They were talking about how the Sugar 'N Spice Cupcakery may have connections to this murder that needed looking into. And one of the officers suggested that it may be part of a bigger string of murders. He admitted that he wasn't the one who made that connection, but rather it was something he'd overheard at the office this morning. No matter, Kate wasn't going to get tripped up by a couple of officers when she was so close to putting all the pieces together herself!

Boldly, Kate marched into the dining room and sat down at Eddie's table. He was just about done with a cup of coffee and was likely nearing the end of his meal, but Kate pulled up the chair anyway and introduced herself. She made it sound as if she was just another tired wedding patron who'd been stuck there overnight. Pretending not to know who he was proved harder than she thought, because every time he looked at her without speaking, she became slightly nervous. Hopefully it didn't show.

"So I saw you arguing with your son up there during the toasts, me and my dad used to fight like that about everything. Silly, right??" Kate laughed and picked up one of the untouched pieces of fruit from the fruit bowl and popped it into her mouth. "These strawberries are amazing, I can't believe you didn't eat any…"

Eddie never moved a muscle the entire time she

was speaking. He sat stoically across from her, and it looked as though he was trying to get a read on her. A couple of times, he would glance behind her, and Kate assumed he was looking for Julius to escort her out of the room. When he found no one, he spoke.

"My son knows I do not care for his choice of bride." He paused, but didn't move. "And as children do, sometimes, he did not take his father's advice and choose a more appropriate match. That's neither here nor there, if you're getting at what I think you're getting at. The fact of the matter is, I love my son and respect his wishes to marry whoever he chooses."

"But you would have chosen differently," Kate said plainly, studying another strawberry instead of his face.

"That is correct. But again, irrelevant."

There was a loud commotion in the foyer, and Kate turned around to see what it was. There went Lucie, being escorted out of the room by two police officers, with her hands behind her back. Her sister was being arrested!

"I'm sorry I--I have to go. Please excuse me." And with that, she left Eddie Wendell sitting there.

Lucie was fighting the officer's hands but he wouldn't let her arms budge as they walked.

"What is going on here!?" Kate demanded. But when the officer started to speak, Lucie interrupted them.

"No no, I'll tell her! Selena had me accused of having something to do with not this murder....but all the murders. All of them! And without even letting me speak they're arresting me. Isn't that funny! HA!" She fake-laughed very loudly in one officer's face and he was not amused with her sass.

"You, sirs, may NOT arrest my sister. I need her to help me solve this case!"

The officer who was walking next to them stopped mid-stride and chuckled. "You're going to have to solve it without this one suspect, so have fun with that." And he turned to follow Lucie and his coworker out the front door. Kate followed them and screamed many more things at them, but was not-so-politely asked to leave the premises after making too many ridiculous demands. Shocked, Kate does just that. No one else was going to get permission to leave this place before the murder was solved, so she relished the opportunity to do so. Not twenty minutes later, she was in her own home. Here, she could think. And shower.

After both of those things, and with no word yet from Lucie, Kate went to the bakery to do the one thing that always seemed to ease her mind: whip up some cupcakes. Maybe she could whip up a batch, do some deep thinking about how Selena was connected to all the different murderers in the past, and then use the cupcakes to win over the hearts of the officers that were currently putting her sister in a jail cell for no reason.

Upon arriving, however, Kate finds Selena in her industrial kitchen with Lachlan. She stood back at the doorway, just as she had done with Lachlan in his own work kitchen, and watched them talk. Lachlan was angrily accusing Selena of being an insider to all of the awful events they'd attended. Selena, on the other hand, was trying to seduce him. Of all the things Selena was horrible at, having the audacity and capacity to try and seduce someone while she was being yelled at and accused of a crime was really just stunning. Lachlan was having none of it, much to Selena's disappointment as usual, and he managed to back away from her so convincingly that she actually didn't follow him.... which surprised Kate. Selena leaned over and put her elbows on the countertop and typed something furiously on her cell phone. Kate took that opportunity to slip out without being noticed and go back to her house. The cupcakes could wait.

Chapter 7

The next day, Kate was awoken by a knock on her door. It was Lachlan, and he look stressed beyond belief. It was obvious that all of this was finally starting to get to him; Kate had never seen him look older than he did at her front door. After getting them both situated with some tea, she listened as Lachlan explained that Selena was accusing him of attacking her. He'd already dealt with the police that morning, and he made it sound like it was no small feat to convince them she was lying. He'd spent an hour being questioned at the police station.

"And I drove straight here. I--I'm sorry. I didn't know where else to go," he said sadly.

"That makes totally sense, actually. You'd want to come straight to a non-crazy person who doesn't think you're a murderer." Kate smiled when Lachlan offered a half chuckle.

"I'm not really sure what to do, and I need help. Will you help me?" He was so sincere, and so beaten down by everything that he was suddenly starting to realize, that Kate actually felt a bit sorry for him. The weight of it all had finally gotten to her yesterday, and it felt just as heavy to her then as it looked on Lachlan's face now.

"Okay, well the best thing to do is just get into it. Let's start with what we know, work our way through it, and hope to figure everything out before we are both arrested. Sound like a plan?" The hopefulness in her voice seemed to lift his spirits and he got up to refill his tea. "What we know, most recently, is that everyone was released from custody at the event hall yesterday. They were told to all go home, and that no one was allowed to leave the city until further notice. So for now, everything is being done remotely. This means that we don't know where Blake or his father are, we don't really even know where Selena is."

"I know where she was last night," Lachlan scoffed under his breath as he was sitting down.

"Yeah, I'm not gonna lie, I saw you two." Kate admitted.

His eyes shot up and met hers. "I promise you, she is crazy and I didn't have anything to do with her. Promise."

"Calm down there, Casanova. I saw that part, too." Kate smiled. "Not that I have any real claim over you, I just--it was nice to see her get turned down."

Lachlan smiled at her earnestly. "She will always be turned down by me. I only have eyes for one girl and she's a pretty amazing amateur sleuth. Hard to top that."

The moment lingered there in the air for a few seconds as each one took the time to appreciate all that wasn't being said. After a few moments, Kate got up to switch on the small kitchen television while they worked things out. Maybe the news had caught on by now and would be reporting something.

"And in breaking news, two murders at a local wedding last night." The reporter's calming voice took a moment to sink in.

"Did she say two murders?" Kate asked Lachlan. He nodded, glued to the tv.

"One Ruma Wendell, recently married to Blake Wendell of the famous Wendell family. And one Nazim Kumar, cousin of the groom. The surviving spouses of the victims, Mr. Blake Wendell and Mrs. Lola Kumar, are not available for comments but are expected to give us an official word from both families later in the day. Both families are very prominent in our community and we are saddened deeply by their loss. We here at Channel Four offer our condolences to their loved ones."

"Nazim is Lola's husband!" Kate shouted, slamming her cup onto the table.

"Looks that way..." Lachlan answered. "What now?"

"Don't know...Blake and Lola are unavailable for questioning, so you know what that means."

"We go find them and question them?" Lachlan asked, already getting up from the table.

"Yes sir, we do."

Chapter 8

W hen Kate and Lachlan arrived at the hotel, staff informed them that although everyone had officially been released back into the community, several members of each family were still in the facility. The hotel had graciously offered many rooms to accommodate the heartbroken family and friends. Kate snuck around until she found Lola, who was grief-stricken. She had new clothes on, which should make anyone of that stature feel more put together, but Lola looked as though she had stayed out all night, instead. Her hair was a mess and her clothes were shifted in a way that made her appear very haphazard.

"I'm heartbroken, Kate. Heartbroken."

"I heard on the news that you all are somehow related...you and Ruma. Is that true?" Kate asked.

Lola nodded. "Nazim is Ruma's cousin."

This fact reminded Kate of something she'd seen in her internet research the day before, and she whipped out her smartphone to look it up. Her fingers flew over the keys and her intense focus must have piqued Lola's curiosity because her sobbing stopped and she leaned over the shoulder of her new friend.

"Right here, look." She turned up the brightness on her phone and zoomed in so they could easily read it together. "It's an old article I ran across yesterday about

Julius that mentioned…..yes right here. It says that one of his family members was killed in a feud with Nazim."

"I remember that," Lola admitted. "But I never know in this family what is the actual truth and what is being given to help the family members grieve. So I still don't even really know what happened."

"That's not an issue; I'll figure it out for you." Kate got up, determined to find out the full story for Lola, and to save at least part of the Sugar 'N Spice crew from going to jail. "I intend to talk to Eddie about it."

Lola started to object but Kate was already out the door.

Kate looked everywhere for Eddie before giving up. She walked out the back entrance, the service entrance of the kitchen, which led out into a small alley that was used for large trash bins and some odds and ends storage. She heard it before she even opened the door all the way. Two men, at least, were fighting. Hopefully she hadn't been seen, but she braced for impact just in case. The door closed most of the way, hiding her inside, but she left it cracked enough to hear them. When they shuffled in just the right way, she could see them both, and it was Eddie that was getting in most of the hits.

"Boss, wait!" Julius grunted. It was pretty obvious that Julius was letting his boss have the upper hand in the fight, and his body language and voice seemed to suggest that he was trying to be respectful while his boss beat some sense into him. "I didn't--"

"Yes you did, boy! And you had no right!" Eddie must have had plenty of practice recently, possibly because his life was more risky than most folks, because he was quick on his feet and the punches he threw were fast and accurate. "You killed her. And you ruined Blake's life."

"But you didn't approve of her!" Julius ducked one fist but let the other one land hard on his shoulder which nearly knocked him to the ground.

"Yes but on what planet would I ever want her killed at my own son's wedding? Now I have to deal with the heartbreak, which will take much longer to mend than if you'd accidentally done her in six months down the road. What is wrong with you?? People will be talking about this for years! And to top it off, he'll think I had something to do with it!" Eddie landed a fist on Julius's jaw, which caught him by surprise because he was just about to speak. "Of course, you're going to be doing plenty of talking until then, reminding him every day that this was all your doing." Eddie said the last sentence in a growl.

"Boss, please." Eddie stood up straight to take a break while Julius spoke. He spoke too quietly for Kate to hear, at first, so she used that moment to text the Chief of Police. She watched as Eddie spit to the side several times while he listened to Julius. Only moments later, there was shuffling behind her and three policemen pushed her out of the way and burst into the alley. Julius started to run, but Eddie caught him by the shirt and threw him toward the men, who dragged him away. Moments later two more men showed up and dragged Eddie off, as well. Kate hid behind the door as they were dragged away, that way they wouldn't see who called in the fight, but she was more frustrated than anything because that ruined her chances of being able to speak with Eddie and get the answers she needed.

She needed help. She needed Lucie out of jail.

Chapter 9

Lachlan surfaced about the time Kate was trying to call him. Together, they devised a plan for Lachlan to squeeze the truth out of Selena. He was less than enthused about it, but still on board because it would produce the fastest results. They were both pretty certain that if he tricked Selena into thinking he was falling for her charms, and then was rejected, that she may spill a few beans in anger. At least, that was the plan.

"Don't worry," Kate assured him before they spilt. "I have no doubts that you'll be able to win her over. She is quite taken with you, and quite ridiculous."

"Yes, let's hope so. But…" He leaned in toward Kate and put his hand behind her neck, pulling her to his lips. He brushed them with his, but didn't kiss her. "Let's hope she talks before she accidentally kisses me." Kate's head was swirling. "Because that would make me puke."

Kate laughed almost directly into his mouth and put her hand on his waist. "Yes, let's hope for that."

Kate was smart enough this time to find a good hiding spot, and also pull up the video camera on her phone. Just in case Selena confessed to everything, a video of it would make quick work of everything! She quickly changed her mind and video called the police chief, turning the volume on her cell phone all the way down so no one would hear or suspect anything. If they get the information they need, she thought, then they can drive over and arrest her on the spot!

Lachlan winked at Kate and strolled into the venue. Selena flashed him a dazzling smile from the far end of the bar, twirling a lock of her dark, thick hair around her finger flirtatiously. He leaned casually against the wall a few feet away. Kate watched uncomfortably as he looked Selena up and down, grinning.

"You look great," he said, doing his best to sound convincing. She batted her thick eyelashes and giggled.

"I know," she stated simply. Seeming slightly bemused at her quick response, he chuckled slightly and took a step closer, resting his elbow on the bar next to her. He locked eyes with her, trying with great difficulty to not pull away, and sighed.

"It's such a shame, Ruma and Nazim. I just wonder what could have happened to them," he pried.

Selena bit her lip, her dark eyes twinkling mischievously. "Can you keep a secret?" she asked quietly, gracefully placing her hands on the countertop.

"Anything for you, Selena," he crooned, brushing his fingers against hers. She stared at his hand for a few moments, then gazed deeply into his eyes again and leaned a bit closer. He could feel her breath on his lips as she said,

"Poison."

Kate drew a quick, deep breath, glancing at her phone to make sure the chief heard. He nodded and slipped into his car, driving towards the suspect's location.

Lachlan's eyes widened as he let out an almost silent, "No."

"Oh yes," Selena countered, her thick lips stretching over her perfect white teeth in a malicious grin. "I helped Julius poison Ruma and Nazim."

Lachlan tried not to look mortified, but he realized that standing right in front of him was a heartless killer. She could even have poison on her lips at this moment, waiting to kiss him and do him in. He made a mental note to not let her get any closer.

"Hey, that's pretty clever," he lied. "But why, may I ask? I mean, you're really talented, everyone knows that…"

Kate held back a chuckle from where she was standing.

"I am, indeed. I'm so glad you noticed." She placed her hips closer to his deliberately, but luckily for Lachlan, he was appalled by her and his countenance didn't waiver. He did, however, pretend to let it fluster him.

"So if you're so incredibly talented, and clever," he nearly choked on the words. "Then why get into all this poisoning business? I mean, it seems kind of risky."

"Risk is sexy, Lachlan. I thought that's why you liked me."

"It-it is. I just wondered why you would take such a chance for one incident. Like…why? What's in it for you? Do you know this Julius guy or something?" He tried to continue seeming interested, but it was really hard to not ask too many questions at once and tip her off.

Selena shifted her weight, uncomfortably, and for a moment Kate was afraid he'd shown his hand. In only a moment though, Selena smiled slyly.

"You know? I really don't want to tell you. A girl's got to have some secrets."

It's now or never, Lachlan, Kate thought. The police will be here soon and you need to get as many details as you can out of her. She nearly gasped out loud when she saw him lean in as though he was about to kiss her on the lips. She hadn't considered that he might go that far to find out the truth, and it hurt a little because she would never resort to that for information. To her surprise, he faked her out and just got crazy close to her, and switched gears to get a stray eyelash. Kate was pretty sure the eyelash was fake, but it worked because whatever he whispered in her ear had rattled her. Selena was adjusting her hair by pulling it up into a ponytail and then letting it fall a few times.

"Well I guess it's no secret that I don't like Kate, right?" she finally admitted. "And I don't really like Lucie either, for that matter. They're both just so fake, and you can tell. I mean, you can tell, right…"

Lachlan nodded as if to say obviously.

"Well I really just wanted to ruin their lives. And I figured all of this would drive them nuts." Selena gestured out toward the empty room.

"All of these…..people at this wedding? Oh you mean this murder?" he asked earnestly.

"No. I mean all of them."

Lachlan stared at her for a moment, and Kate's jaw dropped. Lucie was right all along.

"I don't understand," he finally said, his brows pulled together.

"All the murders" Selena's gaze was locked in on his, and she barely blinked.

Lachlan was at a loss for words. He just sat there like a log and stared back at her. Kate wanted so badly to clear her throat or throw something at them to get his attention, and make him press for more answers. But she knew that would ruin the tension and sharing that was already happening. Eventually, he came out of his initial shock and fell back into character.

"Wow, Selena." He let out a whistle. "That is impressive. I mean really, really impressive. I never would've guessed that because all the murders were actually committed by other people. So I guess you're pretty much a mastermind if you pulled all that together without tipping off anyone's suspicions."

"Yes, exactly. And how's Kate doing? She's miserable, just like I'd hoped. No doubt she's taking all this to bed with her every night, which is a glorious thought that what I'm doing literally keeping her awake."

"So how do you even find these people? I mean, they obviously already wanted to kill whoever the victims were, but how did you work yourself in there?"

'Well, that's a woman's touch. Men are easy to control, and women are very keen on drama. I simply set out and perked my ears for drama, then watered the ground where the seed had already been planted. So I didn't help with anything that wasn't already going to happen. Really, I was just doing a job, like I do here. Assisting people." Selena looked downright convinced, as was made obvious by her nonchalance.

At that moment, the police broke in and arrested Selena. On their way out, the police Chief nodded his thanks to Kate, and let her know that Lucie would be released shortly.

"And don't worry," he assured her. "We've been taking really good care of her. Once I saw who the boys had brought in, I made them wait on her hand and foot. She's been fully taken care of."

Kate smiled. She was so glad to hear that, mostly because it would make Lucie much easier to deal with when she picked her up from the station. This way, she would be more apt to grab a cup of coffee and listen to the crazy details of the last five cases they worked on together.

"You know, Miss. You really should consider joining our squad; you've got quite a knack for solving crimes." The officer grinned at her, hopefully.

"Sir…." she said, taking Lachlan's outreached hand. "I just may take you up on that."

Selena Sharma Cozy Mysteries

Murder By Butter Chicken

Chapter 1

“In a few words, describe your father. I know from my research that he's a billionaire rice tycoon back in India, which seems deliciously amazing. So tell me something personal about him.” The spritely blonde reporter's eyes widened, as if she were interviewing a celebrity and couldn't quite play it cool.

“Tough to please,” Selena rattled off without looking up from her bowl. As soon as she'd said it, she felt her heart sink. The way a teenager's heart sinks when they realize they're fixing to get in trouble for something. Her big brown eyes opened up as though she'd been startled and she wiped a strand of hair from her face with the side of her hand.

“Please…please don't print that.” The girl looked down at her paper and scratched out what she'd written and smiled back at her.

“Well I'm just dying to know what it's like to have a rich family. I mean, why even work?!”

The girl was really enjoying herself in her little dream sequence at Selena's kitchen table.

“What, does he want you to marry a rich guy or something…”

Selena rinsed the onion off of her hands and dried them before returning to her prep work. “As a matter of fact," she looked the girl straight in the eye. "Yes, he does." The reporter's eyes grew wide again. This girl would be terrible at card playing, Selena thought. "It's not uncommon for your family to....make very strong suggestions in whom you marry. Because the marriage should benefit everyone, not just two people. I'm not saying I agree with that, entirely, and don't write that down either. But the gentleman he wants me to wed is no gentleman at all. So I won't be doing that."

Selena found her favorite bowl and combined tandoori masala, ginger, garlic, and some yogurt while the girl was still writing something on her notepad. No doubt it was something that would get her in trouble, but that certainly wouldn't be a first. She'd already been such a huge disappointment to her father that there would be no pleasing him, anyway.

At only twenty three years of age, Selena was quite proud of who she'd become so far, in life. She attended university, earning a hospitality degree from the University of Surrey, UK. Spending three years practicing the industry she loved, and one that she was sure she would spend her whole life loving. Hospitality was in her bones. She didn't want to marry the awful son of a textile king in India that her father had chosen.

It didn't matter if it would have been a good match for the family, that man was atrocious! Always lying and cheating on his girlfriends, she knew this about him and had barely even met him, that's how bad his reputation was. No way was she going to be linked to that forever. They would have the finest things, of course, the nicest houses and cars, but she grew up that way. The Sharma family lacked for nothing, so she knew that wasn't enough to satisfy someone for a life-time. Maybe this reporter would like to marry him, she mused while stirring.

"Oooooookay, I think I have everything I need here. I was hoping for a much more exciting mini-story about your father just so I could get some of those readers who love juicy gossip. But you didn't seem to want to get into that too much, and I want to respect that. I WILL say, I am so excited about the upcoming cooking event. I think it'll bring in a ton of new people, and I love visitors! Thanks for letting me come out and interview you, it's my first time writing a real story for the bigger town paper so I really appreciate you being so fun to interview! By the way, what's that you're making, is it for the event?"

"No, no. This is dinner tonight for the guests. Butter chicken is always a favorite, so I try to have it at least once a week."

"Well it smells delicious already, and it's not even cooked yet!" With that, the reporter hugged her gently so as not to shake her hand while mixing, and trotted out the back kitchen door, causing the sweet little bell to ring that Selena loved so much.

What was there not to love about this town? Not long after uni, Selena Sharma, daughter of the billion-aire rice tycoon, stayed in a local caravan park here in Pottsville, Australia, and never left. Her father would have been horrified. Everything about the Tweed Coast area struck her as home. Pottsville, a seaside town on the gorgeous far north coast of New South Wales, had beautiful beaches and there was never a lack of relaxing activities. Anytime Selena felt overwhelmed or like she needed a break, she could swim, read on the beach, scuba dive when she was feeling really adventurous. Those really adventurous times usually came after the monthly, very long, phone calls to India with her father. After those, it always seemed her soul needed some recharging.

While her father was essentially a good man, he was definitely set in his ways. Rousi Sharma, lifelong inhabitant of Mumbai, India, constantly reminds his only daughter that she should pull her head out of the clouds and return home immediately and start her life as the family connection to one of the largest textile entities in the world. She should be proud to honor her family in that way, he always told her. Anytime she felt bad about not upholding her part in the entire family's happiness, she just walked right out the back of that kitchen door, smiled and the little bell sound she heard, and took a walk.

After graduating, and finding herself in Pottsville, Selena soon bought an old guesthouse about seven kilometers out of town and turned it into a profitable guesthouse and cooking school. It wasn't too tough to get the loan for the place, even though she was stretching her limits and borrowing heavily from the bank. Much to the groans of her father, who could have easily purchased it outright for her if he so desired. Luckily for her, the young man at the bank took a liking to her and made the whole borrowing process go much more smoothly than she'd anticipated.

The ultimate goal for herself, the thing that she kept on sticky notes on her bathroom mirror and all around the kitchen to remind herself that she had a goal and was moving toward it every day, is to open a string of takeaway cafes called Selena's Spice. She would franchise them and eventually make the man who taught her a guest chef there. That was the dream, anyway. Her passion for Indian cooking was a strong fire in her heart and her work ethic was just as strong. Selena would show her father that she could make her own way in the world, do things her way and in her own time. He made something of himself, so one would think that'd be an admirable quality in a daughter, but only time would tell.

For now, a walk. The chicken could sit in the fridge for a while and she would finish up when she returned, just in time for the guesthouse dinner. Hopping down the few steps out the back door, she let the door latch behind her, without bothering to lock it up. No one ever bothered anything around here, which is one of the reasons she loved it so much. The building itself had so much charm, and she was instantly attracted to its architectural beauty. The place not only had great bones, it was filled with the charm of a building twice its age.

In only three short years, Selena had turned it into a highly successful guesthouse that was always booked to capacity. Not long after the guest business got going, people began remarking about Selena's cooking skills and the wonderful dishes they were having every night at dinner that they just couldn't find anywhere else in town. There were restaurants of great quality in the neighboring areas, Banaglow and such, but not much in the way of Indian cuisine. And her patrons assured her that even the best Indian restaurants as far away as Sydney paled in comparison to "The young beauty running the guesthouse in Pottsville".

She made quite a name for herself very quickly, and succeeded with ease and oodles of hard work, as she did in all areas of life. If she wanted something, even if she couldn't make sense of it at first, she made it happen. And when someone questioned her? Even more so, if someone told her it could not be done. That was that! She made it happen even more quickly and efficiently. Selena Sharma was devilishly tenacious and resourceful. Aside from the heavy borrowing to actually purchase the building, she scraped and did what she could on a shoestring budget for everything else. The building, though, was so worth it to her. She couldn't see herself being as inspired anywhere else in the world.... when she saw it....she just knew. Like falling in love.

Love? She giggled to herself as she jogged out onto the pathway leading down to the shops. The thought of pretending to love the atrocious textile prince nearly made her vomit in her mouth every time she thought about it. The idea, however, was just becoming more comical to her, lately. The more time she spent out on her own, the happier she was. Being alone was a very empowering feeling, and Selena was in love with making her own way in the world, and nothing could stop her from achieving anything she set her mind to. In her spare time, which she had plenty of because she practiced the art of self-care every evening before going to bed, she loved to read biographies and autobiographies of people who have made something spectacular with their lives but didn't have life handed to them on a silver platter. People like Oprah Winfrey, Andrew Carnegie, and Dhirubhai Ambani. She even loved to browse the social pages and catch up on all the gossip about Bollywood stars, although some were not that inspirational.

While her story was a bit different, in that she had everything a child could possibly dream up, she still felt very inspired by how much people are able to change their lives in a short time. Each person only gets one lifetime, and that isn't even that long if you really think about it. So to be able to go from poverty to being self-sufficient, even highly successful, and changing your family tree for generations to come.....that's an amazing feat. Her father didn't see it this way, of course, but Selena was convinced she could help him see her as an individual, and an adult, soon enough. She just had more hard work to do, and that was fine by her.

Coronation Ave was a beautiful spot to turn around and head back to the guesthouse, but not before stopping into the Detective's office to give him a hard time. Detective Cameron Stewart and running her blog were her other two favorite things to do in her spare time. And since she was already nearby, the Detective Stewart must be paid a visit.

The heavy door to the station groaned loudly as she opened it, causing the secretary to turn her head. Noticing that it was Selena, she tilted her chin down and looked over her glasses, smiling. "He's in there, honey," she gave a wink and pointed toward the lounge. Selena gave her a fake salute and headed down the long hallway. Normally civilians wouldn't be allowed to go traipsing through the station, but Selena was an exception.

Not long after moving to Pottsville, she befriended the Stewart…sort of. It was more like she made herself indispensable to him, actually. Among her other talents, Selena had somewhat of a knack for solving crimes, which both amazed and frustrated Detective Stewart. It wasn't clear why she had such a way of reading people, and figuring things out that even had whole teams of officers scratching their heads, but she did. And she did it with flare, as she did most things.

Once she realized how annoyed this made Cameron Stewart, she made sure to tease him after every case that she consulted on. It drove him batty, and Selena loved driving him batty, because she had her eye on him from the first day they'd met. Though she would never let on, she found him very handsome and let her thoughts fall to him often. Her favorite thing about him was his voice. He had the gruff voice of a seasoned officer for a gentleman of such a young age. It was no secret that Stewart worked very hard at his job and had a passion for justice, his work ethic and dedication was admired by all, not just Selena.

After witnessing a hit and run in high school, he made it his mission to bring justice to as many cases as possible during his time on earth. It was his life's calling, and he took it very seriously, which Selena really respected that.

"Morning, Detective!" she chimed when she rounded the corner. Stewart was standing near the coffee pot talking to another officer and Selena could almost feel his eye twitch from where she was standing. No doubt he wasn't expecting such a cheerful interruption this early in the morning.

"Morning, Selena," Stewart groaned without turning around. "Come to pester me, eh?"

"Never, officer. Just wanted to remind you to be at the festival on time so you can try some of the best Indian cuisines around, especially Satchin Singh's butter chicken. They are sure to win a prize. And I don't want you missing out."

"I'll be there." Detective Stewart turned to face Selena with all the seriousness he could muster in that handsome face of his. "You won't be causing me any trouble, now, will you?" One eyebrow crept higher than the other and his mouth turned up in a half grin. Selena curtsied playfully. "I'll do my best."

Stewart nodded, and she left him to his work. The jog home was always more pleasant when she'd seen the policeman. His energy was contagious and always lifted her spirits.

No sooner did she shut the front door behind her at the guesthouse, did her long-time friend, and the daughter of an Indian supermarket owner, Susannah Singh walk in from the front room.

"Where've you been, Missy? Off pestering Detective Stewart, no doubt?" Susannah gave her a sly grin and shuffled three large crates in her arms, lumbering toward the table in the kitchen.

"Naturally," Selena sang. Susannah was at the guesthouse this morning to do two things: brighten Selena's day, and deliver the morning's spices. "What've you got for me today?"

Her friend sifted through one of the crates with one hand, holding her hair back with the other. Susannah was really such a lovely girl, and always made everyone's day when she came to visit. She pulled out a slip of paper. "Looks like you ordered cumin, turmeric, and saffron...plus three large bags of basmati rice, and not your father's brand," she giggled.

"Amazing, thank you. So...." Selena asked without wasting time. "How's Constable Surti?"

Everyone in town knew that Constable Derek Surti was in love with Susannah. And why shouldn't he be? She was as sweet as they came, very pretty in a plain sort of way, and as quiet as a mouse. The poor girl was smitten with the constable, but was too naïve to really think he fancied her back, and Selena teased her endlessly about it as any good friend would.

"I'm sure he's fine," Susannah answered, playing with her hair. Her cheeks reddened as she hurried into the kitchen and out of Selena's sight. "He came by the grocery store this morning and looked well enough," she yelled behind her so that Selena would follow.

"I'm sure he did, dear." Selena pulled the dish towel from her shoulder and popped her friend with it lightly. As a woman who'd had her fair share of male suitors over the course of her young life, Selena knew enough to recognize a crush when she saw one. If she was any good at setting people up, she would make it her hobby to be a matchmaker. They would be perfect for each other, as the constable was also a quiet sort of fellow. He didn't speak unless he was spoken to, and was generally revered as a vanilla sort of gentleman. He wasn't really much to look at, as far as Selena thought, but when he was around Susannah, his eyes lit up like a schoolboy in a candy shop and it was adorable.

"Are you going to the charity fete?" Susannah asked, changing the subject?"

"Well what else will there be to do in this town on that day, dear? Of course I am going. I'll bet the constable will be there, too," she teased.

"Alright, alright! That's enough out of you. What are you, my grandmother? Are you excited to be a guest judge?" Susannah looked so happy at the thought of Selena enjoying the lime light.

"Your experience at the cooking school certainly makes you a highly qualified judge!"

"Oh yes, it will be so nice to sit back and relax and just eat a lot of food. Is your father ready to become mildly rich with that prize money?" Selena said teasingly.

It made her giddy to think that old man Singh would finally get the recognition he deserved for his wares. The man certainly knew his way around the kitchen better than any female Selena had ever met, and she was pretty well traveled, if she did say so herself. No one held a candle to Satchin Singh's butter chicken. He made one hell of a tandoori chicken, as well, but that butter chicken could make even the hardest Indian food critic melt. Selena could spend all day, every day, in the Singh's kitchen. Of course, she'd have to be of a mind to gain a few extra pounds if that were the case, but it would likely be very worth it.

Susannah laughed and nodded her head. For a shy girl, she knew her father had more talent than most and was fairly confident that he could win every category at the fete, with ease. There was to be a purse of five hundred dollars given out for the best butter chicken recipe. Two hundred dollars would be awarded for the best tandoori chicken. And one hundred dollars would go to whoever had the best vegetable samosas.

"Who's the weird, old fella that's putting on this soiree, again? I can never remember his name..." Susannah asked.

"Mr. Hamish O'Lachlan. That handsome old Scottish coot with all the money." If Selena were a bit older, perhaps quite a bit older, she would probably be more into him, even if just to irritate her father. Mr. Hamish O'Lachlan was loud and brash, and would be sure to vex him exceedingly. Family gatherings would certainly be something to behold, she imagined. And even though Selena was quite a bit younger than he was, he had made his fair share of passes at her, so it isn't like he would be that hard to get ahold of. All Selena had to do would be say the word and he would whisk her away to wherever she wanted to go, and she would likely never have to work again. That would go against everything she was, and everything she stood for, of course. But it was always a hilarious fallback plan to think of on her bad days.

"How did he get so much money, anyway, Selena? I don't remember ever having had a benefit before he showed up to this town….and now we seem to have them all the time. For any old occasion. It's like he can afford to do just…anything."

"No one knows, actually. I've tried to find out, myself, but never had any luck with it. I'm sure if I'd go out with him once or twice he would spill the beans, but that seems an awfully unbearable way to get some juicy town gossip. He doesn't seem terribly strange to people, so they just don't care how he became so rich! It's kind of funny when you think about it. It's like it gives him a pass to do whatever he likes." Selena laughed and imagined him as a voice-over actor with his thick, Scottish accent. That would certainly be a fitting job for Mr. O'Lachlan, though she didn't imagine it would pay quite that well. His voice drove the ladies mad and he loved to work a crowd of women with it, he would have them eating out of the palm of his hand within minutes with just one bad limerick. Selena thought that was probably why he did such things as throwing galas and picnics, and big parties for every occasion…to fight the boredom of being incredibly wealthy and to give the ladies something to fuss over. He probably considered himself to be a bit of a Sean Connery type, although Selena could never quite see him that way.

For the last four years, the benefit had been renowned for its amazing food, including the Indian foods that were so widely talked about in the Northern Rivers. It was also well-liked for its fun rides and fantastic baking prizes. Everyone in the town loved to go, as it gave them something to look forward to every year. All the proceeds from the rides and games went to whatever charity organization Mr. Hamish O'Lachlan chose, and the whole event even attracted people from many neighboring villages like Byron Bay, Clunes, and Lismore.

Selena couldn't wait for the day when she and her celebrity guest chef would be celebrated at the events. She could one day expand her guesthouse and fill it even fuller, and then wow the guests with her and her guest chef's masterpieces. She had a long list of possible guests that she would choose from, and it was her favorite fantasy.

Selena's friend, Sally, would be driving into town for the festivities and to spend some quality time with her. Selena loved her friend, she was a fine young woman, but she wished Sally would get her act together quickly and settle down with a nice young man.

When Saturday finally arrived, Selena helped Susannah unload the truck with her father's contest entries. There were plenty of strapping young men around to help them, but Selena always made sure that she had a hand in as many things as she could, physically. It never hurt anyone to get their hands dirty and unload a truck or two. It connects people, working together in that way, and it was one of her favorite qualities about herself—her wiliness to do the hard work. The two women had arrived early enough to the event that it was very quiet, though everything was already set up and ready to be enjoyed.

The children's rides had been set up overnight, the caterers had already set up the restaurant tent and snack bar, and the local carpenter, along with the assistance of several farmers, had set up the stage and judges table inside the large food tent. Selena followed Susannah carefully toward the long table along the far side of the tent that was labeled Contest Entries. A young boy, no doubt a child of one of the workers who would be there for the day, held the rope aside for them to pass by without dropping their food.

Selena was quite impressed with the wide range of dishes and treats that were offered at this particular fete. It seemed that the little village cooks had outdone themselves this year. She'd already decided that once the judges visited the tables later that afternoon, she would put her name down to purchase six of Sonny Kumar's samosas. "His samosas are really the best in the county," she told Sally, who had just walked up beside her...keeping her voice low so as not to offend old man Singh, who considered himself this year's samosa champion. Sally, whose favorite meal was a hamburger and fries, shrugged and smiled before wrapping her friend in a good hug.

"What are you doing here so soon?" Selena asked, knowing that Sally would likely be quite bored just hanging out several hours before the actual judging was to take place.

"I came early so I could hang out with you! Surprised?!" Sally flipped her hair playfully. Careful not to knock the samosas from her hands, Sally leaned forward to kiss Selena on the cheek. Selena walked past her and set the samosas onto the smaller, round table, covered in an elegant burgundy cloth, eyeing the other entries.

"Wow," she murmured. "They've really outdone themselves this year. Will you go ahead and mark me down for six of Sonny Kumar's samosas, please? I don't want to forget, but I need to get these arranged on the tables properly. I don't want Susannah thinking she has to go and do it by herself."

Today would be a very eventful one for Selena, in more ways than one.

Chapter 2

It was nearly lunchtime when the winner of the butter chicken was declared, and it was a very well-deserving entry. Arjun Das would take home first prize and the five hundred dollar purse. Much to the dismay of Sonny Kumar and Selena, Varun Ganguly took home the honor of best samosas. Apparently they were "fuller flavored to the palate" than Sonny Kumar's, which Selena disagreed with whole heartedly. But since she wasn't the only judge, her voice was not the final decision. No matter, it would be more for her to purchase for herself, she thought. The guests at the guesthouse would enjoy the heck out of them for the rest of the week. And she would even keep a tray or so back for herself to eat during her self-care time in the evenings.

As for the best tandoori chicken, that prize actually went to Susannah, who had entered and won in that category of her own accord. The look on Constable Surti's face when she was announced as the winner was the only consolation Selena had after Sonny Kumar's samosas being snubbed. The constable looked positively in love.

As she had taken to doing every year, Sally walked Selena back to the restaurant tent to have lunch with her. It was Selena's favorite part of the day, because she could catch up on the gossip from her friend's small town, which wasn't too far away. She filed this information away systematically, to be retrieved later if needed. Her brain worked much like Detective Stewart's in that way, and he often, though begrudgingly, complimented her on it.

Usually, Selena and Sally would have hamburgers and chips in the restaurant tent after the judging portion of the morning was over, but today Selena caught her friend drooling over the chicken tikka masala, so they settled on having that instead. Between the chicken tikka masala, the samosas, and the Indian desserts that they'd managed to round up from the sweets tent, the two of them were perched happily under the tent for the better part of an hour. For dessert, they each had a slice of fruit tart from one of the award winning trays from another category. Selena knew she would have to do a few extra laps of her ten acre property tomorrow to wear off the extra calories she devoured today, but it was well worth it.

As Selena was scooping the sauce from her last bite of pie, there was a commotion near the back of the tent. Someone was choking, and apparently no one knew what to do besides sit and stare. That is, until Arjun Das stood up and knocked his chair over, causing Varun Ganguly to shout at the sight of his friend writhing on the ground for breath. At that point, people started clamoring around them, unsure of what to do.

"Someone find Detective Stewart and a doctor!" someone screamed, trying to pry Arjun Das hands from his face so he could help. Soon, though, the gentleman stopped thrashing, and relaxed his hands, then relaxed his whole body into Varun's arms.

"Oh my God!" Varun cradled his friend, pushing the hair back on the top of his head as if he were petting a cat. "No no no….."

"How can that be?" Sonny Kumar whispered as Selena trotted up behind the crowd.

～

Detective Cameron Stewart rushed through the front of the tent. He'd been visiting the fete on his day off, just like everyone else, but was happy to help. Frantically, he searched for the choking victim. All he'd been told was to get to the food tent immediately because someone was choking. Pushing through the crowd, he knelt down next to Varun and carefully helped him stand up and passed him off to a nearby onlooker.

"You there!" He pointed to an older woman who looked as though she could speak well enough. "Which table was he at?"

The old woman pointed to her right with a shaky hand.

Stewart spoke loud enough for the entire tent to hear. "No one touches that table, you understand? Don't even pick up your purse. Leave it there; I don't care if it's inconvenient. Don't touch it." There were a few grumbles, but everyone stayed away from it.

Constable Surti trotted into the tent, and Stewart

gave him some sort of signal to manage the crowd, which he did.

"Excuse me, ladies and gentlemen," he said only loud enough to be heard. "You heard Detective Stewart. Stay back."

Stewart opened his mobile phone and dialed the only funeral parlor driver in town. Sullivan's Funerals had been a part of Pottsville since 1973, a family run business now in its third generation. Since the town was small, it didn't have its own autopsy facility or morgue, so Arjun Das would have to be transported to Lismore, some thirty kilometers away, for evaluation. Detective Stewart was pretty certain he was dealing with a man that had choked on his food but needed to be sure.

It was very sad, but hardly the reason to make people wait any longer than they had to. He would take some snapshots and get a few statements and let everyone get back to the event if that's what they wanted to do. The crowd was already growing restless.

~

It wasn't twenty seconds before Detective Stewart's eye was twitching. The body had only been gone a few minutes, and already he saw that Selena was set into motion. The young woman was a dear soul, and he very much liked her, but nothing irked him more than having her know things first. Stewart didn't want to be shown up again by Selena Sharma, Pottsville's would -

be amateur sleuth, over a highly trained, academy graduated detective.

She was bustling about, getting as many people as
she could to talk to her about anything they might have
seen. And, of course, everyone wanted to talk to Selena
anyway, seeing as how she was so beautiful and charming and driven, so it didn't take long before she had
talked to three people before Detective Stewart could
even make his way over to her.

Her hair, he noticed, was long and straight and
pulled back just the slightest on each side and held their
by a straight pin. Even in the midst of the craziness,
he was taken aback by her happy and lovely countenance, and her ease of talking to people. He had often
thought of trying to convince her to train to be a police
officer, just so he could partner up with her and spend
more time with her. No doubt the pair of them would
have every mystery for the surrounding three counties
solved in three days…now if she just wasn't so tire-
some.

"Stay here if you want, dear. I'm going to talk to
Sonny Kumar. That man's up to something." Selena
patted her friend on the shoulder and rushed away, but
not before the Detective grabbed her gently by the forearm.

"Leave it alone, Selena. It's nothing."

"It's Selena Sharma to you, Detective. And I'm just
going to talk to someone. It's nothing." She winked at
him and hurried away. Detective Stewart sighed in frus-

tration knowing that anything involving Selena wasn't just about nothing. She was obviously acting on one of her hunches again, or woman's intuition of whatever she called it, and they were usually right, much to the displeasure of Detective Stewart.

"Selena!" It was Sally, trotting toward her, looking as though she was saddling up to say something brave. "Don't go," she suggested, taking her by the hand. "I know you like to help the police, but can't you just sit this one out?" Sally knew her friend had a reputation for getting caught up in police matters, and it didn't matter if she figured things out first or not, she was still a bit of a nuisance to the police force.

Selena kissed her friend on the cheek and walked briskly to the other side of the food tent, sliding in and out of mini crowds that had formed, making her way through them easily. Being so slight of frame had its advantages, especially when trying to weasel in and out of a crowd. Sally watched her briskly stride out from under the tent, appreciating from afar that Selena really was cut out for her favorite hobby. And amateur sleuth did have a nice ring to it, so she let her friend go.

Sonny Kumar was startled when Selena sat forcefully into the chair next to him. "Hey there!" Selena said loudly, patting the man on the leg. I heard what you said back there, why was that? What made you say "This can't be?"

The color drained from Sonny Kumar's round face. "I have no idea...did I say that? Probably something I mumbled from shock."

Selena didn't buy it. There was still plenty of time left in the day to have a cup of tea with the man and sort things out, so she suggested just that, recommending a little trip home to Sonny Kumar's house to help him deal with his shock. Surprisingly, Sonny Kumar agreed, and the two walked arm in arm right past Cameron Stewart on their way to the parking lot.

He stood up and looked at them, eyeing his nemesis as though it would change the fact that she was taking a witness home with her. If he tried to stop her, she would only cause enough of a fuss to delay his entire day, so he let her go and returned to questioning witnesses at the table closest to the crime scene. It didn't seem to be going well; all the people at the table could say was how shocked they were that anyone would want to kill Arjun Das.

Chapter 3

Detective Stewart wouldn't be going home tonight. Everyone else would probably stay at the fete in order to shell out their money to happily give funds to the children's shelter. Stewart, however, tossed his notepad and hat back into the car and rented a cabin at the Pottsville Caravan Park, near the beach. Thankfully they had a room for him.

"I find it strange," Selena said on the phone to Stewart once he'd reached his cabin for the evening, "that Arjun Das was poisoned in the food tent."

The detective sighed; he was going to have to hear her out, one way or another. And after all, she had helped him on quite a few cases, so the woman at least deserved a hearing. "Why is that, Ms. Sharma? A food tent seems like a perfectly normal place to poison someone to me." He pressed his eyebrows together with his forefinger and thumb, and sat down in the desk chair in the cabin. It felt like it was going to be a long night. The crashing waves made it feel almost like he was on holidays, but alas he wasn't. Nosy Selena would keep him in the real world.

"Poisoning someone is a private affair, Detective," she said plainly. "One never randomly poisons somebody. It's usually targeted and personal."

Stewart waited for a minute, processing his response. He didn't want to blow her off or seem ungrateful for her assistance but once again she was meddling in police business. And he didn't want to make it seem like this was news to him, but he had to admit, she had a good point. She went on to talk some sort of nonsense about Sonny Kumar mumbling a phrase under his breath at the crime scene. Selena seemed to think that Sonny Kumar assumed he, himself, would be the victim. The idea struck Stewart as the most ludicrous thing he'd ever heard, but he nicely mentioned that it was "far-fetched" at best, and promised to appease her and keep her posted.

"No need, my friend. I'll figure it out." And she hung up. Stewart sat back in his chair, shoulders slumped thinking to himself, here we go again. He looked to the ceiling of his room, sipped his tea and grimaced at the thought of Selena not only being involved, but being right.

The next day, Stewart decided to investigate Selena's hunch and take a trip to Arjun Das's cottage. Yet, before he had the chance, the forensic science team from Lismore called him stating that they'd found a threatening letter in his study desk. He wondered if anybody else had received a similar sort of letter, and told them to wait for him at the cottage.

Chapter 4

Selena called the Detective from her house at eight o'clock that following morning, having already put several more hours in on the case, and she felt more energized than she had in months. Selena was an early riser most mornings, happily preparing breakfast for her guests, and taking delivery of Susannah's spices and pottering around re-arranging the fresh flowers that adorned the lounge and hallways in the house. But sinking her teeth into a case, invited or not, gave her an extra spring in her step.

"You see, Detective Stewart, I went straight to Sonny Kumar's house yesterday after the festival. I knew you'd trust me with him, and you were right to do so." She loved rubbing it in the Detective's face that he pretty much let her have her way with things, and she waited for him to respond to her jab.

"And?" he asked impatiently, letting out another sigh; something he would do often around Selena. It sounded like he was traveling somewhere, and she didn't want to actually waste the man's time, so she hurried through the account of the previous night.

"When we got there...I told him I just wanted to have tea with him and would buy some of his delectable samosas, hoping the idiocy of the timing would catch him off guard. It worked, of course, and he allowed me in. We weren't five minutes into the tea and pastries before he started to shake. I really am good, eh?" Selena laughed at her own joke but Stewart was seething on the other end.

"Oh yes. The best, Ms. Sharma. Can you tell me why he was shaking or are you just going to leave the story at 'I made an old man shake'?"

"Now listen here you little smarty, he isn't much older than you, so watch your tone. And of course there's more. He fetched an odd letter from a stack of papers in his kitchen and let me read it. It just said 'Lying is a mortal sin.' What do you make of that, Detective Stewart?"

"I've no idea." She could hear him put his rackety car in park and shut the door, and was sure he'd hang up soon, so she blurted out the rest.

"The only other thing he asked me was what kind of poison was used to kill Arjun Das. Since I'm not privy to autopsy reports…yet…I told him I thought it was probably arsenic. A few drops in his tea would have sufficed, don't you think? Anyway, before I left, …he said something strange."

He just said "There were three of us…" Sonny immediately looked as though he'd regretted saying anything at all, but when I turned around to ask him what he meant, he merely crumbled into my arms in a sobbing heap. I couldn't really make out much more of what was said after that. It's very lovely that he entrusted me with such emotions, but he's a very heavy gentleman, you know. And I'm not exactly built to hold up a grown, sobbing man for so long. So for the thirty minutes after all the strangeness happened I was just me trying to get out of there without being rude."

Stewart was quiet for a moment. He had to admit; thinking about Selena trying to hold up such a large man while he was crying as hard as he probably ever had in his life, was quite comical. It was made even more comical when he thought of her face. She always thought she was so clever, but he imagined that in that moment she didn't feel very clever at all.

"You might want to get it from him before he destroys it. He's a bit off his rocker at the moment. And you may want to visit Veejay Raj, as well. He's a cantankerous old coot who probably won't let you in the door, of course, so I would be more than happy to accompany you if you like?"

"Veejay Raj?" he asked, sounding out of breath.

There was a knock on Selena's door, so she switched the mobile phone to her other ear and straightened her blouse. It felt good to be this active in the morning. She opened the door just as Detective Stewart was flipping his mobile phone closed. He slipped it into his pocket and gestured toward the inside of the house, asking to come inside.

"Well I never! Come in, Detective. Anyhow, Sonny Kumar and Veejay Raj testified to a crime some years ago" It was so nice to be carrying the conversation on now, face to face. Especially since Detective Stewart had such a nice face. "Before you and I were ever in this area. Whatever the old case was, the suspect that was accused didn't commit the crime. Sonny Kumar refreshed my memory, but that's really all he'd tell me."

"Isn't he an invalid or something? My wife visits him for church, I think." He followed Selena through the foyer of the bed and breakfast and she poured him some tea. They adjourned to the verandah and took in the view of the grassy valley to the distant mountains, where they discussed their next move; Selena now firmly entrenched in the case regrettably accepted by Detective Stewart.

"We need to get over to Veejay Raj's place" Stewart exclaimed finishing his tea and retracting his attention from the engulfing view and re-focusing back on the job at hand. "Let's see if he has received a letter also?"

Chapter 5

After ringing the doorbell at Veejay Raj's house for the third time, the Detective shot Selena a knowing look and walked quickly toward the back of the house to check the other door. "Wait here," he instructed. And, as she sometimes was inclined to do, she did as she was told. Before long he opened the front door and informed her that Veejay Raj had, indeed, met his Maker. Selena was aghast.

"Was it poison?!" she yelled, pushing past him and searching for the kitchen.

"No, no," he replied.

"Are you sure? How can you be certain?"

"I know for a fact it wasn't poison because she was stabbed with a letter opener."

Selena pulled to a stop before entering the kitchen. She didn't need to see that to be helpful to the police force, so she turned to Stewart.

"Detective," she said, adjusting her slacks. "Was it his letter opener or someone else's? And did you find a strange letter, as well?"

"I didn't see one, no. I came to let you in. But I'd be willing to wager that we will find one if we look hard enough. And as to whether it was his letter opener, well hopefully there are some fingerprints on it we can lift."

~

Cameron Stewart dropped Selena off at her home, and she immediately phoned her friend at the Lismore's Northern Star newspaper office. She was trying to obtain a copy of the article about the trial Sonny Kumar was speaking of. And even though she had little hope of the gentleman finding it anytime in the next few hours since it happened nearly thirty years ago, he mentioned that he knew the case quite well.

It was apparently one of his first journalistic feats, and he even attended the trial, which he remembered clearly. On a year or two into his sentence, the person who was found guilty committed suicide, yet the story didn't end there. A full twenty years later, the witness of the crime came forward and said that they hadn't seen the criminal's vehicle properly. The men—Arjun Das, Veejay Raj, and Sonny Kumar— were even charged with perjury.

"Of course, they never went to jail," her friend said. "But I'm pretty sure suffering their own conscience was punishment enough! That poor man that hung himself, it's so tragic."

Selena thanked her friend and hung up, walking to the window to think clearly. It was sure lucky that she knew how to make friends everywhere she went. It was one thing she learned growing up with most everything else given to her. One of her favorite things to do was to size people up and see if she could figure out a way to turn them into an alliance for her in the future. It wasn't so much that she was lying or trying to deceive people, but she knew there was absolutely nothing wrong with making friends everywhere she went, and if she could just be pleasant enough around them, then they would remember her in the future and be more inclined.

Amazingly, it always worked out in her favor. She often thought that this was one of the things that made her such a good business person, her ability to make great connections and network with anyone, no matter their personality type. She was so agreeable, in fact, that she could talk to anyone in any position. It was probably why it was so easy for her to talk to Detective Stewart the way she did. She never looked at herself as being less than anyone else.

The day was clear, hardly a cloud in the sky. Momentarily Selena's mind drifted back to her days in the UK; dark, dreary, cold wet days and she thanked her lucky stars she had made the decision to move to Australia where the sun and clear blue skies were in abundance. But back to the case in hand. Someone is making those men pay for wrongly accusing an innocent man, she thought. But who would do such a thing?

She put her teacup and saucer in the sink and decided to go for a walk to clear her head. And a call to Detective Stewart to update him was in order, as well. He took notes on everything she said, and meekly thanked her for her contribution. The two of them agreed that

Sonny Kumar was next on the list, if they were worth their weight as police officers. Well, at least one was, officially. They decided together that he needed to be protected and Detective Stewart arranged for Constable Surti to stay with him until they could sort things out.

"We'll wait for the forensic report on the letter opener and go and catch our killer," Stewart said.

"Awwww, Detective. You said we. I'm flattered."

"Alright, now. Don't go getting a big head, Selena." Stewart mentally cursed to himself to be more careful when freely talking about the case using the collective 'we' in the conversation. But at the same time he did have to give Selena her dues; once again.

On the way home, Selena would pass the cemetery and decided to take a look at the headstones of the victims from thirty years ago. Maybe she could find some inspiration or direction there. It was all she could think to do while they waited for the report. Surely, something would come to her, it always did.

As she walked past the graves, she poured over the names carefully, trying to remember details from stories she'd heard over the years about the case. The cases were well known enough to people who were keen on talking about that sort of thing. And being in charge of the guesthouse, Selena had heard many a conversation about this sort of story over the years.

She wasn't really one to eavesdrop, officially, but she thought it part of her duty to be involved in her guest's experiences at the house, and she also considered it to be learning about the region that she now calls home. It was her great pleasure to live a little piece of each guest's life as they passed through her acquaintance. And many of them had spoken of this, and stories like these, during their stay with her, and she was pressing her mind for the most accurate details and trying to separate it from the hearsay she'd overheard during all those times.

Leaning against a tree, she took in the whole place for a moment. The cemetery had a commanding position in the town with many old tombstones of the district's early settlers and pioneers. That's when she saw the fresh flowers. On one of the headstones, a bouquet of fresh flowers was arranged neatly on top of the stone. It caught her eye because she had seen an identical bouquet of flowers at the fete the day before, though she couldn't remember whose they were.

Chapter 6

"Susannah Singh!!" Selena shouted into the air. Susannah Singh had received a bunch of flowers identical to this one! Derek Surti had given them to her for winning the tandoori chicken prize at the fete! When she approached the headstone that the bouquet was laying on, she exhaled sharply. The script was as plain as day.

"Lying is a mortal sin and you never did, Beshin. May you rest in peace."

"Oh bless you, Sally, for this wretched mobile phone. I've used it more today than I ever thought I would!" She kissed her mobile phone held in her shaking hands and dialed Detective Stewart's number.

"You can't be serious, Selena. You can't be serious."

Yes, Selena insisted that he get Constable Surti out of Sonny Kumar's home immediately. He could tell from her breath that she was running somewhere and she seemed quite worked up about the Constable, so he decided to humor her. She hadn't been wrong yet, though he couldn't quite understand how the quiet Derek Surti could manage to kill as housefly, much less a human. Two humans, no less!"

"Oh thank God!" Selena leaned on the fencepost of

Sonny Kumar's house to catch her breath, more than relieved to see that Sonny Kumar was standing on the front porch with Detective Stewart. "Where's the Constable?" she demands immediately.

"Oh he's gone to get some milk at the store, Ms. Sharma. He's such a good lad," Sonny Kumar is as clueless as ever, yet here he was, standing there bragging about the kindness of a man who was going to kill him.

Selena looked to Stewart. "If he thinks he's been found out, he'll run."

"I still don't underst...." as Stewart was cut off by Selena.

"He's our murderer, Detective. Sonny Kumar would have clearly been his third victim."

Sonny Kumar put his hand to his mouth to cover a gasp, though the news did not come as a complete shock to him. Seeing the look on Stewart's face, Selena offered her explanation.

"Arjun Das, Veejay Raj, and Sonny Kumar committed perjury during Beshin Patel's trial thirty years ago. Their statements sent Beshin to prison for life, where, as I told you before, he committed suicide. Ten years ago, the three of them admitted to their perjury about the suspect's vehicle and Beshin Patel obtained a pardon posthumously.

"However," she held up her index finger in the air. This was her favorite part. "The guy's admissions of guilt came too late as far as his son was concerned.

Derek wanted them to pay for what they'd done to his…. father. Yes…father!"

"His mother, you see, suffered the wrath of the town gossips for years until she eventually reverted to her maiden name—Surti. She and her son moved away, embarrassed and ashamed, but Derek wanted retribution for the loss of his father. He's been planning this for a very long time Detective. Remember what I said earlier – poisoning is not random. It's a private affair and in Derek's case it was very, very personal."

Within moments, Stewart had called in an arrest of Derek Surti at the local convenient store, where he was reported to have been picking up gasoline and matches. Later on while going through his wallet, a worn, crumpled portrait photo of Beshin Patel would be found; the father he had lost because of the actions of Arjun Das, Veejay Raj and Sonny Kumar. Now he would pay for their injustice.

News spread fast in the small township of Pottsville; shocked at the arrest of their local police constable. But life must go on. Susannah still managed to show up on Monday morning with the delivery of goodies and spices from her father. Never once had she considered, she told Selena, that Derek's interest in the Indian cooks of the town was anything but harmless. Murder never is though.

Murder of a Bollywood Queen

Chapter 1

Selena Sharma's birthday was coming up, and it wasn't something she was too keen on thinking too hard about. There wasn't anything wrong with birthdays, but they always reminded her of home. Not that she minded but it was cause for her father to ring and as well wish her a happy day, demand that she returns home. But that was the furthest thing from her mind. There were still plenty of things to be done here in Pottsville, Australia, like starting her very own Indian café franchise, Selena's Spice. A contented smile consumed her as she realized that her dogged determination to succeed was a direct trait of her father, Rousi Sharma, India's rice king. He would be proud of her one day.

She was drinking her first cup of tea of the day, standing in the large kitchen of her bed and breakfast property, Selena's Place, she ran on the outskirts of town, flipping through the paper. There wasn't really anything noteworthy happening in the small town of Pottsville, New South Wales. One of the quieter cities in Australia, it was a favorite of Selena's during her travels over the years from the UK. She recalled that this was another bone of contention of her father who wanted her to give up her gypsy ways and settle down and start a family. He even had her husband picked out; the son of a textile millionaire. But for Selena, Potts-ville was a better choice. For some reason it struck her as the perfect amount of quaint and city life, kind of a cozy village and it suited her perfectly since she decided to move here.

She bought the bed and breakfast just off Cudgen Creek Road, and was the strange 'Indian girl' of the small town. Everyone loved her, even though she was a bit forthright. Rousi Sharma taught her to stand up for herself, now regretting it often. Her mild blend of Indian and British accent, not to mention her much talked about wealthy family, was much the talk of the district and it certainly helped in getting onboard with the local community councils; great venues for Selena to listen in on the town's gossip.

Disappointed in the lack of enthusiastic news reporting for the week ahead, Selena refreshed her tea and strolled over to the little picture window over the sink. Clad only in her bathrobe, she was caught off guard by the knock at the door.

"Who on Earth would be ringing me at this hour?" She wasn't expecting any deliveries from Susannah Singh as she had only stocked up on rice, turmeric and cumin powder two days ago. Being Sunday it couldn't be the mailman either.

Nevertheless, whoever was at the door was knocking so adamantly that they couldn't be kept waiting. She hurried to the front door, careful to look quickly through the foyer to make sure no guests would see her in her robe, and shuffled to the door. When she opened it, she gasped a little, and was greeted by the flushed cheeks of Detective Cameron Stewart of the local police force.

"What's the matter, Detective?" she asked, making sure the robe was closed all the way and pointing to his reddened cheeks with her free hand. "Cat got your tongue? Or has it just been a while since you've seen a stunning beauty in a bathrobe?" Selena laughed as she liked to tease the Detective. This would be one man her father would not have to push her to marry. But this would be unlikely and she would never make her feelings known publicly. For now the teasing was most enjoyable.

Detective Stewart cleared his throat mid-laugh and asked to be let in. He didn't look, Selena thought, like he was really in the mood for joking. Though she was glad she got that one in, because seeing his cheeks flus was worth all the flack she would catch for it later. She waved her arm out in front of her and gestured for him to go into the kitchen quickly.

Cameron did as he was told and shuffled in with a medium sized box under his arm. Following Selena he couldn't help notice that she cut a model appearance in her robe, although his poker face would make the outside world none the wiser.

"Cameron, you're soaked. Do you want some dry clothes? I'm sure I can find you something around here?"

"Aaah, no thanks, Selena" The thought was going through Detective Stewart's mind as to how Selena would have some men's clothing in her possession considering she was single. A slight pang in the heart reminded him of his true feelings for his 'beauty queen' friend and he thought better of it to ask about the clothing. But the thought did linger for a while. Romance and a hard working detective didn't always marry up and he hoped that he hadn't left his run too late. Cameron shook his head and refocused.

"So how can I help you Detective? Let me take your coat."

Cameron let her remove his coat, and she draped it over the back of one of her kitchen chairs close to the auger; its heat warming the room. Eventually, when she saw that he wasn't going to stop pacing her kitchen floor, dripping wet, without saying anything, she made him a cup of tea. Selena tapped him on the shoulder, breaking his train of thought. Cameron grumbled a bit and nodded his thanks to her, taking the saucer from her hands.

"Thanks, it's been raining all night, and I just never dried out. I appreciate the hot tea, Selena. It's got a musky spiciness to it" Cameron remarked trying to sound like a tea connoisseur, hoping to impress Selena.

"Very good Detective Stewart. It is Darjeeling tea; one of the finest in my country" Selena smiled; impressed that Cameron Stewart was showing his gentlemanly qualities.

"Well, hopefully you don't catch pneumonia and end up in hospital. You really should take better care of yourself. Now what brings you here? Do I need to call the station and let them know where you're at?"

"Ha ha no thanks. I'm a big boy, I sure they're not worried. I appreciate the sentiment. But I'm not really speaking to anyone at the moment." Stewart replied sheepishly.

Selena's eyes perked up and one eyebrow danced across her forehead. "Oh really?" Her mind flitted towards the box wondering if it could be a Valentine's Day gift since the 14th of February was only next week. Maybe a birthday present?

"Yes, really. Don't go getting all excited about it, it's nothing like that." Stewart was quick to deflate Selena's enthusiasm.

Selena grinned widely at her friend. "Oh I think it's exactly like that, Cameron! You know me, and it's nearing Valentine's Day, even! This must be your gift to me" Selena paused with a smirk "a juicy secret case to be solved on the quiet. That's very kind of you. Ha ha you know it's my birthday soon, right?"

Cameron's heart had smashed the 150 beats a minute; his cheeks flushed and mouth gaped open until he realized Selena was once again teasing. She dipped her head to him "Now what have you got for me, here Detective?"

"My socks are soaked through, Selena. I'm freezing and I don't want to be here all day, I'm knackered.

I came to you because I don't want to be airing out my dirty laundry all over town. I'd much rather come to you, since you have a way with these sorts of cases, than to have it broadcast all over town. It's from my Aunt in Cabarita Beach, she sent it in the post and I wanted you to have a look at it before I took it to the Station."

"Alright alright, settle down, as you Aussies would say, buddy. You look shaken, positively pale, what's going on? Why do you want me to look at it first?" Selena asked.

Cameron handed her the box, and Selena eyed him carefully. Whatever was in the box has him pretty worked up. "It's probably a book of some sort, I'd imagine."

She pried the lid off with one hand, and half expected there to be a dead rat or something inside of it. When the lid finally came loose, Selena swallowed hard. Nestled into a crimson-colored piece of fabric was a jar. The jar was cloudy inside, and had a liquid in it, held securely by a firm piece of cork. Inside the bottle, which Cameron looked away from as soon as she opened it, was a slender finger. It was floating in some sort of liquid, and upon a quick smell of the bottle, Selena assured him that it was formaldehyde. She could see the color in the Detective's face grow lighter, and he looked as if his stomach was a little queasy.

Selena regained her composure quickly and squared her shoulders at the kitchen table. "This is not what you were expecting, I take it?"

The Detective shook his head and brought a fist to his mouth, looking as though he were about to be sick. "No!" He shouted, suddenly upset. "I thought it was an old book or something that she had gotten."

Only a few moments later, Selena was showing him to the front door. Detective Stewart apologized profusely for the interruption and confusion, and excused himself to the police station at Lismore to try and figure out what the package was all about.

Selena watched as he went back to his car, not quite fully dried out yet, still holding the plastic bag under his arm. He had barely wanted to wait for her to wrap it up, but she'd insisted, so that he could maintain privacy. Those goons at the police department had no business asking questions about a beat up old shoe box; just yet anyway.

Chapter 2

Selena Sharma, beloved bed and breakfast owner and part time sleuth of Pottsville, New South Wales, freshened her tea and returned to her kitchen table. No sooner had she grabbed her iPhone, opened Notes and begun to jot down some points, her mind raced with all the things she'd taken in.

She wasn't given much time before the Detective had replaced the lid on the box, but in that short time, she'd gathered that it was a young woman's finger. Brown skin, not Caucasian. It was a ring finger, probably belonging to a woman in her twenties. She guessed it belonged to a young woman, in a relationship, since the finger was still adorned with a friendship style ring.

Getting dressed quickly in her favorite denim jeans, a light cashmere jumper and a pair of sensible flats, Selena hopped into her car. The sporty car, a 2008 Mercedes 250 SLK, red with off white leather, perfectly engulfed everything that was Selena Sharma in a nutshell. It was classy, fun, sporty, and full of life. And it turned heads, which she loved.

She climbed into it and checked her hair in the rear view mirror. She couldn't get the "ring finger in the box" out of her head, and she wanted answers. Those answers sure wouldn't be coming from Detective Stewart, as soon as she'd opened the box; the man had clammed up like a school boy on his first date. This left the ring, itself, as being the only other lead in the case.

She'd seen many rings like this one advertised on television; it was no ordinary friendship ring. An expensive jeweler in Lismore had been advertising rings exactly like these for months. They were very unique, and Selena admitted to herself that she'd envied them on more than one occasion.

With Valentine's Day approaching, the jeweler had been offering the rings at a reduced price. Nearing the shopping center where Lismore Family Jewels was located, Selena pulled into the car park located underground. She usually hated driving around in town, mostly because people were in general impatient asses, but this morning the drive had not been so bad.

Trotting up to the entrance of the shopping center, Selena was pleased to see that the early morning crowd was much thinner than normal today. The shops were opening one by one, and she took a seat on a bench outside the jewelry shop. It was one of the last ones to open, which Selena took note of. She was careful not to look as though she was staring, and she carefully eyed the man inside the shop who was directing the other sales clerks to their stations. It was time to have a chat with the man.

Meanwhile, as Selena rose to confront the jewelry store owner, Detective Stewart was leaned over his desk at the police station with his head cradled in his hand.

"Auntie, auntie….listen…" he said quietly.

"No, you listen, dear. I sent you no such package. I'm certainly not dead, and I have all of my fingers! So whatever you found in a jar inside a box has nothing to do with me. And quite frankly, you're making me nervous. You sound quite shaken up. You should get some sleep…or make a cup of tea."

As he was trying to hang up the phone, the Detective Stewart's Sergeant bursts through the door and tries to interrupt his conversation. The young officer had no tact when it came to when and where he was invited to speak, and was always in a hurry. Cameron liked the guy, but Sergeant Davidson always seemed to be running late, and everyone else's time suffered for it. He hung up quickly and turned to Sergeant Davidson with a sigh.

"Sir," the young man was breathing heavily, as though he'd sprinted down the hall….and everywhere else he'd been that morning. Carrying more than a few regulated kilos, that wouldn't surprise. Thoughts of booking Davidson for a medical ran through Stewart's mind.

"Sir, I've only found three women reported missing in the last few weeks. These are the only three that fit the description from the forensics lab." Sergeant Davidson handed him three pieces of paper fresh off the printer. The finger apparently belonged to an Indian woman in her early twenties.

"She's had a manicure pretty recently," Detective Stewart said aloud. "Now we just need a body to go with this finger."

Chapter 3

Back at the shopping center, the little bell on the door dinged as Selena walked in. The man she assumed was the manager looked surprised to see her for some reason, and checked his watch absentmindedly.

"Are you open?" she asked.

"Yes, yes Miss," he replied. "We'll be here until six."

"Ah very good! I'm in a bit of a hurry and was wondering if you could be a darling and show me one of those Valentine Day rings you advertise on television."

The man eyed her curiously, wondering if it was custom for Indian women to pop the question in a relationship. Normally it would be a man looking at the rings. Whatever the case, the manager thought there must be a lucky man involved taking an admiring glance at Selena's firm figure.

"Oh no, no dear. I'm not doing the buying! I just wanted to ask you a few questions about them so I can leave a few well timed casual hints for a special friend." Selena said with smile that would spice up any man's vindaloo. When he returned with a tray of rings similar to the one in the jar, her face lit up. "Oh, they're beautiful!"

The man went through the usual list of reasons to buy such beautiful and unique rings, but Selena stopped him mid-sentence.

"Do you remember, perhaps, selling one of these to a woman sometime in the last month or so?"

Taken aback, the manager took two actual steps back. "Why on earth would you want to know something like that? It's mostly men who enquire about these rings"

"Yes of course, I just…one of my friends had one just like this and I was wondering if you were the one that sold it to her." After another half hour of clever fibbing, Selena left the jewelry store with three names and addresses of men who had purchased a ring from the tray in the last three months.

One of the names, Selena noticed, was for a young man who lived on the same street at the Detective's aunt in Cabarita Beach. It might be a coincidence, but Selena doubted it. These things were seldom coincidences; they were generally revered as juicy, wonderful details that led her to solving a crime that the police department couldn't handle.

Returning to her car, she threw down the top and pulled out of the park way, headed for the police station. When Detective Cameron Stewart saw her breeze through the station doors, a picture of beauty, his skin tingled then crawled a bit. He knew he shouldn't have involved her in this, though knowing her she already had the perpetrator tied up in the trunk of her car begging to be fingerprinted. He hated when she came to the station, why didn't she just phone him with her hunches as she usually did? No time for personal insecurities, Detective Stewart needed to talk with Selena.

Chapter 4

Just as Detective Stewart was approaching Selena, Sgt. Davidson rocketed in from behind an office door.

"Sir! A woman in her twenties was just pulled out of the river...she's missing her ring finger."

Stewart nodded to his sergeant and kept walking toward Selena. As much as he hated involving Miss Sharma on cases directly, he had to admit she'd been an incredible amount of help on many occasions. He'd be a fool not to ask her.

"Well," he said when he reached her. She jumped a bit when he came up from the side, and it made him happy to have startled her. The Detective imagined that it probably didn't happen very often. "Let's go."

"What's that, officer? Are you taking me in?" A sly smile wandered across her face and she put her hand to her chest dramatically. "I'm sure I didn't do anything..."

"Alright, alright." Stewart grinned and laced his hand through the crook of her arm. "Come with me. Something's just come up...literally." Selena's eyebrows danced across her face and Detective Stewart shot her a grin. "In the river."

He knew she loved this part, where things were just

starting to get interesting for the normal police force was the part where Selena started working her magic. As much as Cameron Stewart hated to admit it, the little boy in him loved watching her brain work.

"Happy to go along, Detective! But I'll take my own car if you don't mind." Selena turned her nose a bit in false protest. "It's much more stylish than a police panda car."

"That may be perfectly true, Selena. But I won't be able to debrief you if we're in two separate vehicles." Selena looked disappointed, but ultimately caved in pretty quickly. "It'll be fine, your car will be fine here, and we'll come back and pick her up later. The boys will make sure she gets lunch." Stewart winked at her.

Selena was happy to oblige the Detective. The opportunity to be close to him outweighed riding in a Toyota Camry surrounded by its cheap plastic. Having a man in the car, smelling his after shave made Selena feel more complete. In some ways it reminded her of home taking Sunday drives with her father through the rice paddies to the mill. She felt safe then and Detective Stewart did the same. He was a simple man; no pretenses unlike the jerk her father wanted her to marry back home. He may be the son of a textile magnate, but he must have got the rags when it came to clothing. Cameron Stewart was kind; the jerk was full of himself.

As soon as they pulled out into traffic, Selena pulled three sheets of paper from her tote bag and waved them at Cameron while he was driving. "Let me debrief you, first. These three gents all bought rings like the one we discovered. And one of them lives very near your Aunt. What do you make of that?"

Unexpectedly, Detective Stewart grabbed the papers from her and pulled out the one that lived near his hand, he folded it up and slid it into his jacket pocket while steering with one hand.

"No offense, Selena, but I really don't want you getting involved in the case in this way. This perpetrator seems to be especially vicious, and I don't need to lose you due to your lack of police training. It was dangerous going and getting these." He looked at her, and rolled his eyes at the grimace she was sending across the cabin of the police car. "What?! It was dangerous. How did you even get anyone to—you know what. Never mind. I don't want to know."

Before long they pulled up to the pier on the banks of the Brunswick River where the body had been discovered. There were a handful of officers walking around and some police tape being strewn about in places that made sense to Selena. She loved the excitement of the scene and started to get out of the car.

"Huh uh. You stay here." Detective Stewart pointed his finger to the seat like he was instructing a toddler. "I'll come get you when I need you. It's dangerous down there and you're in proper shoes. No sense in dirtying them up if you don't have to."

Reluctantly, Selena agreed, but not without a significant amount of scoffing. Five minutes later, though, as

Cameron Stewart was getting his bearings on the scene, he saw Selena traipsing down the embankment toward where he was standing. There really was no telling that woman what to do. Selena always did exactly what she wanted, even as a small child back home. She had her father wrapped around her little finger and she knew it. Later she would defy his orders to return home, instead flying straight to Australia. Rousi Sharma cursed the day he let things get so casual, but she was his only child.

"Selena, seriously! You're going to break your ankle! Didn't I tell you to stay in the car?" Stewart trotted out from under the pier offering to give her a hand. She accepted, as any lady would do, and didn't say a word until they were settled underneath the pier again. She motioned for Detective Stewart to get back to whatever conversation he'd been having, and after rolling his eyes a few more times, he did just that. She undoubtedly just didn't want to miss any details, and Stewart couldn't fault her for that. But when the body was rolled over, Selena let out a gasp holding her right hand over her mouth, her big brown eyes wide open.

"Do you know her?" Detective Stewart asked.

"Yes, it's Susannah Singh's cousin, Maahi" Selena whispered, her voice crackling. "I just don't believe it. She's a Bollywood star back home. She's been out here for a couple of months on holiday."

"You won't be saying anything to Miss Singh just yet" Cameron moved to comfort Selena placing his arm around her shoulder and steering her back up the hill.

"I did notice something in the mud up there on the hill." Selena commented pointing to where she had walked from. "I didn't want to disturb it because I knew the forensics team would want to get a picture of it in situ, but it's worth looking at." Stewart was always impressed when she used proper police terms, but he always immediately pictured her reading Agatha Christie novels late at night.

"Show me," he said. Selena glanced back over her shoulder, tears filling her eyes, as she thought of the terrible plight her friend must have endured at the hands of her killer. Her mud stained clothes, hair strewn across her face was so contradictory for a woman who carried herself in such an elegant manner.

"It's ironic Detective" Selena went on "Maahi in Indian means river. What a way for her life to end."

The two of them climbed back up the hill some ways and Selena pointed to the ground. "I believe that's a ring box, Detective Stewart."

"Stay right here." He started back down the hill and stopped mid-stride, turning back to her and reaching his hand out in kindness. "Please."

Moments later, he came back with a forensics photographer, and when they gotten what they needed, he slipped on a latex glove and pulled the box from the mud. Turning it a few times in his hands, he didn't say a word, and then dropped it into a clean evidence bag. On the outside of the box was the name Lismore Family Jewels.

Chapter 5

The Detective and his team confirmed that Percy Tendulkar, a local real estate salesman, was one of the names on the slip of paper that Selena managed to rustle up, had purchased the ring on the severed finger. Once they reached his house, Tendulkar told Detective Stewart that he purchased the ring at the jewelry store in town.

Apparently, and Stewart wasn't even the slightest bit convinced of his story due to the trademark shift eyes of the person telling it, he'd asked Maahi Singh, even though he had only known her for two months, to be his Valentine on the river bank where they had found the box. The two of them walked back to the restaurant on the promenade where they then had a lovely dinner to celebrate their new confirmed love.

They drove home separately, and since it was a week day on the evening he proposed, Percy assumed Maahi had driven back to her parent's house. That was, as he claimed, the last time he saw her. The next day, Maahi's mother listed her as a missing person.

In Stewart's mind, there were too many unanswered questions in the case. Selena wondered why sending the package to the Detective personally was something the perpetrator chose to do, it seemed a bit bold. And why did the attacker use his aunt's address? Selena suggested to Detective Stewart that it could have been done on accident, or possibly to derail the investigation. It was, she thought, a strange thing to do for a serial killer, though.

The following day, Cameron Stewart phoned Selena to inform her that there was a second body with the same description.

"Have you received a shoe box for this one, too?" Selena asked.

"No, I sure haven't. Not that I've seen, anyway. Maybe it was a fluke?"

"I doubt it. Strange things are rarely a fluke. Hold on a moment, please." Selena walked to the door where the postman had just come in. She'd seen him there, in the foyer of her bed and breakfast, a thousand times.

Today, though, the sight of him stopped her in her tracks. He was holding a shoebox and the clipboard he normally carried when she was required to sign things. The only person that had her address that would have anything to do with the case, other than the Detective himself, were the shop assistants at the Lismore Family Jewelry Store. "Send a car to the guesthouse. Immediately! I'll call you back."

She knew that within ten minutes there would be a car at her door, so she sat tight with the box and readied herself for whatever was to happen next. A fresh coat of lipstick and a pair of earrings later and she opened the door for the officer. The baby faced police officer, whose name Selena could never remember because he was a very forgettable person, sat quietly with her and sipped his tea like a timid gentleman in training until Detective Stewart arrived.

"Okay, Selena. A lot has happened in the time since you had me send the car. Bolton, you're excused. Thanks so much."

The young man thanked Selena for the tea and set his cup and saucer in the sink before leaving as quietly as he'd come in.

"This guy is killing these girls because he was refused; at least that's my theory. His own proposal to his girlfriend was refused, and the profiler and I truly believe he's acting out on other people because of it. It's pretty basic, but you get the drift.

Anyhow, he bought the rings at the jewelry store in the mall, and when I swung by to question the manager you spoke to, he wasn't around. The other workers mentioned that he'd gone on an unscheduled vacation."

"Mmmm…I could go with that Detective but I have another version." Detective Stewart rolled his eyes. He was going to hear Selena's view whether he wanted to or not.

"Valentine's Day is still somewhat frowned upon back in my country Detective. The traditionalists believe that it's Western propaganda and by infiltrating the young Indian people with this commercial love practice, the true values of India are being lost. Since all the victims are Indian, I think we should be talking to Ritesh Patel, the manager, from the jewelry store" Selena concluded with a smug look on her face.

"Yeah, my thoughts, exactly." Stewart piped up trying to regain control of his investigation. Once again it seemed that Selena had delivered the trump card. "I've got his address. Want to ride along?"

Selena nearly jumped from her seat. "Do I!"

At the town house complex, the site manager informed the two of them that Ritesh Patel had not gone on vacation as far as he could make out…he'd left altogether. Mr. Patel had moved out three days ago.

"He was never a problem," the manager said. "He even paid the last month's rent. He mentioned that his girlfriend had taken a job out of town and he wanted to follow her. Seemed a good enough excuse as any, I'd say?"

"No way is she moving for a job. That woman's been abducted," Selena whispered to Detective Stewart as they walked back to the gate. "I'd wager these three killings are a warning to her that she should be adopting old Indian values of love and not these trashy Western ways…or else!"

Stewart scoffed. "That seems a bit far-fetched even for you, Selena. But…."

Selena raised an eyebrow as they walked. "Does it?? Then give me another explanation. Do you recall the….." Selena pointed to her forehead inviting Detective Stewart to recall that Patel had a red dot on his forehead. "Mr. Patel is a devout Hindu. Very religious I would say."

"Ok....you're probably right as usual. It'll be faster if I just admit that out loud. If you're right—"

"Don't tease me, Detective. You know I'm right. Even more little grey cells than your favorite Hercule Poirot. "

"And if he thinks his girlfriend is like the other three, then he'll kill her too. We've got to find her before that happens."

Chapter 6

"**P**erfect! You did perfectly, thank you so much." Stewart slammed the phone down and jumped from his chair, slinging his jacket over his shoulder. He quickly dialed Selena's number with his free hand.

"Selena! The clerk at the Cabarita Beach Jewelry Store just phoned to say that Mr. Patel ordered a pendant and was having the word 'kama' engraved on it. He told him yesterday to come back today to pick it up. And he's phoned us this morning. Sergeant Davidson and I are on the way to apprehend him. Davidson is going to pose as a clerk and I'll be waiting outside when he shows up."

"His girlfriend is probably being held somewhere in town, Detective. Did you ever get any information on her?"

"I didn't, but I'm hopeful we'll get it out of him. That's why Davidson is posing as the clerk, he'll try to get her name and address before we grab him. He's wearing a wire so I can hear the address when he does, I'll send a team out immediately after."

An hour later, with Davidson in place, Patel walked into the shop. The other shop assistants were on lunch, and Patel strolled right up to the counter, where the Sergeant did his job exactly as he was trained. He asked for the name and address of the girlfriend for insurance purposes, which is something that Ritesh Patel knew to expect as common practice. In this case, however, Patel actually refused to give the information.

"I'm the one buying the pendant and I'll use my information for it. I value our privacy." Patel told him. "If she refuses the pendant, it will still be paid for, and I'll keep it as a keepsake."

Davidson did not argue, as he knew that would only raise Patel's suspicion. Detective Stewart, however, heard the whole conversation in his earpiece and simply waited for Patel to come out. When he left, Stewart would simply follow him, convinced he'd lead him to the girl.

While he was waiting, however, he received a call from the Lismore Police Station. The desk sergeant reported a woman had called in a reported that her daughter didn't come home last night. She was worried, and the daughter's name was Anita Kumar. Her boyfriend's name was Ritesh Patel. The hairs on the back of Cameron Stewart's neck stood up, he thanked the sergeant and gripped the steering wheel.

As soon as Patel exited the store and pulled into traffic, Stewart followed him at a safe distance. They were headed to the southern end of town as best as he could tell. Something about the direction they were headed didn't feel right, and sent goose bumps down his arms. The main road, Tweed Coast Road was busy, even for a popular seaside tourist town and he didn't want to lose the guy in traffic. He called in to have a few unmarked cars dispatched to assist in an eventual chase, just in case.

Fifteen minutes later, Patel dropped down into a car park below the popular Cabarita Beach Hotel. Detective Stewart followed and watched him exit the vehicle, and he received word that a local police constable was on site near the car park elevator. Carefully, the officer followed Patel to his room and radioed Stewart the location: Room 651 on the sixth floor.

A few minutes later, Stewart and the Hotel security officer met the constable outside the room. He listened for any noise, and when he heard a faint string of muffled sounds followed by a very audible scream, he used the security officer's master key to open the door.

As the three men burst in, they saw the young woman being held over the balcony railing by Patel. Anita Kumar fainted just as Detective Stewart reached her, luckily he grabbed her arm firmly enough that he could swing her back toward him and she collapsed into his chest. The police constable slammed handcuffs onto Ritesh Patel and forced him to the ground.

That evening, after a long day of filling out paperwork and then filling Selena in on the details, Detective Stewart left to stay the night at his Aunt's house in Cabarita Beach.

In the morning, they would go shopping together for a special book for Selena's birthday. It would be a tall order, Stewart thought, because it would have to top the early birthday gift of her being able to help on another case. And he knew it would be hard to top that. Stewart's aunt noticed a twinkle in Cameron's eye and wondered of things to come.

About The Author

CT Mitchell's debut murder mystery, Dead Shot, was an international crime & mystery bestseller, reaching the number one position in category in the Amazon charts both in the UK and US.

This was followed by Amazon #1 mystery novels best-sellers (in category) Dead Ringer, Dead Wrong and Dead Boss. The Detective Jack Creed Box Set – a collection of short story novellas compiled from C T's first 4 novellas was a runaway crime fiction success smashing the Amazon UK & US markets for this emerging Australian crime fiction author. High Stakes, Murder at Stonehaven and The Thin Line followed suit feeding C T Mitchell's growing global reader base. In April 2016 C T launched his first full length mystery thriller novel, Murder Secret.

In mid 2015 C T released his first cozy mystery short story novellas introducing Lady Margaret Turnbull, Father Douglas and The Kate Mackenzie culinary cozy mysteries to his diversified readers immediately claiming Amazon's #1 Hot New Releases both in the UK and US.

In 2017, Indian amateur sleuth, Selena Sharma joined the stable. Her books have much appeal in India and the sub-continent and there's already talk of a television series or Bollywood movie in the making.

C T Mitchell splits his time between both Brisbane and Cabarita Beach – a sleepy seaside village in northern NSW, Australia – the home of his award-winning books. To grab two free mystery bestsellers, please visit his website, or follow him on Facebook or Twitter.

http://www.CTMitchellBooks.com

And don't forget to connect on:

http://www.twitter.com/theshortreads
http://www.facebook.com/ctmitchellauthor

More Short Story Books by C T Mitchell

Detective Jack Creed

Detective Jack Creed Box Set (Books 1 – 4)

Or buy the books individually
Dead Shot
Dead Ringer
Dead Wrong
Dead Boss

Detective Jack Creed Box Set 2 (Books 5-7)
Or buy the books individually
Dead Stakes
Dead Lucky
Dead Silence

Dead Set The Complete Box Set

Lady Margaret Turnbull Cozy Mysteries

Lady Margaret Turnbull Box Set

Or buy the books individually

Murder at the Fete
Murder in the Village
Murder in the Cemetery
Murder in the Valley
Murder at the Manor
Murder in the Frame

Murder in the District Cozy Mystery Box Set

Father Douglas Cozy Mysteries

Murder and the Mechanic
Murder and the Jewelry Box

Kate Mackenzie Culinary Cozy Mysteries

Deadly Vows
Deadly Liaisons
Deadly Soiree
Deadly Birthday
Deadly Finale

Deadly Mix Cozy Mystery Box Set

Selena Sharma Mysteries

Murder by Butter Chicken
Murder of a Bollywood Queen

Grab any of the above books at

www.CTMitchellBooks.com

FREE Downloads

Grab 2 FREE #1 Amazon eBooks at

www.FreeCrimeBooks.com